ARC D'X

STEVE ERICKSON

Poseidon Press • *new york* • *london*

toronto • *sydney* • *tokyo* • *singapore*

POSEIDON PRESS

Simon & Schuster Building
Rockefeller Center
1230 Avenue of the Americas
New York, New York 10020

POSEIDON PRESS is a registered trademark of Simon & Schuster Inc.

POSEIDON PRESS colophon is a trademark of Simon & Schuster Inc.

Designed by Barbara M. Bachman

Manufactured in the United States of America

10 9 8 7 6 5 4 3 2

Library of Congress Cataloging-in-Publication Data

Erickson, Steve.
  Arc d'X/Steve Erickson
  p.   cm
  I. Title.
PS3555.R47A89   1993
813'.54–dc20
                                        92-30968
                                        CIP

ISBN: 0-671-74296-5

On an April night almost midpoint in the Eighteenth Century, in the county of Orange and the colony of Virginia, Jacob Pollroot tasted his death a moment before swallowing it. He had, then, a moment to spit it out and save himself. This moment was lost not because he was slow-witted but because he'd become a monster of appetites; his had not been a life of spitting out things. The taste was sweet, slyly familiar. He'd tasted it before, in some Indian campaign of his youth or some night with one of his black women. But he had only the time now to look up from the stew that was his dinner, gaze at the house around him, and see through the steam of the poison his slave Evelyn standing in the doorway of the kitchen.

He raised his hands to his throat. The pain began almost immediately in the pit of his stomach, widening in a circle to his bowels below and his brain above. He pushed away from the table and lurched across the room; Evelyn watched without glee or concern. "Jesus you've killed me," Jacob wailed, crashing into a wall of dishes. For a moment he lay shuddering on the floor. Some would later say his hideous noises were the leakage of a black life hissing out of every orifice.

Evelyn walked up to the body. She stood over it long enough that she might have been contemplating giving it a good kick. She looked up to the faces of the other slaves in the windows, who were staring in stupefaction not, she knew, simply at Jacob Poll-root's death, but her own.

At Evelyn's trial there was a thorough recounting of Jacob's barbarities, and testimony as to Evelyn's constant debasement at Jacob's hands and his savage treatment of his slaves in general. All this was accepted not as reasons that might justify Jacob's murder, but rather as the motives that proved Evelyn had done the deed. Evelyn herself said nothing. She sat throughout the trial as impassively as she'd watched Jacob topple across his dinner. She wasn't invited to speak; her trial wasn't seen as a legal right extended to a person to defend herself—since by Virginia law Evelyn wasn't a person—but as an object lesson for a system that occasionally needed one. The case certainly created alarm throughout the county. The court found Evelyn guilty and sentenced her to be burned at the stake, once the spring rains stopped and the town could find wood dry enough for it.

The rest of Jacob Pollroot's slaves would later create the legend that on the first of May when Evelyn was torched alive, she received the inferno's lust with the same stoic self-possession as she'd received Jacob's so many nights. But it was a difficult legend to maintain in the face of Evelyn's screams, so terrible they stunned even those who had witnessed such executions before. For days afterward the pale and shaken townspeople still remembered the screams, transparent portholes in the flames through which could be seen Evelyn's aghast face. Her ashes smoked for hours in the twilight. The smell of them carried in people's hair and clothes, and the cloud of smoke rose high into the Virginia sky, visible for miles around.

It was visible in the next county. A Virginia squire driving his wagon down the muddy road toward his plantation looked up to watch it rise above the mountain. A dark knowing murmur swept through his own slaves riding in the wagon and walking alongside; on the hills and in the fields slaves stopped their work to look up at the smoke. At that moment the squire, hearing the dangerous din of their black prayers, wanted nothing more than a strong wind that would scatter the smoke, though a full gale force would not disperse its memory. Next to him on the wagon seat the squire's five-year-old son watched the smoke too. Into the night the little boy smelled it. He smelled it in his food and his bath. In the air outside his bedroom window that should have been ripe with the scent of spring rain, he smelled nothing but the burning body of the black female slave. He woke in the middle of the night vomiting; and lying in bed the next day, depleted and delirious, his five-year-old head was filled with excruciating visions: staring into the nothingness above him, he waited for the woman's ashes to fall from the sky, to clot the branches of the trees and hang from the rafters of the house like black snow. The boy's name was Thomas.

Thirty-four years later, down the hall from Thomas' boyhood room, as the smoke of revolution settled over the countryside, a nine-year-old slavegirl called Sally stood in another room watching her mistress' last hours. Along with Sally were her mother, brother and most of the other houseslaves. In bed a dying young woman glided in and out of consciousness, gripping her husband's hand. The heavy blue curtains were closed to the sun; the dank smell of childbirth and the woman's dying mixed with the fragrances of lilac and musk, which a bedchamber slave frantically wafted through the room until Sally thought she'd gag. Thomas finally wrested himself from his stunned bewilderment. "Please," he whispered, so low Sally could barely hear him, "no more perfume." It was the only thing anyone had said in hours, and the stricken husband returned to his silent vigil.

In fact the mistress of the house had been weak and in poor health as long as Sally could remember, and had lain on this particular edge of death for some time. The smell of placenta and blood that still hung in the bedchamber was from the birth of the mistress' third daughter. Throughout the recent weeks visitors had come to the house from across Virginia not to offer best wishes to the sick woman but to pay respects to the departed one, since news traveled prematurely that she had already died. All summer Thomas walked the halls of the house in a trance. Racked first with the sorrow of his impending loss and the denial of its inevitability, he'd nearly come to that point where such denial becomes anticipation, as a consequence of which such sorrow becomes guilt. His hand perpetually in hers, he was both ready to pull her back as she was sucked into the afterworld and to squeeze her fingers goodbye in his encouragement that she go.

At night in their quarters the slaves talked about what would happen to them when the mistress was gone. It wasn't that they feared their treatment at the hands of the master. The master treated the slaves better than the mistress, actually; no one had ever seen him beat a slave or order a slave beaten. Once in town Sally watched with awe as Thomas, who at more than six feet tall towered over most men, seized a stick from a handyman who was beating a slave. Thomas neither bought slaves nor sold them; he'd inherited his from his father. But most of the slaves belonged to the mistress when she married Thomas, and over the years of their marriage the master had remained incomprehensible to them when not appearing simply eccentric. He was dreamy and distracted and perhaps, for all anyone could tell, a bit addled—a lawyer who never had any clients, a tinkerer who built peculiar contraptions with arcane functions. To the nine-year-old slavegirl Sally there was something godlike about his calm. She was mesmerized by his immaculate silence, his chaste reflectiveness. The rest of the slaves were more unsettled than reassured by his strange otherness. They didn't know what to make of it when Thomas occasionally rode off to Williamsburg to propose laws that declared no one would own any more slaves.

Thus, standing at the deathbed of the mistress on this September afternoon, the watching slaves were as much distressed by the uncertainty of the moment as by its gravity. When the sun finally fell and the blue curtains were pulled aside from the window, the mistress woke from her stupor with a start. "Tom," she said calmly, "I want to tell my children goodbye."

Thomas visibly shuddered. Slowly he turned to look over his shoulder. For a breathless moment Sally thought he was looking at her; she raised her hand to her chest. But in fact Thomas was looking at Sally's mother, who turned and left the room and then reappeared with the two older daughters, Patsy and Polly. The wetnurse brought the baby, Lucy. Stoic and purposeful only moments before, the mistress dissolved at the sight of her two little girls, calling to them hysterically with her arms open. Patsy, at ten the older of the two, gamely went to her mother, but the younger

Polly, terrified, turned and ran straight into Sally, clutching Sally's skirt. Sally's mother gently pulled Polly away. The mistress sobbed uncontrollably. Thomas stared at the scene in devastation. Sally's mother took Patsy and Polly from the room. The wetnurse approached the mistress tentatively with the baby whose birth had killed her; the dying woman only shook her head once and seemed to lapse again into unconsciousness. A quarter of an hour later she began to speak as before. "It's not right," she said, "that they should have another mother."

Thomas looked up in surprise. He'd assumed she was asleep.

"It's not right," she said firmly. "Tell me."

"What?" said Thomas.

"Tell me please, Tom," she begged, "that our little girls won't call some other woman mother."

"But how can they have another mother?" Thomas asked blankly, confused. "They have only one mother."

"Then you won't marry another," Sally heard the mistress say, "they'll be our little girls forever. I'll be your wife forever as you'll be my husband."

"You'll always be my wife," Sally heard the master say.

"Tell me," the woman whispered. The sun had fallen behind the hills, and the room was dark.

Sally heard him say, "Yes."

She died an hour later, not long after someone lit the candles. All the summer goodbyes Thomas had squeezed into his wife's hand were forgotten. He rose slowly as the life left her, and as he stared down at her there was in the candlelight on his face no goodbye, no yes, only no, only horror and incredulity; and then he made a sound like nothing any of the slaves had ever heard. It was so terrible, so wordlessly abysmal, that nine-year-old Sally ran from the room. The slaves were torn between their instinct to embrace the master and their fear of approaching the source of such a sound. The sound didn't stop. Sally's older brother James grabbed Thomas and took him from the bedchamber. Sally's mother tended to the corpse as the young slavegirl stood in the hallway where James led Thomas to the library. Other slaves now came into the hall from outside, and Thomas' two little girls also came running in, Patsy with her face in her hands and Polly crying. In the library was a sudden crash. Sally got to the library doorway to see Thomas on the floor, a small table in pieces beneath him where he'd collapsed. Sally didn't see him again for weeks, during which Thomas remained in the dark library speaking to no one.

Sally wouldn't realize it until years later, but her mother had originally belonged to the mistress' father, who—as was not uncommon in Virginia—had a taste for fucking his female slaves. Such an encounter begat Sally. The mistress' father, then, was in fact Sally's father; Thomas' dying wife was in fact also Sally's dying half-sister. This was as much a bond between Sally and Thomas as the deathbed assurance he would never remarry, and as would be yet another bond made between them five years later, one not so easy to break as a promise.

For another summer Thomas grieved, remote and celibate, unresponsive to the women of Virginia who flirted for his attention. Some of these women were single, some already married, others widowed by revolution and disease. In his shy and remote manner he kept their company and considered their sexual offers, among which only the adulterous ones tempted him. For the most part he remained to himself. For weeks, sometimes months, the spellbinding pain behind his eyes that he'd known as a child returned to hold his head in its crush. The slaves could hear his moan in the darkened library, where Sally sometimes glimpsed her mother applying cold rags to his face. Finally the headaches would wane. From the back porch Sally watched Thomas ride off alone in the afternoons, the wild hills his only direction, desolation his only rendezvous.

Thomas resolved after still another summer to leave grief behind and not know it anymore. He made plans to sail with his oldest daughter Patsy for France, booking passage on a ship and reserving all its berths so that they'd sail alone. He decided to take with him Sally's brother James as his personal valet and servant. On the afternoon of departure all the slaves of the household as well as the fieldhands followed the carriage—driven by James and carrying Thomas and Patsy—down the road waving goodbye. Sally's mother was the last to linger, watching the road until long after the carriage was out of sight.

Thomas' ship took six weeks crossing the Atlantic, docking at Le Havre almost two years to the day after the death of Thomas' wife. From Le Havre, Thomas and Patsy and James traveled to the French village of Rouen. There they stayed in an inn overlooking the town square. In the middle of the night Thomas woke to a dreadful smell that turned his stomach. Thinking he was going to be sick, he jumped from his bed and stumbled to the window, throwing open the shutters; what filled his lungs wasn't fresh air but the very thing that had awakened him. The night was full of it. He recognized it as the smoke of the burning black female slave that had risen from the next county thirty-six years earlier; slamming shut the window he backed away from it as though an apparition would appear any moment. Thomas wasn't remotely a superstitious man, so he didn't easily accept the prospect of apparitions. He was, on the other hand, habitually tormented about his slaves, whose ownership he could barely bring himself to accept but whose freedom he could not bring himself to give. He returned to bed and, his face buried in his pillow, to sleep. The next day he was reminded by one of the villagers that, three and a half centuries before, the girlwarrior Jeanne from Arc had been tried and burned at the stake in the square below Thomas' hotel window. On the road out of Rouen, from his carriage view, he almost believed he could see streaks of ash in the morning rain.

They arrived in Paris a week later, after dark. Their carriage entered the city from the west, through a gateway in the outer wall, and then spiraled its way into the heart of the city along the inner concentric walls. The streets reeked of cognac and sex. Merchants and rabble-rousers, soldiers and whores jostled each other; women opened their dresses and breasts to the passing coach while insurrectionists, ankle deep in open sewers, exploded with streams of incomprehensible diatribe. Down every avenue tunnels wound off into an ominous darkness that was broken only by the flash of light from a door thrown open, in the momentary glare of which could be seen people engaged in acts so unfamiliar it was impossible to grasp just what they were. Patsy shrank from the onslaught. Her father gazed deliriously. The city seemed to Thomas the size of a country. The carriage continued descending from one ring of walls to the next; by the time they reached the rue d'X and the Hotel Langeac that would be their home over the years to come, Patsy cried for Virginia. Thomas, on the other hand, felt liberated by the way the city had already violated him.

Paris was electrified by the news of Thomas' arrival. Clergy and aristocracy greeted his appearance with alarm, while French radicals and American expatriates made pilgrimages to the Hotel Langeac where they might discuss philosophy and revolution with him. Thomas spurned the invitations of the French elite who wanted to take his measure and instead passed his time in bohemian circles. His liaisons with women were limited to bubbly libertines and deeply discontented wives who wouldn't threaten the vow he'd made to his own in her last hour. His most serious affair was with Maria, the wife of an English pornographer who abused her, often leaving her alone in Paris for weeks before snatching her back to London.

The winter after he'd come to Paris, Thomas received the news that Lucy, the last child born to his wife, had died of the whooping cough at the age of two. Not able to trust anyone else to keep at bay the grief he'd resolved never to know, he arranged for the passage to France of his other daughter, Polly. He sent word to his sister in Virginia that Polly was to come as soon as possible, in the care of whatever female slave seemed suitable.

B y t h e t i m e s h e was fourteen they called her Dashing Sally. She was tall with wide hips and round breasts; her smile was sweet and hushed, her voice watery and melancholy. She had brown eyes with flashes of green, and skin that was too white to be quite black and too black to be quite white. The dark hair that fell down her back she tied with a long blue strip she'd torn from the curtains that hung in the mistress' bedchamber that fatal summer, after they'd been taken down and discarded. Some said that Sally was already the most beautiful woman in Virginia. As is true with any such beauty, it was lit from within by her obliviousness of it. It stopped men where they stood and pushed to the edge of violence the friction between husbands and wives. But her sexuality was still a secret, to no one more than herself.

Every several weeks the master's sister would visit the plantation to see that everything was in order. With her she'd bring the master's remaining daughter, who had been living with her since Thomas went to France. Polly liked these visits because she could play with the slave children; in particular she looked forward to seeing Sally, whose skirt she had clutched on the day of her mother's death. Polly trusted Sally and felt secure with her, and was not displeased that she could sometimes order Sally and the other black children around. When Thomas sent for Polly it was assumed she would be accompanied on the voyage by either Sally's mother or one of the other women of the household. Polly, extremely willful at the age of eight, had only dim memories of her father and sister; she had long since stopped missing them and had no interest in leaving Virginia. In protest she threw terrible tantrums.

When it was evident that nothing short of physical abduction was going to get Polly to France, a plot was hatched. All talk of the trip was dropped, time passed, and one day Thomas' sister and Sally's mother took Polly and Sally to look at the big ship docked in the Norfolk harbor. With the permission of the ship's captain, the two girls were allowed to come onto the boat and play. For several hours Polly ran along the keel of the vessel from bow to stern, laughing and shouting until she collapsed on a bunk in one of the cabins and fell asleep. When she woke it was dark and the room was moving. She sat up and started to cry; Sally was on the bunk next to her. "Where are we?" asked Polly.

"We're on the boat," Sally answered.

"I want to go home," the little girl said. She looked around her. "It's dark."

"I know. It's night."

"I want to go home."

"Well, we're going to see your father and your sister," Sally finally brought herself to say.

"I don't want to go to France!" Polly cried. She jumped up from the bunk and ran to the door of the cabin, flinging it open as the night sea sprayed her face. She looked up at the mast of the ship swaying in the dark above her. Sally tried to pull her from the door but Polly pushed her away. "You tricked me," she screamed at the older one.

"Yes," Sally admitted.

"I order you to make the ship go back. You have to. You're a slave and I'm a Virginian."

Sally walked across the dark cabin to close the door. By the bed she lit a lantern. "This isn't Virginia," she said, "this is the ocean." She sat back down on the bed. "I'm sorry we tricked you. It wasn't how they wanted to do it. They never wanted to send you away at all, it's what your father wants. I didn't want to go either." Sally folded her hands in her lap and looked off into the corner, thinking of her brother James. "My mother's not too happy about it."

Polly didn't care in the least about Sally's mother. "You tricked me," she repeated bitterly.

"I know," Sally said.

As the ship crossed the Atlantic, however, Polly reconciled herself to the adventure. They sailed not to France but England, where Thomas was supposed to meet Polly in London and take her on to Paris himself. Sally, it was understood, would immediately return to America. But at the rue d'X it had become apparent to Thomas, over the course of the month, that a rare opportunity to see his lover Maria was about to present itself. When Polly and Sally got to London, Polly's father wasn't there to greet them. This left the little girl even more nonplussed; so, as well, were the American couple in London whom Thomas had alerted to take Polly in. After a few days, just as Sally was about to embark back to Virginia, word came from Thomas that he wouldn't be traveling to London at all and the American couple were to send Polly along to Paris in the company of whoever had come with her to England. On general principles Polly threw the most spectacular fit of her eight-year life, though she was secretly pleased that Sally would be staying. The American woman, Abigail, was appalled. "It won't do," she said to her husband John one night, "that girl's got to go back home on the next ship."

John pretended to misunderstand. "She hasn't seen her father in over two years," he answered. "He should have come to London to meet her though. Inexcusable."

"I'm not talking about Polly," Abigail said impatiently, "I'm talking about the other one." She didn't look at her husband. "She's rather useless. Why they sent her instead of an older woman—"

"I think they explained that," John cut her off. John cut off people all the time, but he never cut off Abigail; they both realized it at once. "It was the only way they could lure Polly onto the boat. She was the only one who could have gotten Polly across the ocean at all. Give her that, at least." He shrugged. "She's not an unpleasant girl."

"What do you mean," said Abigail.

"I mean she's not an unpleasant girl."

"Don't be disingenuous with me."

"What the hell—"

"You know what he's been like since his wife died," she said quietly. "All those stories about his carryings-on in Paris—"

"Political enemies—"

"Yes, I know," she said, "and I don't doubt his enemies make it all much worse than it is. Listen, I think the world of him. I believe I'm closer to him than you are at this point. I've always thought there was something of the saint about Thomas—"

"Well," John began to protest, "I don't—"

"Yes, well, you two have had your differences lately. That's politics, and I defer to you on politics. But I'm talking now about Thomas' passions."

"Do you suppose Thomas has passions?"

She was astounded. "Do you suppose he doesn't?"

"I've never thought of him as a passionate man."

Abigail stood in the doorway of the study looking down the hall, past the stairs, to the back quarters where the slavegirl named Sally slept. She folded her arms. "Thomas is the most passionate man I know," she said into the dark of the hallway. When John didn't answer, Abigail said, "She shouldn't go to Paris." She wanted to ask her husband if he thought Sally was beautiful, but it was a foolish question. The answer was obvious, and whether he told her the truth or a lie it was bound to hurt.

"She's only a girl," John finally said after an uncomfortable interval.

"She shouldn't go to Paris."

T h e y   d i d   n o t know her. The city did not know Sally on the drizzling autumn day the coach delivered her, along with Polly to the rue d'X; the street did not know her when Patsy dashed from the Hotel Langeac into the rain and mud to sweep her baffled little sister up in her arms. "But who are you?" Patsy finally turned to ask Sally amidst the family reunion, as the slavegirl lingered before the fire in the hotel's front room; and Sally answered, "It's me, miss." They had spent many afternoons playing together in Virginia. "Father," Patsy said, looking at Sally from head to foot in consternation, "it's Betty Hemings' little girl!" On the stairs Thomas stood with an elegant young Englishwoman and a black man who Sally realized, after some moments, was her brother; they all regarded her with troubled curiosity. "But why did they send someone so young with Polly?" Patsy asked, though in fact Patsy was only a year older than Sally, and it was Sally who looked like a woman. "Isn't it odd?"

"She tricked me," Polly exclaimed petulantly. It was the first thing she'd said.

"Yes, I'm afraid so," Sally said. James stood at her side, studying his hands nervously. "Miss Polly wasn't at all keen on making the passage. They decided I was the only one who could get her onto the ship."

"It was a shrewd maneuver then," said Thomas.

"It was a bloody trick!" the eight-year-old cried.

"Don't say that word," Thomas admonished, "obviously you spent too much time in England." He disappeared up the stairs with his daughters. James followed in silence with the bags. Sally stood shivering in the foyer as the other woman remained on the stairs watching her. "I'm sure," the woman finally said, "it would be all right with Mr. Jefferson if you wish to warm yourself for a moment by the fire. Then your brother will show you your quarters." The woman left and Sally was completely alone for what seemed a long time. She realized it was longer than she'd ever been alone. No one else was in the hotel foyer; the only sound was the crackling of the fire and some footsteps upstairs, and the flow and ebb of the din from the streets. She could hear the voices of passersby outside speaking words she didn't understand. This isn't Virginia, this is the ocean, she'd said to Polly on the boat. She looked at the door of the hotel and had a thought she'd never had before; she so terrified herself by it that she immediately left the fire and went upstairs, where she found her quarters across the hall from James'.

It was a tiny room but it was her own. There was a wooden bed with posts; at night she'd take the long blue ribbon from her raven hair and tie it to the post above her head. She'd shake her hair loose and let it cover her bare shoulders. High above the bed was a small window in the shape of a crescent moon, and through it came the light of torches in the middle of the night and the angry tumult of growing mobs.

Sally was shocked when James later explained that the woman on the stairs was the master's lover. "But don't you remember," Sally said to her brother, "he promised his wife he'd never marry again," and James answered, "He'll keep that promise. Mrs. Cosway is already married." Sally saw the woman twice more. Two days after arriving in Paris she served the couple breakfast. Both Thomas and Maria were lost in their thoughts, staring silently out the window of their suite at the ceaseless rain: he appeared too depressed to eat and she, regarding Sally once, lowered her eyes and never looked back up. But just as Sally was about to leave Thomas asked what she could tell him of Virginia, and so the nearly dumbstruck fourteen-year-old sat in the suite for the next hour trying to update him on what had happened since he'd left. The more she talked and answered his eager questions, the more evident was his wistfulness for home and the more Maria seemed to wilt beside him. For the rest of the day Sally was ecstatic at how she'd raised his spirits.

Then one afternoon a week later, coming up the street after taking Polly for a walk, Sally saw a coach in front of the hotel being loaded with luggage. Thomas and Maria stood together in the hotel door. Both of them looked very unhappy. They held each other's hands and said nothing; as she turned to the coach, he was ashen. Several feet from the carriage she stopped for a moment and he raised his arms as though expecting her to come back. But Maria boarded the coach staring straight before her; and Thomas, more crestfallen than Sally had seen him since his wife's death, whirled around and disappeared into the hotel.

The headaches began after that. They were worse than any he'd had since that terrible summer five years before. As then, he hid in the dark of his room, only occasionally receiving the visitors who arrived every day in an endless stream. Through the double doors Sally could hear their monologues punctuated by pauses in which Thomas' whisper was barely discernible. Sally would close the hallway windows to shut out the sound of the crowds who gathered every day in the streets, listening to speeches. "Why are you closing the windows," Patsy said to her one unseasonably warm afternoon.

"I thought your father would appreciate the silence," Sally answered.

Both girls were immediately struck that she'd called Thomas "your father" rather than "the master." A moment passed before Patsy said, "Perhaps for a while, until things outside calm down."

Mortified by her faux pas, Sally could only mutter, "Paris is an excitable place." Outside it did not calm down. The afternoon grew more volatile and Thomas remained in his sanctuary, emerging each afternoon only to ask if a letter had arrived from Maria in London, then vanishing back into the dark. Finally Sally summoned all her courage and early one evening entered Thomas' room. She brought some cold rags as she'd seen her mother do in Virginia. She carried them in a smooth peach-colored porcelain bowl. Thomas was lying back in a chair that reclined. Sally waited in one place for several minutes and, her courage slipping, was about to leave when Thomas looked up. "Who is it?" he said.

Am I so black, Sally asked herself, that he doesn't know me in the dark? "It's Sally, sir."

"Sally."

"I have some cold cloths for your head, if you'd like."

"Yes," Thomas whispered after a bit. He said, "Sometimes I think the pain's about to leave, but midday it returns."

Midday, she thought, when he hopes for word from her. Thomas lay back in the chair. Sally set the bowl down on the desk beside him. She wrung the excess water from the rags; she squeezed the rags over and over until her hands were red. Nothing would be so appalling as to put the rags on his head and have a drop of cold water run down his face. Her hands shook badly as she held the rags above his forehead; she had to set them down for a moment and collect herself. His eyes remained closed, waiting.

She was aware of someone behind her. She turned and Patsy was in the doorway. Without meeting Sally's eyes, Patsy came and silently took the rags from Sally's hands. Thomas didn't stir. Patsy placed the cold rags on her father's head; she never looked at Sally or spoke. Sally bowed her head slightly and left the room.

Thomas lay in the chair and felt her hands on his head. He was having a vision of the King of France hanging by the neck from an archway in Versailles. It wasn't an unpleasant vision, though in all truthfulness Thomas found the king an amiable fellow, perhaps even well-meaning in a weak and ultimately pointless way. But there he was, nonetheless, dangling from the rafters of Thomas' mind; when Thomas himself actually felt the wind blow through the king's hair, he realized the slavegirl was stroking his brow. After a while he opened his eyes and saw, quite unexpectedly, his daughter. "Oh," he said.

Patsy sat down in the next chair. "How is it?"

"It comes and goes," Thomas said, "I was telling—" He stopped. "It comes midday, and then goes." He pulled the cold rags from his forehead down over his eyes. He'd recently come to talk about things with Patsy the same way he used to talk with his wife, but Maria wasn't something he could talk to her about. "It will eventually pass," he said. "As it always has before."

"Father," Patsy finally said, "what about James and Sally?"

"James and Sally?" he said.

"How long will they stay in Paris?"

Thomas lay back in the chair, his eyes closed again. Patsy found this disconcerting. It was like her father to be private, but not evasive.

"As long as it's . . ." He shrugged. "Helpful."

"I would think you might want to send them back to America soon."

"Why? It's a dangerous voyage this time of year. We certainly could use them here, especially now that Polly's with us. It seemed to me you and Sally were friends once."

"We were little girls, father. When some things didn't matter."

"What things?"

"Do James and Sally know they aren't slaves in Paris?"

Thomas sat up. He pulled the rags from his eyes and looked troubled. "I don't know," he said. "I would think James will figure it out if he hasn't already."

"And then he will tell Sally."

"Yes."

"Do you ever think of telling them?"

"Yes."

"Will you?"

"I don't know."

Patsy asked, "Doesn't it still trouble you? It used to trouble you. I mean, the slaves."

"Yes."

"Everyone here says it's rather dreadful."

"They're right. It's rather dreadful."

"So why—?"

"Because we're weak," he answered, before she could ask.

That night Thomas dreamed about the hanging man. He hung from a beam just below the pain in Thomas' head, not in the king's palace but a bare room of empty shelves and tattered deep-blue curtains. The hanging man was gaunt and old, not at all like the king; it wasn't long before Thomas realized it wasn't the king but himself, hanging in the study of his home in Virginia. The home was dilapidated, ruined, which Thomas somehow found more shocking than his own body spinning in the smoke that curled in through the window. Sometimes in this dream Thomas was standing below looking up at himself, and sometimes he was up there hanging from the beams of the ceiling looking down at his slaves, who were watching him. James will cut me down soon, Thomas thought in his dream. Sally will put cold rags around my scarred neck and run her fingers through my hair. But Sally and James didn't come, and the black faces below were pitiless. For a moment in his dream he believed it was his slaves who had strung him up here, but then he knew that wasn't it. Then he knew he'd done it himself. He regretted it now and wanted down. He wanted to call out to his slaves to cut him down but he couldn't get out the words. As the smoke came in through the window, as he could feel the heat of the fire outside, his only hope seemed to be that a flame through one of the windows would lick the rope and drop him to the floor. He recognized the smoke, of course; he knew it all along. He knew it the moment he first smelled it. And as she burned outside, somewhere unseen but certainly burning, the smell that he'd known since he was five years old, that had caused the first of these pains in his head and the first of his many visions, now became the smell of his own freedom. His best hope was that she would burn so hot, that her immolation would be so intense, the very heat of her black annihilation would burn the rope that held his life. At that moment he loved the smell. At that moment, as the rope choked him tighter, he inhaled its sensuality; he was filled with desire for the burning slavewoman. He could see his slaves below him. He could see them shrink back from the sight of his erection. It would become so big that the weight of it would snap the rope above him and send him groundward, and then send him through the window to the pyre, where he would thrust himself into the ashes of her thighs.

He woke in this pandemonium. No spell was broken. He didn't shake himself loose of his dream: his dream went on and on, across the bedroom and into the hall. He knew he was awake, he knew he was in the Hotel Langeac and not his house in Virginia; but the smoke was still there. It was as unmistakable as his desire. His head didn't hurt now. He was filled with exultation at his new conviction, born in his dream, that no ashes of a burning woman would ever rain down from the sky, as he'd believed when he was a child, but that such ashes were only the soft sensual harbor of his desire, waiting between her legs. He followed the smoke to her quarters. What if James, he wondered, should try to stop me? I should have to flog him then, or sell him. He had never flogged or sold a human being. It thrilled him. He felt like a master, a king.

In her bed, Sally lay with her face in her pillow, her eyes open. There was a melee outside her door, coming down the hall, though she couldn't be sure what was happening. Then she knew.

The revolution, she said to herself, has come.

The revolution, she said to herself, has come. But when she looked up at the crescent-moon window above her bed, there was no light from torches, there were no voices from the streets. She heard her door open; she didn't move. She lay still with her face in the pillow, but she didn't turn to look. An uncomprehending terror gripped her: a secret had come stalking her to Paris. Something she'd never known, something she'd never wanted to know, was in her doorway. Like the child she still was, she thought if she lay still he would leave. He'd think she was asleep and therefore inviolate. But he didn't care whether she was asleep.

He closed the door and with no hesitation came to the bed. He didn't touch her to see that she was awake; he didn't grab her roughly, but without thought at all to either roughness or kindness. She looked up into his face in the dark; his eyes were wild. He took the sheets and blankets that covered her and threw them on the floor.

"Sir?" she said. He took hold of her sleeping gown by the neck and pulled it, and she heard it tear. "Sir," she could barely choke it out again; he tore the rest of the gown off her. Naked, she now pulled away toward the other side of the bed, but he grabbed her by the wrist and pulled her to him. He took from the bedpost the long blue strip that she'd surreptitiously shredded from the curtains that had hung in his bedchamber in Virginia. It's my fault, she thought, for taking a piece of the curtain to tie back my hair: "I didn't know," she said; "I thought it was all right." He tied her wrists with the cloth. "Please," she said, but he held her tight, and then, when he loosened his robe, she saw him. In a panic she tried to bolt, but her wrists were bound and he held her by her legs. She fell back onto her bed. Behind her he pulled her hips toward him so she was on her knees, and took her long black hair in a knot in his fist. Before he buried her face in the pillow she had one last chance to gaze up at the crescent-moon window, to look for the light of torches, to listen for the sounds of voices. The window was black and silent.

He separated and entered her. Both of them could hear the rip of her, the wet broken plunder, a spray of blood across the tiny room. She screamed. She screamed so her brother James would hear, so the whole hotel would hear. She didn't care if he killed her for it, if he pulled the hair out of her head for it, she screamed so they'd all know that their secret had found her. It was their secret, she'd seen it in all their faces, in London and Paris. But he didn't strike or kill her, and then she knew it had been a secret to him too, and he couldn't bear to live with it anymore. She screamed as the tip of him emptied his secret far inside her.

It thrilled him, the possession of her. He only wished she were so black as not to have a face at all. He only wished she was so black that his ejaculation might be the only white squiggle across the void of his heart. When he opened her, the smoke rushed out of her in a cloud and filled the room. It thrilled him, not to be a saint for once, not to be a champion. Not to bear, for once, the responsibility of something noble or good. Didn't he believe that one must pursue his happiness? Such a pursuit is as ruthless as any other. This possession made him happy, until he came. Then he sank out of his own sight, refusing to look at himself or what he'd done. He fell asleep, half on the bed and half on the floor.

For a long time she lay naked beside him, shuddering. Her face was turned away from him, but she could feel him there; if she could have moved she would have, but she could not. Nothing was more terrible to her than the silence, because she'd screamed so loud there was no way they couldn't have heard her; she knew they were all awake in their beds in the hotel, James and Patsy and Polly, all lying staring in the dark still hearing the screams to which they didn't respond. In these first moments she hated them and then she hated herself, for the way they would despise her now. So she lay shuddering, silently awake, and they all lay awake, except him.

Finally Sally slept. When she woke, before dawn, it was he who awakened her.

It was, actually, the soothing coolness between her legs that awakened her. When she opened her eyes and saw him, she lurched. Then she didn't move.

Her hands were untied, the blue ribbon back on the post where it had hung. Blood still streaked the bed. Beside the bed, he knelt on the floor. He held in his hands the cold rags she'd brought for his head the previous afternoon. Sitting on the bed beside her naked body was the peach-colored porcelain bowl. He touched the rags to Sally's thighs and wiped the blood from her, rinsing and squeezing the rags and putting them to the new wound between her legs, holding them there for a long time. He went on applying the damp rags until finally she stopped shuddering.

When she heard him bury his face into the rags between her legs and sob, she went back to sleep.

When the blood stopped, after he'd taken her many times over the weeks that followed, he didn't wash her with the rags anymore. It was the hemorrhaging of his conscience to which Thomas tended. If he couldn't quite forgive the way he fucked her, he accepted it as the dark thing that allowed him otherwise to be good.

Toward the end of the year, when he thought Sally was strong enough, Thomas brought a doctor to the Hotel Langeac to inoculate her for the pox. For several days and nights Sally lay in bed with terror and pox coursing through her; it was left to Patsy and James to care for her. They silently brought her food and, in the same silence, mopped her brow. Their eyes burned with hate. When the fourteen-year-old girl felt how she was banished from the heart of her own brother, her loneliness was without horizon.

Thomas, of course, didn't come to her during this time. So at first Sally was grateful for the fever. But finally she would have gone through anything to be free of it, and in her spells and exile from everyone around her, she imagined that the white spillage of her dark god might cure her like a potion. Feeling his rejection, she even heard herself call for him. When the fever of the inoculation finally passed and she'd spent another couple of days in bed recovering, she crept to the hotel kitchen one night and smuggled out a carving knife. She told herself she would lop off her tongue before she ever allowed it to call his name like that again.

Thomas and Sally didn't speak of what was happening. He wouldn't have chosen to speak of it, and there was no one for her to speak about it to. She was shunned by everyone as the living black secret that spread through the hotel and down its stairs, out its door and into the street. There this secret took the form of the heads of dead deer and the carcasses of dead rabbits stuck on gate tops and pinned to doorways, draping the pillars of the Pont Neuf and lining the walls along the rue St-Lazare. By the end of the first day the stench of dead animals was as political as the cognac and sex that Thomas had smelled on his arrival in the city two years before. The people in the streets said the dead carcasses were a protest against the law that made it a crime to kill the game of the aristocracy. But Sally knew the carnage had emerged from her uterus in the gush of his afterflow, beasts with their fur slicked by semen dashing crazed into impalement on the spires of Paris. The heads of people would be next.

The heads of people will be next, she whispered to him on the first night he came to her after her fever had gone. He'd taken her and then fallen asleep by her. Now at night there was always torch-light through the crescent-moon window above. I called you from the fever, she said to his sleeping face, drawing the carving knife out from beneath her pillow, because I'm so alone, and for that moment I would have rather had you up inside me than been that alone: that's what you've done to me, she said. That's the worst thing, that you've made me actually long for your defilement. Next time I'll cut off my tongue first. He was sleeping in the light of torches. She looked down to between his legs and an idea gripped the knife in her hands; instead she pressed the blade to his throat. Her own face was inches from his. She had the feeling he wasn't asleep at all. Something about his breathing was different; she put her eyes right up to his as though to look in. "Master," she said, "we'll carve your head and put it on a pike outside, with a rabbit. Your head on a rabbit's body, and a rabbit's head on yours. That's how Patsy and James will find you tomorrow." She wanted to goad him now out of his pretense of sleep. It would be just like him, she thought, to die without anyone's ever knowing whether he'd been awake for his own death. How godlike. She put the knife away and lay back on the pillow, waiting for a lion to emerge from her and crash through the hall, down the stairs and into the foyer, spearing itself on the iron poker with which the ashes of the fire below were stirred.

The next time he came to her she was awake. She heard the door open and let herself go limp in his hands. He took the blue ribbon from the post and tied her wrists. But instead of taking her from behind, he knelt on the floor by the bed as he'd done when he washed her with the cold rags. On the ceiling above her was the riot of light through the window, a blazing crescent-moon in the black. When she had almost lost herself in it, she was shocked by the feeling of something she'd never imagined. It was several seconds before she realized it was his mouth she felt on the small red hinge of her thighs. It didn't hurt at all. It didn't hurt in the least. She lay transfixed by it, not daring to look down at his hair the color of fire brushing against her in the dark. She felt his tongue slip inside her. Her inner mutilation hummed to it; the shudder she felt from it was unlike the one in which his first depravity left her. The crescent-moon grew on the ceiling above her. As he continued with her the furor of the streets outside retreated to the low hum of her inner passage. The next shudder took her by surprise as did the one after, and when she felt herself plummeting into the blaze of the crescent-moon, when she felt herself grab the fire of his hair and pull him to her, she knew, with rage, that her violation was total: when she came she knew, with fury, that this was the ultimate rape, the way he'd made her give herself not just to his pleasure but to her own. Then he turned her over and plunged himself into her. But it was too late. If he'd intended to make his own possession of her complete, she had also, if for only a moment, felt what it was like not to be a slave.

"G r e a t   m a n' s   w h o r e ," James said to her when they were alone. Her eyes filled with tears but he wasn't moved. "Just don't think," he went on, "just don't think for a second you're not as black as black."

"I don't think that," she insisted, "I've never thought it. I would be even blacker, if I could."

"Liar!" James said. They were upstairs standing in the hall of the hotel. Patsy had gone out and Thomas, who was now American ambassador, was at Versailles. Polly was in another part of the hotel with the concierge. "You're a liar or a fool," James said, "to wish to be even blacker in this world." He leaned in so close it frightened her. "Remember this, little sister. He's not your father or your husband, and never will be. So don't get into your head any such foolishness. No silly-young-girl ideas. He's your master, and all his white jism will not make you white enough to be the wife or daughter of a great man."

Sally turned and ran, crying. She hurried to her own room but, looking at her bed, she could barely stand to be there. So then she ran to James' room. When he came into the doorway she searched for anything she could throw at him; grabbing his chamber pot, she hurled it. The morning's piss slopped all over James and the door. "Damn!" James cried, and lunged at her. He flailed at her as she covered her face with her hands. He would have kept flailing but stopped when he realized he'd have to account for the marks on her beautiful face. "Christ, I can't even hit you," he said disgustedly, "it would only bruise his property."

She sat on the edge of his bed glaring up at him. "Oh, don't let that stop you, James," she said, "don't you worry about that. He can't tell anyway. He comes to me at night and I'm still black enough he can't see me. So you just go ahead and beat me, because I'm still black enough that he'll never know."

In the middle of his room, looking at his sister, James put his face in his hands and let loose a convulsive sob. After a moment she got up from the bed and put her hand on his hair. He pulled her to him and they stood together, the reek of urine rising around them. They spent the afternoon washing down his room and their clothes; they didn't talk anymore except at one point when James, on his knees scrubbing the floor, suddenly said, "We're not slaves here." He said it to the floor that he was scrubbing. She had wet clothes in her arms. When he looked up at her from the floor, she rushed with the clothes down the hallway.

Thomas returned from Versailles the following day. He called Sally and James into his chamber, which was still dark from the period of his headaches; he was sitting not in his reclining chair but in an upright one, behind a desk. His hands were on his head, and all Sally could see of him was the same red-gold hair she'd clutched so fervently in the night. Thomas told Sally and James he had decided to pay each of them thirty-six francs a month in wages. He said he regretted not being able to pay them more, his debts being what they were. He rose from the desk and walked around the room, his head barely missing the low ceiling; he went on to explain that he'd arranged a tutor for Sally, who would learn French, and for one of the city's finest chefs to teach James how to cook, so that on returning to America they wouldn't have to leave behind them the pleasures of Parisian cuisine. Sally could see how her brother wanted to leap over the desk and kill Thomas. She saw it on James' lips: we're not slaves here. I could kill you, she knew he was thinking, and in Paris it wouldn't be a slave killing his master. They might hang me for it, but in Paris it would be hanging one free black man for killing one free white one.

That afternoon Thomas and Sally rode through the city in his carriage, from one clothes shop to the next. Never concerned about his own attire, always wearing old pants and threadbare shirts and coats, Thomas was particular about choosing for Sally dresses that were elegant and simple. He bought shoes for her and an expensive pair of wine-red gloves. Sally wore the gloves in the coach on the way back to the Hotel Langeac. "Do you like them?" he said, the first words that had been spoken intimately between

them, and she answered, "Yes, I like them," and she was astounded at how his face lit up. "They're beautiful on you," he
blurted, "all of these clothes are lovely on you," and then, embar-
rassed by himself, he withdrew into silence.

She didn't thank him for them. In the time she'd been in Paris
she had come to construct the first foundation of who she was.
Used as she was by him and abandoned as she was by the rest of
them, the only one she could turn to was herself, and when she'd
first turned there and found no one, she had no choice but to make
a person where nothing but beauty had been. The person she'd
made wasn't going to thank him for a pair of gloves and a couple
of dresses. They weren't compensation for anything; they were the
gestures of a man taking care of his possession. That night she
wore only the wine-red gloves as she lay naked on her bed. She
believed that when he came to her, when he took her wrists to
bind them with the blue ribbon that hung on the bed post, the
generosity of his having given her the gloves would be desecrated
by their sex. Lying for hours on the bed she began to touch herself.
It was in the early morning that her door opened. "Sally," he said
to her in the doorway. He'd never spoken on these occasions.

"Yes, Thomas," she answered. The familiarity of his name
shocked both of them.

"I want you to come with me," he said, and she raised her hand
to him from the bed. He took it, and as he pulled her from the bed
he could feel the wetness of the glove's fingertips. She brushed up
against him as she stood and looked into his eyes to taunt him.

"Are we going somewhere?" she said.

"Get dressed," he answered in the dark. Twenty minutes later
they were in his carriage again, riding through the city with dawn
still an hour away. When Sally shivered in the cold Thomas moved
from the opposite seat to sit beside her, a thick blanket pulled up
around them. They rode in silence beyond the city walls and then
on the road east out of Paris, passing along the way the farms and
villages that lay beneath the winter snow. Finally the sun came up
over the trees. Sally could see an abbey on the other side of the
valley. Sometimes, when she arranged the blanket around her,
Thomas looked at the gloves on her hands. As they approached the
abbey he broke the silence. "I received word last night," he said,
"that Patsy has requested to join the convent." He added, "She's

angry with me." The carriage stopped at the abbey gate. An old stooped abbess trudged wrathfully out into the snow to meet them.

"I'm Patsy's father," Thomas said to her in French, stepping from the carriage.

The abbess regarded him coolly. She peered at Sally over Thomas' shoulder. "Christendom knows you too well, monsieur," she said. "Your visit is irregular. The girls are already underway with their chores and duties."

"I'd like to speak to my daughter, please," Thomas said.

"For a moment," the abbess answered. She led Thomas and Sally into the church. Sally continued to shiver in the cold. The church was also very cold, its stained windows gray on one side and colors squinting through the ice on the other side where the sun was rising. The abbess and Thomas did not speak. The abbess vanished and Sally sat in one of the pews as Thomas paced up and down the church aisle. When the abbess finally reappeared in one of the doorways, Patsy was with her. Near the altar the abbess hung back, watching. Patsy began to cry when Thomas took her in his arms. He gave her a handkerchief and, after she'd wiped her eyes, she looked at Sally. "You bought her some clothes," she said in a small voice.

"Yes," Thomas answered.

"Why did you bring her here?" Patsy's face was still buried in his handkerchief.

Thomas gestured to Sally and said gently to his daughter, "This isn't her fault. She doesn't deserve your fury, your fury's with me." He took Patsy by the arm and they began to walk around the border of the church. In her pew Sally watched them circle in silence. For a long time they just walked, not talking at all, as though in the early-morning carriage ride from Paris Thomas had no luck trying to figure out what he would say at this moment. In the empty resonance of the church the buzz of their voices finally reached Sally, but it wasn't until their third time around she made out the words. "Do you know," she heard Patsy plead, "the way they say your name here? In the street the common people say it when they need to fill their hearts with hope. I never believed," she said bitterly, "that my father was just another fine Virginia aristocrat, having relations with his slavewomen."

Thomas led Patsy to a pew, where they sat down. He continued to hold her hand. "There are things," he said, "a man can explain least of all to those whom he most owes explanations. Something happened to me after your mother died. Something happened to me after Maria left." The abbess watched intently from the altar. "I'm not here to make you promises," Thomas said to Patsy. "I'm here to try and dissuade you from a decision I believe you're making not because it's what you want but because you're angry with me. I want to dissuade you from this decision because it will hurt you more than me, because you're only using your own life to reproach me."

"I've heard that Grandfather Wayles had many slavewomen," Patsy said.

"Yes."

"I've heard—" She looked at Sally.

"I believe," Thomas said, "that Sally is Grandfather Wayles' daughter."

"Then she and Mother were sisters?" Patsy said angrily. "Then she's my aunt?" Patsy asked in disbelief, pointing at Sally. "Will she next be my mother?"

The abbess hurried over from the altar now. "It's most irregular, monsieur," she announced in French, hovering at their side. "It's time for the girl to return to her chores and duties."

Thomas stood up from the pew. He looked down at Patsy and sighed. "I'm taking you home. You're still of an age that I can make these decisions for you."

"You should think of the child," the abbess protested.

"Of course."

"It's unfortunate," said the abbess, "that your own hatred of God blinds you to—"

"I can appreciate that she's politically valuable to you," Thomas said to the abbess in English. "She is after all the daughter of someone your church fears and despises. But I'm taking her back, for as long as I have something to say about it, as her father. Later Patsy may decide for herself."

"For your daughter's sake, let's pray she never comes to share your contempt for God and his works."

"I have nothing but reverence for God and his works," Thomas answered. He was already walking toward the door with Patsy under his arm and Sally behind them. "It's the base machinations of power conducted in the name of God for which I have con-tempt." Outside, the carriage was waiting where Thomas and Sally had left it. With his daughter and lover, Thomas stepped into the carriage while the abbess seethed in the doorway. "I'll send some-one in a few days for her things," he said.

Outside Paris they stopped at an inn to have breakfast. While Thomas and Patsy ate in the guest room by the fire, Sally sat in the servants' quarters in back. Through the window of the kitchen she could see the snow of the winter and through the door of the kitchen she could hear Thomas' and Patsy's laughter. In her fine Parisian dress she quietly picked at her meal while the other ser-vants watched; the wine-red gloves lay on the bench beside her. The servants offered cheese and bread with jam. After a while they turned their attention from Sally to discuss kings and repub-licans.

By the time Thomas and Patsy and Sally returned to Paris it was a gray wintry noon. Bedlam rose from the city like a swarm. The boulevard St-Germain was raucous, enraged people stopping coaches in the streets and rocking them back and forth to overturn them while the passengers frantically hurled money out the win-dows. Throngs made the bridges impassable. From her window Sally could see approaching on the horizon of the Seine an angry black-and-red current. The revolution was trickling in by river, a rebel navy of flaming boats advancing to seize the docks and block the king's commerce; one by one the boats beached on the quays. Sailors stormed ashore with torches burning beneath the black winter sky.

People were reaching inside Thomas' carriage. They grabbed at Thomas and Patsy and at Sally in her fine Parisian clothes. Some-one yanked one of the gloves off her hand and, when she reached to seize it back, she was almost pulled from the coach. The turmoil became uncontrollable. The carriage was about to be pitched over the side of the bridge into the river when someone shouted, "Mais c'est Jefferson!" and then there was a hush, and the recurring murmur, "Jefferson," over and over. A roar rose from one end of the mob to the other. "Jefferson," men and women cried, "the people's champion!"

The crowd grew larger, cheering his name, people dashing from shops and looking from windows. Those around the carriage now reached in not to grab Thomas but simply to touch him; soon it became clear he would have to say something to them before they'd stop. He opened the carriage door and stood on the step of the coach and the crowd shouted at the sight of him, the giant with his hair of light and his old worn disheveled clothes. For a long time this wild demonstration continued. He kept trying to talk but no one could hear him amid the furor. "My dear friends," he said in his halting French, once the mob finally became quiet; his voice was so soft that inside the coach Sally could barely make it out. No one in the rapt crowd was so rude as to call for him to speak up. "My dear friends," he started once more, fumbling his hands, "please forgive the poor French of an American savage," and people laughed and the cheering began all over again.

When it faded, he went on. "My friends in this country," he said, still stumbling and nearly inaudible, "which I've come to love as though it were my own . . . what can I say to you that wouldn't be presumptuous? What can I say that won't be a . . . small whisper against the bold shout of your streets. The witness I bear here humbles me, and I'm not worthy of it—" and someone in the crowd began to protest but Thomas continued, "—I'm not worthy of it, but I'm grateful to see it."

He stopped. Behind him the revolution continued upriver. In the cold of the winter his words left tiny clouds before his face. "I'm a poor champion," he finally said after a moment. No one spoke. "I'm only as bright as the whitest light in any man can be, tempered as it is in every man by whatever black impulse he can't ignore. At my best I have only been the slave of a great idea. It's an idea which no man holds but which rather holds him. It's to no man's credit that he has such an idea, it's merely his good fortune that such an idea possesses him with such force and clarity that he can't help but serve it. What you do here stirs the slaves of the world to life. What you do here leaves the world's sleeping tyrants with no dreams but the endless counting of the few remaining days left to them. You should remember," and now Sally almost thought she could hear his voice break, "that whenever a poor champion fails a great idea, it's not the failure of the idea itself. The idea is as great as it ever was. It survives its poor champion and goes on and on. You should remember that when the final reckoning comes with God in his heaven, when the final battle of old prophecies is fought here on this sphere, it will be between those noble enough to have been slaves, and those arrogant enough to presume themselves masters. Let no one doubt on whose side God will be."

It seemed to Sally, there in the carriage, like a very long time before the crowd responded. When they did it was with a clamor like she'd never heard before. "Jefferson, Jefferson!" they screamed and, overwhelmed by the violence of the adoration, Thomas swung himself back into the carriage as though to cower from it. He was pale. The crowd escorted the carriage on its passage across the bridge; all the way across the city back to the Hotel Langeac people ran alongside, shouting and announcing to others on every new street that it was Thomas who was in the coach. At one point he summoned just enough nerve to look to the seat across from him where Sally sat, and then he looked away, out the window to the adoring people. When he couldn't stand to look at them, he stared down at his hands that had held Sally captive in the dark. When he couldn't stand to look at his hands, he looked somewhere else, until he ran out of places on which he could set his gaze, and closed his eyes.

By the end of winter he'd taken her to his own bedroom. By the middle of spring she slept all her nights there. Before everyone she openly called him Thomas. Sleeping in his room she couldn't hide the carving knife beneath her pillow anymore, so she kept it wrapped in the one glove she still had from the day on the bridge when she'd lost its mate to the crowd. At night after sex, when she was still awake, it seemed to her that she felt the bed beneath her flutter as though it were alive with wings, waiting to take flight.

The storm gathered in Paris. While winter chilled the turmoil in the streets it also raised the price of wood, further enraging the populace. One morning James found Thomas' carriage dismantled in the snow, broken to slivers and burned in stoves all over the neighborhood. By spring no one could afford bread. Bureaucrats frantically distributed stale crusts among the people while marauders ambushed flour wagons and hijacked grain barges. Roving bands torched the vineyards of the aristocracy while rioters looted merchants' houses and scattered the innards up and down the avenues. An anarchy of bodily fluids flooded the city, torrents of blood and shit and vomit running in the gutters. Soldiers vacillated nervously in their alliances, from the king one moment to the people the next. Among any accumulation of citizens and soldiers there was certain to be shooting, though who would fire upon whom was never known until the shooting began, at which point soldiers might suddenly become revolutionaries. "You must remain in France," James told Sally, "you mustn't go back to America with us."

"With us?" she repeated.

"He's agreed to set me free," James stammered, "if I return to Virginia as his cook."

"In other words," she retorted, "he's agreed to set you free if you remain his slave."

"Don't twist this around, little sister," James said angrily. "It's not the same, I'm not the one he beds. He'll never free you in America. He couldn't if he wanted to, not if he wants to continue as a white man having a black woman's body."

After this conversation she hid the knife wrapped in the glove behind the headrest of Thomas' bed. Tied by the wrists she listened to the beating wings of the bed beneath her, his cock far up inside her on the night Thomas said, We're going home soon. He pulsed with the news. He throbbed with the prospect of having her on American soil, where her slavery was irrefutable and the delight of her body was his with the crack of a whip. Until she felt him throb and pulse like that she hadn't really known what her answer would be. Will you take me back slave or free? she asked, and felt him stop, desire fading before her question. Collapsed on her breasts he lay still long enough for her to believe he was unconscious until he said, I cannot take you back free.

"You've freed my brother."

"It's not the same."

"Then I'll stay in Paris," she replied, and for a long time they were this way, his head in her breasts and her wrists bound.

When she woke it was in a panic of her own. In this panic she realized for the first time she'd never see him again. If in the way he had debauched her she became isolated from everyone around her, then he was her only human connection, defiled though that connection was. At this moment she wanted him to drink her dry as before. She felt not only like a jilted lover but an abandoned daughter, and thus his sex became not only a master's rape but a father's incest; like the molested object of any such incest, she not only reviled but cherished it. There in the dark it was more than she could stand. It wasn't enough simply to remain in France, it wasn't enough to free herself by an act of no: only an act of yes would see her through the nightful panic. She tore her wrists apart, the frayed ribbon of his dead wife's bedroom curtains exploding in bits of blue. She seized the knife from behind the headrest of the bed and, raising it above her head, brought it down into him; she could hear the penetration.

She threw herself back from the knife and tumbled out of bed, sobbing. She picked herself up from the floor to see fly out of his body a hundred black moths which filled the room. She grabbed her dress and rushed into the hall naked; she was still pulling the dress onto her as she dashed from the Hotel Langeac out into the July night.

On the balcony above her, Thomas watched her go. He'd been standing there for some time, since rising from bed unable to sleep. The loss of Sally was different from the loss of Maria or the loss of his wife; in them he'd lost a part of what he constantly revealed of himself to the world. In Sally he lost a part of what the world never knew, of what he had never known about himself, and now he believed he'd never know it. In the short run this was a relief. In the long run he knew that what he couldn't release between her legs would eat away his heart. He had no choice about America. As a free black she could not sleep in his white American bed. It was the nature of American freedom that he was only free to take his pleasure in something he possessed, in the same way it would ultimately be the nature of America to define itself in terms of what was owned. So he had no choice about that. If he'd had one he would have freed her, so long as he could have her. Once, if he'd had the choice, he would have freed them all, before it became easier for him to believe it was too late for such a choice, that such a choice had already been made for him. Now he watched her run down the street and disappear into the dark. Not very far away, over the spires of the city, was constant gunfire, into the light of which she'd rush to be obliterated by the flash of freedom. He turned from the balcony, back to the hallway, only to be overtaken by a plague of black moths. Calling out in alarm, he swatted them frantically as they flew over the balcony's side. In the doorway of his bedroom lay one of the gloves he'd bought for her; he found somewhat less curious the gash in his bed where the knife was plunged. On many nights while feigning sleep he'd felt the knife against his neck as she spoke to him. Just the previous afternoon he'd taken it from the glove and inspected it, before replacing it where she'd stowed it away.

She left without anything. She didn't have her clothes or the money she had saved from the wages he paid her. She knew a few French words and phrases from her tutoring. All night the city was rocked by explosions and rioting; she wandered the Parisian maze, now grateful for what had been an unbearable summer's heat. Only before dawn, on reaching the river, did she become cold.

On the banks of the river an old man gave her bread and wine. Then she walked eastward into the rising sun until it became too hot, at which point she left the riverside and meandered back up through the Right Bank. When she came to the rue St-Antoine, an enormous mob was gathering at the gates of a huge black building with eight towers and walls as high as fifteen men. Around the black building was a moat. For an hour Sally sat in the shade of an inn next to a perfume shop. A pregnant woman explained that the crowd intended to invade the prison, free its captives and seize the gunpowder held by the garrison stationed inside.

As the day dragged on and the heat became worse, the demonstration by the prison grew angrier. More people were pouring into the square and a huge cheer greeted an arriving wagon of guns, followed by a cannon that had been liberated at Invalides. As negotiations went on inside the prison between its commander and a representative of the crowd, the mood of the throng fluctuated between wild celebration and mounting frustration. People passed out in the street from heat and drunkenness. Others shouted insults at the soldiers high above them on the prison ramparts, while the eyes of horses hitched to carts of straw became lit by a dark malevolence, as though the animals were possessed. Sally was gripped by the exhilaration and fear that winding its way through the streets of Paris at this very moment was word that Thomas was dead, murdered by his lover. Suddenly, perhaps irrationally, she was certain the news would sweep the crowd and she'd be recognized by someone. Any minute someone would say, Yes I know this girl, the black one; and point to her, and hold up the glove that had been taken from her that day the mob almost pushed Thomas' carriage into the Seine. She wore this glove, the witness would say, I took it from her myself. Sally was watching the prison, wondering how it would be to spend the rest of her life in one of its towers, when the shooting began.

Where the fire came from first wasn't clear. It might have been from the prison itself or a hotel across the street. But then there was a tremendous volley, muskets exploding and the crash of cannons from the high walls of the prison, answered by the crowd's own cannon. The wagon horses reared as the straw was torched to fill the square with billows of smoke, obscuring the vision of the soldiers above. The window of the perfume shop erupted in a rain of glass, and a maelstrom of fragrances overwhelmed the square, mixing with the smell of smoke and wine and blood; a warning from someone in the crowd was followed by the loudest explosion of all, and Sally looked up just as the drawbridge of the prison came thundering down, cut loose by someone who had scaled the walls. People began rushing through the prison gates. The water in the moat beneath the bridge sizzled with the debris of smoldering iron from guns and cannons. Through the gates a howl rose from the people as though it were coming from the black towers themselves, and as the stampede threatened to carry Sally along with it, all she could think of was getting away. She was trying to turn against the momentum of the crowd when the pregnant woman grabbed her by the arm: "But where are you going, mademoiselle?" she said, before sliding lifelessly to Sally's feet, the back of her head smoking. Sally felt herself lifted off the ground by the surge.

A horse with its fiery wagon bolted wildly in the riot, people trying to make way for it. Reaching into the flames of the passing wagon, Sally hoisted herself onto it.

Across the square and past the drawbridge, through the revolution and into the dusk, she rode down the Paris streets with a ball of fire at her back. She could feel its heat. When the heat felt like his body, when it felt as if it were going to take hold of her hair and make her submit to it on her knees, she leapt from the wagon and rolled into a gutter, where she lay watching the flaming wagon disappear down the road before she lost consciousness.

Sometime in the night she picked herself up from the gutter. She walked until she came to the city gates. She left the city behind and continued in the dark toward what she believed were the woods in the distance, where she finally fell asleep again in the grass.

S h e   s l e p t   a long time.

She was vaguely aware of morning and the sun in her eyes. Far away in her mind she thought she should wake up and go, before someone came along and arrested her and took her back to prison, or abducted her to sell her. In her sleep she laid end to end all the dead masters with knives protruding from their gullets. But worse was that in her sleep, the sun sliding across the sky, she missed Thomas, and all she could hear was the rip of his body when she'd killed him, and all she could see was the black moths flying up out of him, and she wanted to gather them all up and put them back inside him and take back the knife and close him up, and feel him drink her as a father drinks a daughter.

When she woke it was late afternoon, and she was on a terrain unlike any she'd seen.

She stood up slowly and looked around her. Her head pounded and she was very thirsty, her life drunk dry. There were no woods. Beneath her feet where she'd slept so many hours wasn't grass but cold cinder. She was on the ridge of a large mountain; to one side of her, far down below her, stretched a plain of the black cinder, and to the other side was the mountain's crater. The horizon of the mountaintop was flat, as though its peak had been lopped off by God, and from the pit of the crater beneath her feet rose a steady stream of smoke and the light of a fire.

She was very thirsty. She wondered if someone had picked her up after all and deposited her far from Paris. But she didn't remember anything like that.

She walked down into the crater toward the light. The fire grew brighter, and soon she came to a house.

It was twilight when she reached the house. It sat on a small plateau overlooking the crater's mouth, and it wasn't like any other house she'd known. It looked like no French house, no English house. It didn't look like any house she'd seen in Virginia. It wasn't like the house a white man would live in, but closer to the ramshackle slave quarters on Thomas' plantation, except that it seemed to be made of the very rock of the mountain. On the porch of the house slept two large gray dogs, who raised their heads to greet her. She passed the dogs and paused at the door, afraid to knock; but she was very thirsty, and perhaps someone would give her some water. The crater loomed to her side, its smoke rising and dying in the darkening of the sky.

She stood at the door of the house, her ear pressed close to it. But she didn't hear anything and finally she rapped her hand on the wood. The door opened, and she saw herself.

She saw herself standing in the doorway, looking back at her. The two of them stared at each other agape; the only thing momentarily reassuring to Sally, the only reason she didn't scream and run immediately, was that the other one looked as amazed as she. If Sally had had the presence of mind she would have raised her hand to feel if it was a mirror; but she wouldn't have felt a mirror in any event. Sally instead put her hand to her mouth, too late to stifle her cry; the other one cried out too.

"Polly?" She heard a voice from a back room of the house. At the sound of Polly's name her first reaction was that it was Thomas' voice, but it wasn't Thomas; and then the voice said again, "Polly, what is it?" And then the speaker stepped out from the back room.

Sally had never seen him before. In his midfifties, he was of normal build, not as tall as Thomas but older; he had a wild mass of black hair speckled with white and gray. Thick spectacles made his eyes loom like blue crystal balls. As he tottered in the doorway his dissolution was profound, beyond simple drunkenness, and though Sally was at first relieved and disappointed to see that it wasn't Thomas, the sight of the older man with the black hair roared out of unfamiliarity into the psychic zone of distant but unshakable recognition, remembered more than prophesied. He looked at her and screamed, in a gasp whose sound died midair.

The color of his drinking vanished from his face and for a moment he was on the verge of fainting; the other Sally inside the house stepped toward him as though to catch him. But he caught himself, gazing from one woman to the other, and Sally felt her fear transformed by his own into something they shared that neither of them understood. Now he said not Polly's name but her own: "Sally," and he choked on it. Like the earlier cry it didn't all come out, part of it caught in the ventricles of his heart where it had been a long time.

Sally turned from the door. She ran past the gray dogs and the porch, back up the side of the crater toward the ridge of the mountaintop. She ran down the other side of the mountain toward the black plains. She hadn't a thought in her head now of water or prison or slavery. Later she would have liked to believe it was a dream; she'd have given anything to believe it was a dream. But at this moment she knew it wasn't a dream and so she ran parched and exhausted and half out of her mind. She never looked back at the crater or the house or herself standing in the doorway watching her go; when she finally reached the bottom of the mountain she went on running and stumbling across the black plain. Sometime in the night a wagon picked her up. Sometime in the night she felt and heard beneath her the turning of wheels; she felt and tasted on her lips the trickle of water. Into the night she didn't dream or think at all. The wagon took her back to Paris.

In the early hours of morning she pulled herself off the back of the wagon and again wandered aimlessly as she'd done after burying the carving knife in Thomas' sleeping body. It wasn't until she saw Thomas that she stopped.

It was dawn and, pulled by the tides of the city, Sally found herself returned to what was the center of the Parisian moment, the black prison with eight towers. Smoke still hung on the square. Blood had long since overcome the scent of lilac from the perfume shop. People streamed freely across the prison drawbridge in and out of the prison gate; high on the dark red pikes that surrounded the square were the heads of garrison soldiers. Women wept over the cobblestones where their men had died.

Thomas moved from widow to widow, talking to them, holding them in comfort. To each of the widows he gave some money. It reminded Sally of when she was a little girl and one day had seen him seize the whip from a man beating a slave. She sat dazed in the street, amid the glass of the perfume-shop window, watching. Pieces of glass glittered in the dawn sun.

He finally saw her. He stood in the smoke staring at her. When he came toward her she couldn't help but find his judgment terrifying. He looked at the glass all around her: "You're going to cut yourself," he finally said. Picking her up he caught himself on a shard in the folds of her tattered dress he'd bought her; together they watched his hand bleed. As he carried her in his arms she tore from her dress, as she'd once torn from the discarded bed curtains in Virginia, a long strip and wrapped it around his hand. She wanted to fall asleep in his arms but said, "Put me down."

He put her down. Her knees buckled beneath her and he had to catch her to keep her from falling in the street.

"Three conditions," she said. "First, I will be the mistress of your house. Second, you will never sell me to another. Third, you will free all our children when they come of age."

"I trust," Thomas answered, "you agree in turn not to murder me in my sleep."

"You're in no position to negotiate," she murmured sleepily.

"If I accept your conditions, do you promise to go back to America with me?"

"I promise," she answered, and only in the last moment, before completely submitting to exhaustion, did she open her eyes to look up from his shoulder at the shadow that crossed his face. Nothing much astonished her now. It was the cloud of black moths descending on them.

Except that it was much greater than a cloud, much more than a plague of moths: they filled the sky from one end of the square to the other and then, as they lit on his coat and his brow and his bleeding hand, the man and girl realized they weren't moths at all and never had been. He touched them and they crumbled in his fingers. They left a black smudge. After waiting for their dreadful rain since he was a boy of five, he realized with a gasp that they had finally fallen, the ashes of the slave named Evelyn who poisoned her master Jacob Pollroot forty years before.

T h o m a s   s a y s ,   I   n e v e r saw Paris again. In the beginning my dreams were of the Paris I'd come to after my wife died:
languid gardens and rambunctious streets, the sensual exuber-
ance, the ferocious quest. As the news from France traveled to
Virginia over the years following my return, my dreams changed
and in the last one I was walking the rue d'X and felt a tide about
my feet, some thick hot river; and then I saw bubbling up from the
gutters the blood, and I looked up to a wave of it rushing toward
me. Often I've defended it. Often I've said to those who here de-
cried it that the nutrients of the blood of tyrants are drunk by the
soil of freedom's storms. But in my dreams the blood keeps rising,
flooding the terrain until no soil remains. And if I could never
openly condemn it, now I would secretly hate Paris for how it
betrayed what it fought for if only there were not more intimate,
firsthand treachery to despise.

On the other hand, some small more intimate treachery on the
part of the King of France might well have saved his head. . . . He
needed a slave of his own. He needed some black vessel to receive
the blackness in his heart and soul and leave him strong enough
for the right and good. He needed to commit some trivial duplicity,
betraying his vain, viperous little Austrian queen; in so identifying
the part of him that cried for redemption he might have redeemed
his country if not his throne. Now his blood bubbles up with all the
rest, and so does his queen's.

One should not make the rash promises of one's ideals before so
many witnesses. I told her I would never marry another. Perhaps I
wouldn't have anyway. Perhaps I said that not so as to ease her
passage into death but to deliver myself to the forbidden that I had
denied myself so long even as I hungered for it. In a year I'll be
fifty. I passed some time ago that point where I was closer to the
end than to the beginning. I spent all the years up to that point as
the slave of my head's convictions rather than my heart's passions,
and never felt as alive as the first night I took her. Never felt as
alive as those moments when I knew I'd done something that could

never be forgiven. In the nights that have passed since, I accepted such moments not as the crimes that contradicted what I believed in but as the passionate chaos that justified and liberated the god of reason living within me. I've asked myself whether I love Sally. I believe I have come to love her, even if it's not the way I loved my wife. Sally was the woman who was there when I was closer to the end than the beginning, when I wasn't so willing to surrender my moments only to my convictions. Surrendering to passion, I came to believe my convictions not less, but more.

When I was young, the state of Virginia did not allow a man to free his own slaves. Such was the bond between the slave and the man who owned her. Such was the state that would not loosen such a bond. At the age of twenty-five I offered to the state a law that would allow a man to free his slaves, freeing not only the slave but the man who owned her. The state was outraged. Twenty years later I took her in the Paris night and cannot free myself from it: such is the bond between us. And no law will set me free of the thing I own, the thing that possesses me in return.

I believe in time the black one may be whole. The state hates me for saying so.

I've invented something. As the germ of conception in my head it was the best and wildest and most elusive of my inventions. It's a contraption halfcrazed by a love of justice, a machine oiled by fierce hostility to those who would ride the human race as though it were a dumb beast. I've set it loose gyrating across the world. It spins through villages, hamlets, towns, grand cities. It's a thing to be confronted every moment of every day by everyone who hears even its rumor: it will test most those who presume too glibly to believe in it. But I know it's a flawed thing, and I know the flaw is of me. Just as the white ink of my loins has fired the inspiration that made it, so the same ink is scrawled across the order of its extinction. The signature is my own. I've written its name. I've called it America.

In the autumn of 1789 Thomas left Paris with his daughters, valet, and mistress and set out for home. On the night they came within sight of the Virginia coast their ship caught fire and the entourage, with as many of their possessions as could be rescued, were loaded into small boats and rowed ashore. The ship burned behind them in the sea. On Christmas Day James drove their coach over the familiar hills of Thomas' plantation, which Thomas and Patsy and James hadn't seen in nearly seven years; and suddenly the horizon filled with the black faces of slaves rushing to welcome them. For the last mile the slaves followed the coach to the house, shouting at James and cheering when the carriage door opened and Thomas emerged, followed by the two daughters. But the commotion stopped still at the sight of the beautiful black slavegirl who took her master's hand to step from the coach, dressed in her fine European clothes. Without a word, staring straight ahead of her, Sally kissed her stunned mother and then vanished with Thomas into the house, as unmistakably pregnant as she was elegant.

The child died at birth. It was a small girl, who would have had the face of her mother and the firelike hair of her father. Over the next ten years Sally bore Thomas several children; it was the last, a son named Madison, who would later identify Thomas as his father, though Thomas' "legitimate" family—his daughters and their own children—were bound to deny it, as they would in fact deny that Sally was Thomas' mistress at all. They would have denied Sally's very existence if it had been possible to do so persuasively. Thomas never acknowledged his children by Sally, nor did he treat them in any fashion differently from the way he treated the other slave children of the plantation. But as Madison grew older he would often, from a distance, be taken by visitors for Thomas himself; and later, as each child turned twenty-one, Thomas quietly fulfilled his agreement with Sally and gave them their freedom, at which point, one by one, they disappeared in the night, to reappear in other places and other lives.

Her own identity, which she'd begun to construct so tentatively as a free woman in Paris, was now given back to the role of possession, without whose possessor life meant nothing. She did not completely forget the person she conspired to make in Paris, in the moments when she wouldn't thank him for a pair of gloves: now, when he returned from his travels, she'd thank him for such gifts by closing the bedroom door and dropping her dress from her shoulders. What life was solely hers she came to pass over the years making jewelry, which she'd store in a black wooden box with a rose carved on the top, or give to the other slaves who came to regard Sally with a nearly mystical awe. It didn't occur to her that this jewelry might have value. She made it for her own pleasure, often from the beads of Indians whom Thomas would sometimes take her to meet in the hills. Thomas had great respect for the Indians' resourcefulness and honor. Sometimes it seemed to her that he felt special kinship with the savagery of their existence and envied the harmony in which they lived with that savagery. Sometimes, it seemed to her, he talked of them as though they were white. Sometimes he talked of them as though they were better than white. She noted this with wonder and rage.

She took charge of his bedchamber and the rest of the house, also as they'd agreed on the rue St-Antoine, the enormous fury of Thomas' daughters notwithstanding. She kept out of the sight of visitors to whatever extent was possible, though the visitors never stopped coming. Often they'd wait for Thomas in the parlor of the house, anxiously anticipating the appearance of the famous fiery philosopher-king while wondering with baffled alarm about the tall beggar who seemed to have wandered into the house from the woods outside and was now shuffling down the hall toward them in rags. The stories of Thomas' eccentricities and quiet outrages only grew with his fame, and inevitably became more frenzied during his campaign for political office. There were stories that he was broke and in debt, which were true. There were stories he hated the clergy, which were true, and God, which were not. There were stories he was going to ride at the head of a great slave army and lead a new revolution. And then, in the shadow of the Nineteenth Century that advanced at twilight across the Virginia hills, there were stories he kept a beautiful black woman in his bedroom. These became the currency of doggerel, newspaper articles and songs. With some variations, the name of the woman in these songs was always the same. Dashing Sally, Dusky Sally, Black Sally.

When Sally heard the stories she feared Thomas would send her away. She thought to confront him one night and ask what he was going to do with her, and to remind him of their contract that he never sell her; but she didn't have the courage and she was too afraid of what he might answer. She lay awake many nights wondering about what was going to happen to the children whom Thomas never acknowledged. Thomas, however, didn't send her away or sell her. He answered none of the charges made about Sally, either publicly or privately, and denied no rumors; the greater the controversy grew, the more his allies pressed him to answer and deny, the more his daughters now used this turn of events to try and banish Sally from their lives forever, the more he kept his silence. However he may have been haunted by the rape of Sally and the betrayal of his conscience, he would not compound these things by denying her.

One night, as she slept in his bed, the door opened and she turned and saw his silhouette in the light from the outer hall. "Yes?" she asked.

"I'm elected" was all he said. Then he went to the window of their bedroom and sat in a chair in the dark, and was still there when she finally drifted back to sleep.

He was gone when she woke the next morning. She got up from the bed and drifted through the house, where the day had already begun; she was a little alarmed at how late she'd slept. "Have you seen Thomas?" she asked everyone, but no one had seen him at all. He didn't return in the afternoon or the evening.

He didn't return the next day, or the day after, or the following day. She stood on the porch late into the evening, staring out at the road and the wooded Virginia hills. The other members of the household watched her and whispered to each other. Visitors to the house were turned away with the news that Thomas wasn't home. The weeks passed, and then the months.

A year passed, and then another. Sally struggled to keep the plantation together but everything began to dissolve in the mists of ruin and decay. The walls of the house smeared like colors in a hot steam, and everyone at the plantation became more inert. One night she announced, "I'm going to find him." James loaded her a small wagon of supplies including food, blankets, the black box with the rose carved on top full of her jewelry, and the carving knife she'd wrapped in one ragged red Parisian glove. Leaving her children in the care of her mother, she set out with the wagon and two horses, down the road she'd watched so many evenings waiting for his return.

For a brief moment it occurred to her perhaps he'd returned to Paris. But Paris had been all terror and Bonaparte in the years since they'd left, and nothing was there for him anymore. She drove the wagon westward as its supplies slowly dwindled. Sometimes she slept in those inns that would give a black woman a corner to stay in; usually she slept outside. She could feel the eyes of the Indians watching her from the hills but she worried more about being raped by frontiersmen or seized by whites as an escaped slave. Finally the supplies ran out and all she had was her jewelry box and her knife. She abandoned the wagon and rode one of the horses. She tried to sell the other horse to two men in a tavern one night; when she overheard them asking each other what a lone colored woman was doing with two horses she became frightened and left, without the other horse.

Everywhere she went she asked people if they'd seen Thomas. To her great alarm she was surprised by how many said he was dead. She was shocked by how many insisted there had never been such a man. Every once in a while someone claimed to have spotted him, perhaps even recently; someone told her he'd been seen with the Indians, a thin giant shadow walking with them along the ridge of the mountains.

She did what she had to do. When there was no food left she worked for those who would feed her. When there was no work she begged on the road until her voice was gone. When there was nothing but her body to give for a place to sleep then she gave it. Twice she was captured as a slave when she couldn't produce proof of her freedom, and twice she escaped because both times her captors expended themselves in the pleasure of her. She hated both of them enough to kill them with her knife, but as she'd grown older she had become shrewder about the politics of murdering white men, about the relentlessness with which white people would hunt her down for it. So she didn't avenge her violations but fled them.

She searched a long time. She crossed the great river that lay to the west, and continued on where neither white man nor black had gone, into the land of the red. She collapsed one winter's day from cold and exhaustion and hunger in the middle of a field of snow, and when she woke she was in an Indian tent with several women who were admiring the jewelry from her box. She stayed with the Indians through the winter. She gave them the jewelry. Now all she had was the knife. With it she drew for the Indians pictures in the dirt of a tall man with a head of flame; but she had trouble communicating to them his whiteness, since she was now so far west some hadn't seen a white man. For a while in her own mind Sally pictured Thomas as she supposed the Indians did, black in the sun. Often in her imagination she made him blacker than she. She stripped him nude and placed irons around his ankles and chained his arms, and rode along behind him on her horse, the reins in one hand and a whip in the other.

In the spring she set out again, on a new horse and blanket, wearing the clothes the Indians had given her. She crossed land as red as the Indians, land so red she could only believe the Indians who lived on it had emerged straight from the ground made of its rich red dirt. She rode as the Indian woman of an unknown tribe, and when she met other tribes and they asked her to identify her own, sometimes she said Virginia and sometimes she said Paris, and sometimes she tried to say another word that she'd been trying to say a long time, except it had caught in the ventricles of her heart like her own name in the ventricles of a strange vision she'd once had. For the remainder of her journey the word rested there and she couldn't clear her heart or throat of it, she couldn't bring it to her lips. Under the searing sun of the summer she rode, concentrating on nothing but saying it, and she didn't finally say it until she'd found him.

She found him in an Indian village high on a mesa that overlooked the world as far as she could see it. She stumbled onto the village by chance, meeting some Indians at the foot of the mesa and allowing them to lead her up the path along the mesa's side. They offered her a place to sleep and took her to an adobe house that waited on the other side of a narrow stone bridge that crossed the main mesa to a smaller one. The bridge was so narrow and high that, as she crossed, she didn't dare look anywhere but straight ahead. The house was empty and cool. Some water was in a bowl. Some blankets were in the corner where she could sleep.

As she was falling to sleep, she had a dream. She dreamed she was back in the Hotel Langeac on the rue d'X, back in the bedroom where she'd slept with Thomas. She dreamed it was once again that night when he'd told her they were going home and she'd been devastated by the realization of how she'd miss him, as possessor and master and father, if she stayed behind in Paris. In this dream she once again reached behind the headrest of the bed and took the knife from the red Parisian glove and, as she had that night, raised the knife above her head and brought it down into him. Except this time no moths flew from the bed. This time she could hear the wet sound of the rip of the knife and she knew she'd killed him. When she dreamed this, the word that had been caught in the ventricles of her heart loosened itself and floated up to her throat; she could feel it on the back of her tongue. The knife slipped from her fingers.

She heard it fall to the floor. Which was odd, because she was sleeping on the floor, and there was nowhere for the knife to fall.

She heard a strange sound in the room, and it took her some time to identify it as music, playing very low. At some point, in the low clouds of her sleep, there was also the shriek of a siren, like the alarm of an air raid.

The word was between her teeth. She wanted to bite it in two and taste its blood.

In her sleep she raised her fingers to her mouth and tasted blood after all. Dimly she looked at her fingertips as though pieces of the word would be there.

"America," she said. She woke and there was blood on her pillow. There was blood on the sheets of the bed beneath her. Someone was lying in the bed with her and his head was flowing with blood; and she was startled to have found him again, and wanted to ask what had happened to him and where he'd gone, except that she knew he couldn't answer. Then in the next moment she forgot her dream entirely, only the flotsam of it washing in and out with the tide of her consciousness; and though the tall man in the bed next to her looked familiar, she could no longer remember his name. The music suddenly stopped and she heard the click of the radio. She sat up in the hotel room to look at the two men in suits at the foot of her bed. One was a very large black man and the other was a small white man with red hair. The black man bent over to pick up the knife from the floor and stood there for some time, holding it in a handkerchief and turning its bloody blade over and over.

She looked again at the dead man next to her. She was now awake enough to cry out, and she rose from the bed too fast, becoming dizzy. "Take it easy, Mrs. Hemings," the large black man said. He put the knife in the handkerchief over on a table in the corner of the room and took Sally by the arm to steady her.

"Married name is Hurley," said the small, wiry white man. He was reading from a note pad that he pulled from his coat pocket. "Hemings is her own name."

The black man pulled a chair from the table and sat Sally down. The room was stark. No pictures hung on the dirty white walls and there was no furniture besides the bed and the table and the chairs. On the table were the knife, now forming a small pool of blood, and the radio that had been playing. Besides the door that led out into the hotel hallway there were two other doors, one of them to the toilet'where there were a sink and faucet but no bath or shower. The other door was next to the bed.

"Mallory, is that guy still out in the hall?" the black man said to the other one, who turned and opened the door and signaled to the hotel concierge in the hall. The concierge was a fat man with a handlebar mustache; he was pale and breathing heavily. He tried not to look at the bed where the body was. "Where's this go?" the black man said to the concierge, pointing to the door by the bed.

"That's been shut up as long as I've been here," the concierge said. Bringing himself to look at the body, he blurted, "I don't like this in my hotel."

The black man went over to the door by the bed and opened it. The concierge made a sound of surprise: behind the door was nothing but a wall of dirt. Some of the dirt fell into the room. The black man touched the dirt wall and looked at his fingers; he gnawed on the inside of his cheek, which he tended to do when he was confused. "This has been opened recently," he said. He looked at the dirt trickling into the room through the door. "Someone tried to get out through here," he said. Then he walked back over to the table where Sally was sitting in a daze. She stared at her hands in her lap. The black man sat down in the other chair and looked at her. "Now then, Mrs.—" he started. "Damn," he muttered, and turned to Mallory.

"Hurley," Mallory said.

"Mrs. Hurley," the black man said, "what's your name?"

Sally didn't answer. "Sally," Mallory said, reading from his note pad.

"Thank you, Mallory," the black man said with annoyance, "I know *you* know what her name is. I want to see if *she* knows what her name is." The concierge was still whimpering at the sight of the body in the bed. "Mallory," the black man said, "please take away our friend here and let me talk to Mrs. Hurley?" Mallory took the concierge out and closed the door, and now it was just the one man and the woman. Sally still hadn't said anything and stared at her hands in her lap. "Hey," the man said, snapping his fingers. Slowly she looked up at him. "Mrs. Hurley," he said, "my name is Wade. I'm a policeman. I have to ask you some things and you're going to have to try and tell me the answers to what I ask you."

Sally looked around the room, at the walls and the bed.

"Can you tell me what happened here?" Wade said. She looked vacantly ahead of her and then at the dead man. "Can you tell me who he is?" Wade asked, and she looked at the bloody knife in the handkerchief on the table. "Is that yours?" She reached to touch it. "Just leave it, Mrs. Hurley. Sally. We're going to have to check that out and if it's not yours then you don't want to touch—"

"It's mine," she said.

Wade gnawed on his cheek again. His brow furrowed and he looked around him to see that the door was closed. "Now you should be careful what you say," he said to her in a low voice. "In this city you can be locked up for nothing other than the fact that someone in my position just doesn't happen to like you, which I've done in the past but don't want to do now." Wade was trying to figure out if she was black. It was a tricky situation for him. It wasn't beyond Mallory to be spying for either Wade's superiors at headquarters or some low-level priest up at Church Central; everything was fucking intrigue in this city and here was Wade, a black man in a room with a very beautiful woman who might be black and might have just murdered a white man. So he couldn't cut her much more slack than he'd be able to justify later on.

"It's mine," she repeated with determination. She was determined about it because it was the only thing she remembered now, or thought she remembered, though as the moments passed since she woke she became less and less certain. It seemed important to be able to lay claim to this singular memory. The legal ramifications of the knife's being hers either hadn't occurred to her or weren't as important as the sanity of being able to remember this single thing.

"I've got to take you in then, Mrs. Hurley," Wade said. He got up and went to the door of the hallway, where Mallory was waiting. "You make the call?" he said to Mallory.

"They're coming in now," Mallory said. He looked into the room at Sally and then at the bed. "Should we check out the body?"

"Let the coroner do it," Wade answered, "that's his job." He nodded at Sally. "I'm taking her in. I want to hold off a little while before notifying the husband." Sally turned slightly in her chair. Talking to Mallory, Wade lowered his voice. "You said there's a child?"

"A daughter," Mallory answered. Sally turned back in her chair. "This is the way I like these babies," said Mallory, "open and shut."

"That's because you've got an open and shut brain," said Wade. "When the others get here I want you to go over this place top to bottom. The whole hotel and the streets outside. Go around back and see if you can figure where that door used to go."

"You're going to have to take my altar shift this afternoon," Mallory told him, with no small satisfaction.

"Shit," Wade fumed. "Where?"

"Humiliation."

Wade heard sirens outside from down the street and then the sound of them pulling in front of the hotel. Doors slammed. "That was actually damned punctual," he said. Two other police came up the stairs and into the room. One looked at the body casually and the other, who was new on the detail, turned a little white. More cops were on the stairs and Mallory started giving directions. Another older cop came in and started on the body. "Either of you got a rosary?" Wade asked the first two cops who had just arrived. Rosary was the name they used for the irons and the new cop pulled some out. Wade nodded at Sally and the new cop clamped the rosary around Sally's wrists. Sally looked at the chains on her hands as if she had known all along it would come to this. Wade took her down the stairs. The sound of the chains clanking between her arms and the way she looked at them as she got into the car released in Wade so deep a sense of betrayal he felt sick.

Headquarters was over on the other side of Sorrow, which was the next zone over from Ambivalence where the hotel was, so they had a good twenty-minute ride, maybe longer depending on the foot traffic. Wade took the long way to avoid the Market and part of Downtown. Sally sat next to him in the front seat. He told himself he put her in the front seat so he could question her, though he wound up not saying anything to her; then he told himself he didn't say anything because the more he pressed her the less forthcoming she was going to be, and he knew he didn't believe that either. He just wanted her in the seat next to him and now that he had her there he couldn't bring himself to talk to her. She was so beautiful he just held his breath and felt mean about it.

When he placed her in the cell she gazed around her and then at Wade so mournfully that all he could do was hurry away.

Wade thought about the woman for the rest of the afternoon. The file on her was one of the thinnest he'd ever seen. Sally Hurley aka Hemings, twenty-five years old, married to Gann Hurley, twenty-seven, whose occupation was listed as "artist," whatever the fuck that meant, with one child, two years old. Actual date of birth on Sally Hemings: blank. Place of birth: blank. Parents: blank. Race: blank. How did this ever get past Primacy? The husband's listing as an artist and the Hurleys' address on the edge of the outlaw Redemption zone were little red flags waving in Central's face. Wade wished Sally could have told him more than she did and he wished she hadn't told him the one thing she had, about the knife's being hers, because if she hadn't identified the knife and it somehow came back from the lab clean, there was always the chance she might have slipped through this somehow, though if Primacy wanted to burn her they didn't need a reason anymore than he needed one to lock her up. He was still thinking about this when the alert siren went on across the city and he remembered he was supposed to take Mallory's altar shift.

Wade went through the motions on the shift, his mind still on the Hemings woman. Randomly he narrowed his search choices to

Circles Seventeen and Thirty, both on the far side of Humiliation. Seventeen was on the list of neighborhoods that hadn't been hit in a while; Mallory had gone through Thirty only yesterday, which meant if Wade went back today he might catch someone off guard. Wade wasn't up for catching anyone off guard, so he decided on Seventeen. Even under the perpetually dark sky the white of the circle shone blindingly in his eyes as he drove into the middle and parked in the shadow of the blue obelisk. As with all the residential circles of the city, nine individual units dotted the circumference of Seventeen and faced the obelisk at the center. The units were identical in size and all built of gray brick. The obelisks were so tall that from Downtown the suburban skyline of the city was a range of blue spires against the black clouds and the ash of the volcano to the east.

Wade chose three units in Seventeen as randomly as he'd chosen the circle itself. It wasn't possible for anyone ever to be certain their unit would be inspected during an altar-room search; sometimes, if the cop was surreptitious enough, it wasn't possible to be sure even after the search was over. He found nothing to confiscate in the first; in the second he took a small wooden carving of a woman's head. There wasn't anything particularly subversive about the woman's head, but something faintly enigmatic about the woman's expression made him decide he better bring it in, since there was no telling these days what Primacy considered subversive and what it didn't.

In the third unit he was dissatisfied with the sealing on the altar-room door. He inspected it for a few minutes to see that there wasn't some kind of peephole through which those in the small room on the other side of the door could look out. That was a heavy-duty felony and it would be pretty damned stupid of whoever lived here, but some people were just pretty damned stupid. He clicked on the intercom next to the door. "This sealing's a violation of city ordinance," he said to those inside the room. "Get it taken care of by tomorrow morning's alert." He made a note of the unit. He kept looking at the carving of the woman's head from the second apartment, thinking maybe it was harmless enough and he'd put it back. But it was the only artifact he'd confiscated and he ought to have something to show for the search; the matter was decided when the siren came on announcing the

shift was over. He put the carving in his coat pocket. Sitting in his
car in the shadow of the blue obelisk he could see families emerging from the altar rooms of their units, peering out the windows.
As he started the car and slowly drove out of the blinding white
circle, the crash of the ocean against the city's cliffs in the distance
reminded him of something, but it wasn't until he felt the nausea
that he realized it sounded like the irons around Sally's hands as
she'd gotten in his car at the hotel.

Crossing Humiliation back toward Sorrow, Wade filed a report
over the car radio about the faulty altar-room-door sealing in Circle Seventeen's third unit. To his surprise a response came back
from Mallory, who was already finished with the business at the
hotel and back at headquarters. "Shit," Wade said, "you could
have done your own damned altar search." Mallory laughed with
dull malice. Wade thought Mallory was going to tell him something
about Mrs. Hurley or the hotel but instead Mallory was calling back
about a disturbance "over in Desire," he said, and then abruptly
stopped, and now it was Wade's turn to laugh because he knew
Mallory had just fucked up. Redemption was Primacy's name for
that zone but, because it was an outlaw zone, everyone called it
Desire; Church Central's jurisdiction over it was shadowy at best.
It wasn't a good idea, however, to call it Desire over the police
radio because some ass-licking priest up at Central was probably
monitoring it and now Mallory had fucked up and this made Wade
happy. "Say," Wade answered back, "where did you say that was
again, Mallory?" and he emphasized Mallory's name just so the
ass-licking priest would be sure to catch it.

As twilight fell Wade headed toward Desire and the scene of the
disturbance, a twenty-four-hour strip joint called Fleurs d'X.

S o m e t i m e s e v e r y t h i n g h a p p e n s at the same
time, Wade told himself later looking back on this particular day.
As he finished the altar shift and was heading back to headquarters, he'd already thought about swinging by to check out the day's

graffiti. But if by any chance he'd forgotten about the graffiti, what he saw at the Fleurs d'X would have reminded him.

Wade knew he was going to have to take a better look at the day's second dead body than he had the first. For the cops to get called in about a "disturbance" in Desire, it had to be pretty disturbing; what probably happened this time was that someone panicked before cooler heads could prevail. Desire got away with more than the usual shit because it operated out at the edge of the lava fields just barely within—or without—Primacy's threshold of righteous indignation; the zone's anarchy particularly manifested itself in a huge neighborhood called the Arboretum, a single unit of chambers, lofts, urban caves and underground grottoes linked by hundreds of corridors and passages that shot off in every direction. The Arboretum's nefarious activities included a theater, TV arcade, book outlets and, Wade had heard, a floating emporium of forbidden artifacts, most of which had been seized by police during altar-search shifts before making their way back onto the black market. You needed either a map or a very weird brain to find your way through the Arboretum, and since no map existed because no one person knew everything that was in it, that narrowed the neighborhood's demographics to the very weird. Sailors docked up the coast and drove down across the tip of the lava fields in old bombed-out buses in the dead of night, just to get lost in the Arboretum for weeks.

Wade spent an hour bullying his way through the labyrinth to the Fleurs d'X, where twelve stages and a bar operated twenty-four hours a night, since daylight never invaded the Arboretum. Between the lights and liquor and women the club usually got pretty steamy and crazy, but now it was empty. Bodies on the decidedly rigorous side of mortis probably didn't do much for business. No suspects were waiting in bed with the dead man this time, just the faces of the girls watching from behind the curtains as Wade walked into the club's dressing room. The dead man slouched on the bench was more a kid, really—about twenty, Wade supposed—good-looking and muscular, bare-chested and his head completely shaven. Covering his chest was the tattoo of a voluptuously naked woman with the head of a bird, standing in a sea of fire. Something dripped from the birdwoman's mouth, and behind her was a strange insignia of crossed blue lightning bolts; on the back of the boy's shoulders were tattooed red wings. His eyes stared openly before him, their terror frozen and eternal; his chest was ripped and his fingernails bloody with his own flesh, as though he had attacked his own body. From the look on his face Wade figured heart failure as the cause of death, but that was another thing for the coroner to work out. As with the body in the hotel bed earlier this morning, Wade had never seen this guy before. The nice thing about a bald kid with wings tattooed on his back was that if you'd ever seen him before, you sort of remembered later.

Behind the bar a tall darkhaired woman named Dee, whom Wade had known as a stripper herself in younger days, poured him a drink. He waved it away. "Somebody panicked," he said, "that's how I figure it."

"You going to get it out of here?" said Dee.

"How long's he been dead?"

"All night."

"Outside in the real world," Wade explained, "the night's just starting. In this place 'all night' means anything."

"I would have dumped him myself except I heard someone called the cops," Dee said with some disgust. "I decided it would be better if there was a body when you got here rather than me trying to convince you there wasn't."

"Ever seen him before?"

"No."

"The girls?"

"Nobody knows him at all. Things broke up fast when it went down. Jenny, one of the dancers, became hysterical. It made for a shitty evening."

"So who called it in?"

"You're the cop, you tell me. Could have been anybody."

"Your girl?"

Dee shook her head.

"So exactly what happened?"

"You're the cop, you tell—"

"Is this Jenny here tonight?"

"I didn't want This Jenny around. I told you, she was hysterical."

"It would have been a lot easier for both of us if I could have asked This Jenny a few questions."

"She doesn't know anything anyway," Dee said, "she never even talked to the guy. You going to drink this or not?" She answered her own question and drank it for him, and then poured another. "Actually, Mona's the one who talked to him."

"Who's Mona?"

"Right there."

She pointed to the nearest stage and there was Mona.

Wade had never seen her at the Fleurs d'X before. Nineteen years old, her long blond hair tied back, she stood on stage in nothing but black stockings and black high heels and the pink light. Dee waved her over and Mona came down off the stage, fanning her face futilely with her hand; unlike the other girls, she didn't appear remotely alarmed by Wade. When she smiled, with her head tilted to one side like a child, she had little baby teeth, perfectly lined up and white. She smiled at Wade now, who gnawed on his cheek. "The guy in the back room," he said, "with the tattoos."

Mona leaned against the bar, one arm folded beneath the other, fanning her face with her hand. "Tattoos?" she said.

"The pictures," Dee explained to Mona, pointing to her chest.

"Yes," Mona nodded, understanding now, "it was the pictures," and Wade could tell from the accent she was from the Ice to the north.

"What do you mean it was the pictures?" he asked.

"He said they were changing."

"The man said the tattoos were changing?"

"He was sitting watching," and she pointed over at the stage, "and then we talked after. He came back to where we dress," and now she pointed in the direction of the body, "and I said he couldn't be back there, it wasn't allowed. One of the other girls was with me."

"Jenny," said Wade.

"Suddenly he was very excited. Very upset. He said the tat . . ."

"Tattoos."

"He said they were changing on his body." She looked down at herself and absently straightened the top of one stocking that came up to her thigh. He was thrilled by her fearless vacancy. "He took his hands," and she raised her own hands and curled her fingers to show him, "and clawed at his chest," and she ran her fingers over her breasts, "and tore at the tattoos. I think he wanted to remove them." She wasn't unintelligent, she wasn't without expression. She smiled easily. It was the way she smiled, Wade thought to himself later: with her little baby teeth, vacant of concern and introspection and moral contemplation. As though she could search her soul in seconds flat and find not only everything she was looking for but everything she needed, because all she would ever need was the means that would further whatever needs were immediate, to eat when hungry and drink when thirsty, to cover herself when cold and fan her face when hot, to sleep when tired and fuck when excited, to use the world to survive, vacant of artificial meanings and tomorrows that existed nowhere but in people's heads.

Outside Wade radioed in to headquarters to send another squad car for the body. No one but Wade would have thought much about the dead kid with the tattoos, writing him off as insane or under the influence of some new bootleg drug; but when Wade heard the story about a man who believed tattoos changed on his body, he knew he had to go check the graffiti. He didn't expect the graffiti to have any answers but he did expect, as had been true every day for the past year, the graffiti to have changed like the tattoos. Wade crossed Desire. In his mind he entered Mrs. Hurley's cell and took her as Mona watched, smiling vacantly with her little baby teeth and her head tilted to the side. Wade decided to go by Mrs. Hurley's address; he parked at the center of the circle in the dark, trying to remember which unit was the one. He turned off the lights of his car. For ten minutes he watched the windows for a glimpse of someone who might be Gann Hurley or Sally's little girl. In several of the units people kept glancing out at him.

Finally Wade left the circle and then Desire, driving along the highway that surrounded the city of Aeonopolis. He was happy to leave behind him the sound of the sea against the cliffs to the west; it was replaced by the sound of the evening train on its way into Vagary Junction, passing through the control zone that divided the city from the outlands. On one side of the highway to Wade's right was the silhouette of the Arboretum rising in the night sky, on the other the lava fields to the east and beyond the lava fields the looming shadow of the volcano, its peak flat as though lopped off by God. From the mountain, where a steady stream of smoke could be seen rising by day, came a red glow from the crater's fires. Soon Wade reentered the city. He passed the barbed-wire entry points of several districts and drove into Downtown, finally pulling up to the corner of Desolate and Unrequited. He got out of the car and made his way down the cobblestones of a small alley.

The city was full of graffiti. By ordinance, defacement was designed into the basic urban blueprint; architects built it into their work. In this way Primacy confronted chaos, disorder and revolution by preempting the result of their vandalism, devaluing if not utterly obscuring the occasional scribble of outlaws. Primacy's graffiti took the form of sloganeering, nursery rhymes or, most often, scriptures; but this one Wade had noticed a year before: SONIC MEN, ANONYMOUS GOD, it had read, in dark blue block letters. Wade never really understood what it meant. He only knew that SONIC MEN, ANONYMOUS GOD wasn't the sort of thing the priests over at Central were cooking up. He directed Mallory to direct someone else to remove it. The next day Mallory reported his man couldn't find it. Since he never passed up an opportunity to make an idiot out of Mallory, Wade personally dragged him out to Desolate and Unrequited and down the cobblestone alley to point out the graffiti and ask how anyone could have missed it. Except that now, in the same dark blue block letters, it said BLUES FALLING DOWN LIKE HAIL.

There was no doubt it was by the same hand. Wade walked up and down the alley in search of the previous day's graffiti, feeling more and more foolish; inspecting the wall, he scraped at it with his fingernail as though the sonic men and anonymous god lurked beneath the granite surface. But there was nothing underneath. The message had simply changed.

It continued to change over the next year. Every day that Wade went by the alley at Desolate and Unrequited, the graffiti was different. Old letters disappeared and new ones appeared, or old ones rearranged themselves to form new words. Wade didn't mention the graffiti to anyone or try again to have it removed; since it was always changing, no one could exactly accuse him of neglecting his duty. The messages, after all, were removing themselves. He wrote each down, one after another, in a log he kept. Each came to seem somehow more seditious than the one before, even as each became more obscure, until finally there was one he didn't understand at all: ICH BIN EIN BERLINER.

So when he heard there was a man who claimed the tattoos on his body were changing, Wade didn't entirely discount it. Tonight, stumbling down the dark alley without any other light, he searched for the graffiti by lighting one match after another and tossing them away as they singed his fingers. The last message had been the rather vague and irritating THE RETURN OF THE QUEEN OF WANDS. It seemed urgent to Wade not to miss whatever the graffiti might say today of all days; he found the corner and was down to his last match. He struck the match and held it up to the wall, and was immediately disappointed by the most innocuous and meaningless bulletin yet.

THE PURSUIT OF HAPPINESS.

"You're running out of ideas, my man," Wade muttered out loud. In his dismay he forgot about the burning match, crying out when it reached his fingertips and flicking it in the air where it fell like a dead firefly.

Those who built Church Central on the huge rock that overlooked the sea to the west and the city to the east never imagined any other structure would challenge its predominance on the landscape. Their contempt for God was large enough that they presumed not only to speak for him but to approximate his stature; a few may have convinced themselves that it was God who gave them the rock for the purpose of building the church in the first place.

In the meantime the Arboretum to the northeast grew higher. Those living in the Arboretum didn't give much thought to the Church at all; their descent into the Arboretum's passages was the lateral motion of their mirth at God and Primacy. The Church insisted on jurisdiction over the zone that it called Redemption but everyone else called Desire and continually drew up plans to tear down the Arboretum board by board. That the priests shrank from this finally had less to do with bureaucracy than dread of what might come shrieking out of the Arboretum once its walls had been pulled away. Even heaven, one priest conjectured, needed a hell where the things heaven could not know or touch might be contained.

If Church Central was anxious about the disorder of human desire that lurked in the Arboretum, it genuinely feared the only thing on the landscape that dwarfed both, and that of course was the volcano. The volcano towered high enough in the east that the sun didn't rise above it until a couple of hours before noon; and from the rooftop of Church Central a day never passed that the priests didn't contemplate the curl of smoke that rose from the volcano's flat peak. A day never passed that somewhere in the city a priest didn't fall to his knees and press the palms of his hands flat to the ground, not to prostrate himself before God and beg for mercy but to assess the seismic whispers of the coming infernal scream.

Mostly Church Central feared the volcano because it represented the most alarming of possibilities: that there was indeed a God, who manifested himself daily in the mix of volcano smoke and ocean fog that the residents called the Vog. What's more, God's molten wrath might be reserved not for the hedonists of the Arboretum but the priests' cynical impertinence, though this consideration demanded a moral imagination no one in Primacy possessed enough to fully formulate or understand. But the possibility nibbled beneath the floorboards of their consciences. It was heard at night as the devouring of an approaching infestation. And if moral imagination would not acknowledge let alone speak to the prospect of God's living in the crater of the volcano, it certainly wouldn't account for the fact that if one were to stand on the volcano's peak and look midpoint between Church Central and the Arboretum in the distance, if one were to stand in the highest tower of the Arboretum and look midpoint between Church Central and the volcano, if one were to stand with the priests on the rooftop of Church Central and look midpoint between the volcano and the Arboretum, the crosshairs of these vantage points would have fallen on the small alley off the corner of Desolate and Unrequited where Wade read the daily graffiti like changing tea leaves. But Wade didn't know this either, and the man who would later chart such coordinates only stared at their undistinguished meeting point and concluded it meant nothing at all.

On his way into headquarters the next morning, Wade encountered the rookie who had provided the rosary for Sally Hemings the previous afternoon. That was when Wade heard about the satellite dish the police had found at the hotel. If there was a dish, Wade thought, then there must have been a monitor, but Mallory hadn't mentioned either. "Mallory said not to tell anybody," the rookie added, affecting his most guileless expression but not quite able to conceal the connivance in his eyes. Shit, Wade said to himself, another weasel. Mallory tells the kid not to tell anyone and the kid runs straight to me; the entire force is made up of one ambitious backstabbing motherfucker after another, and that now includes guys who haven't been around for more than a week. "I was trying to get the concierge to cough up the TV when Mallory came along and said forget it, he'd take care of it. He didn't want to book the concierge, either." The rookie said, "I thought monitors and dishes were felonies. Maybe I shouldn't have told you."

It was stupid of Mallory, really. Every time Wade thought maybe he shouldn't underestimate him, Mallory did something silly. "You've done fine," Wade said to the rookie.

"You won't tell Mallory that I—" the rookie started, but Wade was already walking away through headquarters, narrowly missing its low ceilings and brass pipes that coiled from the walls. If Mallory worked fast enough, he could have sold the TV on the black market last night at the Arboretum, assuming he was there to check out the Fleurs d'X business and there weren't a lot of other cops around. For a few minutes Wade was feeling pleased that he had something on Mallory, to balance out whatever Mallory had on him, but the maze of paranoia through which his mind wandered led to another possibility, that Central let Mallory work his black-market scam as a reward for being an informant. Of course, if Mallory was caught red-handed, Central would deny any knowledge of it and Mallory would be on his own. When Mallory walked by his desk Wade, studying the file on the hotel murder, said casually, "Heard you found a dish," to which someone with a little imagination or humor might have answered something cute along the lines of, You mean the little dark one with the huge tits or the blonde with the long legs and funny accent? Instead Mallory sputtered just long enough for Wade to change the subject and wave the file at him. "So what do you have?"

"Have?" Mallory said, flummoxed.

Wade leaned back in his chair. "From the hotel yesterday," he said. "What did you think I meant?"

"Nothing."

"What?"

"We didn't find anything."

"What did the concierge say?"

"About what?" Mallory nearly shouted.

"The murder, Mallory," Wade answered slowly, "there was a body, remember? Blood everywhere?"

Mallory read from a note pad he took from his pocket. He was rattled, the way Wade had brought up the TV and then dropped it. "Concierge says Mrs. Hurley checked into the hotel two nights before."

"Under what name?"

"Sally Hemings."

"What was she doing checking into a hotel in the middle of the night?"

"I didn't say it was the middle of the night."

"All right. What was she doing checking into—"

"Domestic dispute. Told her husband she was leaving. Or, actually, the husband says she just left."

"What's the husband do?"

"He's an actor in the Arboretum."

"Did he say what the argument was about?"

"No."

"Did you ask him?"

"Sure I asked him," Mallory answered.

"She was upset enough to check into a hotel for two days."

Mallory said, as though it explained something, "They're broke."

"They're not living off anything he's doing in the Arboretum, that's for sure."

"She makes jewelry and sells it. Necklaces and earrings and shit."

Wade looked at the file. "She ever clear this jewelry with Central?"

"I doubt it."

"You search their place?

"I thought we were investigating a murder."

"They live off the sale of this jewelry?"

"A couple years ago she inherited some money. One of those things that happens out of the blue, a dead relative she never knew existed." Mallory checked the note pad again. "Madison Hemings. Anyway, that money's gone now."

"Where was Hurley the night before last?"

"Arboretum, he says."

"Was anyone with Miss Hemings when she checked into the hotel?"

"The concierge didn't see anybody. She was up there alone the whole time he knew of. She went out the day before yesterday and came back and told the concierge she'd be leaving. Yesterday he goes up to her room to see if she's checking out and the door's open. He takes one look inside and sees everything and calls us."

"And he never saw anyone else coming or going?"

"He sleeps behind the front desk at night."

When he's not watching his felonious TV, Wade thought. "There's still no ID on the body," he said, opening the file again. "Did you dust?"

"Of course we dusted. She left prints on the door knob and the knife, about what you'd expect."

"No prints from the dead man."

"No."

"And you checked out the premises entirely, the streets outside the hotel and in back."

"Yeah," Mallory said impatiently.

"That other door that was in the room, where's that go outside?"

"We couldn't find any other door outside."

"Did you look—"

"We looked fucking everywhere. There was no damned door outside. That door's been sealed up a long time, like the concierge said."

"Miss Hemings said something—"

"Mrs. Hurley you mean," Mallory said.

Wade licked his lips. "Mrs. Hurley said something when she woke. Did you catch it? It was only a word or two."

Mallory looked at his note pad. " 'A miracle.' "

" 'A miracle'? Are you sure?"

"That's what I've got down here. 'A miracle.' "

Wade kept looking at the file. "And you found nothing—"

"Give me a hint, Wade. What is it we're supposed to have found?"

"A murder weapon."

"Excuse me, but there was a knife with blood all over it—"

"You read this file? Guy wasn't stabbed." For a while Wade and Mallory looked at each other. "Not a stab wound on his body. He died from a blow to the skull."

"Bullshit."

"Hard enough for his brains to run out his ears."

"The handle of the knife," Mallory sugested.

"The handle of the knife? The woman goes to kill this guy with a knife and beats him over the head with it?"

"You know," Mallory leaned across Wade's desk and into his face, "I get tired of you making me feel stupid. There's nothing complicated about this. A woman's in bed with a stiff and a knife has blood all over it."

"I apologize, Mallory. It may not be complicated to you but I'm confused, because if the knife isn't the murder weapon, then—"

"She got rid of the fucking weapon."

"Let me make sure I've got your theory straight. She beats the man over the head. She leaves the hotel in the middle of the night with the murder weapon while the concierge sleeps behind the front desk. She must have gone some ways from the hotel to dispose of the weapon because you searched the hotel and you searched the area around the hotel and you didn't find anything. She gets rid of the weapon and then *returns* to the hotel. She comes *back* through the hotel lobby past the front desk where the concierge is still sleeping and goes *back* up the stairs. She comes *back* into the room where she's murdered a man and leaves the door open, the way the concierge found it, so that people can walk by and get a good look inside and see she's murdered someone. Just to make sure somebody finds her there, she crawls into bed with a knife and goes to sleep next to the murdered man while he bleeds all over her."

Mallory was still leaning over Wade's desk. "I just knew you were going to find some way to get her off," he said. "I could see it all over that big black face of yours yesterday, you licking your chops for some of that black—"

"You should be careful right now," Wade said quietly.

"Yeah, well, we should all be careful, shouldn't we?" Mallory answered. "Woman in bed with a dead body and you're telling me she had nothing to do with it. Well, sure, it's your call. We've all got our secrets and I guess this one's yours. But, you know, somebody up there," and he pointed over his shoulder in the direction of Church Central, "might wonder just who killed this guy if she didn't."

"It won't be the first murder that's gone unanswered in this city."

"It'll be the first one," Mallory said, "where the killer was lying in bed next to the fucking body."

In fact, it hadn't been Wade's intention at all to release Sally Hemings. The discussion with Mallory just sort of evolved that way. Whether Wade liked it or not, Mallory wasn't half wrong: Sally was the only person at the scene of a crime that didn't have any other suspects, except for perhaps the husband if by chance his alibi didn't check out. The fact was that Sally acted like a woman who had killed a man. From the beginning Wade had assumed she did it, though he might have hoped she had an excellent reason; the fact that they hadn't found a weapon only meant Mallory had been too busy working his TV scam with the concierge to do a proper search. Now his petty little political struggle with Mallory had put Wade in the position of having to let her go, at least for the time being. He walked to her cell, turning everything over in his mind.

He almost expected not to find her there. He almost expected to walk into the jail and find her cell empty, a lapse among the city's incarcerated. He thought she might have just disappeared as peculiarly as she'd appeared, that he'd walk back to his desk and find her file vanished with no trace of her having existed for the twenty-four hours she'd existed. But inside her cell she sat on the small bench staring at her hands in her lap the same way she had in the hotel room the day before, appearing only somewhat less dazed at the end of the twenty-four hours than she was at the beginning. Wade watched her awhile before she looked up at him.

"You said something yesterday," he finally spoke, "when you

woke in the hotel. Do you remember?" He said, "Something about a miracle." She licked her lips and seemed to think about it very hard, terrified that there might be still another thing she couldn't account for. Wade signaled to the jailer at the end of the hall, who pulled the lever that opened Sally's cell. Nothing was so sophisticated in this city, Wade thought, as the levers that opened and closed cells. "I'm going to take you home," he said, and she looked at him with the hushed alarm of someone who might be expected to know where home was.

He tried to explain things to her on the way to Redemption. They took the same outer road bordering the city that he'd driven the previous night coming back from the Arboretum. "You're not clear of this," he said to her next to him in the front seat, "not by a long shot. You and your family are going to be watched. There's only so much we have the authority to do in this particular zone, but keeping an eye on you is one of them and arresting you again is another, since the crime was committed in the city proper." He paused. "I'm sticking my neck out for you." It only really occurred to him as he said it. Maybe, he thought angrily, she didn't give a flying fuck. "But my neck's not that long," he almost snarled, "not for you, not for anyone." He still had trouble talking to her. It didn't help that she said nothing in return. "You know," he blurted, "if there's anything you'd like to tell me, this would be a fine time to do it," and he looked at her to see that he wasn't talking to thin air.

She was still there, all right; the thin air hadn't claimed her. She was still there, mute, unaware, and it made him furious. He wanted to stop the car and reach over and shake her, but he was afraid of himself, of what he'd do if he actually touched her and held her in his hands. He wanted just to wrest her from her transfixed attention, until he realized she was transfixed not with her memories or her dreams but something very real beyond the windshield of the car.

She was looking at the volcano. She looked at its flat peak and the smoke that rose into the sky. She watched it a long time, it seemed to Wade, and then for a moment she turned to him, something expectant in her eyes and on her lips. She craned her neck to keep the mountain in view long after they passed it and after Wade had turned the car toward the sea. In the white light of the circle, when he parked the car and she got out, she continued watching the volcano until her attention was interrupted by the redhaired two-year-old child who ran from the third unit into her baffled mother's arms.

It may not have been until that moment that Wade knew for certain he was going back to the Fleurs d'X. Even driving Sally back from police headquarters he believed he could resist returning to the Arboretum. But when the small child ran to Sally's arms, and the mother grabbed her daughter to her breast, Wade reeled where he stood, a huge wavering black blot on the blinding circle beneath his feet. He staggered back to his car. Gann Hurley, tall and thin with long brown hair, stood in the doorway of the third unit watching his wife and daughter.

In the afternoon light the Arboretum was an aberration, something that should have been invisible until darkness fell.

The entrance was obscure, indifferent. At the end of one of the neighborhood's jutting extensions, cut in a grungy wooden wall about a foot off the ground so Wade had to step up, it was by chance or intention the neighborhood's single doorway, wide enough for only one person to go through at a time. There was no actual door that opened or closed. Wade walked down a long narrow corridor as the light from outside grew dimmer. Soon there was nothing but blackness.

For a man as large as Wade the claustrophobia was uncompromising. The corridor wound slowly downward and then back up as the distant sounds of the inner Arboretum became more distinct. Through the walls Wade could feel vibrations from far away, the churning of machinery and the hum of unknown music punctuated by garbled profanities, violent outbursts, high female moans. Then the corridor made a U-turn, opening onto a small chamber where a dirty bulb burned high on one wall, revealing two doorways to the left and one to the right, and another directly on the other side of the chamber. The doors on the left and right opened to other corridors to other intersections, eventually leading to the theater, TV arcade, artists' grottoes and bars, and units where people lived.

The doorway directly in front of him revealed a spiral stairway. Descending the stairs Wade passed any number of other doors; he'd never gone far enough to be sure how many. It had been two or three trips before he realized the sound he heard from the bottom of the stairwell was water, not like a river but a tide that rolled in and out, lapping at the subterranean walls. Deep in the heart of the Arboretum its sensual history was told in the smells of the people who had been there, floors and walls soaked with wine and the juice of lovers' couplings. There was also the Vog that had drifted in when the Arboretum was layers younger, before its labyrinth had crept inexorably across Desire's terrain, the belch of the volcano's most ancient ambitions caught in the Arboretum's inner sancta and frantically drifting from hall to hall in search of the way out. The same panicked search was shared by the lost ones Wade met as he made his way through the neighborhood, their confusion compounded by the narrowness of corridors that wouldn't let more than two people pass: anyone crossing Wade's path, for instance, found he wasn't inclined to back up. Thus the Vog Travelers, as they were called, spent as much time going backward in the passageways as forward. Sometimes one would mutter to Wade, asking where "the door" was. But usually they said nothing, concealing their plight because thieves in the Arboretum preyed on the Vog Travelers who wandered perpetually until they found exhaustion or delirium.

In all the times Wade had been in the Arboretum he'd never seen a single sign. One learned to count and remember. Deep in the heart of the Arboretum were the drawings of artists who scurried from corridor to corridor looking for bare walls, since honor dictated that no one vandalized the work of others. No one wrote graffiti because graffiti was the propaganda of authority. In the final corridor that ran to the Fleurs d'X, a short squat painter without a shirt, grim colors splattered across his chest, rendered with dimensional exactitude the image of another corridor, which had the effect of providing Fleurs d'X its ultimate camouflage, particularly since elsewhere in the Arboretum was a corridor where the artist had rendered the image of this one, complete with two naked girls leaning in one of the doorways. So Wade, who had been to the club just twenty hours before, couldn't be sure it was real until he actually stepped into it.

Once again it was almost empty. Three stages were open; no bodies waited in the dressing room. Wade sat down and Dee, who was watching him, motioned one of her girls over to his table. She was small and dark, with breasts too large for her body. "Where's Mona?" he said. Mona, she answered, didn't come on for another three hours. Wade considered the political ramifications of whiskey and ordered one anyway, and then another; after an hour a fourth stage opened and after another hour a fifth and sixth. The Fleurs d'X began to fill. Wade was aware he should have been back at headquarters some time ago. But each time he thought of Sally Hemings standing in the white circle with the small child whose hair was the color of fire, he'd call over the small dark girl and order another whiskey as he contemplated her disproportionate breasts, shrinking them in his mind. He waited.

When Mona finally appeared from the back of the club, she didn't acknowledge Wade at all; she didn't acknowledge anyone. For a while she served drinks and stood in the doorway where it was cooler, waiting to give her first performance: all the stages were now operating. Wade got up from his table, staggering a bit because he'd had many whiskeys. He went over to Mona's stage where the seats were full of other men; randomly he tapped one on the shoulder. "You're in my seat," he said.

The sailor looked up at Wade. "Fuck off," he answered.

Wade picked the man up and dropped him on the floor. He sat in the chair while the man thrashed painfully on the ground. Mona smiled at Wade with her little baby teeth; on the floor the sailor continued seething, mumbling obscene comments. Mona laughed. Wade laughed too. He ordered another drink.

The dancers rotated among the stages so that a man sitting at one stage long enough would eventually see all the girls. Wade, however, followed Mona from stage to stage; soon men gave up their seats without having to be removed from them. For each dance Wade put more money on the side of the stage, and after each dance Mona picked up the money. She laughed at the money in the same way she laughed at the sailors being dropped on the floor, and Wade laughed back. There wasn't any doubt in his mind she danced for him. He could tell by the way her head tilted to the side and she smiled with her little baby teeth when she knelt on the stage and opened herself; he didn't care so much about her opening herself. He didn't care so much about the secrets of her body. He did feel affection for the roundness of her breasts, which were not too large; he admired that her nipples were always erect. He understood that she might act as though she danced for the other men, he understood she might smile at them in the same way and show them the same things; she had to deceive them, he understood, in order that they would give her their money. But he knew, with more and more clarity as he drank more whiskey, that her dance for him was special, and a promise, and they could laugh together at how round her breasts were, at how erect her nipples were, at how it sent his blood rushing through him, how it sent his very blackness rushing through him.

They laughed at the ludicrousness of how black he was and how white she was, how pale she'd be to his penetration, as dark as the deepest passages of the Arboretum or the ashen Vog that circulated its hallways. Wade gazed on her vacancy in wonder at how it was big enough to receive the white rage of his heart, the white pain of his having arrested the previous afternoon a woman whose file was white, whose past was black, whose whiteness or blackness was blank. The vacancy of Mona's soul could receive Wade's rage and pain without either of them making the slightest impression on her except for the way their sensations pleased her or interrupted her boredom; Wade believed if he could just ravish this blond child in the wide-open spaces of her vacant soul he would not only free himself of the way Sally Hemings' captivity revolted his conscience, but celebrate it. Mona was the refutation of everything Sally stirred in Wade, including the sound of chains that followed him all day and night. If Wade could have opened up Sally and split her in two, he believed the opposite who would have stepped out of Sally's dark voluptuous rubble was Mona; at this moment he saw and felt all this even as he couldn't identify it in the dark. Perhaps all he saw was his anticipation of the time to come when he would wish he'd never laid eyes on Mona. It was, however, Mona's job to be laid eyes on. She liked the men at her feet; more than anything else it may have been why she danced at the Fleurs d'X, for the way men had to look up at her, leaning their heads so far back it was difficult for them to breathe. They had to gasp for air just to catch the merest glimpse of what she showed them, and it seemed to her an entirely reasonable price for them to pay.

When he passed out, he heard her laughing in his ear. From down in his unconsciousness, as his bulk slid from the chair to the floor, there bubbled up to his mouth a gurgle of laughter in return.

He woke in the dark, the lights of the stage above his head gone dead. He pulled himself up on the chair and looked around at the club, which was empty but for a single dancer on one of the far stages, dancing to a single customer while several other men lay sprawled on the floor to the side. One of the dancers worked the bar; Dee was gone. Mona was gone. Walking out of the Fleurs d'X, Wade held his hands before him as though the doorway wasn't real but an artist's rendering. He was almost disappointed when it allowed him to leave.

Sliding around the corner of the passage he continued blindly ahead. He'd gone some way, turning several corners and moving the length of several passageways, before he vaguely realized nothing was familiar. The light and air were dank and the walls close, and suddenly the whiskey inside him lurched to his throat and he vomited on the floor. "How do I get out," he whispered. He turned another corner to find himself back at the Fleurs d'X, two naked girls in the doorway watching him approach. "Oh," he said, when he slammed the palm of his hand into one of their faces and it was nothing but a flat wall. He continued to barrel down hallways that became tighter and tighter, becoming more and more lost until he stepped through a doorway and found himself almost tumbling down a hole, catching himself on the rail of the stairwell that had originally brought him from the surface.

Outside the Arboretum, in the Vog of dawn, he lay across the front seat of his car. Before he dozed off he promised he would never see her again. It wasn't a prayer; Wade didn't pray, one of the few acts of subversion he allowed himself. I'll never see her again, he repeated, and then asked, Her? wondering to whom he made the promise, and which of two women he meant. At police headquarters no one said anything to him. No one asked where he'd been all the day before, or why he looked the way he did. After a while he felt almost clean and unscathed, as though nothing had happened. Throughout the day he got up and walked over to the window to look out and see what time of day it was and feel therefore that his life was real after all. Sometimes he caught Mallory glancing over at him, but decided today he wouldn't worry about political intrigues; at any moment he might get a call from Central to explain why he'd released Sally Hurley, but this had the potential for being just a bit more overwhelming than he could deal with, so he dismissed it. He wanted to go home and sleep, and late in the afternoon he did.

He lived at Circle Four in Humiliation. He arrived during an altar-room alert, from which he was exempt; he drew the curtains of the windows and lay on his bed in his darkened unit listening to the radio before drifting off.

He woke in the middle of the night and looked out the window. The Vog enveloped the blue obelisk at the center of the circle. He wanted to have Mona in the Vog against the white of the circle in the middle of the night. Against the white where no one would see her and against the night where no one would see him and they would be invisible this way, all that would be seen was the drama of their loins, the black of his rod and the pale red of her rose. The next day he had the distinct feeling of things slipping away. Over and over he read Sally Hurley aka Hemings' file. What would he say if they asked why he let her go? He kept feeling Mallory watching him. In the afternoon he left headquarters, driving through the city across Downtown and the Market. He pulled the car over at the corner of Desolate and Unrequited and walked down the alley to the day's graffiti.

It said, I DREAMED THAT LOVE WAS A CRIME.

He got back in the car and drove out of Downtown. He was back on the road that ran between the city and the lava fields, driving through the merciless black shadow of the volcano. The shadow went on and on, it didn't seem to end. Shouldn't there be an end to this shadow? he asked himself. He parked for a while, perplexed by the endlessness of the shadow; but he wasn't in the shadow of the volcano anymore, he was in the shadow of something else. Last night he just sort of lost his head, he told himself. Took a wrong turn somewhere and got confused. Drank too much whiskey, for one thing. Too much damned whiskey and not keeping his head straight: he wouldn't make that mistake again.

Her breasts were so round. Not so large, not so small: round and perfect like her little baby teeth. The thrilling vacancy of her laugh when she took his money.

Three stages were open in the Fleurs d'X, three dancers. One was the girl who had brought him his whiskey the night before; now, writhing across the stage, she was well served by the extravagance of her breasts. He knew it was hours before Mona came on. He sat at the side of the room and signaled one of the other girls for a drink. Not too many whiskeys today, he assured himself. Maybe he wouldn't even wait for Mona, maybe he'd leave before she came. From over behind the bar Dee brought Wade's drink herself and sat down beside him. Wade put some money on the table and threw the drink back, just to get things started. Not too many today.

"You like one of my girls?" Dee said.

"I've reevaluated the matter of her tits," Wade answered, still watching the dancer on the stage.

"Mona has an early shift tonight," said Dee, "your lucky night. Mine too, because it means she's on before most of the sailors get here and that means fewer customers you'll be tossing around the room. Let's not let things get out of hand this time."

"I'll decide when things are out of hand," Wade said. "That's my job, to decide when things are out of hand."

"Is that what you're doing, your job?"

"I want another of these," he said to the shot glass. "Not too many today, but I'll have another. When does she come?"

"Another hour," Dee answered, nonplussed. She snatched the empty shot glass and headed back for the bar.

Sometimes everything happens at the same time. Life seems quite normal and then suddenly everything changes rather abruptly, first this and then that, and you think, Sometimes everything happens at the same time. But it also might have been true that it was happening all along, all your life, some small impulse always denied that wasn't going to be denied forever. It wasn't that you changed, it's that who you really were was always there but denied, and then you stop denying it. And there you are suddenly face to face with who you really were all along. There you are face to face with your lucky night. That was the secret of Fleurs d'X, Wade told himself, sipping his third, well maybe it was his fourth, whiskey: that you believe, as you step into doors that are entrances or doors that are pictures of doors, that you're stepping into the dream of Fleurs d'X until one night, your lucky night, you understand you've been stepping in and out of your own dream all along, and that everyone else was stepping in and out of your dream as well. Then it doesn't matter any longer what time of day it is outside. He waited to explain this to her. When she got to the club and took off her clothes and stood in the doorway ignoring him— he knew she wasn't really ignoring him, he knew she was thinking about him every moment that she pretended not to even be aware of him—he waited for her to drift by so he could take her by the wrist and tell her. By his fifth whiskey, or perhaps his seventh— they were little whiskeys, and he was a big man—she came just close enough for him to catch her.

He didn't sit at her feet tonight, he didn't follow her from stage to stage. That wasn't necessary anymore. He caught her by the wrist; in the dark she actually looked surprised to see him, but that was the dark for you, it fooled you, because she knew he was there all along, she knew standing over there in the doorway and serving drinks to the men, to all the men but him, she knew all along he was there. So she couldn't have been surprised. "You stepped into *my* dream," Wade explained, "it's not that I've stepped into yours. It's that you've stepped into mine." She tilted her head to one side and smiled: Yes. Like that. Her vacant beauty like an open plain with nothing but the sky for as far as one looked. Looking into her was like descending concentrically through a maze to a door at the center, where you expect to find a confessional and instead step onto a veldt that stretches as far as the eye can see. A hysteria of nothingness, inviting him to mount it, empty himself into it.

But then she shook herself free of him. She looked at him and for a moment he actually believed it wasn't so different from the way she looked at all the others. He gnawed on the inside of his cheek. He pushed away the whiskey; he wasn't at all sure she understood. He didn't watch her dance, the dancing wasn't important anymore. The ritual of her dance and his money had performed its necessary function but it was time for new rituals, or none at all.

He got up from his table as she was dancing, turned his back on her, and walked out of the club. Dee watched him go.

He waited. He'd never been much for hiding and waiting, but in the shadows of the Arboretum it wasn't so hard. In the shadows of this corridor or that it wasn't so hard, except that the corridors were so small. Waiting for her now he sometimes wondered what time of day it was, but he knew that wasn't a real question anymore. So it was impossible to say when she left the club that night, because in the Arboretum there was no when. Wade followed her. They walked for half an hour. They took corridors and flights of stairs he'd never seen before; they passed huge arenas where the blue squares of forbidden TVs hung haphazardly in the pitch black, transmitting nothing but waves to an unseen audience in the shadows.

Soon they were in some other part of the neighborhood altogether, an older section where the smells and colors were deeper than he'd smelled before, the Vog hanging in clouds where the corners turned. She never looked behind her. He made no concerted effort to hide himself; she might have looked over her shoulder at any moment and seen him. It didn't seem possible she could miss the sound of his heavy steps. It didn't seem possible she could miss the roar of his blackness against the blank silence of her back. Off the stage, dressed, she looked smaller. He trained himself in those minutes to know her step so that even in the blackest passages, so black that even the white of her body, even the gold of her hair was denied light, he could hear her. In the blackest passages, she surely must have heard him.

By the time she got to her place, he guessed they'd crossed the Arboretum to the other side. Later, when he was inside her flat and saw the window, a porthole that stared out at the volcano, he knew he'd been right. She had a padlock on the door and went through her pockets to find the key. It was dark but she knew the key and she knew the lock. As she opened the door he was standing only ten feet away, gnawing on his cheek until he could taste blood; at that moment the only thing in his head was the only thing he didn't want to think about, and that was her, not Mona but the other one, who was free of his dream and the world it claimed as its own. Mona was closing the door behind her when he caught it with his hand. She wasn't alarmed to see him, but when she tilted her head to the side in that way of hers, she didn't smile, and he missed her little baby teeth. "Your lucky night," he said.

W h e n   h e   f i r s t   s a w the stone, Wade had no way of knowing he'd been in the Arboretum three nights.

They had simply stretched into the one long endless night that always possessed the Arboretum, though at some point it occurred to him that outside the clocks must have noted his absence. It occurred to him in the amber haze of her cognac, the aquadream of her opium, the porcelain delirium of her body, as he lay naked among the dusty cushions of her flat, his body glistening with the tide that washed out between her legs with its smell of sea and flowers. The clocks outside know I'm not there, it occurred to him; and he was just lucid enough to translate this into its more banal consequences. But he'd think about this only long enough to tell himself not to think about it, instead to gaze at her sprawled unconscious at his feet, disheveled and tangled. She gurgled with the sound of him inside her.

From his stupor he gazed dimly at the door, which he'd secured on the inside with the lock that had been on the outside when he first arrived. He was trying to remember what he'd done with the key. He reached blindly for the cognac and knocked something over, and heard the splash and saw the rising amber cloud around him. To the catastrophe of the spilled cognac he said something even he didn't understand.

He sat up from the cushions and pillows that were propped beneath him. He took her long yellow hair in his hand and studied it stupidly; he ran his hand down her back to her thigh. He pulled her beneath him and heard her unconscious moan of dread, the response of her recesses to the realization that her vacancy wasn't big enough for him, that her vacancy wasn't one moment larger or smaller than her own body and she couldn't hold all of him. When he exploded in her he spilled out of every crevice, he ran down her chin and hung from the lobes of her ears like pearls. She didn't laugh anymore like when she picked up his money after dancing for him, she didn't laugh like when he picked up the sailor from his chair and dropped him on the ground; her laughter had turned to the resistant whimper that made him soar, until exhilaration got the better of him and, in the throes of the way he fucked her and the long endless night of the Arboretum, he said, "Sally."

It stopped him the moment he said it. It turned him befuddled, and she felt it. He looked down at her beneath him and, there through the part of her lips, were her baby teeth and the smile of victory.

He let her go, she fell limply beneath him. He staggered to his feet, the name he'd spoken ringing in his ears, except that as the moments passed he wasn't at all sure he'd actually said it. He looked at her as she dozed on the pillows, and almost asked if he'd said it, except that he didn't trust her answer. Suddenly he had to go to the toilet; now looking around he realized, for the first time in three nights, that the toilet was a converted altar room. It surprised him, actually, that anybody had ever bothered building an altar room in the Arboretum.

He was trying to think what he'd done with the key as he stumbled around the unit, which was in some disarray from when Mona had torn the place apart (hours ago? days ago?) looking for the key herself. That was when he saw the stone. It was in a small cabinet that sat next to the porthole that stared out at the volcano, smoldering in the night and smoking in the day, except now Wade couldn't remember ever seeing anything in the porthole but night, he couldn't remember ever seeing daylight at all. He touched the glass of the porthole as though it might be a painting hanging on the wall, rendered by the short, squat artist who was slowly transforming all the hallways of the Arboretum into other hallways. Wade put his face to the porthole and peered in. The closer he looked, the drunker he felt. He gazed back at Mona on the pillows, then turned to the cabinet.

On the top shelf was the key to the lock. He had no recollection whatsoever of putting it there. But now more interesting to him were the cabinet's other contents, a small collection of forbidden artifacts from the black market: a child's doll and a pair of dice, mildly pornographic pictures and a comic book, small wooden carvings like the woman's head he had found a few days ago and still had in his coat pocket, and next to the key a stone. It seemed out of place. Wade examined it. It was flat and smooth on one side, rough and broken on the other, and fit his large hand; but what caught Wade's eye, what sobered Wade for the first time since he'd lost himself to Mona's sanctum, was the writing. It was a fragment of graffiti. But the graffiti wasn't written on the smooth side of the stone, rather it was scrawled across the rough part where it seemed impossible that anything could be written; and though the beginning and end were lost, the core of the message was unmistakable: *pursuit of happiness*

The actual calligraphy was nothing like the graffiti in the alley at Desolate and Unrequited, which made the coincidence all the more astounding to Wade; and suddenly it became very important to him that he keep this stone. For the first time in a while he found himself chewing the inside of his cheek, where the wound of his confusion had healed amid the cognac and opium and flesh. When he'd gotten his clothes and dressed, he took from his coat pocket the carving of the woman's head and placed it in the cabinet in exchange for the stone, which he put in his pocket. It was heavy and weighed the side of his coat down. He thought it might fall through the bottom of the pocket. He also took the key. He opened the door to the black hallway and stood for some time staring down the corridor to a dark end he couldn't see, wondering if he had the bearings to find his way out.

It was dark outside, as the porthole had told him it would be, as though the porthole were not a window but a crystal ball suspended on the wall, predicting his future.

His car was still where he'd left it, in the part of Desire where there stretched in the daylight hours the endless shadow of the volcano meeting the endless shadow of the Arboretum. The window was broken on the passenger's side. Wade found the night air not invigorating or cleansing but oppressive like a perfume; he felt the weight of the Vog on his heart, and the sound of the waves against the cliffs were louder than he'd ever heard them. In the car he took the stone from his coat pocket and set it on the seat next to him. Trying to start the car he didn't feel so good.

He drove back into town. He went to the corner of Desolate and

Unrequited and pulled the car over to the curb, and opened the door and threw up. He got out of the car and walked down the alley. Even in the middle of the night he knew where to find the graffiti. Even in the dark he knew it wasn't there anymore, that the place where Wade's graffiti had addressed him day after day for the past year would be conspicuously blank. The furor of the spot's emptiness drove his hands to his head, covering his ears.

At home he confronted the evidence of outside clocks that had noted his absence. He parked beneath the obelisk at Circle Four and opened the door of his unit; more disturbing than any havoc was the way the unit had been ransacked so carefully. It revealed the precision of authority, the invasion of those who didn't have the time or enthusiasm for superfluous destruction. Wade recognized the work because he'd often done it himself in the past. Standing in the doorway of his unit, his arms hanging limply at his side, he heard someone behind him; he turned and saw, stepping from the dark Vog into the light of his doorway, the rookie who had rosaried Sally Hemings and told him about Mallory and the satellite dish at the hotel. For a moment the rookie didn't say anything. "What?" Wade finally asked.

"Yes sir," the rookie said. "They posted me here in case you came back." He pointed behind him and Wade could now see, on the other side of the circle, another car beside his own. "Everyone's been wondering what happened to you, sir," the rookie said. After a moment he added, "It's four o'clock in the morn—"

"I didn't ask what time it was," Wade said.

"No," the rookie replied coolly, and now Wade realized something was wrong. Now there was no telling whose side anyone was on. "No, you didn't ask what time it was, but I thought I'd mention it anyway. I have to ask you to come with me down to headquarters." He stepped aside as though to give Wade room to pass, even though he was standing outside, in the clear, where even Wade had room to pass. Wade hated being in the clear. He hated having room to pass. He wanted to make the rookie back up in a corridor; he missed the psychic geometrics of passages and doorways and chambers.

There were more cops at headquarters than he'd expected to see at this hour. Most of them were sleeping slumped in their chairs, but they woke quickly when Wade walked in. Wade went to his desk and aimlessly moved some things around on it; looking down at the desk he caught sight of himself. He looked himself up and down. His coat hung on him like a rag, and his tie and belt were missing; he became vaguely aware that he smelled of sweat. Was there the smell of sex and liquor too? Was there the smell of blood, or was that in his mind? Was that the smell of still being in a dream, or the smell a dream leaves on you when you wake from it? In the middle of headquarters he felt everyone examining him. The only one in the room who didn't get up from his chair was Mallory.

"Look at you," Mallory finally said. He leaned the chair back; his hands were folded in his lap. He appeared very relaxed. "You're not presentable. *They* want to talk to you but you're not presentable. Well," he said, bringing the chair forward and now rising from it, "no time now for making ourselves presentable. *They* want to talk to you." Mallory headed down a back hallway and stopped midway to turn, a withering look on his face that asked what Wade was waiting for. They left through the back door and got in a car. Mallory was behind the wheel. "Whoa," Mallory said, recoiling from Wade with relish. "You smell unpleasant, Wade. Like you just crawled out of the deep shit you're in, except you couldn't have done that, because it's much too deep for that. Deep deep deep. Way deeper than you're going to be crawling out of any time too soon." He laughed and shook his head. "We went around the bend on this one, didn't we? Mrs. Hurley, I mean. Black Sally. I mean, I think she's a shade, what do you say? Next time we bring her in, those of us who are still on this case I mean, which we can presume will not include yourself, those of us who are still on the case will get a better look at her. A good look. All the nooks and crannies. I'll give you a report when I come see you on visiting day, let you know what you missed. I'm sure they'll let you have visitors every now and then. It'd be inhuman otherwise. You have to seriously fuck up not to ever get any visitors. Well, shit, now that I think about it. You may not be seeing anybody for a while, now that I think about it. Well, I'll find some way to let you know. Don't think your old buddy Mallory would leave you wondering about something like that. I'll find some way to let you know just how black it all gets down deep inside. I say she's a horse of a different color, once you get a better look. The good part, especially. I say the good part's not even built the same way. I say you touch it, you bite it, and the juice that comes out is more like blackberry than cherry." Mallory thought a moment, driving down the highway. "When you come, Wade, is it white?"

Wade looked at Mallory and then stared in front of him as Mallory drove west in the dark, toward the rock. There was only one road up to Central. It was lined with small lanterns that hung from posts all the way up the side of the rock, but they didn't light the road particularly well, their glow rendered increasingly vague smudges as they ascended into the night Vog. At the rock Mallory and Wade parked the car and took the lift up. From the lift they walked to the main doors. The sound and spray of the sea was all around them, mixed with the ash of the volcano. It was impossible to see, in the mist, anything of the sea or the volcano or the white round building itself. Inside the building the huge plain lobby was dark and empty.

Wade had been in the lobby before. He noted that Mallory didn't seem such a stranger to it either, more impatient than intimidated. Over to the left were administrative offices and down a hallway was the Church's confidential archives. At this moment the only other person Wade could see in the building besides himself and Mallory was a clerk leaving the archives, a man in his midthirties with a wild mass of black hair and thick spectacles that, in the glint of the hall light, made his eyes appear like blue crystal balls. He didn't look like a priest. The archives clerk glanced furtively at the two cops as he passed; behind him Wade heard the main doors open and close with the clerk's exit.

Wade and Mallory waited. There was no place in the huge lobby to sit. Finally through a single door to the right came a man in the white robes of a priest. He signaled to Wade to follow him and with the flick of his fingers dismissed Mallory. "See you, Wade," Mallory said as the priest led Wade back through the door he'd just come from. Wade didn't look back.

The priest and Wade took another lift. The priest neither said anything nor looked at Wade. When the door of the lift opened on a long hallway as austere as the lobby downstairs, the priest indicated a room at the hallway's far end. Wade stepped out and the door of the lift closed behind him.

The doors of the room at the end of the hallway were open.

Wade was now forcing himself to focus better; he was manifestly aware of the way he smelled. He was still trying to understand if the smell of sex and liquor was real or wafted in the corners of a dream-memory. He got to the end of the hallway and inside were three priests seated around the outside of a crescent table. In the hollow of the crescent was an empty chair. The room was white and the priests were in white; one of the priests looked up suddenly at Wade in the doorway as though Wade's blackness had rudely announced him. He studied the policeman with unmistakable disapproval and pointed at the empty chair.

Wade sat in the chair for almost as long, it seemed, as he'd waited in the lobby below. The priest who had looked up at Wade wasn't paying him attention anymore; he was reading some papers while the other two priests were busy making notes. Behind the priests were windows that looked out onto the night. Beyond the glass of the windows Wade could see bright searchlights illuminating the waves of the sea below. The room was insulated so Wade couldn't actually hear the sea, but sometimes it seemed everything vibrated slightly as though from the force of the waves against the rock. The head priest was still reading his papers. He didn't look at Wade but rather at the papers when he said, "Wade," and since it wasn't a question as far as Wade could tell, Wade didn't answer. At the policeman's silence the priest finally raised his head. "You've been with us for some time." Wade still didn't say anything. The priest studied his papers and said, "Your work in the past has always been satisfactory, Wade. Occasionally a bit cavalier, perhaps even eccentric, but we allow for a man's personality in his work." He smiled tolerantly.

Wade began to say that no one had ever mentioned before that he was either cavalier or eccentric. Wade couldn't remember ever having been—up until the last few days—cavalier or eccentric. He started to chew the inside of his cheek but stopped himself and instead took a deep breath.

"Where have you been?" the priest said.

Wade was focusing. He needed to swallow because his throat was tight, but he knew if he swallowed hard the priest would see it and he felt as though only a hard swallow was separating him from incarceration, not in a police cell but in one of the cells in the rock below his feet or the penal colony to the south, reserved for political heresies. He'd heard many times over many years about the justice of the priests, which was far less benevolent than that of any cop. So he didn't swallow too hard when he said, "Under-cover."

For some reason the priest actually appeared surprised by this answer. "Undercover?" he said.

"On a murder case."

The other two priests stopped writing and looked at him now. The head priest leaned forward across the crescent table. "The murder in the hotel downtown?"

"Yes."

"Have you found anything?"

Wade was trying to think quickly. "I'm following a lead. I've reached an interesting point in the investigation. But I've surfaced now in order to get some hard answers. I'm sure you understand what I mean."

They didn't understand at all. Wade knew they didn't understand, because nothing he was saying made any particular sense. Finally the priest nodded, "Yes, I see." After a moment the other two priests nodded as well. "Wade," said the head priest, narrowing his eyes with concern, "there was a woman. She was at the scene. When you found her she was holding the murder weapon. You held her twenty-four hours and then let her go."

"There was no murder weapon at the scene."

"A knife," the priest corrected, reading his papers.

"The deceased wasn't stabbed."

"But there was a knife."

"But he wasn't stabbed."

"But there *was* a knife."

Finally Wade had to swallow. He'd been talking some time and felt as though he'd choke, perhaps puking cognac all over the priests' crescent table. "The man was beaten to death," he said.

"Then where is the club?"

"Exactly."

"There is no club," the priest said gently, the words cold in the air and the *is* hissing like a snake. "There *is* a knife."

"I think the husband did it," Wade announced.

The priest seemed astounded. "Really?"

"He's an actor. The Hurleys live over in—" he caught himself, almost having said Desire—"Redemption. I had to go undercover to find what I could. I don't like loose ends anymore than anyone else. I like them less than anyone else. I hate them." He paused. "It's . . . difficult in that part of town. We don't really have jurisdiction there."

"That's a matter of dispute," the priest rebuked him. Wade allowed himself to be properly chastened. "Why didn't you tell anyone you were going undercover?"

"Well," Wade said, allowing a cast of disappointment to cross his face, "it's very hard for me to say this. But I have reason to believe, I've believed for some time, that one of my officers has been selling confiscated forbidden artifacts to the black market. I believe that just recently, within the last several days, he sold a TV monitor that was confiscated at the very hotel where this murder took place. In order to keep me from investigating Hurley's outlaw activities and in the process perhaps uncovering this black-market scheme, this officer I've referred to might have blown my cover and jeopardized the investigation. He's also found it necessary to try and implicate Hurley's wife even as the facts of the matter indicate she's not the murderer. In other words, I believe Mrs. Hurley has been an unwitting smoke screen for police corruption on possibly a wide scale."

The priests were stunned. The two flunkies kept looking at the priest in the middle.

"In retrospect," Wade said, "I understand I made a mistake by not coming to you personally and explaining my course of action. I'd like to add that I also feel badly about my appearance at this meeting. It was my hope to make this report in a more . . . presentable manner. I hope you'll forgive the disrespect of the officer who brought me here so unceremoniously. Next time I'll insist on decorum."

The priest locked in on Wade's gaze. "Yes, Wade," he finally smiled faintly, "next time you do that." The two just looked at each other for a long time. Then the priest announced, with some resignation, "Very well. Let's not belabor the matter."

"What?"

"I mean," the priest waved his hand nonchalantly, "do what you have to do. No use spending a lot of time in territory where we don't have jurisdiction anyway."

Wade thought about this a moment. "Does this mean you don't want me to continue the investigation?"

"Of course you should continue the investigation. After all, someone was murdered. Let's not, however, overcomplicate things."

Wade said, "I'm not sure what you mean."

"Yes you are, Wade," the priest said, "you know exactly what I mean. You're a rather clever man. You've just made it rather clear that you're a rather clever man."

Wade chose his words as carefully as possible. "Is there anything about this matter to which you'd like me to give particular attention?"

"I was just getting to that."

"Yes."

"You know," the priest said, "maybe the woman killed him, maybe the husband. Maybe someone in the hotel, the concierge for all we know. But we'd certainly like to know, as much as anything else we'd like to know, who he was."

"Who . . . ?"

"The man who was killed," the priest said, with some impatience.

"There are no records or information on that."

"In your own word: exactly."

Wade nodded. "I see."

"Find out who the dead man is, Wade, and we might be inclined to close the whole matter. The hell with who actually killed him," laughed the priest.

"Yes, sir," Wade laughed back, "the hell with it."

"I was making a joke, of course."

"The hell with who killed him," Wade went on laughing.

The priest narrowed his eyes and shifted uncomfortably in his seat. "Is there anything else?" he said. He was now anxious to get Wade out of his sight as quickly as possible. The center of the room throbbed with the cop's blackness.

"Anything else?"

"That we need to discuss."

Wade thought for a moment. He looked around the white room. "God?"

"You take care of things on your end, Wade. We'll take care of God."

Wade got up from the chair. He was careful not to walk too quickly from the white room. He was careful not to walk too quickly down the hall. At the lift he waited; there was no button. Finally the door opened and the lift took him down to the main floor, where he found his way out into the lobby.

No one was waiting for him, of course, since no one had expected he'd be coming back. Wade had rolled everything up into one big messy ball that Central was going to have to sort out before they knew what to do with it. Once they got it sorted, they'd take care of Wade; he knew that. So he only had a little time. He took the lift down the side of the mountain and walked down the road into Downtown. The lanterns posted along the roadside down the side of the rock had long since gone out and it was still dark, but the sky in the east above the volcano was a lighter shade of blue than it had been before, a lighter shade than he'd seen it in some time. He didn't care for it.

At the edge of Downtown he took a road heading north. He walked in the direction of the nearest blue obelisk. If he remembered correctly Circle Twenty-two was about half a mile away, just on the border of Ambivalence. When he reached the circle he waited behind one of the units; an hour passed and the siren for the morning altar search came on. In the units of Circle Twenty-two people scurried into their altar rooms and shut the doors behind them. In one unit after another Wade went through the closets looking for some clothes that might fit him; the best he came up with was an overcoat. It was small but he could wear it for a while. He also collected whatever money he could find, though people usually knew to take their money with them into the altar rooms unless they left it out as an arranged bribe. In the unit where Wade found the overcoat he used the shower. He was a quarter of a mile down the road when the all-clear alert sounded; at the edge of Downtown he flagged down a startled cop, who took him to headquarters.

When he walked in, everyone appeared as surprised to see him this time as they had the last. Mallory was sitting with his back to the room; he could hear the silence behind him. He turned and saw Wade and didn't look as happy as he'd been a few hours before. The overcoat was tight around Wade's shoulders and under his arms. "I need a ride," he said to Mallory.

Mallory looked at the other cops standing around and said, "Get somebody else."

Wade said, "I need *you* to give *me* a ride."

"Bullshit."

"Would I be here if this was bullshit?" He lowered his voice. "Would I be here right now if it wasn't a good idea that you give me a ride?"

Mallory kept looking at the other cops as though one of them could explain why Wade was there in the middle of police head-quarters and not chained to a rock somewhere. Slowly he pulled his coat from the back of his chair. "Where we going?"

"I'll tell you in the car."

They left through the same back door they had before and got in the car. Mallory wasn't having as good a time as the last time they got in the car. He kept looking at Wade and Wade kept looking out the window. They had driven deeper into Downtown when Wade told Mallory to turn up Desolate Street; at the corner of Unre-quited, he told Mallory to pull over. "Remember that graffiti I told you about a year or so back?"

"No," Mallory said.

"Sure. That graffiti I told you about. You couldn't find it and I came out with you and then I couldn't find it." Wade laughed. "Remember what an idiot I was, walking up and down the alley trying to find the graffiti?"

"Yeah," Mallory answered slowly, "I guess I remember that."

"Sure," Wade kept laughing, "man, was that crazy. Here, I want you to see this." Wade got out of the car and waited for Mallory, who took a lot longer getting out of the car. They stood together on the sidewalk looking down the alley. "I walked up and down here, remember?" Wade said, chuckling. He looked at Mallory.

"I remember, I remember," Mallory said. Wade just went on chuckling, shaking his head. "Yeah," Mallory went on, "you said it was here and we couldn't find it."

"That's it," Wade said, "we couldn't find it. Come here." He motioned with his hand and Mallory followed him. They walked down the alley. They came to the place where Wade's graffiti had been for the past year and there was now only a blank spot. Wade stopped and stared at the spot, and Mallory stood beside him. "See that?" Wade said, nodding at the spot on the wall.

After a moment of staring at the blank wall, Mallory said, "What?"

"Right there," Wade said.

"Where?"

"Right there. In red."

"Red?" Mallory said.

Wade smashed Mallory into the wall. When he pulled him away, pieces of Mallory's nose pocked the wet red smear where Wade had heard the messages of anonymous men and the Queen of Wands over the previous year. Wade held Mallory up by the collar and said, "You see it now, don't you?" and a strange bloody yawn snorted out of the gape that had been Mallory's face. "Yes, Mallory, in answer to your question, when I come, it's white. When you bleed, isn't it red?" Wade examined the disrupted mass of tissue across the front of Mallory's head. "You're not presentable," he said, dropping him in a heap. He walked back to the car and drove away.

At his unit in Circle Four he showered again to wash off Mallory's blood, and then changed clothes. He drove his own car, with the stone from Mona's cabinet still in the passenger seat next to him, out to the cliffs not far from Desire's frontier. Parking the car in neutral with its front tires at the cliff's edge, he got out with the stone and pushed the car over. As though the force of the car's plunge might pull him along after it, he found himself sitting on the ground staring at blue nothingness, the blue of the sky and the blue of the distant sea where only a moment before the car had been. The crash of the car below was really no louder than the crash of the waves.

He walked to Redemption. An hour after he'd left Mallory's face on the wall at Desolate and Unrequited, he was at the doorway of the Arboretum. It was almost light. Before Wade stepped in the doorway to walk down the long corridor, he looked up at the sky and treasured how he wouldn't have to be offended by its lie anymore.

Mona says, Oooh he shoots me up inside. Ohhhhh. It's not so bad when it's only a feeling like opium, something I can think about when I have nothing to think about. In the dark he isn't there at all, and one night when he says the name of the other woman it means I'm not there either. He slips out and sleeps, I push him away. I get up and go to eat at the place in the south Arbo, I hear him splash inside. When I come back from work I think maybe he'll be gone. One morning when I wake he's gone but I go to work and come back and he's back. I'm back, he says. I'm back for good. He tears my clothes. He wants to tear everything, he does it to me fast. After that he looks at the window and smiles. "Only the night now," he says to the window, smiling, "nothing but night," and I'm looking up at the window and see the morning light come in, shine on his smile. But he just says over and over, "Only the night. Damn the light."

I almost never go outside but sometimes when I do the blue points of the city make me think of when I was a little girl growing up in the Ice, the chimneys of my village the way they line the road coming into town. The smoke of the chimneys the way it rises in the sky like the Vog of the mountain like the smoke of the sea and I'd ride with my father in the wagon down the road of our village and the chimneys line the road like tombs, like the empty trees. And the smoke of the chimneys rises and hangs over the road like an archway. And my father sits nearer to me on the wagon seat to keep me warm, he says, he moves his body next to mine to keep me warm. He comes at night to keep me warm. I hear him in the night in the next room keeping my little brother warm. I hear my little brother's cries and I think, Please don't stop, keep my little brother warm all night. Because when he's finished with my little brother he'll come for me: so don't stop. The louder little brother cries the happier I am. My brother is eight. Mother sleeps in the other room across the hall from mine but I know she doesn't really sleep, I know she lies in bed saying, Please don't stop keeping my children warm. Please don't stop because when he's finished he'll come for me, my mother thinks, lying in the bed across the hall. One night I take what I can carry and walk down the road beneath the long arch of smoke until I'm far enough away that I won't have to pray anymore that the cries of my brother never stop.

I know about the stone. I know how Wade stole it from the cabinet, in its place is a small wooden woman's head. Someone once told me these things are, what, forbidden . . . ? None of this matters to me. Someone once told me that I'm, what, attracted? to these things because they're forbidden, but forbidden means nothing to me, so what's to attract. The stone was more real than memory or love. I could put it between my legs and feel it there. I could push it into me a little bit and it hurt and it was a hurt I believed, not the hurt of the heart or head which aren't real. But after the morning when I found the stone gone he came back and fucked me and afterward when he slept I found the stone hidden in the corner of the flat behind his clothes. I left it there until later when the thing happened with the other man, later when I wasn't so sure about the hurt of the heart. Later when, after Wade had been here a long time, I saw the other man who came to Fleurs d'X with the glasses that made his eyes big, who smiled sadly and was lost in the hurt of his heart. One night he dropped his glasses and I was on the floor in the dark helping him to look, and the way he looked at me when he put them on I knew at that moment he was ridiculous like all the others. I laughed. I laughed at how ridiculous and sad he was. They're so easy to forget, the men. It's the best thing about them, the way they're so easy to forget, the way they're never really there at all. But his sadness is in my head now and I can't forget it, his sad smile makes me feel what I don't believe. And now I wait for him night after night to come. I wait for him to give up what all the men give up. They think it's about them, the way I dance, but it isn't about them, it's about the way they're nothing, and the man with the glasses is only another fool, but his foolishness is in my head and heart and I don't know why, and then one night Wade comes to the club when the one with the glasses is there too. After a while I know Wade's watching him. After a while I know he's watching me watch him, and he doesn't like it.

I liked it better the way things were before. I liked it better when the feeling of a stone between my legs was more real than memory or love. One night I come home from work and open the door and step in and find the floor beneath my feet gone. I look up and the ceiling is gone. I look around and the walls are gone, far away I can see into the other rooms and halls and doors. Wade is there naked waiting for me like always, like always he has that look on his face. His thing is hard. We're there hanging in the middle of nothing, everything's vanished. I scream and he nods. I scream again and he keeps nodding.

When Mona opened the door of her flat and stepped in, she found herself falling.

Wade employed the short, squat artist who transformed the halls of the Arboretum to paint Mona's flat as what one would see if there were no walls, nor any walls beyond them, to the ends of the Arboretum. To paint the ceiling as what one would see if there was no ceiling, to the heights of the Arboretum. To paint the floor as what one would see if there was no floor, to the Arboretum's depths. Now in Mona's flat Wade could look in any direction and see to the far reaches of the Arboretum all the catacombs and corridors, the empty TV arcades and casinos and galleries and stages and bars and clubs, abandoned of borders and supports and people. Everything around and beneath Mona was gone, including the very door she'd just come through; all that was left, besides the furniture of Mona's flat—a couple of chairs and a table, a broken-down vanity dresser—floating amid the beams of the neighborhood high above its cellars, was herself and Wade, naked and erect and strangely serene.

She held out her hands to catch herself but even the furniture implied treachery, as though she might grab a chair and the weight of it would only hasten the plunge to oblivion. So Mona felt she had no choice but to reach to Wade, who was there to take her; and when he took her the two of them became suspended in space, and the growl that came from Wade sounded as though it leaked through an abrasion in that space, perhaps the very sound of the rip itself. He entered her and she clung to him, and in the oblivion's cold she let go of him, having decided long ago she would never let anyone keep her warm again. He continued with her until she reached down and yanked him out of her at the moment of his explosion. The white of his ejaculation danced in the air.

In the middle of the night Mona would lurch from unconsciousness, awakened by the sound and speed of her plummet. She would attach herself to the floor like a golden spider, riding it downward until she fell back to sleep.

Lying on his back with her face in his lap and her yellow hair in his fist, gazing up at his living map of the Arboretum, which is to say the universe of his dream, he could see the Vog. He watched it move through the passages of the Arboretum and billow across the terrain. It was the only thing he couldn't eliminate from his vision, the only thing that didn't defer to his elimination of walls and ceilings and floors; it was the uncontrolled thing of his dream and it moved where it wanted. Following it with his gaze, his eyes riding its untamed rampage, Wade became the greatest Vog Traveler of all, until there was nothing left for him but to rise and leap into its dense heart. When he did this, he hurled himself into his own blackness. He hurled himself into the ash of his own flesh, as though it were the black mouth of a volcano. Inside his blackness he heard the sound of years and chains. In his blackness he knew that it wasn't a miracle Sally had said when she awoke that noon in the hotel room, it wasn't a miracle she had said when the knife dropped from her hand. He knew it was a name, the name of both the man she had killed and the act of killing him; and it was a name he'd known forever, though he'd never heard it before. At that moment he knew a thousand nights in the Arboretum had stretched into one.

In the midst of his blackness, he couldn't be sure when he'd stopped taking her and when she'd begun taking him, but it was sometime after he entered his blackness and found she'd been there all along, just like the other one and the name she'd spoken. He found her drinking it, his blackness; as he lay among the pillows and cushions of the flat, feeling himself grow as black as the Vog itself, his little blonde nymph mounted him and drew into her his every drop. On through the night she rode Wade into the distant vapor of his dream laced with her opium and cognac. Her head back and eyes shut, mouth parted with the tip of her tongue be-

tween her lips, she loosed a weird rattle from her depths that told
him the darkness behind her closed eyes wasn't his and the man
she fucked wasn't him. "Open your eyes!" he heard himself bellow
at her, though he couldn't be certain it came out as anything but a
grunt or a squeak. When he climaxed, a luscious smile burst on
her lips. It was a different smile than he'd ever seen from her
before, a smile for all the orgasms of all the men she'd known
because they were small deaths of those men, life pathetically
blurting into her. "Open your eyes!" he demanded again, terror-
stricken at how, in her submission to his will, her own blackness
ravished his. But she didn't open her eyes, and she rode him down
and down into the dark.

Far away, when the Vog cleared, Wade could see the other man.

Wade looked past the walls of Mona's flat into the Arboretum's
empty core, looked past all the empty catacombs and corridors
and could see the sole figure of the other man sitting in the dark of
Fleurs d'X watching his Mona. And when she returned from dancing he could tell she was no longer the simple vessel of Wade's
dream, she was no longer the transport of what Wade deposited
in her, sloshing against the walls of her womb, but the vessel of
another dream: it may have been the other man's dream. It may
have even been Mona's dream, since the baby-teeth smile wasn't
so vacant anymore, its exquisite emptiness now marred by a meaning. When she smiled there was something else in the smile, a
longing that was not Wade's, the wriggling into Wade's dream of
an alien aspiration like a virus. It was more than intolerable, it was
incomprehensible. It went on for many hours of the long Arboretum night until finally Wade put on the clothes he hadn't worn in a
long time and went to Fleurs d'X to see for himself.

As he sat at one of the tables to the side of the club, it took Wade
a long time to remember where he'd seen the other man. In his
mind Wade traveled down every corridor he'd ever walked in the
Arboretum, peered into every chamber where he might have seen
the man before. The short, squat painter had blotted out everything that ever happened to Wade outside and before the Arboretum, and if Wade hadn't seen the other man just hours before
smashing Mallory's face in the alley and shoving the car over the
cliffs into the sea, he never would have remembered. When it

came to him, when he recognized the man with the black hair and the glasses as the archives clerk who had walked past Wade and Mallory in the lobby of Church Central, it was the biggest intrusion of all, the most unseemly of violations; at that moment Wade almost got up from his table and left the club. If he had, he thought later, Mona might still be with him. But he stayed and, as the minutes went by, his calm gradually became more and more frayed. His serenity was undone by the way the man watched Mona dance, by the way he smiled at Mona and the way she smiled back. When she smiled there was something in her little baby teeth that Wade had never seen all the times she smiled at him; there was a response in her smile to the way the man with the black hair and the thick glasses appeared so sad, the way he smiled at her so halfheartedly, the way he seemed lost and not there at all, his attention arrested time and again only by Mona's fleeting lovely secrets. Then the man began to follow Mona from stage to stage as Wade had done the first night he watched her. Mona's smile became more transformed, from dance to dance, by the sad man's relentless audience. Only when Mona saw Wade sitting in the dark did her smile vanish, and it was then Wade knew he didn't own her anymore.

Hour after hour, watching Mona dance for the sad blackhaired man with the glasses, Wade began drinking little whiskeys just as in the old days, signaling to Dee behind the bar as the sad man dropped his glasses in the dark and, on her hands and knees, Mona helped to find them. When the blackhaired man surrendered the rest of his money at Mona's feet and walked from the club, Wade got up from his table to follow; and as he passed her stage he looked once at her, trapped in her dance, and felt her watch him all the way out of the Fleurs d'X.

The other man was at the end of the corridor. Shred by shred Wade tore the clothes from his own body for the last time and left them in his trail; by the time he reached the stairs, he was naked again. He pulled the other man from the stairs, hurling him against the corridor wall, the glasses skidding the length of the hallway. Dazed, the man groped blindly around him, tumbling into some more profound, unspoken incapacitation. Wade beat him furiously. Blood splattered the corridor walls. The man took the

beating without resistance, crumpling to the floor beneath the assault until in his incapacitation he finally groaned a single word. It
was the only sound the man made.

"Sally."

Wade tottered at the sound of it. If the man with the black hair
had risen up and surprised Wade with a blow of retaliation, it
couldn't have struck with more force or shock. Wade lowered his
hands and stood panting over the man, wondering if he believed
his ears just as he'd wondered before when, with Mona, he'd said
the same name. And then the man said it again, through the blood
in his mouth, utterly unaware of Wade as though there was nothing
and no one there in the corridor but blood and broken heart; and
the reality from which Wade had fled into the Arboretum three
years before floated in the hallway between the two men, in a
word.

He turned to see Mona at the end of the hall. She had followed
the trail of his clothes from the doorway of the Fleurs d'X. In this
last moment he would ever actually lay eyes on her, she looked
almost as she had the first time, naked but for her black stockings
and high-heeled shoes; now in the dank light of the Arboretum
corridor rather than the dark of her flat or the blush of the club,
she seemed more frail, even as Wade was the more naked of the
two. Mona didn't look at Wade at all. She put her hands to her
mouth, gazing at the beaten man beneath him. When Wade
reached out to her, she turned and ran. He called out and started
after her, then was jerked back to his victim as though the name
the man had spoken was a web that bound them. It was the best
Wade could do to reach down and pick up the man's glasses and
hand them back to him.

He trampled his own clothes underfoot as he ran after her. He
was naked when he burst into the Fleurs d'X to find her. The
women stopped dancing to look at him; Dee behind the bar
stopped pouring drinks. He ran down the corridors of the Arboretum toward her flat; turning every corner he expected to run her
down. People cowered before the sight of him; he took no notice
of them. He couldn't understand why, with every corner he turned,
he hadn't caught up with her; it wasn't until he reached the flat
that he knew she was gone for good. The door was open. The lock
dangled from the outside. Inside nothing was amiss, but her depar-

ture hovered in the room, over the floor that was painted to look as though there were no floor, beneath the ceiling painted to look as though there were no ceiling, between the walls rendered to appear as though there were no walls. Her goodbye hovered like the explosion of his desire when she'd ripped him from inside her that first time she'd returned to find he had taken such possession of her world.

Wade sat in the flat by himself for a while. For some reason it occurred to him to look in the corner where he had kept his clothes that were now scattered throughout the Arboretum passageways. The stone with the graffiti, which he'd hidden there, was gone. Wade roared at the betrayal.

They heard it all over the neighborhood. They heard it in the distance, as the roar grew louder and closer. Soon it rushed through the corridors, preceding him as he ran up and down passageways, up and down stairs, through doors and chambers, as he swept the Arboretum from end to end, top to bottom, looking for her. The roar crashed through the Arboretum until the neighborhood was submerged in it, the torrent eventually trickling down the long black entryway and out the single door into the world outside. As the years passed, the roar slowly wound its way into the city. The months stretched into years, to whatever extent in the Arboretum years could be measured, and finally, after he'd prowled the corridors a long time, he came to accept that he'd never find her.

When he'd drunk the last of her cognac and smoked the last of her opium, his charge became a wayward stagger, stunned and endless. When he ceased to be the marauder of the Arboretum's food and drink and flesh, he was left to scavenge its dread and rumor and panic, stalking the maze that grew wider and higher as its core grew deeper and darker. He wandered the Arboretum for sixteen years when a vision came to him, and it lasted only a moment.

He turned a corner of the long Arboretum night and saw Sally Hemings.

He stopped where he stood, slumped against whatever wall was behind him. She came from an unlit auditorium, looking around carelessly with two large gray dogs following at her heels; then she saw the apparition at the end of the hall. She'd heard about the naked giant who lurked in the Arboretum passages; there wasn't much doubt this was he. And he was looking back at her, and she was younger and more fair than he'd remembered. Her dark hair had a touch of fire in it. "Sally?" he said.

Her mouth fell slightly. She watched him in wonder.

"Sally?" He started toward her. For a moment she was frozen, and then she shook herself free of the sight and sound of him, turning to vanish into the shadows.

In his last hour inside the Arboretum, lying in a heap in the transformed flat where he'd lived with Mona, from a stupor he saw three more visions. Even he knew the first wasn't real.

It was Mona, standing before him, looking as she'd always looked. She was naked as she'd always been naked, and wet, her golden hair in strands on her bare shoulders as though she'd just climbed from the bottom of the sea. She stood in a pool of water. Even in his stupor he remembered it had been many years since she'd gone. Her head tilted to the side and she smiled, of course, and even though he knew she wasn't really there, when she held out the stone to him, he reached for it. He closed his eyes and then opened them again and she was gone and his hand was empty. Dimly he nodded to himself.

At first, he didn't think the second vision was real either.

It was Sally Hemings again, as he'd seen her in another part of the Arboretum. He closed his eyes and said her name, expecting she'd disappear as Mona had, and only the echo of her name would be left in the room with him; but when he opened his eyes, she was still there. "I'm not Sally," she shook her head, "Sally was my mother."

He narrowed his eyes and tried to think. "Was?"

"I'm looking for a man," the girl went on, and now Wade could see she was indeed younger and fairer than Sally. "His name is Etcher. He wore thick glasses and had black hair . . ." and he laughed until the effort of laughing exhausted him, and he passed out.

He immediately knew the third vision was real. Three men stood before him; one had half a face. Where the other half had been, his mouth curled in a massive scar upward, the face having revolted against its own nature that it might grow back together. Through the hole in the middle of the face came a smudge of words. "Well well well," he said.

It had taken so much effort before that Wade wasn't sure he had it in him to laugh anymore. But he couldn't help it. Stupefied, besotted and trapped like a rat, looking up at the man with the hole in his face, he figured he might as well let it rip from down deep. "You don't look so good, Mallory," he guffawed from the floor where there was no floor.

Mallory kicked him savagely in the head.

Wade came to in time to see the sky above him, bearing down on him like the wave of the world as the three cops dragged him to the car. "Only the night," he cried, "damn the light!"

When Lauren was an old woman, she would stand on the Kansan desert and watch the leaves. They would dance in dark patterns across her feet, and disappear over the small white hills that filled the dead fields. It was several autumns before she actually walked from her porch to one of the small hills and, turning over a few handfuls of dirt, discovered the rail of a small bridge; she recognized it as a moonbridge, like the ones she'd seen in California years before, from which people had watched the trajectory of the moon across the night sky. The nights that the young girl Kara came to visit Lauren for supper, it was Kara's gaze that found those skies, a mass of starry light for which the adolescent had a thousand names. Lauren fixed a simple meal and they ate on a plain tablecloth in the main room of Lauren's house. They talked of Kara's parents, who lived in Chicago and had sent their daughter to the ranch for children possessed by deep disturbances, odd visions, strange talents. Kara's talent was renaming every star in the sky and following them as they shifted from one quadrant of the night to another; but as she grew older Kara progressed be-

yond the ravages of her deep disturbances, beyond the grip of her
odd visions, beyond the enthrallment of her strange talents, all of
which manifested themselves one last time on the night she found
the bottle.

She'd been waiting for the headlights of the brown bus that
would take her back to the ranch, and had come across a star she
couldn't account for. When she ran from the porch it was not to
the bus but the unaccountable light, which she soon realized wasn't
a star after all but the glint of something lodged in the white earth.
Kara brushed away the sand and dug the object from the small
hill; the bottle had been caught, it turned out, in the railing of one
of the old buried bridges. She held up the bottle and, in the light of
every star in the skies above, saw two blue eyes blinking at her.

The eyes in the bottle were old and sad and nearly blind. At first
Kara thought she could speak to them and that somehow they
understood her; in the same way that she could compute the language of stars, she might compute the language of eyes as they
communicated in return. But she concluded they were useless, like
blue fish in water, and she was only to be their keeper, and so over
the years she kept the bottle wrapped in cloth that the blind eyes
might be protected from the light. The bottle became a secret that
Kara and Lauren withheld from each other, a pact of mutual betrayal maintained not by choice but because the secret was somehow too laden with meaning for either woman to divulge to the
other. The only person Kara ever told about the bottle was the
stranger who came down the road one afternoon as she was near-
ing her fifteenth birthday; Lauren invited him to share a meal and
spend the night in the back room. Georgie was around twenty
years old, good-looking, even pretty, it seemed to Kara. His head
was completely shaved and there crept up around his neck, above
the collar of his shirt, a dark growth. At first Kara thought he was
horribly scarred, until later that night in his room when she saw
the tattoo.

In the light of the small gas lamp by his bed Kara made her
bargain, that if she could examine the nude woman with the bird's
head standing in a sea of fire on Georgie's chest, if she could run
her hands along the brilliant wings he wore on his shoulders, she
would reveal something in return. In the light of the small gas
lamp, she unwrapped from the cloth the bottle with the eyes, and

the man and girl sat looking at them together. Georgie understood this secret was very important to Kara, and in the bottom of his backpack he searched for another forbidden thing of his own to show her: it was a stone, flat on one side and rough on the other, a little larger than Georgie's hand. "But look," Georgie said, when he could see the girl was disappointed, and turned the stone over; on the rough side was written *pursuit of happiness.* Kara nodded, trying to appear impressed. "It's a nice rock," she offered, without conviction, "but you have to admit it's not as good as a bottle with eyes, or even wings on your back."

When the young girl saw the old woman standing in the doorway of her house gazing out at the sand and muttering a strange man's name, Kara knew this was the moment Lauren began to die. A week of uncollected mail sitting in the box by the road greeted Kara's next visit; inside the house she found Lauren slumped in her rocking chair. After Lauren had been buried among the white hills of the plains where she lived, Kara examined the mail and discovered a letter sent to the old woman many years before when she lived in California. How the letter finally found its way to Kansas, how it had taken so many years to get there, was nearly as mystifying as the contents of the envelope itself, one letter enclosed inside another which in turn enclosed another, until the answer at the core simply said *I'm waiting.* But whoever was out there waiting for Lauren would now wait forever, and for Kara it was something like a child's first understanding that everyone dies, this lesson of how love can wait in the heart unanswered.

Kara left Kansas and traveled west. Because her gaze had been fixed so long on the stars, she barely noticed the strange shimmer of everything that passed her, how as she headed west everything was blurred around the edges in its rush to an abysmal moment. She continued traveling until she came to a river, where she took a boat navigated by a young man with white hair growing on his arms like fur. The man had been sailing the boat for fifteen years, the length of her own life, back and forth between the shore and an island less than a mile away; from the deck of the boat she looked for the stars in the sky. They were gone. For a moment, between the island and the shore, there was nothing except the boat in the fog on the water. "But why have you come?" the boatman asked when they reached the island and she was about to step ashore; unseen in her coat, she cradled the bottle with the eyes. "To bury something," she murmured.

The answer was still on her lips when she woke. It was still in her ears when she sat up in bed in the dark of the strange motel. She stared in alarm at the strange man sleeping next to her with the white hair on his body that grew like fur; she had no idea who he was or what she was doing in this motel room. She only knew that whatever her life had been before now was consumed by this night's dream, and that the only remaining trace of that dream was some forgotten thing peering out at her from behind glass, twin blue ghosts joined at the soul by the last thread of memory. Immediately she rose from the bed to check her coat, which lay on a chair, as though it protected something. But nothing was there. Before dawn she slipped from the room and caught a bus at the side of the road.

The bus drove through an endless forest. Watching from the window she couldn't remember having ever seen, on the ground and in the trees and hovering in the sky, so much ice. On a far hillside four days west, Kara lived in an observatory as caretaker and chief stargazer. If it was now beyond her waking consciousness to name any stars, she accepted that beneath that consciousness lurked the names that didn't need to be remembered in order to be known. In the isolation of the observatory she felt safe enough in her exposure to the heavens to walk the dark nightlit cavern of the concrete bubble naked, the bright pink of her bare body the only violation of the black-blue sky and its gray outpost. In this way she felt the freedom of loving something that couldn't be expected to love her back, until—after nearly ten years had passed—she met a man who insisted on loving her more than she could stand.

He lived on the outskirts of the village below the observatory. During the week he worked odd jobs in the village, delivering groceries for his mother's store and building doors with his carpenter father. On the foothill trails that he had walked all his life, his path crossed Kara's one dusk; the trees were sheathed by the glistening silver webs of the iceflies, which emerged from their cold white cocoons every year when the winter melted. The young man had been thinking about a wedding some years before that had taken place beneath these same trees, not far from this particular trail. It was a harsh, wincing memory. He'd been the wedding's best man, a particularly bad best man, ignorant of the rituals of best men, of obligatory dances with the bride and toasts to the happy couple. No one had told him about being a best man; and in the oblivious anguish of his own love for one of the bridesmaids, a girl he would never see again after that wedding, he'd taken her down this same foothill trail as the wedding party awaited his presence in growing confusion and fury. His dereliction of duties as best man became for him, years later, the evidence in his life of his own destructive innocence. He never cared much for weddings after that. Years later, when he had left the village after his disastrous affair with Kara, in a white seaside city far away on the morning of his own wedding, the only thing about his pending marriage for which he felt some relief was that at least he wouldn't have to worry about his transgressions as a best man, being merely the groom instead.

Between Amanda, the bridesmaid with whom he'd walked on the foothill trail, and Kara whom he met on the same trail eight years later, there was Synthia. Beautiful and shattered, cruel and totalitarian, Synthia was the woman that divided his romanticism in two because, of all those he loved, she was least worthy of it. Prostrate in her adoration of an iron fist, and for the way it might piece her together according to its own design after smashing her to bits, Synthia despised the young man for the way there was no iron in his fist, no iron in his heart. Rather his heart was soft for her: she couldn't tolerate it. Rather his hands were gentle on her body: she held them in contempt for how they were respectful of her, for the way they refused to violate the most fragile of orifices, refused to draw with exquisite brutality the starting line of his pleasure at the line where hers never began. That he was the only man who ever gave her an orgasm was something she only hated him for all the more; it was something that only made him all the weaker in her eyes. Synthia was the beginning of the end of his idealism about love, though that idealism would be another fifteen years in dying. She was the end of the division in him between love and sex, and of his naïve conviction that the two—the protests of philosophers notwithstanding—didn't necessarily have anything to do with each other. It was the end of his idealistic supposition that freedom wasn't the price of love, and that slavery wasn't ever the choice of those who had the freedom to choose.

Amanda, the girl he had loved on the foothill trail not far from the wedding party, was the last he loved chastely, and the last who wasn't beautiful. He would have a lot of time, living out his later years as an old man inside the rim of a volcano, to consider why something as corrupt as beauty so held him in its grip. He'd have enough time to consider that perhaps, in his blindness, neither Synthia nor Kara was ever as beautiful as he thought. His blindness was too profound even to know he couldn't see, until in the dim light of the lamp by which he read at night he found himself holding the pages only inches from his face. It was just like history to teach him what love couldn't. He went and got some glasses. He couldn't stand for Kara to see him wearing them, as he crashed into the chamber of the observatory that last night and found her naked below the sliver of night wedged in the observatory dome, the fine hair of her arms on end and the nipples of her breasts erect in the cold. He crept up behind her and before she could protest enveloped her in the warmth of his arms and lit her womb with the fire of his cock up inside her and it wasn't until afterward that she sent him away, not because she hadn't surrendered willingly to the way he fucked her but because, no longer able to resist seeing her, he had pulled from his coat pocket afterward his new glasses and put them on.

She looked at him. She grabbed him with fistfuls of his black hair and, staring at his face on the floor of the observatory, recoiled. With his blue eyes grown huge by the magnification of the glasses, there came back to her the memory of two eyes in a bottle dug up from beneath the sands of a dream, and all the heartbreak of that dream which she'd lived her waking life to avoid. She sent him away that night without explanation or comprehension. She was left more naked to the night than she'd ever intended, whispering "Etcher, Etcher" as she'd heard an old woman whisper a strange name in a dream's doorway on the other side of a dream's river.

And a little more of me died. I was twenty-eight. There were moments in the months that followed when I didn't care if I lived or not, too dead to take an active part in ending my life, too alive not to let the days roar past me until the very sound of them had passed as well, and only in the subsequent quiet could I identify the stirring far inside me as something resembling survival. Some might have said I was weak. I never felt weak. I never felt weak that I could have loved so much. I never felt weak that I could give myself over to love, or throw everything away for it. I never felt small that love could be so much bigger than I. It was later, when others might have said I was strong, that I felt weak, later when no love was as big as I that I felt small. Later when, for the ten years that passed after Kara, there was no possibility of a love like that again in my life, and nothing left to me but to write my books in pursuit of more commonplace glory. To tell the story of everyone else's dreams but mine: Kara's dream and Lauren's dream and Wade's, glib dreams of buried cities and haunted jungles and flooded streets, the erotic fevers that change everyone strong enough to change but me; until finally I changed too. And only when the ten years had passed after Kara, only when I'd given myself passively to my marriage in the conviction that I had metamorphosed from the dead childhood of love's idealism to the dead adulthood of loss' resignation, only when from the dead wisdom of such an adulthood I had come to believe in nothing but the palpable reality that could be drunk from the hinge of a woman's legs, was I surprised by love again. She was black and white. She was quiet and wild, her voice watery and melancholy, her smile sweet and hushed. She was the most beautiful woman I ever knew and for as long as it would last I was a force of nature. And if I had never really known her in order to write about her here, then I would have dreamed her, on and on into my nights with no sight of her ever to break the spell and cast another in its place. Maybe that would have been better. But she wasn't a dream. And until there's another dream, and until there's another spell, this is my last book.

When his affair with Kara ended, Etcher packed his things, settled his affairs, and went to say goodbye to his parents.

They lived in the center of the village. They had so long assumed Etcher would eventually leave that, when the time finally came, they had gotten used to the idea he'd never leave at all. Etcher's mother had moved to the village many years before to be with Etcher's father; she came from a warmer part of the world several thousand miles away, and it took the rest of her life for her blood to thicken with the cold. Etcher's father had been born in the Ice, brooding and stormy. There were only the three of them, mother and father and son, each always something separate unto him or herself, the family a home base they returned to emotionally from their daily routines. The night before his son's departure, Etcher's father got quietly drunk at the dinner table. Having arrived at the point where he believed his dignity was in jeopardy, he excused himself to go to bed. "I hope you'll remember me," he said to the stunned Etcher, "at my best, feet of clay and all," and it was unbearable to the son how in that moment of parting his father considered himself to be a failure in his son's eyes. Etcher watched speechless and confused as his father disappeared through the bedroom door, with nothing more to be said between them— which is to say with everything to be said between them—until fifteen years later, at his father's deathbed when it was too late.

If Etcher inherited both his father's brooding fatalism and kindness of heart, he resisted the lessons of life that teach one to be harder. In some ways Etcher taught himself to be softer. And in defiance of life's lessons that teach one to dim the light in oneself and fight the dark, Etcher intended to do neither. He hated the resignation that life insisted on. He listened, with one ear pressed to the passage walls, to the secret life being lived by himself just on the other side of the life he lived consciously. There was no telling how much good he might have done or how much evil he might have committed had he not been so burdened with a conscience. In the end what he feared most was not his own pain but the pain of others, for which he might bear some responsibility. What he feared was not what his heart could survive but what his conscience couldn't, which included the smallest infraction—his graceless negligence as a best man at a wedding, for instance. Time and again he was ready to believe the best of someone else. Time and again he was ready to acknowledge the worst of himself. Hating the resignation that life insisted on, he would come to be led by his conscience to resign himself completely to life, before saving his life at the expense of that conscience.

At the nearest station, eighty-five miles away, he boarded a train heading south. He was on the train for six days. He was on the train such a long time that at the end, when he stepped from his car onto the station platform, he continued to feel it traveling beneath him; and later from his hotel window, while the floor of his room continued to move beneath him as well, the blue obelisks of the city vibrated like the forests that accompanied him so endlessly they had seemed to him always the same forest, moving with the train. After so many trees the obelisks were a relief, spires of sea and rock, and he was exhilarated by the sight of them before he came—like everyone in his new city—to dread them.

Soon after he arrived he went to work for the authorities. For a while he was a clerk in the immigration bureau, where he did nothing but file forms nine hours a day. Eventually he was moved to a position in the archives at Church Central. This was but his first crime of resignation. Over the next ten years, as a dead man traveling surreptitiously in the body of a living one, like a convict on the run with a forged passport, he committed so many more such infractions that he lost count. Sometimes in the course of a day or night they numbered in the hundreds, small deferences and numb capitulations including the most sensual, the drink that took him indifferently past drunkenness, the woman he fucked beyond his attraction to her. His aggression itself was passive, the inexorable rush of a gale into a vacuum. He was in the perfect city for deadness and resignation. As he was exhilarated the day he arrived by the blue obelisks of Aeonopolis, so as well he was placated by the repetition of the sea, so as well he was reconciled immediately to how the city's clerical powers had coopted the tedious questions of spirituality and meaning. So as well he came to anticipate the sirens of the morning and twilight and the time spent in the dark of the small altar room of his unit, where he sat praying to no one and feeling nothing and being no place.

For all of this deadness his memory could never abide the melancholy of another's misery. It was in the early months of his arrival that he walked out of a bakery one morning to be met by an old beggar so hideous and pitiful that when he shoved his open palm in front of Etcher and pleaded for a piece of bread or a coin, the other man was frozen where he stood, even as his mouth was full of bread and his hand full of coins. Etcher fled without giving the man anything. All day he tried to work in the rubble of his moral paralysis, until he couldn't stand it any longer and, claiming sickness, left work to return to where he'd last seen the beggar. The beggar was no longer there. All night Etcher looked for him. Exhausted, he finally found the beggar at dawn; into the stunned beggar's hand Etcher stuffed a wad of money, and fled again. After this episode he never again left empty any human heart that gaped like an open wound. He gave money to whoever asked, as though to ward off the thrusts to his own heart by the things that made him ashamed of life. In the same way he taught himself to become softer, so the immune system of his conscience withered away, unprotected by the antibodies of experience. Among a crowd of hundreds at the teeming Market, a nation of beggars immediately identified him and closed in, no matter how he might hide his face or avoid eye contact, until it seemed they were at his doorstep at dawn, until they had mobilized as a guerrilla army monitoring his various routes, hobbling in pursuit on crutches or little wheels.

It was both the ultimate act of resignation and the ultimate answer to his conscience, his marriage to a schoolteacher for whom Etcher fulfilled an increasingly desperate agenda. Her name was Tedi. She was small and pretty like a doll if not like a beautiful woman, her face framed by gold ringlets. She had a mind for the numbers of things and their mechanics; beneath her sweetness she was obsessed with doom. Her past was strewn with men whom she regarded as having betrayed her and against whom she plotted her vengeance, in exact calculations and with a precision like the plumbing of a building. It didn't hurt that the small school in town where she taught her little pupils was situated amid the most wrathful and indignant of Primacy's graffiti. Gazing at the messages around her she took inspiration. But because even Tedi understood that vengeance was a short-term satisfaction, and because her temperament for it didn't quite match her instincts, she was only left with doom in the end and the realization that its mathematics was more inevitable than any she might concoct to thwart it. Thus she hid in her unit from passing meteorites that might fall from space, searching her out as though with radar; and hidden from the danger of the outside world she was left with the doom that lurked in her like an infection.

Etcher felt as though he'd been jostled among an aimless throng of people and then had bumped into Tedi, at which point he looked down at his cupped hands to see they now held her beating heart. She wouldn't take it back. He couldn't give it to someone else. He couldn't drop it on the ground where it might be trampled underfoot by the throng. He somehow accepted responsibility for this heart by the fact of his having it, and by his inability—even in the depths of his deadness—to be so cruel as to simply refuse or desert it. She closed in on him and he allowed himself to be closed in on, because he'd come to believe, now six years after Kara, that he'd never love like that again and that at the age of thirty-five the dead calm of adulthood called for this final moment of peace. Thus he had never stopped disbelieving in his own blame. That he didn't have the courage to hurt Tedi sooner only doomed him to devastate her later. This culpability became all the more profound when, having given in to her plans for marriage, he gave in to her plans for a child. They both expected she would become pregnant immediately.

He awaited it hopelessly. He waited for his blank passivity to manifest itself as a small life, an unknowing infant whose existence would foreclose forever the possibilities of Etcher's own escape. As he waited, he drank more. He scored liquor on the city's boulevards, sometimes in broad daylight. But he never considered this petty outlawry as an attack on his passivity or even an aberration of it, but rather as more complicity, since the intent and effect of the drinking was to make passivity more tolerable. Like any functioning drunk, Etcher managed his hangovers as well as the hour of the day and the quality of his inebriation would allow; the priests would reprimand him on mornings when he showed up for work obviously toxic from something more than bitterness. In the hollow of his life he fashioned a routine that wouldn't let him forget how his life was over, spending longer hours in Central's dark corridors beneath its high empty rafters that were startling for the way they were immaculate of graffiti, reveling dully in his role as power's flunky and authority's file clerk. As time went by he found less occasion, as he'd done in the early days of their relationship, to leave work in time to pass the windowless downtown street of Tedi's school, sometimes waiting for her in back of the classroom staring at the blackboard, where her messages ran off the edge of

the slate onto the walls, around the corners and down the hallways
—nothing but Tedi and little children and Primacist messages and
classroom shelves of bibles and hymn books.

But offhours, in the shifts between his employment and his marriage, his drunkenness allowed him a fantasy. In this fantasy he
ran through the streets of the city during one of the daily searches,
with everyone huddling in their altar rooms, as he had his way
with freedom, flush with the same rage of pleasure he'd poured
into the flesh portals of so many faceless women. These fantasies
were, in a sense, the same authoritarian fantasies of those who
held power, a wild howl of sensuality derived from the submission
of others. He'd merely been, he realized now, ten years too soon
for Synthia, who had so longed for someone to make her yield to
this sort of submission. She'd marvel now, if he were to happen
upon her, at the steel of his hands that pinned her beneath him
until he finished with her, at his integrity dribbling away inside
her. But there was something else about his fantasies that had
nothing to do with power. There was something about his fantasies
that would have appalled the totalitarian Synthia, that had to do
with anarchy and a lurking subversion ticking away inside him
along with the weeks and months during which Etcher waited for
Tedi to become pregnant and, mysteriously, she did not. In the
dark of the archives he came to realize that with every passing
month fate kept giving him another opportunity to make a break
for it. He also came to realize that, each time he turned down the
chance, it might be his last.

He was excited and terrified by the growing sound of the ticking.
On the afternoon he discovered the archives' back room, the ticking was loud enough to be indistinguishable from that of his heart.

His duties in the archives were to keep in order the records of
the city's affairs, and to file and search out records for the priests
who used them. The door in back of the archives was so inconspic-
uous that Etcher always assumed it was a closet or storage space
of some sort; it wasn't only locked but had the dusty, uncracked
look of not having been opened in a long time. Etcher worked for
Central seven years before he saw a priest wearing the white robes
of a church leader unlock the door one afternoon, enter and then
close it behind him. This was the first sign to Etcher that whatever
was beyond the door was not a closet. The second sign was that

the priest didn't emerge from the room for two hours. When he did, he had a large book under his arm and was looking for a place to put it in order to lock the door. "Want me to take that?" said Etcher.

The priest jumped at the sound of Etcher's voice. It was as if he were unaware Etcher had ever been there, though Etcher was in plain sight and had always been there. "No," the priest blurted, reluctantly putting the book on the ground and fumbling through his robes for the door's key. He locked the door and left.

The next morning a different priest brought the book back. This priest wore the pale-blue robes of a second-level clergyman; Etcher recognized him as an assistant to the one who had been there the day before. As he unlocked the narrow door, the assistant asked Etcher to locate a file for him. When the priest disappeared inside the room Etcher, rummaging through the archives' files, saw that the key to the room had been left in the lock.

He had no idea why he did it. He knew that if he'd been too hungover to think of it, or so sober he might have thought about it too long, he never would have done it. But now Etcher walked quickly to the door, took the key from the lock, and put it in his pocket.

When the priest in the light-blue robes came out of the room, closing the door behind him, he would have turned to lock it except that Etcher said, "Here's your file." The priest took the file and stood there several moments examining it. "I also pulled these, in case you need them," Etcher said.

The priest looked up into Etcher's monstrous blue eyes floating behind his glasses. "No, I don't need those," the priest said. Then he walked away, still reading the file.

It was shortly after noon when the priest returned. Frantically rushing to the door in back, he stared at the lock for a minute in disbelief. He turned to Etcher. He was pale as he said, "There was a key."

"I'm sorry?" said Etcher.

"There was a key," the priest repeated. He wiped his mouth with his hand. "Did you see it?"

"In the door?"

"Yes in the door," he nearly shrieked.

"I thought you took it," Etcher said.

"What?"

"You took it. You came out and took the key. Remember? I gave you the file?"

"I took the key?"

"And then I gave you the file."

"Are you sure?"

"I thought so. Perhaps it fell out of your pocket."

The priest kept wiping his mouth. He looked at the door and then at the floor around his feet as though the key might materialize. His eyes were twitching when he said, "You remember me taking the key. And putting it in my pocket."

"I think so."

"No," the priest said emphatically, "you *do* remember it. If anyone asks, you remember I took the key and put it in my pocket. I didn't leave it in the door. I put it in my pocket and it fell out somewhere along the way. Where nobody would find it. Where nobody would know what it was if they happened to pick it up. We'll get another key made. We don't have to bother anyone else about it. I took the key from the lock and put it in my pocket and you gave me the file, you remember that. If anyone should ask."

"Yes."

"I didn't just walk away and leave it in the door. I didn't do that."

"Yes. I mean no."

An hour later a locksmith appeared to make another key for the door.

For several months Etcher kept the key hidden away, occasionally considering whether to dispose of it, not simply because it was incriminating but because he'd never really thought about opening the door to see what was behind it. Etcher wasn't concerned with what was behind the door. It was never his reason for taking the key. He took the key simply for the taking, and he was struck afterward by how easily he'd done it, how easily he'd lied about it when the priest had returned looking for the key in panic. It was only later that he was tempted to press his luck and actually open the door; and then he was unnerved by how tempting it was, though curiosity as to what was behind the door was never a part of it. It was the act of opening he couldn't resist, as it had been the act of taking. And as every month passed in which he expected Tedi to tell him she was pregnant and that his fate and responsi-

bility were decided, as every month went by that he was once again
reprieved by some conspiracy of biology and destiny, his own reck-
lessness grew more irresistible until the moment came when, in
the latest hours of the night, he gave in to it.

He would try to open the door, he decided. He assumed the
locksmith had changed the lock anyway when he made the other
key. He would try to open the door, and when it wouldn't unlock,
he could then dispose of the key, the temptation having been succumbed to and thwarted.

The locksmith, however, had not changed the lock. In the dark
of the archives, the door opened.

Etcher had been right about its being a very small room, the size
of a walk-in vault. There was nothing inside but the books—nearly
a hundred of them, all like the one the priest had removed and the
other priest had returned. The books were old and dusty, in grimy
red covers that had no titles or authors' names but were simply
identified, on labels that ran along the edges of the shelves, as the
Unexpurgated Volumes of Unconscious History: and at that moment Etcher almost turned from the vault and slammed the door
behind him. At that moment, though he had no idea what the
volumes meant, suspicion crowded subversion in his brain; instantly Etcher somehow knew that if he were to be discovered
here, he'd disappear forever, that no one would ever see him
again. That the breach of entering this room with these books was
more than simply treason, it was heresy. He lingered long enough
to pull one and then another volume down and open them. In them
were listed events Etcher had never heard of. The volumes told of
people no one had ever known and countries no one had ever seen.
He read of lives no one had ever lived and pored over maps of
places no one had ever been. Every sound of Church Central, every
creak in the walls and every footstep in its distant quarters, reson-
ated in the vault until, with dawn just over the horizon, his nerves
could no longer stand it.

He was terror-stricken, some minutes later, to hurry from the
archives into the lobby of Church Central only to see, there in the
middle of the night, two cops.

He could tell they were cops. One was a large black man and the
other a short man with red hair; they appeared tense. He was
certain they had been waiting for him, tipped off by a witness in

the shadows or an alarm miles away. But in fact the cops paid Etcher little attention. They just stood in the middle of the lobby as Etcher walked furtively past them. He got all the way to the door expecting them to call out after him, and it was only when they did not, it was only when he left the lobby and building and, outside, felt the cold sweat on his face and the night air in his constricted lungs, and only when he got home to find Tedi sleeping, with no fateful news on her lips, that he truly believed he'd gotten away with it. Then he couldn't sleep. Then he wanted a drink, but after he dug his forbidden bottle out of the cupboard where he kept it, he changed his mind and put it back. He was seized by the impulse to rid himself of the key for good; outside in the middle of the night he walked around the circle's obelisk, muttering to himself. For a long time he tried to think of where to dispose of the key, and the more he thought, the more the impulse for getting rid of it sub- sided, until he decided—much to his own dismay—that perhaps getting rid of it wasn't so necessary after all.

He allowed himself then what he believed would be his last subversion: keeping the key. The fires of subversion in him were banked; he felt spent, calm.

After several days passed, however, and then a week and then two, Etcher realized nothing had changed. If the target of his sub- version was his own life, nothing about the few clandestine mo- ments he'd spent in the archives' vault had delivered him. The moments in the vault were like a drug that had been taken and experienced and then had worn off, leaving him jangly and unset- tled and blinking around him at how his circumstances had re- mained untransformed. And though there wasn't any way in which stealing into the vault could transform the circumstances, an un- conscious impulse insisted such an act would slowly change Etcher himself until he'd crossed the rubicon of his subversion and there was no way back. He had no idea what such a point of no return would look like. He had no idea what *he* would look like once he'd passed it. He clung to the notion that he would easily see this point approaching in the distance before he got there, allowing him enough time to change his mind.

He began working late in the archives every night. He drifted further and further from home, spending first five minutes, then

ten, then half an hour in the archives vault studying the Unexpurgated Volumes of Unconscious History and their blasphemous reality. The more alien this reality was to him, the more he intuitively
believed it. Thus he surely and deliberately found for himself a
corner with no exits, where he had no choice but to plot his own
revolution against a reality that had no history, and in which he no
longer had faith. His breakthrough act came on the night that he
not only opened the vault to invade its contents but took one of the
volumes from the vault, carried it through the lobby and out of
Central, into the dark of the city. It was the volume that included
all the entries between Heathen and Holy. Etcher not only chose
this volume because of what happened that afternoon but soon
realized that but for what happened he might not ever have taken
any of the books. He might well have just lurked forever in his
corner of no exits, never finding the courage to fulfill his plots.

The woman who walked into the archives that afternoon seemed
lost, gazing at the walls around her. With her she had her two-
year-old child, who bore a striking resemblance to the mother
except for the fire in the little girl's hair.

Somewhere between twenty and thirty, between white and
black, her eyes somewhere between brown and green as her wild
dark hair fell across her face, the woman impressed Etcher less
with her beauty than the audacity of her presence, since he'd never
seen anyone walk into the archives but a priest. Indeed, a priest in
the lobby also stopped to look at her, as struck by her as Etcher.
The woman was very shy as she approached, pulling the small girl
behind her. "I was wondering—" she began in the quietest voice
like water, when she stopped, staring at the looming blue eyes
behind Etcher's thick glasses almost as Kara had looked at them
almost ten years before, as something sprung loose from the
oceanbed of a dream. For a moment Etcher found himself once
again on the brink of a terrible rejection, though nothing had ever
passed between him and this woman to be rejected.

It was a long minute before she shook herself from the sight of
him. The little girl, in the meantime, was running up and down the
aisles of the archives. The priest in the lobby appeared mortified.
"Polly," the woman said to the little girl, "come here." The child
didn't pay much attention. The mother shut her eyes in weary

futility. She looked at Etcher again, struggling for composure. "I was wondering if you could help me," she said. "I'm trying to get some information on a relative. I've been—Polly!"

The child returned to her mother's side.

"What are you doing here?" Etcher said in panic. He kept looking over at the priest in the lobby.

"His name was Madison Hemings," the woman tried to explain quickly. "He was a distant relative, I think, perhaps an uncle or cousin—"

"This office isn't open to the public," Etcher cut in. "We don't have that kind of information."

"Oh," she answered, "I'm sorry."

"You should go to the police for that sort of thing."

"No," she shook her head, "no, I can't go to the police," and before the little girl could take off again the mother scooped her up into her arms. "Well, thank you anyway," she said very quietly, and walked from the archives across the lobby as the priest and Etcher watched her go.

Etcher was miserable for the rest of the day. He wanted a drink, after not having had one since before the first night he'd entered the vault. It was instead of drinking that he took home with him that night the volume that covered material from Heathen to Holy; when he was sure Tedi was asleep, when he'd finally fended off her constant pleas that he come to bed, he went into the privacy of the altar room, shut the door behind him and, in the faint glow of the light above, opened the book. He didn't really expect to find an entry for Madison Hemings. The only Hemings listed was a woman named Sally, briefly identified as the slave and mistress of the leader of a country Etcher had never heard of.

As though searching out a forsaken beggar, he spent the weeks afterward looking for her. He left his unit early in the mornings so that he might spot her on the way to Church Central, and he no longer worked late in the archives in the evening, so that he could search for her on the way home. He thought he might see her in the city's voggy unlit streets, where the only sounds were the engines of cop cars and passing buses and the clanking of deserted trolleys. He thought he might hear her whisper in the Market where the vendors waited motionless and mute behind food stands and clothes racks that buyers selected from in silence. He thought the ragged peddlers who slept with their wagons in the back alleys and hobbled to him out of the sooty magenta dusk might sell him an answer from their pile of lamps and rags and dishes and candles, or trade one for something of value. Several hours a day for several weeks he wandered the city with the graffiti of the church peering at him from the city walls through the Vog and shouting in his head amidst his own voices of subversion and disarray. When he returned to the unit at night he told Tedi he'd been working late, in the manner of adulterers who lie about affairs. They fought about sex. He slept in the outer room and held in his dreams the woman who had come looking for Madison Hemings. He didn't drink.

He used the channels available to him, sending to police headquarters an official Primacy request for a file on Hemings. When it came back he was only mildly surprised to see that her name was Sally. The cop who brought the file said, "A lot of activity on this one lately."

Two days later in the white afternoon glare of her circle on the edge of the outlaw zone Redemption, Etcher stood in the shadow of the obelisk. He waited a long time before walking up to knock on the door. It opened before he reached it. The man in the doorway was several inches taller than Etcher, several years younger. He had long dark hair and wore a T-shirt. Clutching one of his hands was the little girl Etcher had seen in the archives several weeks before.

"Excuse me," Etcher said, "I—" and he stopped, not knowing what to say. All the way across town on the bus he'd tried to figure out what he was going to tell her; the sudden appearance of her husband only distracted him more. "I was wondering if I could speak to Mrs. Hurley," he said.

Hurley raised his thumb and pointed over his shoulder. "Come on, Polly," he said to the little girl, and they walked across the circle beyond one of the other units. Sally came into the doorway where her husband had been. She wore a plain dress, the earth and ash and blood tones of which, in the sun behind Etcher, weren't unlike the color of her skin. Her hair was loose. She was even more startled now by the sight of Etcher than she'd been in the archives. Etcher took off his glasses, rendering her a blur.

"Come in," she said. Etcher stumbled into the unit and immediately ran into a table. "Are you all right?" she asked. He groped for a place to sit and she led him to a couch.

"My name's Etcher," he finally said. "I work at Central. A few weeks ago you came to get some information."

"Yes," she said.

"I didn't mean to be rude," he said. "But there was a priest in the lobby, and the archives aren't open to the public. I didn't want you to get in trouble."

She said, "How did you find me?"

"Well, some things aren't so difficult when you work for the Church." He didn't know what to tell her and he wasn't sure why he was here. He didn't know whether to tell her about the entry in the volume he'd taken from the archives. Thinking about this on the couch he put his glasses back on instinctively, which he always did when he was confused, when, for instance, he couldn't hear what someone was saying. The unit around him was dark, the furniture worn. There was a table on which sat a drawer full of beads and trinkets and small silver chains, a pair of pliers and the finished results of some necklaces and earrings. Otherwise the room had been overrun by little stuffed bears and tigers and storybooks and puzzles with missing pieces; there was a small wooden train that went over a small wooden bridge through a small wooden tunnel. The walls of the unit were barren except for pictures drawn with crayons and a crude poster curling at the corners that announced GANN / ARBO.

Sally got up from the couch. "Gann always keeps it dark in here," she said. She pulled open the window curtains and the light blasted her in retaliation; she put her hand in front of her eyes and stepped sideways into the obelisk's shadow. She returned to the couch and sat down, the obelisk still casting its black denial across the top of her face. It nearly obscured how sad she appeared, sitting beside Etcher on the couch. She looked as though she would break if she learned one more secret, which was why he didn't tell her about the entry in the book from the archives, or if she suffered one more betrayal, which was why the news was on the tip of his tongue. He thought the most tragic thing about her was how her sorrow made her more beautiful. It seemed the worst trick of her beauty, that the chemistry of sorrow would make it so much more luminous. Her touching sweet smile was most lovely as the smile that obviously masked heartbreak; it was when her heartbreak was unmasked, as when the shadow of the obelisk dissipated into a gray twilight pool that poured from her face and flooded the unit, that her beauty somehow defied either the rules or definitions of the earth. Etcher could neither bear to look at her nor bear not to.

"Well," he said, "that was what I wanted to tell you." They sat on the couch a moment in silence and he thought he should get up and leave. He pointed at the drawer of jewelry, the necklaces and earrings. "Did you make these?" he asked.

"Yes." She picked up one of the necklaces and held it against her brown neck.

"It's nice," he said. At first he was being polite. But he reached over and touched the necklace; she placed it in his hand. He'd never seen a necklace like this. Strange charms and primitive symbols hung from its links. "Have the police ever searched you during an alert?" he asked, and realized how abrupt the question sounded.

"I . . . don't know," she said. "It's hard to be sure. When you're in the altar room you never know if they're here or not. No one knows if they even come out to this zone."

"This is the kind of thing they would confiscate. You should hide it," he said.

"Oh."

"Are you from here?" he said, and that sounded abrupt too.

"No." The certainty of her answer wavered in the air. "Are you?"

"I come from a village far away to the north, up in the Ice."

She said, "I come from somewhere else too."

"Have you been in the city long?"

"I— Awhile. As long as we've been married, anyway. A couple of years, anyway. We married when I became pregnant. Are you married?"

"Yes."

"Do you have children?"

His mouth was dry. "Yes. May I have something to drink?"

"OK." She stood and got him a glass of water and brought it back. She sat down and said, after a moment, "How many?"

"What?"

"Children."

"None," he shook his head.

"Oh," she said, "I thought you just said you had children."

"No, not at all."

"I thought you did."

"How old is your daughter?"

"Two."

"Did you tell me that before?"

"I said we got married when I became pregnant."

"What's her name?" he asked, although he knew what her name was.

"Polly."

He drank his water. "I hope I wasn't interrupting anything. I can go."

"Gann was just taking Polly for a walk."

"I hope it's not a problem, my coming here."

"No. I'm glad you came." It immediately sounded to both of them like a strange thing to say. They were moved by it, and uncomfortable. "Have we ever met before?" she asked.

"At the archives," he nodded, "about three weeks ago."

"Yes, of course," she laughed. "I mean, did we ever meet before then?"

"I don't think so."

"Do you want to have children?"

"Why do you ask?"

"Because we were talking about children."

"Tedi wants to have children."

"Does that mean you want to have children?"

"Uh." He took another drink of water. "I promised."

"You promised?"

"Tedi. My wife."

"That you would have children?"

"Yes."

"Because she wants it?"

"Yes."

She looked toward the front door. "You should be sure about what you want," she said resolutely.

"Maybe you're never sure what you want," he said. "When I got married I thought, No one's ever sure until they do it. If you wait until you're sure, you never do it." He realized he had just made his marriage sound less like a capitulation and more like a grand gamble.

"Are you sure now?"

"No."

"But more sure than you were."

"No."

"I'm sorry. I didn't mean— Well, it's strange to be having this conversation."

"I should probably go."

"I'm sorry."

"What for?"

"I think I said the wrong thing."

"No. I came by to say I'm sorry about the other day."

"We're both sorry a lot."

"Well, let's agree not to be sorry anymore."

"All right," she laughed.

The altar alert came on.

They were both startled by it. "Is it that late?" she said.

"I forgot about it," he said. "Most of the time I'm working in the archives and I just hear it in the distance."

"I guess all the priests don't have to run into their little rooms like the rest of us," she smiled.

"No," he agreed. She got up from the couch and walked over to the back wall and opened the altar-room door. "Your husband and child?" he said.

"Who knows," she said. She stood in the open doorway. "You can come in if you want."

He got up and went over to the room, and she closed the door behind them.

In the dark he felt, with a lurch, what he thought was a spider's web brushing his face. But it was a string, which Sally pulled to turn on the light overhead. This altar room was even smaller than most. On the floor against one wall was a mattress. There was a pillow. There was a little pink horse with a saddle and long green

hair, and children's books in the corner. There were a couple of
other books that didn't appear the sort Primacy approved; Sally
retrieved them quickly as though to hide them from view, though
there wasn't anywhere to hide them. There was also a half-drunk
bottle of wine, which she now regarded with mortification. She
glanced at Etcher.

"Let's drink some wine," he said.

"Really?" she said. They sat on the mattress. She handed him
the bottle. An altar was in the corner. It was a very unorthodox
altar, like the jewelry Etcher had seen in the front room, filled with
primitive icons and forbidden fetishes he didn't recognize. In the
center of the altar was a black wooden box with a rose carved on
the top. Etcher had been studying the altar awhile when she said,
"Probably not what the Church has in mind."

"It's not your regulation altar," Etcher admitted. He took a long
drink from the bottle. It was the first drink he'd had in several
weeks, and he found very satisfactory all the possibilities that
washed into his mind with the wine. He realized he'd been sitting
there staring at the altar for some time when he said, "We forgot
to hide the jewelry."

"It's just jewelry," Sally said, somewhat defensively.

For the first time in a long time, the tide of wine brought the
possibilities into Etcher's mind rather than taking them out. "I'm
not the Church," he said to her.

"What?"

He offered her the bottle and she took a drink. "I'm not a priest.
I don't care about the books," he said, nodding at the books she
had tried to hide. "I don't care about the wine. I buy my own from
a bootlegger." He waved it all away. "Don't care about the altar
either," he said, amazed at what the one drink had done to his
head. "Do the cops come out to Redemption?"

"Every once in a while you hear of someone put on report or
taken in. No one seems to know if it's an official Church zone or
not."

"That's because the Church doesn't know if it's an official
Church zone. According to the Church everything's theoretically
an official Church zone." Etcher took the bottle back from her.
"They're of two minds. The first is that it's easier to keep things
under control if they try to control the zone, and the second is that

it's easier to keep things under control if they leave the zone alone." He looked at the door. "I gather your husband doesn't take it too seriously."

"The only thing Gann takes seriously is Gann."

"Will he be back soon?" Etcher asked, still looking at the door.

"I don't know. He may have gone to the theater."

"Where's the theater?"

"In the Arboretum."

"He took your daughter to the Arboretum?" The slush of the wine in his head was settling just enough for him to take another drink. "Is that a good idea?"

"It's a good idea if Gann thinks it's a good idea." She said, "I don't mind the searches. I don't mind the seclusion from everything. Gann never comes in. Sometimes I bring Polly." She smiled and held up the pink horse with the green hair.

He said, "I like the box."

"What?"

"The box." He reached over toward the black wooden box in the altar, then drew back.

"It's all right," she said, handing him the box, "you can look at it." He held the box and opened it; it was empty. "I haven't figured out what to put inside."

He ran his fingers over the rose carved on top. "It's very beautiful," he said. It was voluptuous in its blackness. At that moment he could smell her next to him; he adjusted his glasses. "Where did you get it?"

"I don't remember. I thought I had lost it, I thought I'd given it to someone. And then I came home one day and there it was." She asked, "What's it like up in the Ice?"

"I haven't been in a long time. I had to leave."

"Do you have family there?"

"Yes."

"I guess you don't want to talk about it," she said.

"Everything's white except for the forests, which are dark and go on forever. Everyone's white, with white skin and white hair, except me. I always had the feeling it was because my hair was black that I couldn't see, that all the color of my vision rushed up into my hair, which was the flag of my blindness." He added, "I was in love."

"I want to live in the Ice someday."

"Are you sure?"

"Yes."

"Well."

"What?"

"Just . . ." he shrugged. "Is that where Madison Hemings is?"

"I don't know," she said. "Actually, I assume Madison Hemings is dead."

"Who was he?"

"That's what I've been trying to find out."

"But how do you know there was a Madison Hemings?"

"I inherited some money from him. The postman brought it, like the propaganda newsletter every month, or the tax bill. It's all gone now."

"The money?"

"It just came in the mail."

"But how do you live?"

"With difficulty."

"Does your husband make any money?"

"No."

"But someone must be supporting your daughter."

"I've been working on the jewelry. It's hard when there's Polly, she's at that age where she wants attention all the time. She's just beginning to figure out she isn't a baby anymore, and she doesn't like it. It's easier being a baby. It's easier being helpless."

"But her father."

"Her father loves her. I wouldn't want to give you the impression he doesn't. He wanted Polly the moment I told him she was inside me."

"You can't make the money and take care of the house and your daughter all at the same time."

"It's hard."

"It's not right," he said furiously, feeling the wine.

"I've been thinking about trying to get a stall in the Market. Do you know how I do that?"

"You have to apply to the Church for a license, like getting a unit."

"Would I have to go through the police?"

"One way or another the application winds up going through the police." He said, "Perhaps I could help you."

She said, "They think I killed a man."

He was less shocked than skeptical, having read the police file. "You'd be in jail if they thought that," he said.

"Maybe they aren't sure," she said.

"They don't have to be sure. They can put you in jail because they're as sure as they are unsure, or as sure as they want to be. They can put you in jail because they like the idea. They don't like the idea or you'd be in jail."

"I believe I did it."

"What?"

"I believe I killed him." She took a drink from the bottle of wine.

"Why do you think so?" he finally asked, not sure what else to say.

"I remember doing it. I'm sure I remember. I remember the knife. I know it was mine. I remember holding it in my sleep."

"You remember a knife?"

"Yes."

"You remember killing him with a knife?"

"Yes."

"But he wasn't killed with a knife."

For a moment it didn't register, then she turned to him. "What?"

"He wasn't killed with a knife."

"How do you know that?" she said.

"I saw the police file. It's how I found you. He wasn't killed with a knife. He was knocked over the head."

She began to cry.

"Hey." She continued crying, shaking her head. "I'm sorry," he said, a little baffled.

She shook her head. "Why didn't they tell me? Why did they let me go on thinking I'd done it? Didn't they know how I felt?"

"Sure they knew how you felt."

"They didn't care."

He felt curiously spent, having divulged to her a secret he didn't know he had. "This is the Church we're talking about."

"It's hateful." She sat in betrayed silence.

He said, "I stole a book."

"What?" she finally answered, preoccupied.

"They keep it locked away in a vault they never open. It's a history book. But it's . . . another history." On the mattress he slumped beside her. "The history of our secrets." He was suddenly tired; he closed his eyes. "The history inside us. And I stole it." He closed his eyes, waiting for her to say something, and when she didn't he slowly let himself go to the wine's languid calm. He was only half aware that the glasses fell from his face. He kept waiting for her to say something. He had told her about the book because he didn't want to leave her alone with her crime. His body was tense but he let go of that as well; he knew he was collapsing against her and he tried to hold himself back. For a moment he opened his eyes and then he shut them again.

He was only distantly aware that it had become dark around him. The light beyond the lids of his eyes went black, and he heard the clicking of the light above him in the altar room, the light attached to the string that he thought at first was a web brushing his face. In the rise and fall of her breath next to him he came to believe that, far away, he heard the sound of the sea against the cliffs. He knew he'd fallen asleep when he didn't hear the all-clear siren but rather remembered it from moments or hours before. "It's the all-clear," he murmured so long after it happened that even he was vaguely aware his murmuring made no sense. "Doesn't matter," he told himself, "not in Redemption. Cops don't come to Redemption anyway."

"Redemption," he finally heard her say in the dark, "is the Church name."

"Yes . . ."

"Desire," he heard her say in the dark, "is our name."

He nodded, though there was no way she could see that in the dark. "It's dark," he said.

"Do you want me to turn the light back on?"

"No." He fumbled for his glasses.

"They're here." He felt her hand him his glasses.

"Don't turn on the light."

"I won't."

"Are they back?" He meant her husband and child. He couldn't hear anything beyond the altar-room door.

She knew whom he meant. "I don't know."

"I don't hear anything."

"We would probably hear Polly if they were back."

"Can you see anything?"

"Not in the dark."

"Like me."

"Maybe someday we'll go together to the Ice," she said.

"All right."

"I meant to say that before. But it didn't seem right."

"It seems right."

"It didn't seem right, considering everything."

"Considering everything, it seems right."

"You should be sure of what you want."

"I know."

"I mean, about having a child. It's too big not to be sure." He nodded. She couldn't see him nodding in the dark. "I'm sorry," she said.

"There's something monstrous about my life."

"Of course not."

"The bigger my life is, the smaller I am in it."

"I shouldn't have said anything."

He dropped his glasses beside him and fumbled until he found her hand.

"I've been owned by everyone," she said, and in the dark he heard the resolution in her voice. "I've been owned by this one and that one, my whole life. And the biggest thing I ever did was to free myself. I did it with a knife. I cut myself loose. And now I find out I didn't do it after all. Do you understand? I find out I didn't do it. You've freed me today of the burden of having killed a man. But if I didn't kill him, it means I'm still a slave. God damn everyone who's ever owned me," he heard her say. "The police and the priests, and Gann, and the one before him."

"The one before him?"

"Why do I feel close to you? I feel close to you, heart to heart."

"I know."

"Redemption is their word," she said.

He pulled her to him in the dark, or perhaps she pulled him to her. It was better in the dark, that neither one of them would ever know who had first gone to the other. At first he couldn't quite dispel from his mind the idea that she could see him in the dark even though he couldn't see her, because he didn't have his glasses and he couldn't get over it, the idea that without his glasses he was either blind or invisible. But now that she pulled him to her he knew he wasn't invisible.

In the black altar room the air was thick with wine. He clutched her dress; its tones of earth and ash and blood, not unlike the color of her skin, ran between his fingers. The feeling of its cotton, not unlike the touch of her body, ran through his hands. His head pounded with wine and blood. For a moment he thought of the glasses, he worried they would be smashed underneath, and then the idea of it—his smashed glasses—went straight to his head like wine and blood. When he kissed her he emptied wine and blood and the freedom of smashed glasses into her mouth.

The air was thick with possession. The sound of the wine bottle against the wall was thick with defiance; and then the crash of the altar in the corner, though it sounded very far away, much farther away than the corner, though it sounded like the distant collapse of another altar in another country, was thick with submission. In the dark he felt her breasts fall from her dress. They fell so heavily it shocked him. He wanted to pull the string on the light above and assure himself it was she. But he knew that even with the light on there would be no assurance because he couldn't have seen her anyway, his eyes spinning like wild blue suns in the sudden light, all their vision leaked into the black of his hair. He caught her beneath him. As he'd been stunned by the heavy fall of her breasts, he was now struck by the speed of her nakedness: possession was everywhere. It opened itself to him, bared its wrists.

When he took her in the dark of the altar's ruins they both knew it was more than she'd ever given and more than anyone had ever taken, and that neither was enough. She was touched that Etcher would make love to her so tenderly but she felt no choice except to insist on ferocity: possession was everywhere, and now she demanded it. She'd be restrained by him or, if he couldn't restrain her, she'd devour him. In their struggle either her best nature, the part of her that spent her whole life coveting freedom, would triumph or her true nature, the part of her that spent her whole life choosing slavery, would abide; and in this moment in the dark she would accept either the triumph or the abiding, whichever it might be, as the truth of who she was, until once again her other nature stirred inside her and she wrestled with its relentless nagging. "You," she said, because she couldn't remember his name, "oh you," she said, waiting for him to claim her. But he wouldn't do that. The part of him that would enslave her was overwhelmed by the part of him that would free her, if it was up to him to free her, which of course it was not: it had always been up to her to free herself. So he felt her grip him inside, he felt her contractions swirl around his invasion of her; and he would have thought, in the dark, that his hair had gone white, the wine and blood and freedom of smashed glasses rushing to the only moment of him that was real, lashing the uterine passage to that place inside her where nothing is possessed and nothing possesses.

The tears rolled down her face. He felt them in her hair. No light penetrated the black of the altar room, instead the black rushed from her. It poured from the middle of her, more blackness than she'd ever believed was hers, the truth of her rushing out even as the blackness of the altar room became wan with the tears that rolled down her face. It was only at that moment she realized her wrists were tangled in the string of the light above; and now at the moment she slipped from its bondage, in the jerk of her wrists, the room's light flashed on and off long enough to leave a small rip in her memory through which she couldn't bear to look, even as her lover saw everything. And there was that suspension again, not unlike the one they had felt when the all-clear siren had sounded. Everything was still, the dark was clear of wine and possession and choices; neither of them could be certain she had said she loved him or he had said he loved her, but all that mattered was that he was sure he had said it and heard it, and she was sure she had said it and heard it, and both were sure it was true. And in the dark there was no telling whether it was wine or tears or blood or the torrent of blackness that passed between them, but in the slick of their love they slipped into each other; and only much later did he hear a little voice on the other side of the altar-room door. "Mommy," it said, and started to open the door, and then another voice, a man's voice, said, "Don't open that, Polly."

In the dark Sally pulled on her dress. It was intact, untattered. Etcher found his glasses; they were intact, unbroken. But everything else was in pieces. "Sally," he whispered. "Yes," she whispered back. Beyond the door a child and the child's father waited.

At that moment Etcher couldn't be sure he would ever have her again; he grabbed her to him, by her hair. He would have crushed her into him.

She opened the door and the little girl stood looking up at her.

It was night, but the curtains had been drawn again, as when Etcher first arrived. Some of the beads and trinkets of the jewelry on the table had been strewn on the floor, where the child had played with them. Gann Hurley was sitting on the couch reading a handbill. He didn't even look up; to have looked up at his wife and the other man would have been a concession that whatever passed between them mattered to him in the least, that he could be affected by anything that was beyond his control. At the front door Sally stood holding her daughter; for a moment the little girl looked at Etcher and then turned away. Etcher gazed back at Sally in confusion. "Will you be all right?" he finally said.

"Yes."

Will I see you again? he wanted to ask. But he was afraid of ruining everything.

He left the circle, and after waiting a long time caught a bus on the road back into the city proper. Whatever I do now, he said to himself on the bus, staring out the window at the volcano in the distance, I cannot do for her. I cannot assume she'll be mine. I must act on the assumption she'll never be mine, that it will never be less impossible than it all seems at this moment. I must act on the assumption that I'll never see her again, except for a passing moment in the street or the Market, and that love has been left hanging in the black space of a small room, and that in the light, with a husband and a child, she'll feel very different tomorrow, if she doesn't already. Therefore, whatever I do now ultimately has nothing to do with her. It has to do with the life I've been living. It has to do with the man I've been and who I am now, without her, and what my life is now, without her.

He went home and left his wife.

It had never been in his temperament to understand power. In all of his passivity he had never felt the oppression of other people's power over him, which was why he resigned himself so easily to it; his resignation was born not from his fear of others, after all, but himself. Nor was it in his temperament to revel in power, which was why he had never understood why women like Synthia needed him to exert power over them. He had thrilled to his own power only in the throes of sex, when he didn't have the presence of mind to know that pleasure wouldn't last forever, and in the flush of freedom, when he was too innocent to know he wasn't free.

Now he seized the power that came from that collision of sex with freedom called love.

Etcher didn't tell Tedi about Sally, because when he left Tedi it wasn't about Sally. When he left Tedi he didn't believe anything would ever happen between him and Sally. What happened between Etcher and Tedi was about Etcher and Tedi, and in his new power he tried to leave Tedi without abandoning her, if such a thing was possible. But he came to recognize the limits of leaving without abandoning. For months afterward, he would go by Tedi's classroom—with the children and the blackboard and the shelves of books and bibles and texts—to marvel at the limits and power of her rage. He understood that this may have helped nothing. He understood that something about his enlistment of Tedi as a co-conspirator in his own leaving might be dishonest and cruel, and that he couldn't deny her the right to her rage. Sometimes, outside the school, in the windowless downtown street, he took the full force of her fury as her efforts to contain that fury broke down and she broke down with them, the spectacle interrupted only by an occasional passerby. The best Etcher could do was promise not to lie to himself. He wouldn't pretend it was all her fault, or pretend her pain was less than it was, or tell himself she was better off. He didn't believe she was better off. He believed that in meeting her and being with her he had accepted responsibility for her heart and its dreams, whether or not that was something any person could rightly do for another, and had now broken those things; when she ran from the street crying he was left with the sound of the shattering, her dreams in pieces on the ground, the sound of them crunching beneath his feet like glass as he walked away.

Two months after his marriage ended, Etcher left Church Central one night to the smell of wine in the air. All the way down the rock he smelled it. The wind brought it from the sea to the west through the windows of the lift, as though it were a red-wine sea beyond the shore rolling in and out to the pull of a red drunk moon beyond the Vog. Etcher might have thought he wanted a drink. He couldn't remember the last drink. Yes he did. Sure he remembered the last drink. He remembered the bottle of wine in the corner of the little altar room, the sound of it in the dark. It was better to believe that the smell of wine in the night air only meant that he needed a drink; he preferred to believe that. He needed to believe it had nothing at all to do with that last time. At this moment Etcher might have craved a drink even though he hadn't drunk anything in a long time, because it was easier to deal with his thirst than his hunger. If he had believed in omens he might have known, coming down the rock on the lift, what was there at the bottom. And if the smell of wine from the sea wasn't omen enough, there was, when he stepped from the lift, the empty robe lying in the path. It was a priest's white robe. Etcher had never seen one just lying on the ground like this, as though the person inside it had suddenly vanished. The wind carried it a couple of feet. Etcher picked it up. Once he would have cast it away immediately, as though it would implicate him in some crime. But now he casually threw the robe over his shoulders and walked on, and not much further from where he'd picked up the robe, at the bottom of the rock, he found Sally waiting for him, her hair blowing like a wild ash weed in the wine wind.

"I couldn't get you out of my head," she said.

"Where have you been?" he asked.

He asked it as though they had made some appointment hours or days or weeks before that she hadn't kept. He had imagined seeing her so many times that to see her now in the night and the Vog was somehow utterly expected and utterly unreal at the same time. It was so exhilarating it frightened him. He would have settled for just this opportunity to see her and hear her tell him, "I couldn't get you out of my head," and then watch her walk away. But she didn't walk away. There was no way of being sure she was happy to be there; she didn't appear happy or unhappy. At the bottom of the rock, on the base of the path that led to the lift, she was as dark as the night around her, she was blacker than he'd seen before, even in the black of her altar room. She was beautiful in that chemistry of her soul by which torment lit her beauty, the only light of her being the light in her eyes, and they walked along the cliffs in the night until they passed the point where a small wooden fence ran out and there was no fence at all, just the rocks and the emptiness beyond them, the plummet to oblivion at the border of where they now loved each other and every embrace was a risk.

When she became cold he wrapped her in the white robe of the priest. He didn't notice anymore if the sea smelled of wine. "I'm leaving Gann," she told him. He didn't say, "Good" or "I'm glad," he only nodded, and the Vog leaked from the place where they stood as though that place was scorched by their heresy, rolling out across the cliffs and up the coast. It was the first and only moment Etcher ever believed Aeonopolis had succumbed to the rest of time, which in turn had succumbed to a magic rage wild beyond the fingertips of magicians: and Sally and Etcher didn't presume to hold that moment, they didn't wish to stop it as lovers do. They knew the moment wouldn't wait for them. They knew it would go on spinning out from beneath their feet all the way out to sea for as far as they could see. They merely hoped to get as far as the momentum of the moment would take them, to distill the fury of their heresy into a thrust that would propel them over every moment that hadn't already been reduced to shambles by her astonishing face. It was a heresy that broke ten spells in exchange for the one it cast. Standing where they stood with the sea and the Vog and the night at their backs, in his arms she gazed up at him and cried out, "But you look so . . . happy," though she meant something more, she meant a frightening rapture, and though she understood his love she didn't understand his faith, and if he couldn't persuade her to share his faith he shared her incomprehension of it, and wondered at his desire to possess beauty and own it, because he never really believed it was possible. He didn't believe in his own faith. It was a measure of the power of that faith that it believed in him.

Operating through the Church bureaucracy, Etcher got himself another unit, and a unit for Sally in another circle in another zone. He gave Tedi most of his money. By the time he had paid for the licenses of the units, nothing was left; he didn't care about this. In his seizure of power he believed anything was now possible in his life, with or without money. In that collision called love, nothing was property, which was only the most banal currency of power. Etcher was his own force of nature, not accountable to property or money or bureaucracy or the emotional blackmail of his marriage that had held his life hostage. It had nothing to do with these things but rather with power and the smashing of his own resignation when he began, with blithe temerity, to smuggle from the archives the Unexpurgated Volumes of Unconscious History one by one until, some six months later, the vault that had held them was empty.

The first night he went to see Sally, after she'd moved into the new unit, the door was answered by her tiny incarnation. She was three feet high, the replication of her mother but for the fire of her hair and her eyes, which were as blue as Etcher's own. For a minute Polly stood looking up at him, considering his presence. Then she slammed the door. It took him another minute to work up the courage to knock again.

He hadn't known many children in his life. He had never been much of a child himself, cocooned in the otherworldly blur of entirely too much reason and silence that missed the point of tantrums and manipulation. The child who greeted Etcher at his lover's door was just beginning to learn the power of tantrums and manipulation, in a never-ending fight to win the fleeting attention of a self-involved father and haunted mother. She was ready to draw the line at Etcher. She recognized immediately that he was out of his element, and at her mercy. She was charming, hilarious, beautiful, brilliant, strange and shrewd, but she was not merciful and, worse for Etcher, she was two. Like any true barbarian, she'd ruthlessly exploit Etcher's essentially civilized nature by which civilized people ultimately perish. Across this breach there was nothing left for Etcher and Polly but to bark at each other.

Struck by the vision of a dog in a forbidden children's book that her father brought home from the Arboretum one night, Polly had the new interloper read her the story from front to back and back to front, over and over, while she barked each time a new dog made an appearance. She commanded Etcher to draw pictures of more dogs, rarely to her approval, until the circle's obelisk was plastered with them, chartreuse and purple and aqua dogs wet with the spray of the sea and the dew of the Vog. "Dogs, dogs, dogs!" she chanted, marching around the room, until finally he rebelled: "No more dogs!" he snapped and Polly exploded in laughter, the sound of his breaking point music to her ears. Her laugh was so big for such a little person and so untamed that he laughed too, and the more she laughed the more he laughed, and the more she laughed in return. Over time he came to impose order. Over time he came to be for Polly the agent of order. In the presence of her mother she rebelled against it, but when it was just the two of them, Polly and Etcher, she submitted. Then her rebellions took the form of crawling up into his lap, peering into the mammoth blue eyes behind his glasses, and solemnly announcing, "I am not your friend." He refused to mollify her frustrations. He refused to attend to her tantrums or humor her manipulations. He'd leave her in the middle of the unit screaming her head off while he went into the altar room and closed the door behind him, leaving it ajar just enough so that she knew she hadn't been deserted.

As each crisis passed, a new order took hold. In the doorway of the unit Etcher would watch her fearlessly chase the seagulls across the white circle in the bleary sunlight from behind the clouds. In the blast of the white circle she'd lift her little arm and, with one little finger, point at the vision of the gulls in rapt silence, as though witnessing in them something no one else could see, a secret revelation glimpsed amid the clockwork of the real, between the gears and wheels, to be forgotten when she was older and knew more, and understood less. Between Polly's order and Etcher's, no-man's-land was the time between waking and sleep, between real and dream, when the two-year-old lay in the dark and, if sleep didn't come immediately, called out to anyone who was there. Her bed was filled with so many little animals it seemed impossible to Etcher anyone could sleep there. It also seemed to him a sign of the little girl's possessive aloneness, in a little world that was always filled with people of whom none could be counted on to stay more than a passing moment.

More and more it came to be Etcher who was there when she called. Polly's father was off with the theater, often unseen for days. Polly's mother would take her jewelry box over to a neighbor's and try to work, eking out an existence for her and her daughter. When Etcher took Polly in his arms and carried her out into the circle at night, walking around the obelisk while Polly searched the Vog for the sight of a star, she clung to his neck like someone who had felt the earth shift beneath her too many times and had learned within moments of her own birth how sooner or later everything passes away. She clung hard, silently. Sleep did not loosen her grip on him. And yet in the night when Polly called for her father and he wasn't there, when she called for her mother and she wasn't there, the appearance of Etcher at her side was small consolation. Etcher never quite got used to Polly crying at the sight of him because he wasn't her father. He never got used to the fact, even as he came to understand it, that no matter what he might do for Polly, the sight of him could never delight her, could never make her heart soar, could never bring the spark to her eyes as did the sight of her father. He never quite got used to having the responsibility of being a father without its glory; he never quite got over the small fantastic hope that maybe she'd somehow gotten from him her blue eyes, which she shared with neither her mother nor father. He was never quite sure exactly when it first broke his heart to realize that Polly wasn't his, and never could be.

There was no doubt that Gann Hurley adored Polly more than he adored anyone else in his life or world. He adored Polly for the way she was an extension of him; he adored her for what of himself was in her. Perhaps, Etcher thought, it was this way with all fathers. Hurley had married Sally, after all, for the child she would give him. He had insisted on the child and, because Sally couldn't stand to be dispossessed, she gave him his child. Gann's passivity was of a different strain than that of Etcher, who hoped to move through his own life upsetting it, or anyone else's, as little as possible. Gann consumed lives. His passivity was the vacuum into which lives were sucked. If someone had pointed out to Gann that in choosing to have this child he'd made a fundamental choice about the rest of his life, a choice that entailed a fundamental sacrifice of himself, he would have been confounded if not contemptuous; he would have considered the suggestion that something of himself had to be given up to fatherhood a blow to his integrity. Because his world spun so utterly to his own gravity, reasoning with him as to the wisdom of its various revolutions was like arguing with the sun, with which Gann felt a certain kinship.

Much later, when everything came apart, Gann would look at Etcher in disbelief and say to him, "You went through all of this for a woman?" Maybe this was his retaliation for Etcher's having taken his wife, though Gann would never have seen the situation as Etcher's taking his wife, even if that had been the situation, which it was not: it was that his wife had left him, a version of events Gann also rejected. But that Etcher had come slowly but surely to absorb Gann's responsibilities, that Gann came to live off the fitful sense of honor that Etcher's love created, was the price of Etcher's folly. If lives were to be used, Gann was certain that Etcher's particularly cried out for it. Gann obliged him. That it often came to be Etcher who put the food in Polly's mouth and the clothes on her back and a roof over her head was only the result of the role Etcher had chosen for himself; no one had chosen it for him. And if Etcher could never quite understand how Gann could live with that, he nonetheless couldn't completely disagree with it either, the role being the appropriate price for what Etcher saw at the end of his particular night, the glimmer of light that might be happiness. He had felt himself turned alive by not one woman, but two.

Now, with all his power, he ran for that light. Every moment was shot through with its possibility. In so running he would hurl himself into a new life and a new Etcher, because he never before had really believed in happiness; his rush toward the light was the leap of faith of one who had never before had faith. In the pandemonium of his love he arrived at the archives late and left early, carelessly filing the forms and papers however it amused him. He never craved a drink. In her bed at night, in the contraband love stolen within inches of her sleeping child, he smelled the wine of her and the ash, he smeared himself with her until his body was black with the cinders of her soul. He got on his knees before her and hissed her name in the archway of her womb, and took in his teeth the bud of her blistered dreams. He never relented. He ignored her pleas to stop. He parted the fur between her thighs and slipped his mouth over her red silk bell that rang at the tip of his tongue. "No, please," she moaned centuries away on some unfathomable street of no numbers; and it was his new power that he loved her so much that her no meant nothing to him. On into the night nothing of him moved but his tongue in her, nothing shook his grip of her body or the seizure of her breasts when there trickled down the uterine avenue the gorgeous bitter oil of her black egg. The taste of it flooded his brain like the drug of a star. He said her name. He said it into her, it wound its way up inside her. It hung in the center of her and encircled her heart, sealing off all means of escape, it caught in her throat and filled the back of her mouth. It bled into her eyes and she saw her own name before her written in his terrible alphabet. It crashed the barricades of what they believed and invaded the realm of what they dreaded until for him there was nothing anymore to dread except the limits of his voice to speak her name, the limits of his mouth to swallow what her body flushed onto his lips, the limits of his fingers to hold her fast until he'd pleased her beyond what she could bear. And in those moments on his knees before her he understood how love made a person whole by obliterating him, how it made a person bigger than he'd ever been by taking from him everything he thought he valued, how it could touch a person with the biggest and most obliterating determination of all, the conviction that he could die for someone, that he would die for her.

For Sally those moments were excruciating. She couldn't remember Gann having ever given her an orgasm or having ever given any indication he cared to; now she clung to some uncomprehending unworthiness, never believing herself deserving of the climax to which her new lover dedicated himself. When the no slipped from her lips at the surge of her body onto his own lips she had no idea what it meant, though she had the sense of having been pleased like this before, and of how the orgasm was at once a transcendence she never believed in and a capitulation she could never forgive herself for making. In the dark she tried to make out the place and time into which these climaxes hurled her. In the dark she tried to make out the name and face of the man who knelt before her. She was overwhelmed by his insistence on beginning his life anew. She could barely stand the burden of his happiness. She could barely live up to the possibilities of her own happiness. He gave everything and took everything, and since she couldn't get over the feeling that, where he believed there was everything, there was in fact only nothing, the fraud of it filled her with remorse. She knew, in the dark delirium of his pleasing her, that she'd been borne out of being owned into this blackness where she owned him; and in that blackness the one clue to who she really was was there right in front of her, and farther from her reach than ever. And thus what she released onto his lips from the center of her was the echo of a distant memory that would determinedly abort the birth of the person in her who had sworn never to be owned again. She wouldn't settle for happiness without meaning. She clutched his black hair that fell across her thighs. When his tongue found in her the clearing where the small child waited, in the embrace of the small child's arms was a small white baby seagull not yet strong or knowing enough to fly from the blinding white circle that engulfed it. Like the tragic alchemy of her face, by which her beauty was released by sorrow, Sally could only fly alone. She could not fly with the only lover she'd ever known who believed in her wings.

Three months after her affair with Etcher began, Sally became mysteriously ill.

It began in the middle of her, in the small of her back, as if the small white seagull was growing inside and beating its wings for release. For some time it was merely pain, and then one morning it overcame her and she collapsed. For an hour Polly wandered the unit, absently playing with this toy or that and crying to her unconscious mother; finally she opened the door and wandered out into the circle, where Cecilia the neighbor saw her. Cecilia went out to talk to the child. "Mama's sad," Polly told the woman. "Well, let's go see what she's sad about," Cecilia answered, taking the little girl's hand. Cecilia found Sally shuddering on the floor. When Etcher returned that night Sally was in bed, the pillow beneath her wet hair a ring of sweat. What dismayed him most was her whiteness. She was as white as anyone he'd ever seen in the Ice. He held her all night to conjure the blackness back into her; in her ear he coaxed her with advice, he beseeched her to breathe the night deep into her lungs, that it would flush her body with the tinge of twilight. The next morning she seemed to have rebounded.

But that night she was worse. Etcher returned from work to find Polly alternately poking at her mother's somber daze and playing with her mother's jewelry, having strewn them from one end of the unit to the other. Now Sally was white like ice itself. Her lips were cracked and her hair was matted; the black lines of her eyes and mouth were the very scrawl of death. One moment he'd touch her and she was clammy and cold, the next she was on fire, and she was only fleetingly aware anyone else was there. Polly began to cry. Etcher was astounded. He scooped up the child and wrapped her in the tiny pink blanket of her bedding and paced the floor with her as Sally moaned to the sound of her daughter. "Why is Mama crying?" the little girl bawled. After almost an hour she finally fell asleep. Sally croaked with thirst. In the fit of her fever she hurled her blankets off her. The sheets of the bed were soaked beneath her. Etcher lifted her from the bed and set her on the couch as he plundered the various drawers and shelves for more bedding. He changed the sheets and put Sally back to bed; now she was freezing. He buried her with blankets and laid himself across her. She shook violently beneath him.

It continued all night. All through the night Sally thrashed in a rage of heat and cold, as Etcher would lift her from the bed and remake it, changing the sheets that were wet with her sweat. His hope was that she would expel the disease in the torrent of her fever; he held her so close and she was so hot that their embrace seared him, and when he wasn't holding Sally he attended to Polly, who woke hourly through the night and called to her mother. When her mother didn't come she cried. When she cried Sally stirred from the sleep that Etcher spent the night fighting for. At dawn, when the little girl tumbled from bed and came over to pull her mother's hair, Etcher bathed and dressed Polly, fed her some breakfast, and took her to the neighbor. "Help me," he begged.

"Where's her father?" Cecilia answered, taking the child.

For the first time Sally seemed to sleep peacefully in the morning light. Etcher, allowing himself to hope the crisis had passed, crossed downtown on the way to Central; he didn't make his usual morning stop to see Tedi. At the archives in the early afternoon he was gripped by a sense of something ominous. He took the lift up to one of the offices on the next level, where he found one of the priests. "I have to go now," he told the priest.

"What are you talking about?" the priest said, taken aback.

"I'll return when I can." He had found a new capacity for ruthlessness in his life. It was part of a new power that didn't allow for second-guessing in the matters about which he'd found a new determination. When he returned home, a moment beyond the door's threshold he discovered a metamorphosis taking place. Laid out on the bed she was drained of color or cognizance. The blood in her was as still as stone. She was lividly caught in some abyss that denied Sally Hemings had ever existed. He put on his coat and went to the next circle and found a doctor.

The doctor came back with Etcher. He took one look at the woman on the bed and said, "She's dead."

Etcher gazed calmly at the doctor. "Let me explain something," he answered, "she's not dead."

"It's in the hands of God," the shaken doctor protested.

"Let me explain something." Etcher looked down at Sally and back at the doctor. "Things have changed around here, so you can't be expected to have known. I've been running for the light, is the thing. I've been running and I'm almost there, and the light isn't going to flicker out just at the moment I reach it. It's not going to happen that way. You have to take into account the new power. You have to take into account the new capacity for ruthlessness." He said, "There's been a shake-up, so to speak." He pulled the doctor down to his knees. "God works for me now." He thrust the doctor's face into Sally's, whose eyes were open and still. "Listen: she *breathes*." The doctor listened, terror-stricken. "You can't be expected to have known," Etcher assured him. The doctor and Etcher watched Sally for a long time.

She breathed.

The rest of the night Etcher kept the doctor there by the scruff of his neck. He pressed him into mixing concoctions and formulae; but the doctor, at a loss as to what was wrong with Sally, couldn't treat her. Finally, when Etcher lifted Sally from the bed in order to change the sheets for what seemed the hundredth time, he turned around to find the door wide open; the doctor had made his escape.

Not long after, the doctor returned with the police. The cop in charge was a small wiry man with red hair and a mass of bandages where his nose used to be. The sound of his words seemed to leak out of everywhere but his mouth, which now jagged sharply skyward; there was no way for Etcher to know he'd seen this cop before, in the lobby of the Church in the middle of the night. The police left the doctor with Sally and took Etcher crosstown, up to the rock.

At the rock, Etcher was met by the priest who had left his key in the vault door months before. He didn't say anything but took Etcher by a lift to a top floor of the Church, where Etcher had never been in the nine years he worked as a file clerk. The door of the lift opened on a long hallway, at the end of which were two open doors and, beyond them, a white room. The priest led Etcher to a small office off to the side of the hall, where another priest in a white robe was sitting at his desk waiting for him.

Etcher had seen this priest before, at one time or another. He'd never spoken to him. The priest in the white robe looked up at Etcher from his desk and motioned for him to take a seat. The priest who brought him disappeared.

The priest in the office was curt and officious. "You're Etcher?" he said.

"Yes."

"You've been working here for a while, haven't you, Etcher?"

"Yes."

The priest wasn't looking at Etcher. He was making notes on something that had nothing at all to do with Etcher. "You're very lucky to be able to work for the Church," the priest said. Etcher, thinking this over, didn't say anything. The priest looked up. "Do you want to keep your position as an employee of the Church?"

"I'm not really sure," Etcher said. "Actually, I've been giving this matter some thought."

This wasn't the response the priest had expected. "You're not sure?"

"Well . . ."

"There are reports, Etcher, that you've been acting rather

strange lately. There are complaints about your recent work habits and behavior."

"Complaints?"

The priest stopped taking notes and put down his pen. "Do you find this amusing?"

"I don't think so. I mean, I haven't thought about whether it's amusing. In the larger scheme of things it might appear amusing. At some later point, I mean."

The priest studied him.

"At some later point, it might—"

"Be quiet." The priest had thought this was going to be a routine disciplinary session. He resented having to give it extraordinary attention or energy. "I'm putting you on suspension," he said. "I hadn't intended to do this. I assumed we would straighten this out in short order. I hadn't anticipated your attitude, your impertinence. In several weeks we'll reassess the situation. Maybe then, after several weeks without pay, you'll appreciate your position. Maybe you'll take the matter more seriously."

"The problem is, I need the pay."

"Yes," the priest answered coolly, "I understand that. It would have been constructive if *you* had understood that before we had this discussion. Perhaps next time you'll be less cavalier. More prudent."

"You don't seem to understand," Etcher explained, "I can't take a leave at this time. Not until I figure out what I'm going to do. I have a friend who's very sick."

"*You* don't seem to understand," the priest retorted, incredulous. "I didn't say this was a leave, I said it was suspension. It isn't something that you have any say about whatsoever."

"Oh no. That's not true. I have complete say."

"I beg your pardon?"

"It's not your fault. You couldn't have known. But things have changed."

"Changed?"

"I have the books."

The priest blinked. "The books?"

"The old red ones. From the vault downstairs. The Unexpurgated Volumes of Unconscious History, such as they are." Etcher said, "I have all of them."

The priest went as white as his robe. He went whiter than the people of the Ice, he went whiter than Sally Hemings' disease. His mouth finally curled into a desperate smile. "It's preposterous."

"Well, it's understandable you would think so," Etcher admitted.

"You've taken your life in your hands," the priest croaked, "if you've so much as touched a single one of those books."

Etcher laughed. "Well, now that you put it that way, that's it exactly. I've taken my life in my hands." He laughed for several minutes. When he stopped laughing he added, "There's been a shake-up."

The priest jumped from his chair and ran from the room.

Etcher sat waiting nearly forty-five minutes. He became tired of sitting and waiting; he was worried about Sally. He had finally given up waiting and was walking out of the office toward the lift when the priest returned. He appeared to Etcher to be in something of a state. "Come with me," he gasped.

They walked down to the other end of the hall, through the open doors of the white room. Several other priests were sitting behind a crescent table, in front of which was an empty chair. The head of this group, sitting in the middle between the others, said, "Sit down, Etcher."

Etcher wasn't sure he'd ever seen this particular priest. "I've been sitting for an hour," he answered irritably. "I have a sick friend."

"Sit down," the head priest said again, motioning to the empty chair. Etcher sat. After a moment the priest leaned forward, his hands folded on the table in front of him; the other priests leaned with him. "The books are gone," he brought himself to say, after a moment.

"That's what I explained to the other one," Etcher answered.

"Did you take them?" the priest said. Something was funny in his voice.

"We've gone over this," Etcher told them, shifting in his chair to indicate the priest he had spoken to in the other office, who was now standing behind him in the doorway. "Didn't we go over this?" he said. The priest in the doorway wrung his hands in response. "We went over this," Etcher said to the head priest with impatience.

"Do you know what you've done?" the head priest said.

"Yes. I've taken the books."

"Where are they?"

"I have them."

"The police are on their way to your unit at this very moment, to find the books."

"Well, I certainly wouldn't keep them there, would I?" Etcher said.

"We'll check the unit where you used to live with your wife," the priest said. "We'll check the Hurley woman's residence as well."

"What's the matter with you?" Etcher snapped. "The books aren't in any of those places—you can turn them upside down for all I care. I would have expected," Etcher said to the head priest, "that at least *you* had figured it out. I would have expected that at least *you* knew there's been a change."

"You don't know what those books are."

"Of course I don't know what they are. Who's more dangerous, a man who knows he's carrying a bomb or a man who doesn't? The man who knows, and has to get rid of the bomb as soon as possible, because he realizes that any moment it's going to go off? Or the man who doesn't know and is walking around without a concern in the world, while the bomb ticks away in his suitcase? The chaos of the situation lies in his ignorance, because he doesn't know enough about the situation to get the hell out before it's too late, to give up his control of the situation before it's too late. Look." He took his glasses off and put them on the crescent table. He raised his fists above his head and brought them down, smashing the glasses.

The priests sitting around the outer rim of the crescent table cried out, covering their faces with their arms. Their white robes sparkled with slivers of glass and blood. Etcher raised his hands to his face; in the blur of his vision he could make out only the smear of red on his fingers. He lifted his eyes to the white of the room, to the vibrating hum of the sea: it was the light he'd been running for, here in front of him. He could barely make out the priests; the white blur of them wasn't nearly as impressive as the smear of red. Reaching across the table he wiped his hands on the head priest's robes.

In the heat of their shock, which he felt on his brow, he heard the gasp of history. He heard history open its mouth and silently gape, no sound coming from it, only the silence that consumed everything around it. If there had been a sound it could have been a cry, it might have been a laugh, most likely it would have been the utterance in which a cry is indistinguishable from a laugh. In a city that lay outside of history, in a church that presumed itself unthreatened by the collision of time and memory that named its own truth, it was the joke of their arrogance that they presumed history might be locked away in a room without a single guard. They presumed their power was such that no one would ever turn a key and walk in and carry history out under his arm. What they now wouldn't have given to have placed a guard by the door. What they now wouldn't have given to have put on an extra padlock. What they now wouldn't have given for a bell that rang in alarm, or a whistle that blew; and what they wouldn't have given to have entertained a single thought that once told them, Perhaps our hold on history is not so secure or inviolable. Perhaps our confidence in God isn't so justified. None of them said anything at this particular moment. Maybe they tried to say something and Etcher simply couldn't, in the blur of his new freedom, see the contortions of their shock or insult.

"I have to go," he explained, turning to leave. It was almost an afterthought when, pausing in the doorway, he said, "I'll be back when Sally's better. When I think it's the right time, I'll return the books." He walked down the hall, took the lift to the lobby, and left the Church and the rock behind him.

He found her alone when he got home. The doctor was gone. As far as he could tell, no police had searched the premises. She was alone in her bed, just barely revived by her terror. The curtain of the window was cracked, the sun had shone in her eyes all afternoon; she hadn't the strength to move where she lay, let alone get up and close the curtains. Now Sally, sensing a presence, barely raised her head from the pillow to see who else was in the room. Etcher knelt at her side. Her yellow eyes, circled in black, welled with tears. He had to lean very close to hear her, putting his ear to her lips, when she whispered her first words in days. She said, "I'm afraid."

"Don't be afraid," he answered.

She said something else. He leaned so close he was afraid she'd smother beneath him.

"What?" he said.

He could hardly hear her when she asked, "Am I going to die?"

"No," he told her.

"Do you promise?"

"Yes."

"Am I going to get better?"

"Yes."

"Do you promise?"

"Yes."

"I don't think so," she said.

"Yes."

"I don't think I'm going to get better."

"I promise."

"Are you sure?" she cried, the smallest of cries.

"Yes."

He went to the window. Outside he could see the blur of Cecilia and Polly playing in the circle. Polly looked up just as Etcher was peering out the window. She ran to the door; Etcher opened it. The little girl stood in the doorway awhile and looked at the woman on the bed who was her mother. She was afraid to approach, and then Sally turned slightly, slightly raised her hand to her little girl, slightly called her little girl's name. Polly ran to her side. Tears ran down Sally's face. She thought she remembered something somewhere far in the past when she was a little girl herself, a dying mother in a house far away, beckoning her children to her. But she didn't see how she could have a memory of anything like that, other than in a dream.

When Polly had gone with Cecilia, Etcher drew the curtain closed. He went to the door and bolted it. He piled all the furniture in front of it—the dresser and table, the chairs, Polly's toy chest. The night came. Etcher took off his clothes and got in bed next to Sally and put his arms around her.

Come on then, he said to the door in the dark. Come on, he said in the dark, where he was freest of all, his phony vision left behind him in shards of glass, caught in the robes of phony priests. He no longer needed to see her to know who she was, the woman in his arms. He no longer needed to see her to know she was beautiful or afraid. Come on, he said to whoever would come through this door, to priests and police, to her child or the father of her child. He said it to the city and to history, to memory and the future. He said it to God, he said it to Death. Come on, and try to take her.

This continued the next night, and the next and the next. It continued through the fever, through the horrible chills and the flashing heat. It continued through the wet sheets that Etcher washed and hung to the obelisk in the center of the circle, along with Polly's chartreuse and purple dogs. It continued through the sirens, morning and twilight. It continued for five nights, until finally someone knocked on the door. For some time the knocking continued and Etcher didn't answer. He didn't rise from the bed until, from the depths of her delirium, Sally cried out, "He's here."

"Sally?" the voice outside the door said. It was Gann. Etcher rose from the bed. He looked outside into the dark through the curtains of the window. "Sally?" Gann said again.

"She's sick," Etcher finally said in the window.

After a moment Etcher heard Gann say, "What's wrong with her?" Etcher couldn't see anything in the dark. But Gann was closer, next to the window.

"She's been sick for a week."

"Where's Polly?"

"At the neighbor's."

"What's wrong with Sally?"

"I told you. She's been sick. She has a fever."

"Will she be all right?"

"Go take care of your daughter," Etcher said. He dropped the curtains into place and backed away from the window. He stood for a while listening to Gann's footsteps walking away.

On the sixth night, Etcher woke with a start.

He heard the flapping of the wings before he heard her scream. He heard it inside her, trying to smash its way out, that wild ferocity of even the frailest creature when it's trapped; and she screamed again. He held her. Her body didn't merely convulse, it thrashed in upheaval, and when he put his face right up next to hers, right close to hers, he could see in the dark and in his blindness the horror in her eyes, the startled realization of something about to be delivered. And he held her thighs and pulled her to him even as she fought him off with a new maniacal power; and in the rush of the black spill of her womb he almost believed, though he couldn't be sure, since the room was so black and the vision of his eyes was so black and the spill of her was so black, that there flew from out of her a white baby gull. He could hear it rise in the room. He could hear it flying around him shaking the afterbirth from its wings, insistent on its freedom until the room filled with the rip of the curtain and the crash of the window, and the funnel of the night air poured through. And Etcher leapt from the bed and began, bit by bit, pulling the furniture away from the door, the dresser, the table and chairs, Polly's toy chest, until the way was clear and he flung the door open. He stepped out into the circle and dropped to his knees.

He began searching the ground with his hands. He knew that if he should find there in the glass of the broken window a dead bloody bird, then he had lost Sally. He would have lost Sally and he would have lost the light and he would have lost everything. Only if the bird had made it, only if the bird had broken the bonds of its own wounds and taken flight by a sheer will for freedom, would Sally make it as well; and so he searched on his hands and knees for the rest of the night. On and on through the hours, inch by inch and foot by foot, on his hands and knees he searched the entire white circle.

He never found the bird.

He walked back into the unit at dawn. Stepping through the doorway rubble of his barricade, in the light of the broken window and the afterbirth of her fever, in the trail of her own thwarted death, he heard her say, "I love you, Etcher." And then she went to sleep.

S h e   w a s   s i t t i n g   u p in bed the next day. Three days later she rose from the bed for the first time since she'd fallen ill. Gann returned with Polly. Etcher returned to Church Central.

It was only for a brief moment that it struck Etcher as odd, to be history's file clerk. He barely took notice of the priests. Over the days and then the weeks, they circled him with the solicitous respect that's always accorded a wild sick animal right up to the opportune moment when it can be destroyed. Only after some time had passed did Etcher notice they brought him no forms or papers to file. Quickly his job turned into being some sort of custodian, a watchman on the lookout for anyone who trespassed into his light; for days and then weeks he sat among the archives doing nothing but staring out to the Central lobby. He was thinking about the limitations of his view when his presence was requested upstairs.

In the white room, around the crescent table, they were seated in their half-circle. "We were just wondering," said the head priest, "if you're ready to return the books now."

"I was giving that matter some serious thought this very morning," Etcher answered.

The priests looked at each other with anticipation. "Really?" asked the head priest.

"I'm ready to begin right now, as a matter of fact."

"This is very good news," the head priest said after a moment.

Etcher reached into his inner coat pocket and pulled out a folded piece of paper. He handed it to the priest, who unfolded and studied it for several minutes.

"What's this?" the priest said.

"Page one."

The priest continued studying the paper in his hands. "Page one," he repeated, almost absently.

"Tomorrow I'll give you page two."

"Do you mean to tell us," and it was difficult to be sure without his glasses, but Etcher supposed he heard in the priest's voice a rising hysteria that struggled for control, "that you're going to return the books page by page?"

"I'd like a window," Etcher answered.

"What?"

"A window. In the archives. The view is limited, staring out at the lobby. There's no light in the lobby. I'd like a window. Can you do that please? If you put in a window, I'll bring you pages six through nine perhaps, or eight through eleven. A window on the light. A window on the sea."

A month later, after they had put in the window, he decided he wanted to move the archives altogether. He had them relocated upstairs in the northernmost part of Central, where he could see in one direction the sea and in the other direction the volcano. Here he could always smell the wine in the air, which rolled in with the ocean and bubbled hot in the volcano's crater.

So Etcher had found his light, having been fired by love to defy God and seize history. And the Unexpurgated Volumes of Unconscious History trickled back to Primacy page by page, in no great rush, since Etcher well understood that when the day came years later that the last page had been returned, his life would be over, there would be no more history left to protect him from Primacy, in the same way that if the return of the pages was to stop there would also be nothing to protect him, since there would be nothing for Primacy to lose by ridding itself of him. Everything came down to a trickle of pages. The trickle couldn't be either too fast or too slow. Sometimes, for a window, sometimes for a new view of things, the pages returned in threes or fours, occasionally half a dozen at a time. There were, after all, close to fifty thousand; Etcher could occasionally afford to be generous. It was important to instill hope in the priests. It would be dangerous if they should feel overwhelmed by the futility.

Etcher lived with the woman he loved, in the way he had once come to believe he'd never love again, and with her child whose love he coveted beyond what was possible, beyond what was possible for a man who would be her father if he could, and could never be her father no matter how much he would.

In the haze of his life without glasses, everything was wine and light and pages. But when the thing that emerged from the collision of sex and freedom, called love, collided with the thing that emerged from the collision of time and memory, called history, the dreams began to come to Etcher. And when he woke from them, the light wasn't the same.

In the first dream, nearly a year after Etcher had left his marriage, Sally was sitting on the floor, her knees pulled up under her chin, and she was talking. She told him, in this dream, that she was in love with another man.

He woke from this dream and discounted it. He discounted it even though, somewhere in the back corner of what he'd come to know, he understood that this dream was the expression of an inkling. But he discounted it and didn't think about it again, until the very next night when he made love to Sally and there slipped from her lips a name that was not his, slipped so clandestinely she wasn't even aware she'd said it. But Etcher heard it, unmistakably.

"Thomas," she whispered.

But she didn't believe she knew anyone by that name. Had she been aware of having said it, she would have been as surprised as Etcher, not because she wasn't seeing another man but because his name was not Thomas but Joseph.

He was a large bear of a man who spoke in a hush, and he had a stall in the Market. She'd gone there several months after having recovered from her nearly fatal illness, browsing among the Market's paltry offerings. He made jewelry of a less exotic sort than Sally's—strings of benign white wafers that hung as plain functional necklaces—and had been watching Sally from the other side of the Market; when she wandered over to him he could barely believe his good luck. Then, as she studied his jewelry carefully, he took notice of the necklace she wore.

"Where did you get this?" he said in his hushed voice.

The way he spoke, the way she could hardly hear him at all, felt familiar to her, as well as the way he looked down on her from a height. She was immediately sorry that Etcher didn't look down on her from a height. She was immediately sorry that Etcher, a soft-spoken man himself, now seemed so loud. "I made it," she said of the necklace.

Joseph looked around him, over both shoulders. "They allowed this?"

"I've never . . . subjected it to their approval." She asked, "Do you think I'd have trouble selling a necklace like this?"

"It's a very unusual necklace," he advised her.

She got the idea, then, of selling some of her necklaces through Joseph's stall. She came back the next day to talk to him about it and, though he was dubious and afraid, since he couldn't afford to have the police shut him down, he wanted to see Sally again, so he offered to keep her necklaces and earrings under the counter and show them to anyone who appeared adventurous. Unknown to Sally, he bought some of the jewelry himself, so that she'd return.

Slowly he began to steal her heart.

One night she went home with him, and didn't return to her own circle until late the next morning.

Perhaps it was the jewelry. Perhaps it was that she wanted to be admired for something she created rather than someone she was, since she had no idea who she was and therefore could never really trust anyone who loved her for that. Of course it wasn't her jewelry that Joseph loved, it was the same intangible thing about her that all the men had loved; from the other side of the Market she was the most beautiful woman he'd ever seen as she had been the most beautiful woman a thousand other men had ever seen. But she chose to believe it was the beauty of the necklace she wore that attracted him. And then, if she was touched by the familiarity of him, there was also the way that he was utterly different, because though he wanted to ravish her like the others, he was incapable of it.

They lay together in bed and he tried to will forth the manifestation of his desire. His mind roamed around itself to find the magic click of the cells in his brain that would spark an erection. When he could not, when he suffered in her arms, that need for her comfort and assurance and pity felt more like real need to her than the need others had for her body or soul, particularly her soul, since its contents were so mysterious and unnamable to her. Comfort and assurance and pity were qualities she recognized readily enough in herself that she could offer; they possessed a value she understood. If there was ever a woman who needed to pity a man, who needed to be needed for the heedless assurances of her heart when her body could not be taken, it was Sally; and so she gathered him up. She held him just as the big bearness of him gathered her in his arms and held her. Once she had needed the ravishment. Once, amid Gann's indifference and in the aftermath of a dream from which she woke in a strange hotel next to a strange man in a pool of blood, she needed the carnality of love. But Etcher had satisfied that need, and once he had, Sally in her fashion couldn't quite believe in it anymore, since the slave in her couldn't understand anyone loving her as anything but property;

and when Etcher ravished her not as property but as a person, she could no longer understand ravishment at all, nor his in particular. She believed ravishment was bigger than she was worthy of, which made it unreal. Joseph's love, crippled and pitiful, was real. It didn't overwhelm her in the way of Etcher's. It didn't impart meaning to her life in terms of what it gave to her but in terms of what it asked of her. She had found someone as wounded as she. And so for several months she loved Joseph, the fact of their love sexless if not the intention.

"There's someone else," she told Etcher, not long after it began.

"Then you have to find out what it means," Etcher choked. It was the sort of thing someone believes when he says it but hopes that, the moment he says it, the new infatuation's meaning will become instantly and clearly trivial, and no further investigation will be necessary. It was a fair answer, but not an honest one. She begged him to help her. It was an honest plea, but not a fair one. He'd helped her with everything else, after all; Etcher had been from the beginning the one who helped her more than either of them had a right to. It was unfair of her to ask for his help now because what she really asked was that he accept part of the responsibility for a decision that could only be hers. The night she told him there was another man they made fitful angry love in the middle of which she moaned desperately, "Marry me." Etcher knew at that moment that Sally did not know the meaning of her heart. In a single hour she'd gone from telling him there was another man to a frantic plea for marriage, and everything he'd allowed himself to trust could never again be trusted the same way. At the end of their sex, when she cried, as she had many times before, "No!" to her own orgasm, the no had a new conviction, the no had a new persuasion about it, the no believed anew its unworthiness to be yes, the no believed anew its unwillingness to be possessed.

It might have been easier if Etcher could have hated Sally. But he knew she acted not out of malice but confusion; Etcher's faith in this love was such that it was incapable of comprehending how confusion could be as destructive as malice. "You want to know if he and I have made love, don't you?" she asked witheringly in one of their arguments about the man who didn't even have the same name for both of them, Joseph to her and Thomas to him. But even when Sally scorned Etcher's pain with a contempt he'd never heard from her before, even when Sally scorned his unasked questions, he knew it was really her own heart she scorned. At such moments he wanted to protect her again, as he'd come to protect her since the moment she walked into the archives searching for Madison Hemings. Etcher wanted to protect her from the way the chaos of her heart spilled into the shambles of her soul; it might have been easier, since he couldn't bring himself to hate Sally, if he could have therefore hated the man whose name she knew as Joseph but whom Etcher knew as Thomas. But he couldn't hate Thomas either. It was impossible for Etcher to hate any man for loving Sally; it would be tantamount to hating himself. And so that's what he came to do. Once again he extended the benefit of the doubt to everyone but himself. Once again he was the most convenient target of his own agony and rage, as though he didn't believe anyone else could really sustain the impact of either his agony or rage.

He didn't follow her. He didn't track her through the city, or conspire to confront her infidelity. He didn't spy on her affair around corners. He did, however, wait outside her door. He did sleep at night against the obelisk in the Vog, pulling his coat around him and waiting for her return. He did linger beyond the circumference of her old circle, out in Redemption known as Desire, where Gann now lived alone except when Polly was with him. One night he finally approached, knocking on Gann's door. "Is Sally here?" he asked when Gann answered.

"No," said Gann. After a moment he said, "She got you running in circles, huh?" and it was to Gann's credit that there was no meanness in the question. He seemed to take no satisfaction in Etcher's plight; the odd thing was that Gann had come rather to like Etcher. This, then, was what Etcher had come to: an alliance with Gann.

On a black night that he knew she was with Thomas, at two in the morning when he knew she was going to be with him the rest of the night, he wanted to die. He had neither the passion nor conviction for suicide but he had none for life either, and all the pity he had before for those who never knew the feeling of a love that was bigger than their own lives now became an indifference for life itself. He told himself that if he could, he would have emptied his eyes of her face and his arms of their memories and his heart of its dreams, but his greatest anguish was that as soon as he said it, he knew even on this night he never would have done any of that. He never knew whose slave she had been. He only knew that he was hers.

It may have been at this moment that Etcher was left with no choice but to let go of Sally, since the only other alternative was to let go of his love, which he couldn't do. Because while losing Sally would only break his heart, losing his ability to love like this—and he would never again love like this—meant the shattering of something so profound as to defy its naming with names like love or Sally or Thomas. The faith in love that led him to take his life in his own hands, as the priests had put it more accurately than they knew, was the creation of something more and bigger than love, in the process of which love was nothing more or less than the essential element. Something in him, from that moment on, became just a little cruel. The light in him, from that moment on, became marked with the ashes of a black cremation. And finally, when he came to detest himself for his continuing subjugation to the way Sally hurt him, when he knew he could no longer blame anyone but himself for his feeling of humiliation and betrayal, he stepped back across the chasm, from the side of his heart's blind faith to the side of his heart's naked nihilism: he got another pair of glasses.

When Sally saw Etcher wearing the new glasses, she finally understood what was at stake. Until now she understood only in her head but not her heart that she was at the edge of losing him. She decided the only thing to do was see neither Etcher nor Joseph, perhaps for a long time. She decided that if she was never again going to be owned, if she was never again going to be a slave, she'd brutally have to drag her own life out into its own outlaw zone and abandon it there. Alone she walked Desire's wild shoreline, the city to the south of her and the volcano far to the east, and between the two the rising black hulk of the Arboretum. Beneath her she could feel the waves of the sea slash the rocks and rush into the grottoes under her feet, where fissures ran to the surface; with each incoming wave the water sprayed through cracks in the ground in a hundred geysers as though the earth were crying for her to free herself. Confronted with her new decision, Joseph asked that he might be allowed to see her once a month. Etcher, however, insisted he would not hear from her at all. Sally was furious with his adamant terms. But he was now locked in an effort as desperate as hers to free himself, and when she begged him to stay until morning on what they believed was their last night together, when once again he felt himself nearly seduced by her pain, he refused.

The priests at Central noticed that Etcher wore his glasses again. They didn't have the imagination to understand that at this moment he was vulnerable to everything and everyone, including them; they didn't have enough empathy for the mess and blood and semen and tears of human life to understand that in his desolation he might have given whatever they asked. Instead, mistaking the new glasses for renewed control, they kept their distance even more; and their moment of potential victory slipped past them.

Two weeks after they had parted, Etcher received a message from Sally. He couldn't decide whether to go back. It wasn't because he didn't still love her utterly but because he'd be returning with such crippled faith on his part, to such crippled determination on hers; he had come to see, in the manner of Polly who silently raised her finger to witness in the flight of gulls something beyond what anyone else could see, that Sally's inner turmoil would eventually have to be played out. He did return, of course, convincing himself it could be played out with him as well as, maybe better than, without. And though he'd never understand everything, he would come to understand the hard way that, though Joseph was gone from her life, the ghost called Thomas was not.

Sometimes in the middle of the night as everyone was sleeping, right after the episode in the hotel, when she was still with Gann, Sally would go out into the circle. She would carry with her the black wooden box with the rose carved on the top. After she left Gann, when she was with Etcher, she would continue to rise and cross the circle in a night so dead even the white of the circle was lightless. In the dark she was searching for what belonged in the box. Night after night she waited in the circle for the Vog to break just enough that the moon might peer through, illuminating her search; she assumed she would know what she was looking for when she found it.

It was the rumble of the volcano that launched her final flight to freedom.

The city woke to it one morning as though to a bomb. The ground shook. People ran from their units into the circles and watched the volcano's fireball rise into the sky, spat forth from an earth clearing its throat. The city became paralyzed, silent in its panic, passively waiting for the mountain to roll soundlessly across the lava fields and down the streets in a molten wave. In the distance, to the southwest, the tiny white figures of the priests could be seen on the Central rooftop surveying the coming cataclysm. But after several days passed, when the earth began to calm itself and it was clear the cataclysm would not come this time, the city returned to its deadness, the crack of doom that brought it momentarily to life changing from echo to memory to the finally forgotten.

Sally didn't forget. It wasn't that she was afraid of the volcano, it was that she was liberated by it, as the entire city had been, though perhaps only Sally saw it this way. She saw it as a sign, the voice of the earth, because something had once happened to her in its mouth, once she had seen herself there, though she didn't actually remember this. She didn't actually remember the vision of herself and Etcher in the little house on the volcano's inner ridge. She just knew that the volcano was speaking to her and that her dream of fleeing to the forests of the Ice in the north, far from the barren lava fields of Aeonopolis, was more within her grasp than it might ever be again. It was within her grasp not because she had the means to grasp it but because, momentarily, she had the will, and because it seemed to her the only way she'd ever be free of her life.

"Take me away from here," she begged Etcher.

It was one thing to enter the city. It was another to leave. There were two ways to go. They could go by sea on a boat, or on land by train. If they went by boat they went illegally. If they went by train they would have to get visas from Central. Occasionally Etcher heard about those who slipped into Desire, crossed the zone and made their way past the peripheral highway to where, if they were fast enough, they might jump the train. But there were almost always police on the train until it was far from the city, and with Polly such an option wasn't viable anyway.

Once—it now seemed long ago to him—Etcher had known power. Once, before Thomas, there had been a change, a shake-up. Now in the clarity of his new glasses he saw his power as a stalemate. Police followed him everywhere. They waited for him to lead them to the red books. In fact he did lead them to the books, once or twice a week in the beginning, but they didn't know this; and then his visits became less frequent to Tedi's school, where amidst the graffiti that ran off the blackboards the Unexpurgated Volumes of Unconscious History sat in plain sight, unnoticed and ignored, on the bookshelves with the bibles and references and texts, available to any child who might pull one down and read it like a collection of forbidden fairy tales, with those pages torn from them that Etcher returned to Primacy each day. The books that had once empowered Etcher now imprisoned him. They made it impossible for him to leave. The power Etcher derived from the books ended at the point that Primacy retrieved them or believed it would never retrieve them: Etcher could threaten to toss them into the sea or the volcano, and it made no difference.

Thus Sally would have been trapped as well, except that Etcher set her free. He had watched her writhe too long under the spell of her ghosts and dreams, wriggling for a freedom she could never believe in. He would have to believe in it for her. And so his stalemate with the Church left him only the power to strike the best bargain possible, which was two visas out of the city: one for Sally, and the other for her child.

Standing on the platform at Vagary Junction, eyed suspiciously by the everpresent police, watching the two women of his life wave goodbye to him from their compartment window—the older one in exhilaration and the little one in small confusion—as the train lurched into its own smoke and the Vog in the distance, Etcher actually told himself he'd soon join them, as they planned. He told himself that with them safely out of the city he was free to maneuver more cleverly, more clandestinely, to slip from beneath Primacy's gaze and eventually follow Sally and Polly to the northern Ice. It was, at first, almost a relief to be alone. He hadn't been alone in a long time, since before his marriage to Tedi. It was a

relief to bear only the burden of his own oppression. He told himself that in the three or four or six months before he made his own
escape, Sally would free herself for good, with no one to save her,
and then what she and Etcher had together would redeem itself.
In the back of his mind, since perhaps the first day he'd seen her,
he had been telling himself that there would at last be someone to
save him, and that it was she.

He received letters from her and replied, unobstructed by the
authorities. He had explained to her that while Primacy would
allow a correspondence it would have to be a discreet one; their
emotional revelations had official limits. She could, for instance,
say that she missed him. It was all right, he assured her, to say she
missed him. And her first letters were filled with it, along with the
news of the house she'd found high on a glistening fjord in the
sunlight beyond the treetops, for which Etcher sent the bulk of his
pay each month. She sent back news of the house and her heart's
longing for him, and he saw it all in the lines of her letters, the
magnificent solitude on the high fjord and Polly's Sally-in-minia-
ture with her hair of mysterious fire and her eyes of mysterious
blue running across the white expanse beneath the consuming
sky.

In response, something in him cracked.

Beneath the weight of his own palatable relief, he was cracking
to a relief he couldn't bear. It disoriented him in relation to everything he believed about himself and Sally and what they had; it
disoriented him in relation to his love. He found his conscience
betraying his heart, which is the worst of treacheries, and it only
drove him crazier that he couldn't be with her. He was cracking
beneath the approaching destitution that would signify a failure
bigger than money, that would signify the final psychic failure of
Sally's struggle to be delivered, and of his struggle to deliver her.
He was cracking beneath the surveillance of the Church which
now, rather than letting up, intensified, because in having freed
Sally from the city he had freed her, officially, from the matter of a
murder in a shabby room in a downtown hotel. In a way that would
never have occurred to Sally, in a way even the priests didn't understand, Etcher had accepted the weight of the crime or, more
precisely, the weight of its irresolution.

His success at obtaining the visas for Sally and Polly, then, was more impressive than he knew. In the end Primacy had decided Sally was, officially, expendable. The ramifications of the unsolved murder of an unknown man in a hotel bed had reached that point, officially, where it was riskier to pursue the case than to close the book on it. The strange and violent disappearance of the investigating police officer in the case had made this not only politically preferable but bureaucratically easier, though the police force itself hadn't been the same since. Two years later the case remained rife with undercurrents. The Church didn't like undercurrents. Undercurrents, this one or that, always rose to the surface sooner or later, as happened when Etcher came to the priests and asked to take a leave to go north.

He had still, four months after Sally's departure, not devised any plan of escape that seemed feasible. Everyone knew Etcher was a security risk; no skipper would take him by boat. If he went into the Desire zone the cops kept something of a distance, but the highways beyond the zone and outside the city were always blocked. The trains were always under guard. As Etcher became increasingly frustrated by this imposed immobility, he and Sally had a crisis through the mail. She wrote that Polly missed her father terribly and asked if Etcher could obtain a visa for Gann. Etcher didn't understand why he was responsible for Gann. He didn't understand why Gann, who fancied himself an outlaw, should now receive his help. Let Gann apply for his own visa, he answered Sally. But of course it wasn't just Gann but Polly who would pay the price for Etcher's bitter refusal, to which Sally responded with bitterness of her own. After further correspondence he relented, and went to Primacy for yet a third visa that would be in a name other than his own. And so it was now Gann who left the city, traveling north to live in the house for which Etcher sent money every month as Etcher remained behind to support the three of them. I've become a joke, he thought to himself. I've escorted love across that border beyond which it becomes self-contempt.

So the urgency of his leaving grew, and peaked in the two weeks during which there arrived from the north three extraordinary messages. It was difficult to say which was most startling. The first was from Sally. From her halting, difficult letter, it became clear to Etcher that she was trying to tell him something momentous and not entirely focused, yet somehow familiar. It was written in the voice of a woman who had once told him she had found someone else, except that now the someone else she had found was herself. In the most direct way possible, as direct as Sally's chaos could be, she was telling Etcher not to come.

The second message was from Kara, the only other woman he had ever loved as he now loved Sally. More than ten years after leaving her naked beneath those stars wedged in the observatory dome, he suddenly and out of nowhere received a letter calling him back.

The third message was from home. He knew, before he read it, what it said. He knew, before he read it, his father was dying.

He had begun to know, as imperceptibly as the priests had begun to know it, that nothing had quite been the same since he took from the Church vault the Unexpurgated Volumes of Unconscious History. After his confrontation with the priests during Sally's illness, something began to fray the psychic fabric of this city that existed outside time. A trolley car disappeared. An obelisk moved several feet. In a back alley off the corner of Desolate and Unrequited, in the very spot where the arcs between the Church and the volcano and the Arboretum intersected, official graffiti gave way to heresy, which rewrote itself not simply in the present but for all time: not only was there a different message today and tomorrow, but yesterday as well, and the day before, stretching back as far as anyone had ever noticed. Memory was, flash by flash, undoing itself. When the pages of the volumes began to trickle back into the vault, one or two or five or six at a time, depending on Etcher's whims, the process of this fraying was, for the moment, suspended. Possibly when all the books had been returned to the vault, the trolley car might reappear. The obelisk might return to its place. The official propaganda of the graffiti at Desolate and Unrequited might reassert itself over the surreal nonsense that usurped it. But now, when Etcher came to the priests for a leave to travel north and was refused, the pages stopped and the fraying began again. The priests, sitting around their crescent table discussing the situation, suddenly turned to find one of their colleagues had vanished from his chair. Over the course of the day alarm inevitably evolved into panic: another of them might be gone with the next sunrise. "I'll be damned," the head priest thundered at the others, "if I'm going to wake up tomorrow to find I'm not here!"

A solution presented itself, in the form of a surfacing undercurrent. His name was Mallory and he was a cop. His face was a swirl of scar tissue, having been smashed against the wall at the corner of Desolate and Unrequited two years before. Coming from Mallory the solution was so literal-minded as to be, in the current situation, imaginative. Etcher would voluntarily give himself over to the authority of the police and travel north in the company of several officers, who would present papers signed by the prisoner to anyone challenging their jurisdiction. Mallory volunteered for the assignment not out of a devotion to duty nor even to slavishly impress the priests (as was Mallory's wont), but because he was convinced that Etcher would lead him to Sally Hemings, and that in turn would lead to the man who had obliterated his face and then disappeared off the face of the earth like a trolley car or displaced obelisk or a message on the wall.

Sitting in a church hospital for months picking the scabs off what used to be a nose, Mallory had had plenty of time to figure this out. It was obvious the big black called Wade had gone off the deep end for Sally Hemings the minute he laid eyes on her. He'd made certain she understood she was looking at a murder rap and then cut a deal with her, probably that afternoon in the car driving her out to her circle after springing her loose from jail. He probably pointed out to her how she now owed him everything and how everything was exactly what he wanted; then he spent several days putting together a plan, jumping a train or boat out of the city an hour after he'd left Mallory crumpled in the alley, heading north where he'd been waiting for her all this time. This guy Etcher wasn't anything to the Hemings woman but a connection on the inside, a glorified file clerk who fell under her spell just like Wade and could get her out of town. Now she was stiffing Etcher: Mallory knew this because the police read the fucking mail. Now she was saying she wanted to be alone.

Mallory knew that Wade and the Hemings woman were up there together right now. They had figured the priests would never let

Etcher go, and they were almost right; what they didn't figure was
how smart Mallory was. They just never figured, Mallory said to
himself, what a smart guy I am. Now they were in for a big surprise.
Now let's see Wade try to hide, up there in all that fucking Ice.

At first it was a trick of the wind, the smell of the
smoke. In all the years Etcher had lived in the city he had never
smelled the smoke of the lava fields, the wind from the southwest
blowing the wine of the sea through the streets and in turn the
smell of the smoke north. Now he was heading north on the train,
in the company of a police entourage. They had seized half a car
for his transport. In the dank light of the train one cop sat in the
seat across from him, another in the seat behind him, another by
the door nearest him and the fourth right next to him. The one
next to him was the cop who had come to take him off to Central
the time Sally was sick. One didn't forget him. His name was Mallory and his nose was missing and the whole bottom of his face
lurched upward into a scar; it was sometimes impossible to be sure
what he was saying, words leaking out of various orifices in the
front of his head like the sea that sprayed up through fissures of
the earth along the coast or the Vog that rose from the lava fields.
The chains that the cops called a rosary bound Etcher to Mallory
by one wrist and to his seat by the other. In the pitch of night,
whenever one man slumped into sleep, the slip of his hand would
yank the other man awake, and this went on until the dawn, each
man falling asleep in time to wake the other man. When Etcher
needed to use the toilet Mallory accompanied him. When his heavy
new glasses fell from his face into his lap, he had to wait until the
cop in the seat across from him put them back on.
   It was in the middle of the night that Etcher smelled the smoke.
The smell began unpleasantly enough but then, no matter how far
behind the train left the black fields, it got worse. It went from a
distinct unpleasantness to a horrific stench, and it was then that
Etcher knew the smoke wasn't a trick of the wind anymore, it was
a trick of the soul, and there was no tricking the soul back. It was

then he knew this wasn't just the smell of the volcano but the smell of what waited for him, a moment far north to which his whole life rushed. This was the very smell of his odyssey into the black and it was the smell of the end, of something dead in him that was caught in this particular crevice of time and wasn't to be dislodged, but would go on decaying just beyond his reach, just beyond his capacity to work it loose from where it was caught and grasp it and hurl it out of his life forever. When the smoke grew unbearable, when he was afraid he was either going to suffocate or vomit where he sat, he lunged for the train window to open it, jerking Mallory so hard from the slumber that hissed from the various punctures of his face that the cop believed Etcher was trying to escape. Mallory yelled a strange strangled yell. "My God, that smoke!" Etcher cried. The other cops jumped to their feet, subduing Etcher and wrestling him back into his seat. "Please, open the window," Etcher begged them, and the smoke grew so powerful in his lungs, and his hands were so restrained by the rosaries, that he would have crashed his face through the glass of the window in order to get some air.

Mallory raised his fist to level a blow at Etcher. He stopped only at the last moment, the other cops yelling because the priests had made it clear Etcher was to come back in one piece. "Open the window," Mallory muttered, lowering his arm. They opened the window. But what came through the window wasn't fresh air but a new billow of smoke, like the smell of someone being burned alive. "No, close it," Etcher moaned, now trying to find his glasses which had fallen off.

After six days, only twenty minutes from his home town, Etcher suddenly knew, with a calm utterly mysterious to him, that his father was dead.

He knew he would reach his home and his mother would be waiting for him in the doorway, and she would say, "He's gone." And that was exactly how it happened. They came to his old house on a back road of the village, Etcher in chains with his police guard, Mallory opening the front door for him without knocking. Etcher stepped in to see his mother standing there as though she'd been waiting for him. Two other women were in the room crying. For a moment Etcher's mother was bewildered by the police and the rosary, but then she just said, "He's gone," the way he knew it would happen; he'd died only half an hour before, at the moment Etcher knew it. The son held the mother, Mallory hovering over them obscenely by the dictates of the chains. After another moment the doctor came out of the back room. "He's still back there in bed if you want to go see him," his mother said. "He looks like he's sleeping."

He did not look like he was sleeping. Etcher and Mallory went into the back bedroom and Etcher's father was propped up on the pillows in bed, and he looked like he was dead. Every impulse of life had fled his face, which was the color of sand; his mouth was slightly open. Perhaps if he'd looked as though he were sleeping, Etcher might have remained to say something to him. He might have said goodbye, for instance; he had thought, on the train in the smoke, of the things he might say, but there didn't seem anything that had to be reconciled. Wasn't there always something that had to be reconciled? Wasn't there always some final breach to be bridged between parent and child, particularly when they're so different, when Etcher knew his father had long before stopped trying to identify the ways in which his son refused to live between the incandescence to one side of him and the abyss to the other, attempting instead to straddle both, to place one foot in each? Etcher was filled with regret not that there was something he hadn't had the chance to say to his father, but that his father might have needed to say something to him. When, at the sight of his father's body, Etcher brought his hand to his mouth with a gasp, he pulled Mallory into the gesture like a marionette.

What Etcher most dreaded now wasn't the smoke of his father's cremation. What he dreaded was that the billow of the crematorium would be something entirely different from the smoke he had known for the past six days, something purer and conveying a color of the earth, and then there would be forced upon Etcher the realization that the dark smoke that had pursued him from the city was something else. There was no ceremony. Later Etcher was vaguely troubled by this lack of ritual, though he wasn't sure why, since all three of them in his family had always hated ritual, and the manner of his father's death was therefore in keeping with the spirit of his life. Over the days that followed, Etcher became enraged by the chains. He threatened to intentionally hurt himself. "I'll rip my hands off," he told Mallory. "You can explain to them

in Central how I'm supposed to return their precious books with
my hands ripped off.''

The whole time Etcher was with his mother, however, Mallory
didn't take off the chains. He didn't take off the chains until several
days later, when Etcher went to see Kara.

The observatory was as good as a prison, Mallory figured. It was
made of stone, with no windows, and only a single set of double
doors on the northwest side. The only other way to leave the dome,
as far as Mallory could see, was to jump from the top; he didn't
really think Etcher was going to risk that. He knew Etcher wasn't
going to risk anything before getting to Sally Hemings. So at the
observatory he took the rosary off, more because he was getting
sick of it himself than out of consideration for Etcher, for whom he
had no consideration one way or the other. The other cops waited
outside the door and Mallory patrolled the dome's stone circumference, just for good measure.

As they had approached the dome, Etcher didn't smell the
smoke at all, only the surrounding trees and the bite of the air. He
had nearly gotten to the doors of the observatory when they
opened suddenly and she presented herself, as though to take the
offensive against time and confront both of them with the ways in
which time had deformed them. Her hair was shorter. She was a
little heavier, and older of course. He wore the glasses—if not the
same pair—that had so appalled her that last night. He hadn't
come to answer anything between them, and he'd brought no questions. Perhaps he wouldn't have come at all if he hadn't believed
the smoke was the pyre of everything else ending.

He knew Kara smelled her own smoke. He felt, in the grip of her
hand as they sat beneath the opening of the dome looking up at
the sky, the desperation he recognized as someone smelling
smoke. As calmly as Kara pretended to receive him back into her
life, he recognized the way everything was tinged with this desperation: it was all around him in the trappings of a rendezvous, in
how she would have taken off her clothes and lain naked beneath
the night as she had once before if she hadn't believed it would
send him running from her. They talked. He told her, in terms he
hoped were explicit enough to warn her but implicit enough to
protect what was private, about Sally. She told him, in terms she
hoped would obviously belie her assurance that she expected noth-

ing of him, about what had happened to the sky. It had changed. She had looked up one night a couple of months before and had noticed it immediately. It was just after that dusk which everyone crosses sooner or later, when their remaining days recede before them and solitude suddenly reveals itself to be ghastly and endless. She looked up and it was a different sky. It had different quadrants and different stars. There were different worlds and new mortify-ing suns. Tonight she clung to Etcher, and to what he couldn't give beyond some requisite tenderness that he would have owed to anyone, but especially her.

When she slept, he lay in the dark of the observatory staring up at its concrete shell, and on the inside of the dome watched all his memories. They were big and in color, and roared out of so many years before in details he would have thought forgotten beyond the possibility of remembrance. He reveled in the luxury of being able to raise his hands to his eyes without the shackles of the rosary, and take off his glasses and cover his eyes, hiding his face away from the light of the memories on the observatory dome. To his astonishment and horror he found himself silently calling his war-dens outside to come drag him away. It seemed that, for once, Mallory took forever. In the dark Etcher whispered to Kara, "It's time to go," and had to pry her hands loose from his neck.

"My father is dead" was the first thing he said to Sally when he saw her. Etcher and the cops had continued north across the expanse of the Ice, the trees disappearing and the ter-rain becoming bleaker and whiter until there was nothing but end-less winter, somewhere near the top of the world. The fjord where she lived was jagged and stark. Over its cliffs, which encircled her house, rolled the clouds, each releasing another. At the edge of the fjord gorges cut their way through the earth; the bottoms were filled with water and in the distance there trickled across the ice veins of blue light. A vague gray solstice tumbled across the sky. Polly was the first to see Etcher when he arrived; she ran toward him yelling his name until she got close enough to notice the chains around his wrists. She looked at him confused, not sure whether something was wrong with him or whether she had done something wrong and the chains were somehow for her. When she saw next to him the man with no face, she cried. She turned and ran back toward the house.

"My father is dead," he said, not yet sure whether he had left the death of his father behind him or brought it with him, or whether he had stashed it in the snow somewhere along the way, to be preserved and recovered later. The abrupt gasp Sally gave might as easily have been to the news as to the sight of him. She was flooded with emotion to see him. She had missed him utterly. In the midst of the precious aloneness she had hoped to find, even with her child and the father of her child in the same house, she had still missed him. She had written him not to come in part because she knew that if she saw him again she might not be strong enough to be alone without him.

He knew this too, though it didn't much mitigate his rage. He was alive with indignation over her betrayal. He was still sorting out the matter of responsibility for the fact of his life having become a shambles. The shambles was all the more devastating for the promise of two years before, when his affair with her had begun; he remembered the moment of resolution when he'd left Tedi, ruthless in insisting on his right to be happy. He'd been so certain everything was within his control. Now nothing was in his control. He stood in the middle of Sally's bedroom that was to have been his own as well, facing her and chained to a cop who made little children cry at the sight of him, the father of her child in the room upstairs lying in front of the window that Etcher had dreamed of lying in front of, watching the sky and glaciers gliding past that Etcher had dreamed of watching; and everything couldn't help but seem ridiculous, everything couldn't help but appear as though it had come flying back in his face, in return for his having tempted the absurdity of life by thinking he had any power over it. It was just like Etcher to wonder if this humiliating result hadn't been in the cards all along. He believed just enough in the retribution of destiny to wonder if this place to which he'd now come wasn't the natural price to be paid for every mistake and every resignation, for every brutal truth, every broken heart.

It was a wonderful house. It made everything worse, that it was a wonderful house, because on first sight of it his deepest dream took on dimensions, took on the form of stone and wood, walls and doors, crossbeams and rafters. His deepest dream rose with the staircase that ascended the middle of the house to the upper room and panorama that swept before its western wall. In the southern wall was a door that led out onto the roof of the lower floor. Outside, next to the door, was a ladder. The ladder led up onto the roof of the upper floor, and on the upper floor the world spilled out at the roof's edges, north and east and south and west, in a rush so huge and elemental that even when the winds were still one was afraid of being swept off by the sight of it. Goodbye, one automatically whispered to everything on top of that house, where everything was too big for one to really know whether it was a farewell to the world or to what one believed or to the sheer delusion that, standing on top of the world, one was important at all. It seemed an act of preposterous arrogance to stand on top of such a house with the world thundering down in its blue yowl; and that was the greatest lost dream of all, the loss of that preposterous arrogance, because it was the arrogance of someone in the grip of love's power, and Etcher knew he wasn't that powerful anymore.

He begged Mallory to chain him to Sally's bed.

Mallory complied, not as a favor to Etcher but because he had to find Wade. He knew Wade was there. He knew Wade was hiding beneath the stairs or in some back room. He had begun looking for him as soon as they stepped off the train in the little station twenty-five miles away; he'd asked around in the tiny village. All the way by bus across the desolation of the Ice up to the house, he'd had his eyes peeled for the logical hiding places. But there were no hiding places. There was only ice. When the little girl cried at the sight of him out in the snow and ran back to the house, Mallory hurried behind her pulling Etcher and the other cops along, convinced the kid would tip Wade off and give everything away. Mallory rosaried Etcher to Sally Hemings' bed and ran halfcrazed throughout the house, flinging open closet doors and shoving aside furniture under the rather bemused gaze of Gann Hurley, who was waiting for Sally to bring him his lunch and clean the bathroom and wash the dishes and make his bed. The cop with no face turned the house upside down until he finally reached the top room and the ladder outside. Staring up the ladder, he knew there was no other place for Wade to go. He knew he had him trapped. This frightened Mallory because, confronted with this moment, he was alone; and he didn't want to meet Wade alone. He called down to the other cops, who couldn't hear him. He screamed until he was hoarse and finally one by one they came outside the house to look up at Mallory on the roof of the first floor. "I've got him!" Mallory cried, pointing up the ladder to the very top of the house. The cops, looking at the top of the house from the ground, couldn't see anyone: "There's no one there," one of them yelled up to Mallory, who ignored him, squawking from every open blister of his head until the other cops came back into the house and up the stairs and out onto the roof of the first floor. "One of you stays here," Mallory said, "and the other two follow me," and he started slowly up the ladder step by step until he reached the very top. When the other cops heard his scream they panicked, believing Mallory had found Wade after all. They didn't know that Mallory was crying at the sight of the world, at the sight of the streaming red sky, at the sight of time cascading toward him in rapids.

Downstairs in the bedroom, Sally and Etcher listened to Mallory running throughout the house around them. For a long time they sat together on the bed in silence, following with their eyes the sounds that moved maniacally from place to place. What's he looking for? she finally asked. I don't know, Etcher answered. By the time Mallory had gotten to the very top of the house, his cry of alarm seemed very far away, and neither Sally nor Etcher was paying attention anymore. Each was now listening to his and her own thoughts, trying hard to hear the other's. Etcher could hear Sally's. He had become so adept at hearing her thoughts he almost heard them, he believed, before she thought them. He knew she was thinking that maybe she didn't want to be alone after all; he knew that with him sitting right next to her her confusion had taken yet another turn. Perhaps she expected him to answer this confusion. Perhaps she expected him either to beg her to let him stay—she didn't really understand yet that the police wouldn't have allowed this in any event—or to confess that it had all become more than he could bear and he was leaving her to her confusion alone, as she professed to want. At any rate she waited for him to share some of the responsibility of this confusion: and she couldn't hear, among his thoughts, his refusal.

"Maybe," she said, "you should just come here like we planned. Maybe we should do what we planned all along, and you should come." He didn't answer. "You have to tell me what you're thinking," she said. "Are you angry, are you sad? Are you relieved? Do you want to yell at me, or hit me?"

"I could never hit you," he said.

"But I don't know what you're thinking."

She didn't know, and he could hear her thoughts so clearly. "You've needed to be free since the first," he said.

"I tried to tell you . . ."

The sound of Mallory's searching had stopped.

"All of my life," she said, "he's been there," and he almost said Who? because he knew it wasn't Mallory and he knew it wasn't Joseph and he didn't believe it was Gann. "All my life I could feel him back there, where I remember things that never happened, in this dream that seems to have replaced everything. He's been there all along. I don't know who he is. I can barely see him in my mind. I can barely hear his voice. Until now he was there to blame. He was there as the one who wouldn't let me go. But that's not it anymore. It isn't him that won't let me go, it's me. Once, when I had the chance, I chose something else—love or safety or the home that made me its slave, I don't know, but I chose to go back with him and be his slave and because I made that choice, because I loved him or because I was afraid to be without him, because I was afraid to be free, everything changed. Everything about my life changed. Everything about his life changed. Time and the country changed. Did I return with him just so I'd have one more chance to kill him? Did I return with him just so I'd have one more chance to be raped by him, or to be made love to by him, or to wonder which was which? Why am I like this, Etcher? Why isn't it enough to love you and be loved by you? I know I'm a fool to let you go. No one ever loved me like you. You saved my life. You pulled me from the fever. You adored me more than I deserved. Tell me I'm wrong. Tell me this is a mistake."

He said nothing. He had decided, he had had lots of time on the train to decide, that unless she knew for certain she wanted him with her, he had no arguments left for her. He wasn't going to talk her into anything. He tried to raise his hands to his eyes; he needed to take off his new glasses. They had filled with so many tears he couldn't see through them anymore.

But the chains that bound him to her bed caught his hands and pulled them back. He was left at the mercy of her hands. It was worse, somehow, to be at the mercy of her free hands. They now took the glasses from him, from the eyes of her own bound slave, and wiped the tears from his face for him, again and again.

Two weeks after he died, I had a dream.

I'd been expecting it. I hadn't really mourned my father; I'm not sure I have even now, years later. It may be that I mourned some passing of him before he died, or it may be that the loss still hasn't sunk in, or it may be that on some deeper level I already understood that everything is loss, that our lives are a race against the clock of loss, a race to lose the vessel of our lives before we lose everything that vessel contains. Surely when my mother goes, should she go before me, the aloneness that's almost become a psychological vanity for me, the aloneness I like to think I understand so damned well, will take on dimensions I never imagined; because then the loss of the only two things that all the moments of my life have had in common will leave me utterly alone either to know who I am—as I've always flattered myself I do—or to the desolation of a deluded life. In that case I'll be at the mercy of either God or his antithesis, not the Devil, since I don't believe in the Devil, but Chaos, against which the only weapon God has ever given us is memory.

In this dream about my father I was walking through the corridors of a rest home. It was a very pleasant rest home. The windows were open and the wind that came through was balmy and a pale lovely blue and beyond the windows I could see the trees swaying. As I walked the corridors I saw to the sides large rooms with rows of clean crisp beds, all of which were empty, until I came to the room where my father was. He was sitting up in one of the beds. He looked fine. There was color in his face and he appeared tranquil and happy, perhaps more than I'd ever seen him before. He greeted me. But I distinctly remembered, I completely understood that he was dead; in this dream my sense of time was grounded and I understood he'd died just two weeks before. "Oh," I said to him, "this is a dream."

This is not a dream, he answered.

For some time we discussed this, my father gently pressing the point that this was real. And nothing had ever seemed more real. I could feel the wind through the windows and see the trees swaying outside, and my father was as vivid as he'd ever been. On his lap he held a small plate. On the plate was a small pastry. He gave me the pastry and said, Here, taste this; and I did. He said, You can taste it, can't you? and I could. He said, You can taste it because it isn't a dream; and it was true that it didn't taste like any dream, it was true that I couldn't remember ever having been able to *taste* something in a dream before, taste being the one sense that's beyond my imagination. But I still wouldn't believe him. What my mind had come to believe in as the reality of his death was too strong for my heart, which was confronted with the reality of his talking to me now, and offering me a pastry.

And then I woke, at the beckoning of my mind, which feared that it would lose this argument with my heart. Except I didn't wake to reality but rather into *another* dream, which I later forgot as immediately as I forget all my dreams, moments beyond the thin silver horizon of waking, beyond the edge of the blade of consciousness. Another dream that wasn't in the least important except for the fact that it was there waiting beyond the archway of my last meeting with my father, a place for a coward to hurry when he wasn't brave enough for his visions.

Everyone I've ever told about this has said the same thing. Every one of them has said my father was right.

A f t e r   E t c h e r   r e t u r n e d   t o Aeonopolis, a calm settled over his daily life. But his nights were filled with dreams of his father and dreams of Kara and mostly dreams of Sally, and worse were the waking moments when he lay staring in the dark unable to believe he wasn't with her anymore. "I can't believe what happened to us," he said out loud in the dark. When his nights became nothing but the same dreams again and again, he went looking for another kind of night.

He found himself at the feet of a naked blonde.

In the rosy stupefaction of the wine he wasn't always aware she was there. Sometimes he looked right through her. Her yellow hair was tied back and she had long legs and wore only long black stockings and high heels, and she danced for him though he knew she danced for everyone. Somewhere in the onslaught of his dreams and the stupefaction of the wine he understood the true nature of his exchange with the naked blonde, and realized that in such an exchange it was not the woman who gave herself to the dance but the man, that it was only the man's folly and conceit that allowed him to believe it was a naked blonde giving herself to him, and everything about the exchange was contingent on that conceit. The dance wasn't about her obliteration but his. It was he who lost his persona in the dark of the club, it was she whose persona became all-pervasive in her body's celebration. And so there were moments he took comfort in this, losing himself in the same way a man loses himself in the climax of sex, and there were also moments he wasn't aware she was there at all, when he looked right through her, those moments when there was too much of him to lose no matter how much he might have wished to.

Those were the moments she noticed him. The moments when her spell over him was broken, and her power over him was gone; and she danced to those moments in the expectation of seizing them back from him, and in the hope she never would.

He dropped his glasses one night. The two of them crawled together on the floor of the Fleurs d'X, and when she found them and he put them on he couldn't help but see her then, her breasts close enough to touch and her mouth close enough to kiss. She laughed. "I'm sorry," he said.

"It's all right," she said.

"You're very beautiful," he explained in the dark. "I'm just like all the others."

"Yes," she answered, relieved. He could tell she was from the Ice. Not long after, it might have been the next night or the next—

in the onslaught of dreams and the stupefaction of wine and the time of the Arboretum it was difficult to know or wonder why it was important—when she came to talk to him at the edge of the Fleurs d'X he said, I'm from the Ice too. "You don't have an accent," she said.

"I lost it after I came to the city."

"I never leave the neighborhood," she said, by which she meant the Arboretum, "so I never lose anything." She added, "You don't look like you're from the Ice."

He could tell, even in the dark, that with each passing moment she doubted more and more he was really from the Ice. She believed it was just another fiction of the Fleurs d'X, where everyone had their fictions, the girls most of all. That was one of the attractions of Fleurs d'X, the invention and acceptance of fictions. So he just answered, "I know." After a moment he said, "My father is dead," and was appalled that he'd reduced his father's death to a seduction, only because he couldn't bring himself to so reduce what had happened with Sally.

"My father's dead too," said the woman in the dark, and more than just the cold of the Ice was in her voice.

"Who are you?"

"Call me the Woman in the Dark." Mona was the fiction she offered all the other men, the one that had been claimed by the black giant who lived in her flat on the other side of the neighborhood; and she looked around her as she said it because though the giant wasn't here she knew he was watching from her flat, peering at the living map he'd painted across the walls where she lived. If she'd thought there was any corner of the Arboretum that was hidden from sight in the walls of her flat, she might have taken Etcher by the hand and led him there. Or she might not. It might have been that any violation of her relationship with the men she danced for was too monumental, though of course it had already been violated by the man who lived in her flat. It never crossed her mind to fuck Etcher. She wasn't sure it crossed his either. But she supposed that finally she'd found a man to whom, in some dark cold corner of her life, she might say, "Keep me warm," and it would mean something entirely different from what it had always meant before. "Keep me warm," she might say to him, and not feel colder for it. The dead part of her heart in which her father lived might, should she say it to Etcher, surge with the blood of her life, and in the flush she would dance for only one man and obliterate herself at his hands.

Every night he went to see the Woman in the Dark. She did not tell him her name. He drank again now.

Three months after he'd returned to the city the messages came from the north.

The first came from Kara. It was filled with expectation and insinuating pathos. His responses conveyed as much compassion as their obligatory nature could allow. If he no longer loved Kara as he once had, he nonetheless felt bound to love her for what had happened between them; for the source of his defining anguish to dry completely now would be another betrayal by love too profound for him to live with. But even as his answers to Kara became more perfunctory and less urgent, he wasn't prepared for the simple one-line letter that arrived one afternoon: *I don't ever want to hear from you again.* For the first split second he thought it was a joke; but he knew it wasn't a joke. He thought, for another split second, of answering; but he didn't answer. And so silence followed until, some time later, another message arrived: *Your love was a lie.* Then another: *You led me on.* These memos continued until their terse brutality changed to palpable rage. Now he tried to soothe himself with indignation, that this woman who had rejected him so bluntly and then, after the passage of so many years, beckoned him so summarily could accuse him of leading her on. But it was a cheap indignation, won by logic but without force of argument on the terrain of aging and abandonment and self-remorse: it was easier for her now to believe their love was a lie than to accept the consequences of having once made the wrong choice.

In the midst of these messages came Sally's.

Now at the age of forty, his father and youth and love all passing at the same moment, he might have seemed comic in his new incarnation. This new role was to embody the recent bitter revelations of beautiful women who had come to assume by the nature of their beauty—even when, as in the case of Sally, they never quite believed in that beauty—that their lives were always to be filled with a hundred romantic choices, any of which could at some point be discarded or undone. Then the moment arrived for one woman after another, Kara and then Sally, when a choice could not be discarded or undone: and Etcher had been that choice for each of them. Because his love had seemed so enormous and his faith so pure they found his betrayal all the more incomprehensible. Now Sally was in trouble. Her life had become destitute and terrifying. She didn't call Etcher to help her but to love her again. She called on him to promise her hope. And now Etcher could neither promise nor hope. She wrote scornfully in her letters of how he didn't trust her anymore; he didn't deny it. She wrote scornfully of how she didn't trust love anymore; he couldn't refute it. It infuriated him that she somehow felt love had let her down, when he believed she had let love down. He turned his back on her. His father and youth and love all having simultaneously passed from him, he no longer believed happiness was something pursued timelessly but rather that it was stumbled upon in a moment, seized ruthlessly and sensually with the understanding that it too would pass as quickly as a father or youth or love. But as much as he tried, the one thing Etcher couldn't pretend was that he didn't love her anymore. He couldn't stop the dreams of her. He couldn't stop the voice in his head that spoke to her, or her voice in his head that spoke back.

Then the correspondence stopped and the dreams changed. In the new dreams Sally was sick again, something in her again fluttering for release. As two years before she was in bed dying, the black bloom of her turned livid by fever. At first he thought these dreams were just old memories until in one of them he stopped to look around and saw he wasn't in her old unit in her old circle but in the house far to the north in the Ice where he'd been chained to her bed while police rampaged across the rooftop. He told himself the dreams didn't mean anything. He told himself they were a conspiracy of heart and conscience to provoke him into some kind of flight to her, into rushing back to save her again when he couldn't save anyone anymore. Gann, after all, was there. It wasn't as though she were really alone.

But one night not long after this dream, Etcher saw Gann in a corridor of the Arboretum.

He glanced up from Mona's feet to catch sight of him just beyond the Fleurs d'X door, making his way to the stairwell that held the sound of the tide and led up to the surface; and at that moment he knew something was wrong. Sally was up there alone in the Ice after all, with no one but Polly. A cold dread passed through him. Suddenly oblivious of the Woman in the Dark, he rose to hurry after Gann, dropping his money on the stage and leaving the club behind. He had gotten down the corridor and was beginning to climb the stairs when he felt someone behind him.

The large hands on his back tore him from the stairs and hurled him against the wall. Etcher fumbled to try to catch his glasses as they flew off his face. In the force of his collision with the wall of the corridor, as he slipped bloodily to the floor, he was aware of nothing but that his glasses were somewhere in the hall where he couldn't see them; in the vertigo of his blind haze and the smell of blood around him he was reminded not of when he'd smashed his glasses before the priests but of how far from the grace of love's power he'd fallen. He called out to Gann in his mind, thinking, Something is wrong and I have to find Gann. But what he said out loud, what everything came down to, as it had all come down to since the first moment he saw her, was her name.

He was vaguely aware of someone at the end of the hall. He might have recognized her as the Woman in the Dark if in the light she hadn't been transparent. If he could have seen anything he might still not have recognized the big black man from the church lobby years before, since the big man was more naked than the woman. Etcher reached to his mouth to touch his blood. It glistened from the blur of his hands. He was still saying her name when the large man placed his glasses in his hands and ran down to the other end of the hall.

All the way back to his unit he held out his hands before him and said her name, as though the blood were the medium of their communication and he spoke to her now through his wet fingers. All through the night he lay on his bed with his hands open at his sides. He could tell his hands were still wet with blood in the wind that came through the crack beneath his door. Something's wrong, he told himself over and over; he did not sleep so as not to dream, because he couldn't bear to dream of Sally dying alone in the Ice. It was as well that he didn't catch up with Gann, he tried to tell himself: what would he have said to him anyway? "Gann, I've been having dreams." Now as he lay on his bed he shook himself awake each time he thought he might fall to sleep. He didn't change positions because he didn't want to wipe the blood from his hands onto the sheets beneath him. He had almost slipped to sleep when there was a knock on the door.

Gann, he thought. "Sally," he said.

"It's me," she answered behind the door.

He sat up. "Sally?" he said, astonished. The blood didn't matter anymore, it had conjured her, he thought, and it didn't matter if he got blood on the door when he went to open it.

"It's me," Mona repeated, in his doorway.

"It's you," he agreed, looking at her. She had a coat pulled around her, and appeared cold. He stepped aside and she stepped through the doorway into the dark of his unit. He closed the door and turned on a lamp. He motioned her toward the only chair as he sat on the bed. She sat on the chair for a moment, and when neither of them said anything she got up and came to the bed and sat on the edge of it next to him. In the light of the lamp she touched the battered side of his face, where he'd been thrown against the wall of the Arboretum.

"Are you all right?" she asked.

"Yes."

She took one of his hands. "You're still bleeding?"

"No," he shook his head, "I'm all right."

"I think I caused trouble for you."

"No."

"I think so," she nodded.

"Do you know him?"

"Yes."

"Does he hurt you?"

"Yes. No. I can't go back now, except to leave." They sat in silence, the light of the lamp growing a little dimmer. Glancing casually around the unit, she turned back to him to say, "Do you want to sleep?"

"I can't sleep," he answered, exhausted.

"If you try."

"I mean I can't let myself. I have dreams."

"Oh."

"Do you have dreams?"

"I dream of the room falling." She stood and took off her coat and he wasn't surprised that beneath the coat she wore only the black stockings of the Fleurs d'X. She sat casually naked on his bed. He worried that she was cold. "Should I go?" she said.

"Are you cold?"

"I'm cold," she admitted.

Instinctively he moved to put his arm around her.

"It's all right," she said, raising her hands.

He pulled back. "OK."

She hadn't meant he couldn't touch her. She hadn't really thought through, as she followed him from the Arboretum out of Desire into the city, whether or not she would let him touch her. She had only recoiled from the promised shelter of his arms, not from his bloody hands touching her. Just as instinctively as he'd moved to put his arms around her, she touched herself, since it was her job to touch herself—a vocational habit—since she'd long since come to define all of her relations with men by the way she touched herself in place of their own hands. I'll do the touching for you, was what she said to every man. And so when Etcher came to her not so much out of desire as to protect her from the cold, and when she rebuffed him, she tried to repair the reproach by touching herself for him. Her little gift to him.

There was no blood on her fingers. Her fingers were clean and dry of blood. They didn't mar the butter of her thighs or the precarious labyrinth of her labia to which she attended every moment, pampering its petals and soothing its inflammations after Wade's violations. Watching, Etcher sank into the swirl of her. On the bed next to her he reached out to touch the place where her body opened, that he might raise his fingers to his mouth and taste something other than blood, since taste was the one sense he never dreamed, since taste was the sense that told him it was not a dream. He was inches from her when she knew she had to decide now to let him touch her or not: she never said no, but her abrupt gasp at the moment of truth made him draw back again. He felt a bit humiliated, in his position. In her position, he knew instantly, a man would feel humiliated as well, except that it was the fundamental difference between a man and woman, the difference in their brands of humiliation. "I was made," she explained, "to be seen and not touched."

He nodded. It was the fundamental difference between a man and woman that she would not, in such a position, feel she'd let him down. But she did offer a consolation.

"I can take you from the city," she said.

S h e   a d d e d ,   a s   a n afterthought, since she didn't believe it would matter to him, "It's dangerous," though she might have meant the two of them sitting there together, in the silence and the dark.

"How?" he finally asked, startled.

"Things can happen."

"I don't mean how is it dangerous. I mean how would you get me out of the city."

"Through the Arboretum."

"There's a way out of the city through the Arboretum?"

Her voice dropped. "I can take you and show you," she said. "You have to be sure. No one changes his mind at the last minute. They'll kill you before they let you change your mind."

"The police are watching me," he advised her. "They know you're here right now."

She got up and put on her coat. Looking around, she said, "It has to be tonight. Do you understand?"

"I'm not sure."

"It has to be tonight, if you want me to take you from the city. It has to be now. You'll need money and you can't bring anything with you. Do you have money?"

"Some," he answered, wary.

She knew he didn't trust her. "Well, it's up to you," she said. Her accent was most pronounced when she was speaking colloquially. She leaned over and turned out the lamp, and when she'd turned out the lamp she leaned over and kissed him, in case she never saw him again, or in case he was the sort of fool who trusted a kiss. "I'll be at the Arboretum in an hour. . . ."

"Where will I find you—?"

"I'll find you, if you decide to come. One hour. I won't be there after that. He's looking for me." She opened the front door sound-lessly and sailed out against the rapids of the night. She didn't close the door the whole way and he sat on the edge of the bed looking out the crack of the door until he got up to push it almost shut. With the flash of her blond hair the police would certainly see her leave. In the dark Etcher changed his clothes as quietly as possible and got together all the money that he still had after what he'd sent north to Sally. Then he sat for ten more minutes and waited. He waited for that moment when the police would begin to relax, having seen the blonde leave and decided Etcher had gone to sleep. There would be no fooling them for long but he needed that extra minute or two; once he got as far as the outlaw zone they would fall back a little. He couldn't appear to be up to anything but another trip back to Fleurs d'X. It was going to make the police nervous no matter how you cut it, two trips to the Arboretum in one night; it was going to look unusual. Etcher hoped it wasn't that maniac Mallory who was out there.

It figured that if there was a way out of the city it was the Arbor-etum, though Etcher couldn't imagine what it was short of a hot-air balloon from the top-level tenements or an underground tunnel through fifty miles of cold lava. But he couldn't wait anymore. He couldn't stand this feeling he had, he couldn't stand any more dreams. Whether the Woman in the Dark was telling the truth or lying, whether she was correct or mistaken in what she thought she knew, if there was any getting out of Aeonopolis it figured to be through the Arboretum; and he couldn't wait anymore and that was that, and he got up from the bed and pulled open the door he hadn't quite shut, and stepped out into the circle. He didn't run but walked, not across the white of the circle but around the black edge, and then he slipped out of the circle between two darkened units. He didn't look back to see the police following him. He didn't think about never coming back again.

He walked through the streets of his zone, crossed another zone and came to Desire. He didn't think he was going to make the Arboretum in an hour as she'd said, but then he hoped she'd be late too, miscalculating her own time and distance. When the sil-houette of the Arboretum appeared he kept his eyes peeled for her blond hair; he knew she wasn't going to wait for him and he knew he couldn't afford to wait for her. He was sure the cops were somewhere behind him thinking it odd that he was returning to the Arboretum tonight. He assumed cops had an instinct for these things. There was nothing to stop them from going into the Arboretum if they thought they had a reason, ambiguous as their jurisdiction might be. As he neared the neighborhood there was no sight of her. He paused for a moment outside but knew it was a mistake to stop; it would only make everything appear all the more suspicious. He went inside.

He was halfway down the first corridor when he felt someone in front of him. He felt her fingers run up his face and stop at his glasses. "It's me," he confirmed.

She took his hand. "Come on," he heard her say, and she pulled him down the corridor and around its U-turn, continuing to the interchange chamber where they crossed to the door on the far side and its spiral stairs. Far away below him on the stairs he could hear, as one always heard in the stairwell, the faint sound of waves crashing. Mona went first before him and he followed.

They descended past the three doors to the fourth that led to Fleurs d'X, and then they passed that one. They climbed further and further down, passing another door and then another and then another, the light in each more ominous. Etcher had never gone this far down in the Arboretum. He could see what appeared to be the final door beneath him, the eighth by his count. She stopped before reaching it. "You brought the money?" he heard her ask.

"Yes," he answered tersely.

"This is your last chance to change your mind," she said. "It's dangerous from here on."

"Let's get to the door," he said.

"We're not going to the door," she said in the dark. There was a pause. He felt her reach up and touch his leg. "On the other side of you," she said, "there's an opening."

"The other side?" She meant the other side of the stairwell. It was pitch black. "Let's go a little further down," he said, "into the light of the door."

"That's not where it is," she explained in the dark, "it's where you are, on the other side. Where there is no light. That's why it's there, because there's no light."

He listened and realized that the sound of water crashing in waves was indeed coming not from below him but to his side, in the black of the other wall of the stairwell. He reached out but touched nothing; the wall, and the opening she said was there, was beyond his reach. "I can't reach it," he said.

"No," she said, "you can't reach it."

"How do I reach it?"

"You jump."

"I don't even know there's an opening there," Etcher said, "except that you tell me there is and I think maybe I hear something."

"Do you hear the sea?"

"Yes."

"Next to you, where you are now?"

"Yes."

"Then it's there," she said. "Jump."

He looked at the door down below him. "Is that the bottom of the stairs?"

"No," she said.

"It looks like the last door."

"It may be the last door or . . . it may not. I'm not sure. But it's not the bottom."

"How far is the bottom?"

"I don't know."

He breathed deeply. He kept studying the darkness to the side of him where the sound of the waves was coming, as though he might distinguish some profound pitch of black that constituted an opening. "How big is the opening?"

"I don't know."

He was annoyed. He was supposed to jump over a chasm of undetermined depth to an opening of unknown size, which he could neither reach nor see. He kept staring into the side of the stairwell and he knew no matter how long he looked or waited it all came down to jumping. He took off his glasses, folding them and putting them in his pocket. He raised his leg over the rail of the stairs and climbed out onto the outer edge of the steps, suspended over the dark of the stairwell below him. When he started thinking too much about everything, he jumped.

It was at least half a minute before she said, "Did you make it?"

One foot had slipped, and he'd wildly grasped the first thing he could put his arms around. He found himself sitting for that half a minute listening to his heart pound while she in turn had listened for his fading scream downward or a distant telltale splat or what-ever sound the plunge to oblivion makes, finally deciding that either he had made it or been very polite about the plummet.

"Can you reach me?" he heard her ask from the stairs. She didn't sound far away.

"What do you mean, reach you?" he said.

"Can you take my hand and pull me?"

He laughed.

"What's funny?" she asked in the dark.

"Nothing."

"I told you," she said, "I can't stay here anymore. He's looking for me." He was laughing because one thing was for sure and it was that this woman looked out for herself. Maybe she liked him or maybe she didn't but in either case she hadn't allowed senti-ment to get in the way of his making that jump first, and now that he'd risked his neck once by getting himself across the dark pit of the stairwell, it was his function in the scheme of things to risk it again getting her across. He still couldn't see anything. On his knees he felt the rock's edge at his feet. He leaned out into the dark until he felt her hand, and then pulled her. "You've got the money?" was the first thing she said to him on the other side.

"You're welcome," he answered. Unfazed she led him out through the back of the opening to a tunnel that continued further down into the earth. They went for some way. The sound of the waves grew louder and the air in the tunnel colder. The two of them had gone ten minutes when the path turned to reveal a dark grotto, lit by torches jammed into the rocks. The ocean rushed in and out of the grotto through an opening in the distance that was located at the base of the cliffs far below the city. Inside the grotto was a small dock with several very small boats that wouldn't hold more than two or three people, and standing around the boats were five men talking and smoking and drinking. A couple of them were playing cards. They looked up to see Mona and Etcher climb down the last stretch of the trail.

No one sailed in, everyone sailed out. This wasn't a harbor for sailors on leave but a one-way station for fugitives unlikely ever to come back, and once you got this far the men running the opera-tion weren't about to let you turn around and go upstairs, where you could tell the cops about it. Now they gathered around Etcher and Mona and one of them took his cigarette from his mouth and dropped it on the dock and held out his open hand without saying a word. Etcher gave him the money. The man looked at it and shook his head. He waited.

"That's all I've got," Etcher said.

"It's only enough for one," the man said. Etcher looked at the man and Mona looked at Etcher. Frightened, she struggled with frustration to free her earrings from her lobes, turning them over to the man, who said, "These aren't worth much." Mona took from her coat pocket something wrapped in a scarf and handed that over as well. The man unwrapped it and held it up. "It's a fucking rock," he said.

"It's a forbidden artifact," she said. "Look, there's writing on it." She pointed to the rough side of the rock. "On the other side."

"Give me your coat," he said. "Yours too," he said to Etcher.

"We'll freeze out there without our coats," Etcher said.

"Well, you're not going out there with them," the man answered. One of the other men laughed.

"We'll give you one of the coats," said Etcher.

"You'll give us what we fucking ask for."

"No."

The man sighed. "Didn't anyone explain this to you? Now that you're here you're going out on that tide one way or the other. Either you go out in a boat or you go out without one. You're not going with your coat the first way and you won't need your coat the second way. Doesn't the logic of that impress you?"

"The politics of stalemate impress me," said Etcher. "I'm completely versed in them. You can't let us turn around and go back and if you don't sell us the boat you have to kill us and it's bad business because if I wash up on the shore somewhere it's just going to be a lot of trouble. Really a lot of trouble. I work for the Church and have something they want and they're breathing down my neck and the cops watch every move I make, even now they know I'm somewhere in the Arboretum. Why do you think I'm here? Why do you think I need to get out of this damned city so badly? Why do you think this is my last resort? I'm giving you everything I've got and she's giving you everything she's got and we'll give you one of the coats but not both." He added, "You can have the rock too," nodding at the stone Mona had given the man.

"I don't want the damn rock," the man said. "I'll take yours," he said to Mona, nodding at her coat, and wrapped the stone back in the scarf. He handed it to Etcher, who put it in the pocket of his own coat, which he now took off and wrapped around Mona. The man led them to a boat. It had oars and in the bottom was water and what looked like the tatters of a sail, though there was no other sign of a sail or mast. Around the hull it appeared as though the wood was rotting. "Bon voyage," the man said. Etcher got in the boat and helped Mona in, then he took the oars and pushed the boat off from the dock. Even wearing his coat Mona sat shivering at the stern. Struggling with the oars, Etcher began to row. The men on the dock returned to their drinking and cards, never glancing up to watch the boat's progress.

It was an hour before the boat even got out of the grotto. Only then did Etcher understand the peril of the situation. A low ceiling of Vog billowing into the grotto continued to hang several feet above their heads, so it wasn't until the walls suddenly fell away that Etcher realized they were out on the open sea, where the night came rushing in and the force of the swells threatened to smash the boat back against the rocks. Etcher fought futilely against the waves. They lifted the boat in the air and dashed it back down on the water. Several feet from Etcher at the stern of the boat, behind the gusts of the sea that rained between them, Mona's cries sounded very distant to him, like a shout from the top of the cliffs that towered somewhere above the Vog.

All night the boat was pulled by the waves and then hurled back toward the cliffs. By the early hours of morning the boat had finally made its way out to sea, beyond Central's searchlights; but the shadows of the obelisks of Aeonopolis were still in plain sight and Etcher was alarmed that with dawn the boat would be visible to patrols along the coast. Soaked and overwhelmed by exhaustion and cold, Etcher rowed, racing insanely against the sea and the light of day. Their greatest ally now, he told himself, was the volcano, which delayed the full morning light until nearly noon. He hurried, to whatever extent possible, from one patch of Vog to the other, hoping they might find one to ride up the coast like the lost Vog Travelers of the Arboretum. He kept telling himself that if they could get far enough from the city, around some bend of the coastline above them, then they could rest, sleeping at the bottom of the boat in the sun.

But at the other end of the boat, with his coat wrapped around her in the dark before daylight, the Woman in the Dark said, "I'm cold."

"I know," Etcher said. "In a few hours the sun will be out. When we're far enough from the city, when we don't have to worry about drifting back, we'll sleep in the sun."

"I'm very cold," she said, as though she hadn't heard a word he'd said.

"Think about the sun."

"Even the Ice wasn't this cold."

"Think about a place to sleep."

"Maybe we should go back," she said.

"What?" Etcher was incredulous.

"It's too far."

"We're not going back. There's nothing to go back to. You said yourself there's no going back. You said yourself there's no changing your mind. Think about the sun. Think about a place to sleep. We've come this far, think of how far we've come. It's just a little further." The sea, which had been sporadically calmer, was now becoming rough again. The boat was rocked by a wave and Etcher hung on, but in the dark on the other end of the boat Mona was not hanging on; she was holding herself in the cold, huddling in his coat.

"Keep me warm," she said.

"I will," he answered. "I promise."

"Keep me warm now." She stood in the boat to come to him.

"Sit down," he said quickly.

"Please," she pleaded, still half standing, and she stepped into the middle of the boat. She was in the middle of the boat, coming to Etcher to beg him for the warmth she never asked of anyone, when the next wave slammed the boat and she vanished. In the blinking of an eye Etcher was by himself. There had been no cry, no last glimpse of her going overboard, no hand reaching out for rescue from inside a fatal wave, nothing left but his coat which she'd worn to keep her warm; he'd lurched to grab her when she was standing in the middle of the boat and had only gotten the coat. If she'd been wearing the coat rather than just wrapping it around her, it would have saved her. Now she was gone as though she'd never been there at all, Etcher sitting alone in the night out on the sea with his coat in his hand, looking around frantically for some trace of her in the water. He began to call out to her only to realize he didn't know her name, that the fiction they had invented in the Fleurs d'X was that she had no name. So he couldn't even call to her. He couldn't see or find her. For the rest of the night he didn't row anymore, even after he knew she wasn't coming back, because he couldn't bring himself to abandon her.

As she sank beneath the waves, with far less panic than she would have supposed, Mona thought of Wade running through the Arboretum at this very moment looking for her. Little did he know, little could he imagine as he rushed from chamber to chamber and corridor to corridor searching for her, that she was no longer in the Arboretum at all, no longer in the city, but far away in the ocean's undertow; she wondered how long it would be before he got that feeling one inevitably gets that someone is gone from his life forever. Perhaps, was her last thought, if he'd painted the walls of the flat not with the secrets of the Arboretum but rather in the color and currents of the sea, she would not have left him after all, the aquadoom of her destiny having come to her instead. With the burst of her lungs she announced this doom to the water's surface, a black bubble her only memorial in a night too dark and a sea too deranged for anyone to honor it.

Not long ago I said to a friend, "But of course, nothing's irrevocable." And she was surprised. "Then you've changed your mind," she said, "because up until now everything you've written has been that some things *are* irrevocable." For a moment I felt dishonest or exposed. I was certainly confused, because I hadn't been aware that my view of things had changed so profoundly. I had to give some thought to the possibility that, if I had in fact made this profound change, it was to survive, a necessity I nonetheless couldn't respect because I don't believe the truth of the world changes in order to accommodate anyone's survival. If it's the nature of some things to be irrevocable they remain so however urgently I may need to feel differently. At any rate, I knew it was a process of age. I knew I was now nearer the end of my life than the beginning, and the facts and incidents of that life take on more significance simply because there will be fewer of them, and so I had to believe that they were in fact less fraught with consequence so that I could go on. So that, in the darkness left by passion's supernova, I wouldn't hurtle back into the dead calm that had preceded it. I would defy my own passivity by making the world around me a more passive place, where everything's ultimately inconsequential and nothing's irrevocable, where everything can be returned to the way it was before and every choice includes the option of reversing it when it turns out to be a mistake. Where risk isn't always a matter of life and death. Where at the end of the two years during which you turned your life upside down, rearranging it from top to bottom, you can wind up back where you started, only a bit older and a bit more broken, closer to the end of everything than to the beginning.

And the truth is that I was right all along. Even as the fact of it becomes more overwhelming, more unbearable, some things are irrevocable, if not circumstantially then in the heart and memory, the heart and memory being the only two things that can puncture the flow of time through which hisses the history of the future. Two years ago when I stood with her on the cliffs overlooking the sea beyond that point where the fence ended, we said nothing, we touched nothing, we saw nothing, we were nothing but the two of us together; and afterward nothing, including all the things that had not been said and not been touched and not been seen, would ever be the same for either of us even now when I'm alone once more, as before, and she's gone. In the bid and hunger for freedom in which she'd lived her whole life, she couldn't help but be cavalier about love; love would not undo that bid or satisfy that hunger. Everything that's truly irrevocable finally has to do with love or freedom, but whether you act in the name of the first or the second, one of them ultimately bows to the other and that's the most irrevocable thing of all.

Standing with her two years ago on those cliffs overlooking the sea, even I knew that.

Etcher's treacherous boat found its forsaken shore thirty miles up the coast, on the second day after he'd left the city; and though he'd had his hours in the sun, nothing could warm him. The cold of the sea had sunk so deep into his bones that by the time he made his way to the first little village inland, taking a job stocking the meat locker for a local storekeeper, he was like an animal hurrying to the chill of its natural habitat. In the locker his heavy glasses fogged over and froze to his face. Sometimes he thought about Mona and sometimes he thought about Sally; sometimes in his thoughts the two of them blurred together into a flaxen black succubus so sexually lush it repelled him to think of her. So he didn't think. He worked in the meat locker for four days, drawing wages and hitching a ride out of town up the main highway, by-passing the first station and the second until he reached the third, where he gambled that it would be safe to take a train.

He was always on the lookout for cops. From station to station over the next six days he would constantly change trains, change cars, change seats to the dismay of the conductors. He reached his home village and stayed with his mother one night and then moved on the next day; but he wasn't racing against time. He was traveling on time's train and time's car in time's seat, shifting from one to the other when seat after seat and car after car and train after train eventually fell behind. He had finally given his compulsions over to his fatalism in the same way the sea left him no choice about Mona. On the trains he huddled in the cold that hadn't left him since the grotto.

He finally came to the last little town. He paid a guy in a truck the last of his meat-locker wages to give him a lift the twenty miles to Sally's house. They got there after sundown. The house was dark on the fjord in the distance. The driver said, "You sure someone lives there, pal?" and Etcher lied. He barely heard the truck driving off as he walked up the path, and by the time he got to the house there wasn't any sound at all.

Until, somewhere, he heard Polly crying.

The ice had frozen the front door around the edges and he had to force it open. The house was dark inside except for the faint glimmer of coals in the cast-iron stove, where a feeble fire had been built hours or perhaps even days before. Its warmth had long since fled the house. The frigid blast in Etcher's face was the first

cold to impress him since his thirty-six hours in the boat; he shuddered not at the cold itself but at recognition that he hadn't yet
met the limits of cold, that something in the world was colder than
he was, and that it was this house where he'd once dreamed of
living with the woman whom he would have once died loving.
Stumbling over a squat wooden stool and kicking a toy duck at his
feet, Etcher stood in the dark and listened. For several moments it
was quiet and then once more he heard the crying.

He made his way through the front room. He stopped at the foot
of the stairs before crossing the kitchen toward the back hallway
and listened, peering up the stairs into the blackness to see if
anyone was there. He passed one room after another. All of them
were so dark that Etcher couldn't see the small white clouds of his
breath he knew were right in front of his eyes. In the back hallway
he saw a faint glow shining from Sally's bedroom. Then he could
clearly hear Polly, and a woman's whispers.

A small lamp burned on a table. Next to the table the mother
and her child were in bed. Clothes long since worn and toys long
since forsaken were strewn throughout the room, where the walls
and ceiling were bare of pictures and a curtain was pulled across
the window in a last-ditch effort to keep out the cold. Draped over
Sally's bedroom was a massive silver web. From one corner to the
other a swarm of iceflies had spun a cocoon that glittered like a
giant jewel. The lamp inside gave the jewel its light, fire flashing
off the dense crisscross of ice; and behind the gauzy paleblue mem-
brane of the cell the ephemeral forms of Sally and Polly, moving
with a languid vagueness, resembled the metamorphosis of a black
larva. For a moment Etcher couldn't say or do anything. With the
sweep of one arm and what he thought was a cry, he tore the web
away; but afterward he wasn't sure he'd cried at all. He heard no
echo, and at first neither Sally nor Polly even looked up at him,
barely aware in the stupor of their cold and hunger that anyone
was there.

He called her name. She barely turned her head. She looked so
ravaged and wasted, her face and hair so white like the sheets of
her bed and the crystalline bedlam of ice surrounding her, it was
as if most of her had vanished altogether, nothing but a pair of
deathly distant eyes lying on the pillow and the broken black slash
of her mouth. Huddled against her was the small helpless body of

her daughter, desperately trying to warm herself against her mother's fever. Speechless and petrified, Etcher stirred himself from the grip of his shock to rush to them and throw his arms around them; but he'd forgotten how cold he was, and Polly screamed at the touch of him, and her scream in turn jolted Sally to a grunt so meaningless and unearthly that Polly cried more. Sally instinctively clutched at Etcher not because she was aware he'd come back to her but for his coldness, since she was on fire, and the same cold that the daughter recoiled from the mother pulled closer to her so that she might press her whole raging body against his. Thus Etcher was as consumed by Sally as he was rejected by Polly, who tried to beat him away from her even as Sally wouldn't let him go, the three of them locked in an absurd embrace of ice and fire.

And then he saw that what possessed Sally now wouldn't be delivered so easily as a white baby gull. The thing inside her, part aerial and part amphibian, was in no hurry to hatch from her and expose itself to the cold outside. So it devoured Sally organ by organ and bone by bone, drinking her fecund blackness and then slumbering in the waste of it, fouling its own nest with relish. It had found an ideal host in Sally's purity, which was as marked by chaos and desire as it was devoid of guile or malice, the pure folly of a will for transcendence that at the same moment never understood the nature of what was to be transcended: once she might have cut the thing out of her. Once she might have taken her knife and lopped it off at the root, when it attached itself to her thighs and shot its seed into her womb. But cutting it off would have taken the sort of malice and ruthlessness that Sally's sort of purity didn't allow for; the purity which attracted her destruction was also the purity that left her no defense. From the beginning Sally Hemings had been laced with her own doom. In the web of the iceflies her transcendence had begun. In the dark delirium of her black fire she'd already started the journey. What Etcher saw as degeneration was the first leap upward; as she seemed to him to be plummeting downward, she in turn watched him fade and disappear from whatever her existence was in the process of becoming, as that existence finally surrendered her beauty. For all of her life her beauty had taken away with one hand the freedom it offered with another; for all her life it had unlocked with one hand the chains the other had bound to her; and she didn't want to be beautiful

anymore. She had never believed in it anyway. She believed every
man who had called her beautiful was a liar or a fool, either not to
be taken seriously or to be taken seriously only for how he meant
to possess her. She didn't want her body anymore, she didn't want
her face; she would happily leave her witchy incandescent eyes on
the pillow, her watery dreamwracked mouth in his hand, where
he could hold it like a coin or a plum or a small animal and believe
its kiss was a gift of the soul rather than a twitch of the nervous
system. She would leave behind the bits of her beauty like souve-
nirs, and she'd leave the shell of herself to the thing inside her that
could devour what she was but not who she was, while she went
to a place where the static of love meeting freedom was not to be
confused with history.

He couldn't move her. There was no way he could get her and
Polly through the ice the twenty miles to town, and he had no idea
whether having made the effort he would find anyone in town who
could help them anyway. Nor would he leave her in order to go
find someone who might help: it had taken so much and so long to
get here that he had no money left and couldn't be sure there
would be a way back. As he walked from room to room with the
small table lamp in his hand, he saw that the blast of cold that met
him when he came into the house was more than just the air. The
iceflies were everywhere. The house was a catacomb of webs spun
from doorway to rafter, from crossbeam to window frame, the
corners filled with thousands of cocoons hatching thousands of flies
until they dangled from his elbow and buzzed around his glasses
and his black hair was alive with them. He foraged the house for
kindling to stuff in the iron stove, but after he had chopped up the
furniture with an axe there was nothing left to burn except food
and toys and the house itself. Etcher and Sally and Polly ate the
remaining bread, cans of fish and fruit. When he gathered into his
arms Polly's wooden animals and flutes and trains and the pictures
she'd drawn of birds and kitties and butterflies, to feed to the stove
in a cremation of innocence, he turned to see the little girl in the
doorway of the room as though some child's instinct had alerted
her, bringing her from her mother's bed: "Do you want to play
with my toys?" she asked in a tiny pitiful voice. He was awash with
shame. He looked at the toys in his arms and dropped them to the
floor, and she ran quickly to retrieve her favorite horse, as though

she understood he hadn't really meant to play with them at all and
now she'd rescue at least one when she had the chance.

He took the axe from behind the stove and went into an empty
storeroom on the side of the house, closing the door behind him.
He began to chop. Over the next few hours he chopped up the
room and when he was finished he began on another, carving away
at the house from the most extraneous rooms toward the center.
Day after day he proceeded with increasing ferocity to demolish
the house. With each breach of the house's shelter, with each
assault through another wall, he felt the sick exhilaration of another hope collapsing before the hopelessness of the night that
flooded in through the house's gashes. With his axe he stalked his
own life as Sally did with her knife. He cast on the fire of the stove
the splinters of the house until gradually one room after another
disappeared; he was sure he heard the scream of smoldering iceflies rise through the chimney above the rooftop. Polly was so cold
he would have set the whole house on fire if it was the only way to
keep her warm.

But Sally wasn't cold at all. Sally was hot. At any moment Etcher
thought she'd go up in the dark cloud of her own immolation.
There was no barring her door this time against cops and priests,
God and Death; Etcher was hacking up the doors for the purpose
of the fire. Now Sally lay naked in the webs that were being woven
around her as fast as Etcher could rip them away. Steam rose from
beneath the place where she lay like the Vog that once poured out
from the place where she stood with Etcher on the cliffs of Aeonopolis. When her cries from the heat were more than he could
bear he tore away the room around her, to let in the cold of the
night for which she pleaded from whatever station of the journey
she'd come to. Finally, when the outer wall of the bedroom was
gone, to her momentary relief, he lifted her naked body and carried her through the rubble of the slashed jagged walls out onto
the ice itself, pulling behind him into a pyre bits and pieces of the
house and torching it. The silence of the night, the void of life, was
ghastly. In the light and heat of the huge fire Polly played with her
animals on what was left of the house floor. Sally lay nude on the
fjord with her eyes full of the night and the half-moon above her
and a white mountain in the distance gliding slowly through the
dark like a ship. When Etcher knelt beside her, when he ran his

cold fingers over her body to soothe her shuddering, when he held her breasts in his hands to calm the beating of her heart, he still couldn't be sure she knew he was there.

In his hands like that, you might have been a prayer. In his hands like that, you might have been something he thought he could mid-wife into a new incarnation, strong enough to withstand his love if not your own, wrenching from you the choice that had been killing you since you chose that afternoon in Paris between love and free-dom. After that you always insisted it could never again be one or the other. After that it had to be both or neither; you meant to find on your journey the intersection of the two and convince yourself that they could be the same road with two names. You insisted on seeing the wholeness of everything in life but yourself, which lay in bits and pieces around you like the doors and rafters of a broken house: you thought the men only worshiped the bits and pieces of you. You thought their worship had nothing to do with the whole of you. Looking out at it from the inside, you thought your beauty was a thing apart from you. You never understood how the thing they loved most wasn't your face but your voice, how the thing they loved most was that fountain that trickled up from your heart to your mouth and showed everyone who you were, your heart's bro-ken, wounded aspirations to be better than you were or could be or better than anyone could be. That was what he loved about you. But he never believed freedom and love were the same road with two names. He always believed they were two separate roads and that it was always a matter of moving back and forth between them. On his mouth like that your name might have been an incan-tation; and far away where you are now, beneath the night sky and the halfmoon, you hear him say it one more time.

Beneath the light of the halfmoon, she says to herself, The revo-lution has come.

She turns to him on her bed. She isn't going to bury her face in her pillow this time and pretend to be asleep. She isn't a fourteen-year-old girl anymore who thinks that if she lies still enough he'll go away. This time he isn't going to rape her, spraying her blood across the room, and then absolve himself with cool rags between her legs and tears on her thighs. This time she isn't going to scream out in the hope that the night will somehow rescue her; she isn't surprised that the night answers with an unnatural silence. She isn't surprised by betrayal at all, she expects it; she won't fall this time into the light of the crescent moon above her. She's already well on the way somewhere else. When he comes to take her, without hesitation she greets him with a fierce merciless urgency. With no delusions that she might resist him, she turns instead to devour him back.

In the light of the fire he sees behind her eyes something moving, something that isn't Sally at all, the sudden swish of its tail, the slithering flick of evidence inside her of the thing to which she's abandoned everything of herself but desire. Desire bleeds at her mouth. It ripples to her fingers. She parts her lips to inhale him and take him in her hand. Though he tries to pull away it's a lie when he tells himself he wants to resist her: he doesn't want to resist her. Though he tries to pull away it's a lie when he tells himself she can survive his fucking her: she cannot survive it. She sweeps away resistance as he swept away the web of the iceflies around her bed. She takes him in her hand and drives him up inside her and he hears the response inside, the scamper of something into the swampland; his cock feels the ripple of the marshes. He fucks the thing in her so as to find what's left of Sally at the end of the thing: it's a lie when he tells himself he wants to free her. It's such a huge lie that in his mind it never finishes his own sentence. He's oblivious of the night and he's oblivious of the fjord and he's oblivious of the fire in the distance and, somewhere on the other side of the fire, of the child. And it's only when he thinks of the child that, in horror, he tells himself he has to stop. He can't lie to himself about the child. And when he tells himself he has to stop, it's only then he realizes he's been oblivious of how cold Sally has suddenly become in his arms, beneath his body, holding him in the grip of memory. Desire isn't the only thing left of her after all. The memory is left, a small trace of it in the embers of her slavery that his seed hunts down, the memory of how he loves her and how she loves him and how it's bigger than anything they have ever known or perhaps anyone has ever known, and how it isn't big enough. She whispers in his ear.

"Take care of Polly," she said. And I knew she was gone.

In the light of the fire a shadow scampered across her face, like a serpent taking flight. But it wasn't a serpent. Etcher turned to see

Polly by the edge of the fire. As she'd done on the edge of the city's white circle, announcing with a tiny finger something no one could see in a crowd of birds, she raised her arm and pointed now at the fatal flame of her departed mother.

The wind blew the chains that hung from the northern wall of the Paris courtyard. The wall was over three hundred years old, as were the chains, because they had been laid into the stone when the wall was built, eight sets of shackles that once held the prisoners of dukes and kings and then, after the Revolution, the enemies of the Republic condemned from the highest summit of Robespierre's Mountain. The shackles dangled listlessly, the rain of centuries having long since washed them of their blood. Now sometimes teenage lovers broke into the courtyard in the middle of the night to play with the shackles and Seuroq would hurry out of the house to chase them away. More exasperating than the mirth of the kids running off was that of Seuroq's wife, who found amusing the doctor's indignation at the harmless bondage games—since the shackles could not be locked—being played in his courtyard. Teasing, she would slip into the chains herself, give them a good rattle. "My God, Helen," Seuroq said with shock, and Helen laughed.

"You always were so proper," she said.

"Not that proper, was I?" He softened, momentarily worried that, knowing he was not a demonstrably passionate man, he had in the course of the many years they'd been married denied his wife something. "I wasn't so proper," he asked quietly, "when it mattered not to be proper, was I?" and she took her wrists from the shackles of the courtyard wall and slipped them around his neck, with that smile that was always young.

No one had broken into the courtyard since Helen's death.

Now, with the courtyard's silence interrupted only by the city's distant festivities and its shadows broken only by the twilight through the sieve of the trees, the assistant stood watching the old man through the library window. He's mourning again, Luc thought to himself, though that didn't seem precisely right, since it implied there had been a time in the past eight months when the old man had not mourned. It wasn't that the expression on Seuroq's face was mournful but rather the opposite: his had always been a mournful face, even when he was lighthearted; no one was funnier than Seuroq when he laughed, because his face was perpetually cast in mourning and the contradiction of laughter was comic. Then Helen died and the mourning went right out of his face, the face went blank of its natural pathos; in the light of the lamp on the desk in the library, that was the look on Seuroq's face now, lost somewhere in the thirty-one years of marriage and searching for a ghost. "Dr. Seuroq?" Luc finally called through the window, but as he both expected and feared, the old man didn't answer, staring right through the window and right through his assistant, which left Luc with the choice of either an even more unseemly intrusion, rapping on the window, or leaving without a goodbye. He had more heart for the goodbyeless departure than the intrusion.

In the eight months since her death the world had learned not to intrude, leaving him in his chair in the library and waiting for him to wake from grief, reconciled to the possibility he would never wake. The university had tried gently to nudge the disconsolate widower back into the realm of the living and the learned, coddling him with propositions of study or teaching that he'd find intriguing but not demanding, understanding that the heart's grief makes a person into a child who must grow old again, or takes him to the edge of life's end from which he must again grow young. No one had a formula for grief. For a marriage of thirty-one years, was eight months too much, too little, or about right? That was one month for every four years, more or less. It wasn't the first night Luc had found Seuroq sitting in the library chair staring into the courtyard, with neither a rap on his window nor the call of his name to arrest him from what Luc was young enough to suppose was a particular recollection rather than simply the gruel of light that wore her face.

On this particular night, however, when Luc was watching Seuroq through the library window, something more extraordinary was happening than just remembering. Seuroq had indeed been thinking of Helen: but at the very moment Luc was in the courtyard trying to get the doctor's attention, a number of split sensations were tumbling one on top of the other in a single second, initiated by the wind's rustling the chains on the old courtyard wall and then the instant memory of a night in a very old hotel on the right bank of the city years before, when Helen found the card. Once, when Helen was still married to her first husband, she and Seuroq had a rendezvous in this old hotel; six years later, Helen having long since left her first husband and married Seuroq, the two of them went back as an anniversary of sorts. It was May of 1968. The next morning the tanks rolled down the rue d'X beneath their balcony on the way to the turmoil of the left bank, and the momentum of colossal historic events would steamroll whatever small personal memories of hotel rooms preceded them. Nonetheless, now eight months after Helen's death, the wind rattled the chains and Seuroq thought of that night in the hotel room, when Helen lost an earring and they pulled the bed away from the corner and found the card in a crack where the walls of the room separated. On it was the picture of a dark woman, sitting on a throne holding a rod. A cat lay at her feet and the landscape around her was strewn with rubble; a white moon rose in a blue sky. "The Queen of Wands," Helen announced, "is the card of passion."

"You're making that up," Seuroq had retorted.

What provoked him to think of this? he wondered now in the library. If he had ever had the temperament for rage he might have now raged that everything, even the most absurd thing like the sound of chains in the wind, reminded him of Helen. I am haunted by associations that aren't even my own, Seuroq thought with desolate bitterness.

The extraordinary thing was not that this entire recollection, in which the chains clanked in the wind and Seuroq and Helen made love in the old hotel on the rue d'X and the earring fell behind the bed and the bed was pulled away from the corner and she found the card tucked between where the walls separated, had taken a single second but rather that, shooting through his heart like a pang, it had *taken* a second. Because at the moment of the sound of the chains against the wall, Seuroq had looked up at the only particularly modern piece of technology in his library, a digital clock, which had said 5:55:55; and now, a second later, his reverie

disrupted by the departure of his assistant Luc through the courtyard gate, it said 5:55:54. When he was a child he remembered
waking sometimes in the middle of the night, on the eve of a holiday perhaps, to look at a clock and find the night had acquired
time rather than spent it; even as a child he reasonably attributed
this to his own greedy anticipation of the day. And in his grief over
Helen he might have thought it was another trick on his perceptions, except it was hard to mistake an alignment like 5:55:55, and
he was quite sure that a second later it said 5:55:54. Now the clock
was ticking normally but there was no doubt in his mind that a
second had been lost or, looked at another way, gained.

Being a scientist, Seuroq's first assumption was not of the extraordinary but the ordinary; it was not that he had made some
earthshaking discovery, but that he had a broken clock. He woke
the next morning not to any new enthusiasm for scientific adventure but to the same depression he had felt every morning for the
last eight months, the kind that didn't want him to get out of bed,
that didn't even want him to wake up. As had been the case every
morning, it took all his will to get dressed, have his coffee and
bread and jam, and then unplug the clock from the library wall
and take it down to the electronics store off St-Germain-des-Prés.
On the boulevard along the way banners flapped halfheartedly in
shop windows and from streetlights celebrating the two-hundredth
anniversary of the First Republic in 1793—a muted hoopla, the
French having always found the actual Revolution a happier contemplation than all that business with the rolling heads afterward.
This was at a time, moreover, when people's ideas about freedom
were confused anyway, Moroccans and Slavs and gypsies overrun-
ning the city, not to mention the beginning of the nervous exodus
from Berlin. Even the banners themselves, as had been wryly
pointed out in the newspapers and on TV, were in error. YEAR CC,
they read, in reference to the revolutionary calendar adopted by
the Republic and later discarded by Bonaparte; except that 1993
being the two-hundredth anniversary was therefore in fact the
two-hundred-*and-first* year of the Republic, had the Republic
lasted that long. YEAR CCI was what the banners should have read,
before they were amended by either bad mathematics or a mis-
placed sense of poetry. "The clock's broken," Seuroq told the
shopkeeper at the electronics store.

"Yes? It loses time? Or it's fast," said the shopkeeper.

"It runs backward."

The shopkeeper, of course, found nothing wrong with the clock. "A power surge," he suggested to Seuroq. "You live in a very old building, right?" But it didn't seem to Seuroq that a power surge would have *unwound* the clock by a second; and though his head told him there simply had to be something wrong with the clock, Seuroq's heart was beginning to hear the whisper of the last years of the second millennium. Since it was the heart speaking to him, he could not rule out the heart's agenda—that the psychic debris of Helen's death was gathering like autumn leaves in a storm, blowing together into a meaning; whether the universe cared, Seuroq needed such a meaning. Whether the universe cared, Seuroq needed to believe some purpose might be derived from Helen's death; and he knew this, he recognized the heart's agenda, and in the manner of the scientist tried to factor the heart into the equation. And so, as he returned to his university office for the first time in eight months, to pursue the theory brewing someplace between his heart and mind, he continued to insist on the possibility he was just being sentimental, deriving from Helen's death nothing more than a needy wild conjecture. "What if," he said to Luc, dismissing with the wave of a hand the assistant's apology for having left the night before without a goodbye, "time is relative not simply to the perspective of motion, not simply to what the eye sees from a passing train or a rocket hurtling at the speed of light, but to the heart as well, and the speed at which it travels?"

"What?" said Luc.

What was, Seuroq asked himself, the speed at which the heart travels, in the throes of love or grief or in the fall of its deepest trauma? Across the pages of his logs he calculated until the numbers available wouldn't calculate anymore, at which point he used new ones, remembering as he did the obscure discovery of a reclusive American mathematician in Cornwall forty years earlier who had found a missing number between nine and ten. Beginning with a given premise, he charted the heart's arc across the course of lifetime, from the moment it first took flight until the crash into pieces; and like the clanking of prisoners' chains on a courtyard wall, his head now flooded with a hundred memories of her, ending with her question to him asked in their darkest hour, when they had come close to separating, when they almost lost each other. "But what does life mean, if one isn't loved?" He had argued it might mean many things. But then he had reduced, in scientific fashion, the meaning of all of those things to a common denominator, and it was always love; and humbled by his wife's observation, which she had made with no scientific principles whatsoever, which he had to prove to himself with theorems and calculations and equations even as she had known it in a moment's intuition, he succumbed to the intangible meaning of everything they had been together, and it saved them, until cancer took her and nothing could save them.

Now, scribbling his way through his laboratory at the university, he was flooded by so many memories of Helen he could barely keep up with them, scrambling to translate them into his equations while, over the course of the day and then the next and the next, administrators and other scientists watched him from the hallway through the little window of his door. There was the time he and Helen had driven up the coast and she had unbuttoned his fly while he was driving, and there was the lighthouse on the rocks above the waves as she touched him, and the time they house-sat for a couple in Normandy and for dinner she blackened the fish the way they had it in New Orleans that time they went to the jazz festival, and how in New Orleans at night they slept with the doors of their hotel room open because it was so humid, and the dress he bought her in London when they both knew he couldn't afford it, and how they argued over dinner that night in Vienna about whether she should get a job—she said yes and he said no—and the time a thief stole a bag of asparagus she had just bought in the market off the rue de l'Ancienne Comédie and she was furious when she went back to get some more and insisted none of the asparagus was as good as what she'd just bought, until the grocer took insult and Seuroq started laughing about it.

And the time her mother died, and then the first miscarriage, and then the other one, until they ran out of chances; and the way he came home from the hospital after the second one and walked the house with the baby's blankets in his arms, as he'd practiced doing all during Helen's pregnancy, because he was terrified he wouldn't know how to carry a baby, and how she had lost both the

generation before her and the one behind her and remained un-
defeated even as she seemed born to such losses, until she was lost
to him eight months ago and it seemed to him he should have been
the one to go before her because she was the one that life had
equipped with the wisdom for loss. As he was barraged by one
memory after another, he calculated all the more maniacally, until
he had exhausted every possible trajectory of the human heart and
then two hearts in tandem and then three, until he came to the
heart of history.

Beyond three hearts in tandem was history, and when he reduced the meaning of history he was left not with the common
denominator of love but rather that of freedom. And then his calculations split off in two directions, one into the next room off his
laboratory, the occupants of which he scribbled out of their occu-
pancy until they were standing in the hallway with the others,
watching him through the window; and the other into the hallway
itself, scientists and assistants and administrators backing away
from him down the hall as though he were something oozing out of
the ground. One calculation based itself on history's denial of the
human heart and the other on history's secret pursuit of the heart's
expression: if one heart's story was the pursuit and denial of love
and if history was the pursuit and denial of freedom, what lay at
the arcs' intersection except the missing moments consumed by
memory, the second that was consumed by a memory and then
given back to time, when the clock unwound itself from 5:55:55 to
5:55:54? If it was the lesson of the early days of the Twentieth
Century that the truth could be dislocated from time, the lesson of
the waning days of the second millennium was the dislocation from
time of memory, by which the truth is surmised. A wind had blown
and chains had rustled against the wall and Seuroq had a memory
of a weekend in a hotel with Helen that had nothing to do with
chains whatsoever. Perhaps, he thought at first, the association
was born of some unconscious conviction that a ghost had brushed
past the chains rather than the wind, but once he identified this
conviction he had no sense of having held it: it was the *sound* of
the chains, not their movement, that had triggered the memory, a
sound that had nothing to do with a weekend in a hotel, and that
was when Seuroq realized that a stranger's memory of the sound

of chains had randomly coupled with his, as though memory were a restless thing freefloating in the twilight, like dying ions or dandelion wings, or black notes falling from a sheet of music.

By the time Paris had settled its celebration of long-failed Republics and dead calendars, by the time the misnomered banners had fallen from the windows and the streetlights, Seuroq had found the missing day.

In the labs and the hallways, the scientists and assistants and administrators were giving him a wide berth. They watched his mad numbers as he moved from log to log and desk to desk and blackboard to blackboard. The university called in doctors and wardens in white coats and a couple of police to coax Seuroq out of his frenzy, even to return him peacefully to the numbing dead grief of his mournless mourning; but Seuroq didn't acknowledge them from the fever of his factoring anymore than he had acknowledged Luc in the courtyard. Finally they sent in Luc himself. From the laboratory doorway Luc inched forth as though to nab a butterfly in the cup of his hands. "Dr. Seuroq?" he whispered, and Seuroq answered nothing until, with Luc only feet away, the old scientist suddenly threw up one hand to signal he was on the verge of a conclusion. He dropped his pencil and raised his eyes to the window.

"What is it, doctor?" Luc said very quietly.

He was humoring the old man at first, but then Seuroq started telling him about the missing day, and the more he talked the more frightened Luc became, because either the old man was insane, which unsettled every flimsy foundation a young researcher like Luc had established for himself, or the old man was quite sane, in which case none of the foundations were going to matter much anyway. There it was, Seuroq insisted, pointing to the timeline at his fingertips, a missing day that lay between the 31st of December 1999, and the first of January 2000—twenty hours and seven minutes and thirty-four seconds to be precise, the accumulation, according to Seuroq's calculations, of all the moments over the millennium that grief and passion had consumed from memory and then dribbled back into the X of the arcs of history and the heart, past and present and future rushing toward a dense hole of time into which all of history would collapse. An amazing dark temporal star weighing 72,454 seconds that hovered between the

millennia, on the other side of which everything the past millennium had ever meant might be utterly different, everything history
had claimed might utterly shift, the reducibles of freedom suc-
cumbing to the reducibles of love, or perhaps vice versa.

Even now Seuroq believed he could sense the acceleration toward the vortex; and when night finally fell on this missing day
between the 31st of December and the first of January, we might
all be anywhere, or nowhere, or more precisely anywhen or no-
when, since this was not a black hole of space but time. We might
come out in a lurch onto the year 2493, Seuroq thought to himself,
and then upbraided himself for such a banal conclusion, not having
quite yet reached the further one, that beyond such a day time
would measure itself not by the numbers of the clock but of the
psyche, which was to say that history would measure itself not by
years but by memory, where the heart is a country. Perhaps on the
other side of the 32nd of December or January 0, however one
might mark it, one would see that the millennium had already
begun much earlier, when the Berlin Wall fell, perhaps, or in 1945
when we gazed into the nuclear mirror, or more likely sometime
in the middle of an anonymous night in an anonymous hotel room
when someone exchanged freedom for love or love for freedom,
or entered some irrevocably compromised bargain with a certain
happiness that memory doomed to misery before it ever had the
chance to remember itself, when the promises of history or the
heart first showed the signs of their own betrayal. Perhaps now, in
1993, it was already the Third Millennium, or perhaps it was the
ur-Millennium, and a thousand years didn't have anything to do
with anything, it was just a presumption, like a republic or a reich.

"Dr. Seuroq," said Luc, "can we go home now?"

"Yes," Seuroq answered, "I'm finished here," and when Luc
reached out to touch the old man there was an abruptness about it
that gave way to hesitance, which triggered in Seuroq the last
memory he would have of Helen tonight. "You're making that up,"
he had answered her in the hotel room when she said the Queen
of Wands was the card of passion, and he had reached to take the
card from her and look at it; but between their fingers, his and
hers, the card crumbled, disintegrating with age, as though it were
as old as the hotel. That night she woke him and said she wanted
to go home, so they checked out of the hotel at one in the morning,

to the extreme displeasure of the concierge. In the back of the taxi Helen explained to Seuroq that she had been dreaming over and over in her sleep of the card crumbling in their fingers, and it somehow seemed important that they go back home before everything else crumbled. "Everything else?" he had asked. "Like the hotel," she answered, and laughed as she did when she chained herself to the shackles of the courtyard wall. But it wasn't really the hotel she meant.

In the fall of 1998 an American writer living in the same hotel room first read the news on page seventeen of the *International Herald Tribune,* below the reviews of the latest shows in Paris and London. It would have been more appropriate with the obits, the writer thought to himself later, but at the time he didn't understand the ramifications anymore than anyone else. It wasn't until three months later when a magazine ran DAY X across its cover— or JOUR D'X on the European editions, out of deference to the French scientist who discovered it—that the panic set in and Erickson took the Bullet to Berlin, where they called it X-Tag.

It s e e m e d t o t h e writer that every crucial moment of the Twentieth Century had sooner or later expressed itself in Berlin and therefore it was natural he should go there. But past Hannover the train just got emptier, and by the time it reached Zoo Station at dawn the writer rose from his sleeper to find himself disembarking alone. He took a room on the third floor of an empty hotel in Savignyplatz. The neighbors led lives even more transitory than his: streetwalkers and barflies and whatever tourists were weird enough to stray into Berlin, the kind of adventurous eccentrics who used to pass up Paris or Maui for Amazon villages or Alaskan outposts. A block from the hotel, passing beneath the tracks of the S-Bahn, he looked up one night to the scream of a runaway train hurtling west. The sound and speed were terrifying, the white boxes of the train's windows empty of life, and in the cold blue shine of the moon the tracks of the S-Bahn glistened across the sky like time's vapor trail. The writer braced himself for the crash in the distance, the cry of the train flying off the track into space, plunging into a building or park or the waters of Lake Wannsee. That was the night of the first phone call.

As time passed, his memory of this became less exact. As the present slipped into the final year of the millennium, memory became more and more disengaged from the past, like a door that floated from room to room in a house, taking up residence one day in the kitchen and the next day in the basement. The phone in his room had never rung before. The American couldn't have said for sure the phone even worked. Since there was hardly anyone left in Berlin and he didn't know anyone anyway, he assumed it was the hotel manager; maybe there was a problem with the bill. Erickson answered and there was silence for a moment and then a young woman's voice spoke to him in German. "I'm sorry, I don't speak German," the writer said, and there was another pause and the woman said, in English, "I want to take you in my mouth."

For a split, ludicrous second, he thought it was his ex-wife. He hadn't talked to her in several years—only once since the Cataclysm, and then just long enough to assure himself she was all right, blessed as she always was by dumb luck. His ex-wife lived her life in fear of one disaster or another, ranging from the apocalyptic to the mundane, when more than anyone he knew she was always unscathed by events; in a meteor shower she'd be the one who just happened to be off the planet at the time. Now, for a split ludicrous second, he thought she'd tracked him down, though in the next moment he knew that was impossible. With the phone in his hand he instinctively turned to the window, as though someone were watching. He tried to remember what was across the street—another hotel, where someone might be staring at him from a darkened room. "What?" he finally answered foolishly, and she said it again.

"Are you alone?" she asked, after a pause. Hesitantly he answered that he was. "Take off your clothes," she said; and at that moment he was either going to hang up or do what she said. He told her he had to close the blinds on the window. "Did you take off your clothes?" she said when he came back. They talked some more; she described herself. She had blond hair and nice breasts. She didn't say how old she was, but when he thought about it, which was for only a second, he imagined she was much younger than he. She didn't say she was beautiful. It became implicitly understood, particularly within the boundaries of the fantasy they were sharing, that outright lying wasn't permitted. The thing he would remember later with dead certainty was that, immediately after it was over and he lay spent on the hotel bed, she asked if he was all right. Not whether the sex had been all right but whether he was all right, his intensity having betrayed itself to her. Yes, he answered, and there was a click.

After that he was shaken. He wanted a real woman, not a fantastic one. He even thought of going to the Reichstag, which he'd never done before, but that scene was too strange for him. He pulled on his clothes and opened the window, expecting somehow to see her revealed; below, a camel loped silently down the empty dark street toward the square. It was more than a month before she called back. She left a message with the hotel manager: *Are you really never there,* it said, *where do you go when there's nothing to do at home?* In his mind he imagined her with only a dollop of romanticism—more attractive than plain but not especially pretty, perhaps a bit plump. He wouldn't allow himself to sit in the hotel room waiting for her calls; and yet in Berlin all there was left to do was wait. From his window he watched the dark street for another camel, as though it had been a sign. But when her third call came, the block was empty of beasts, not even the growl of the lion he believed slept in one of the nearby cellars, though he'd never seen it. She fucked him on the phone again and told him when she'd call back, and so already their rendezvous transgressed the spontaneous.

Animals prowled the city. The previous summer, under the cover of darkness, members of the Pale Flame opened the cages in the garden across from Zoo Station; now people were mauled by tigers. In the mouth of the Charlottenburg U-Bahn station the American found what was left of a kangaroo ripped apart by a panther. For months after the cages were opened, the city was the most alive it had been since the fall of the Wall nine years earlier, the orange and yellow and green noise of exotic birds flashing across a sky still smoky from the Night of the Immolation, when the Pale Flame had captured and set on fire seventeen Asian women in the pattern of a swastika. Sometimes the American could still see or hear the few birds left in the gables of the buildings. Beneath the

Brandenburg Gate he was once so startled by a clap of thunder above him he might have thought it was another runaway S-Bahn, if there was an S-Bahn that ran anywhere nearby; but the sound wasn't a train, it was the pandemonium of escaped birds amid the stone rafters, crashing wildly from one archway to the other. The color and music of birds survived neither Berlin nor winter. Slowly but surely one species of escaped animals wiped out the next, with no cops around to pick up the gutted carcasses.

Berliners said you knew which of the '93-'94 exodus were the cops because they were the ones at the head of the throng. Five years later the few police still left were guarding the German government holed up in the old KaDeWe department store, after the ministers of state had returned to the new capital only to find the Reichstag occupied by warring factions of the Neuwall Brigade on the one hand and the Pale Flame on the other. For weeks bureaucrats wandered homelessly the deserted boulevards off the Wittenbergplatz before winding up on the ransacked KaDeWe's sixth floor. Once the most astonishing gourmet food emporium in the Western World, the sixth floor had been picked over thoroughly in the riots of '95, leaving the government not even a roll to nibble or a bottle of wine to suck on while conducting the affairs of the newest reich, which held the dubious distinction of being an even bigger botch than the third one.

Now in Berlin, in the last spring of the second millennium, on X-257 as it was marked on the punk calendar the American writer had bought in Kreuzberg, every nineteen-year-old with a computer was a reich unto himself. He created his own German state and programmed it to last not a thousand years but ten thousand. He invaded weak peoples, wiped out impure races, torched effete cultures, claimed natural living space, and added seventeen new definitions to the term Final Solution. All he needed was the right software and a sector of the city where the juice hadn't been shut off. If the horrific dimensions of his imagination didn't quite have the baroque flamboyance of sixty years before, he made up for it with rudimentary technological acumen, blunt brutishness and a certain obliviousness of irony, since the thrashmetal that served up his anthems would be as unsavory to the Führer as it was passé to whatever decadents were alienated enough still to be here, most of them drifting naked in the sex arcade of the Reichstag basement in search of anyone with a vaccine tag around his or her neck. Berlin, once again and for the last time in this century, lay at the crosscoordinates of history's indecision, the final decade of the final century characterized by dissolution in the East and a contrivance of unity in the West which barely lasted five minutes beyond the contriving, the gravity of authority versus the entropy of freedom, the human race's opposing impulses devouring each other, order consumed by anarchy and then reordering itself. In the anarchy of each individual's building his own reich, each reich imposed its own order, much like the last reich which supposed humanity could be recreated in its image. Humanity knew the attraction of it. It lied if it said it didn't. It recognized the attraction not in its sense of self-perfection but rather in its imperfections which it so despised and so yearned to transcend, that longing for the fire that burned it clean of its humiliations. In the nihilism that was left, in the void of the obliterated conscience, where every rampart had been reduced to rubble, it longed to take care of God once and for all, the smug motherfucker.

Erickson had been in Berlin two months and was eating dinner one night in a restaurant off the Ku'damm, when a couple of Berliners sitting at his table told him about the Tunneler.

A beautiful young American Marxist student went to East Berlin one weekend in 1977 and fell in love with an East German professor. She wound up defecting, marrying the professor, bearing his son, and becoming an East German citizen. Over the years the professor began to suspect, much to his horror, that his wife was informing on him for the Stasi, the East German secret police. He came to believe, moreover, that she'd been informing on him for some time, certainly since she had become a citizen of East Germany and perhaps before that; in fact, as he thought about it more and more, he eventually concluded that she'd been spying on him from the very beginning, that their initial meeting and love affair had been part of a Stasi plan all along. He was convinced that he'd been seduced in the name of the state and that the young American woman had never loved him at all and that even their little boy was part of the political scheme.

Perhaps this was true and perhaps it wasn't. But clandestinely, with the knowledge of only his closest and most trusted friends, the professor entered a plot to escape to the West by underground tunnel near the barren Potsdamerplatz. One morning in the early spring of 1989 he rose from bed, washed and dressed himself, prepared his class papers and packed his briefcase, kissed his wife goodbye and held his ten-year-old son especially close to him, and left his house as he'd done hundreds of mornings over the years, never to be seen again.

A number of high-placed friends who knew of the professor's suspicions concerning his wife were convinced he'd been arrested, and filed a protest with the government. But the Stasi insisted he hadn't been arrested, and that insistence took on some credibility when the Stasi began conducting a thorough search of the city. After some months passed, a new story began circulating. According to this story the professor himself had believed he was about to be arrested and left his wife and child that fateful morning to head straight for the house with the tunnel, where he conveyed his alarm to his co-conspirators. Convinced that the police were about to descend any moment, the professor's accomplices buried him with food and water in what had been completed of the tunnel. No one knew that only seven months later the rest of them would be sauntering across the border from east to west, through the Wall, with tens of thousands of other Germans.

To this day, according to Erickson's dinner companions, the professor still didn't know. To this day, the story went, he was still down in the tunnel. Not understanding the first thing about digging a tunnel, with no map and apparently not much sense of direction, the professor continued digging until finally, after weeks or months, he made a breakthrough, hacking his way with a pick into what he hoped was the targeted destination, the cellar of a house off Potsdamerstrasse west of the Wall. What he found instead was that he had returned to an earlier point of the tunnel. Slowly and gradually he had circled back on himself. His despair and panic must have been unutterable. For ten years the Tunneler honeycombed the no-man's-land of the ghost Wall; amid the new, unfinished Potsdam Plaza one could hear his echoes from underground in the plaza's empty corridors.

The strange thing was that afterward Erickson began hearing this absurd story everywhere, from anyone still left in the city. Whenever he bumped into someone long enough to have more than a three-minute conversation, the tale of the Tunneler came up. He heard it not only in the drunken Teutonic slur of the bars but from other tourists and little old ladies in bookshops and stray bankers from Frankfurt on the U-Bahn, one of whom, standing on the train, pointed at a hole in the underground wall of Kochstrasse station and said to Erickson, out of the blue, "Tunneler." Excuse me? the American answered, not even sure the German was speaking to him, and the Frankfurt banker told him the story of how the Tunneler had dug his way into the U-Bahn and then, terrified he was still in the East, retreated, scurrying back into the blackness. And as Erickson looked at the hole in the wall of the darkened subway he remembered the last time he had come to Berlin, two years after the fall of the Wall, and how he took the U-Bahn from west to east and could still feel the passage from what had once been one side to what had once been the other; the ghosts of division still lurked in the underground. In the case of the Tunneler, however, he'd simply been underground too long, because the fact was that even if there had still been a Wall, Kochstrasse would have placed him not back in the East but in the West, about half a block beyond what was once Checkpoint Charlie.

It was in the rundown Ax Bax Bar near his hotel that the American writer first saw Georgie. He was a twenty-year-old skinhead and reputedly one of the leaders of the Pale Flame, but he didn't appear to be leader of anything; with a face that was almost pretty, his mouth delicate like a girl's, Georgie had a serene sweetness that knocked the edge off any hints of violence, sitting at the table laughing at jokes that didn't include him, told by strangers standing around talking to other strangers. Every time Georgie laughed at one of the jokes, someone looked at him in dismay and moved to another part of the bar. This didn't seem to perturb Georgie either. Erickson saw him again a few days later at another bar in Kreuzberg, and then about a week after that at the Brandenburg Gate.

The American was walking along the desolate stretch where the old Wall used to be, between the gate and the deserted Potsdam Plaza project, looking at the beginning of the Neuwall. In the distance he could hear the escaped monkeys from the zoo that now lived in the trees of the Tiergarten; as he drew nearer to the gate an alligator shot out of the garden, trailing the water of one of the ponds and slithering across the ugly barren scar of the old border to disappear toward Alexanderplatz. The Neuwall was built in the dead of night; the Pale Flame usually came along afterward to kick down the results. Sometimes the two forces battled in the gate's shadow among the patches of moonlight. Begun in 1995 by a coalition of Stasi victims and Stasi informers, the Neuwall's mortar was made from the rubble of the old Wall as well as the reduced paste and pulp of old Stasi files, which numbered in the millions, and whatever pieces of the Potsdam project—a pillar, a post, a demolished corridor—could be spirited away for the effort. The members of the Neuwall Brigade long ago agreed, not formally but implicitly, never to identify among themselves who had been informers and who had been informed upon, an unspoken treaty that was a by-product of why they seized the files in the first place, when the revelations of 1992 were exposing fellow workers and friends and husbands and wives and children to each other. They began the Neuwall not to eliminate freedom but to resurrect the promise that freedom held only when it was denied; they continued the Neuwall as a tribute to the way the old Wall was the spine of the world's conscience, without which humanity was left to its own worst impulses in considering the final resolution between authority and freedom, order and anarchy.

More than this, however, the Brigade believed—for reasons similar to those that brought Erickson to Berlin—that the city's function as the urban metaphor of the Twentieth Century couldn't be fulfilled without a Wall. When the Wall fell and there stood behind it the naked figure of freedom, those in the East couldn't stand the voluptuousness of her body while those in the West couldn't stand the humanity of her face: there was the awful revelation that while at the outset of the millennium's last decade people had pursued and embraced the ideal of freedom, at decade's close they had come to despise its moral burden and absolve themselves of it. The Neuwall was bone white. It bore no graffiti. Earlier, upon its desecration by the Pale Flame and other gangs, someone among the vandals was just shrewd enough to realize they were only completing the concept, that their graffiti had already been anticipated and was part of the blueprint; thus the Pale Flame simply tore the Neuwall down when they could find it, otherwise leaving it unmarked. The Neuwall's only message was written there by the Brigade itself: HITLER WAS ELECTED. Now the Pale Flame patrolled the city in vain looking for blurts of the Neuwall, which didn't follow the path of the old but rather an inebriated, slapstick zigzag through the city. The old denominations of East and West no longer mattered; now what mattered was the mortified memory of a wall. It rocketed wildly up this street and down that one. For all that the Berliners of the year 1999 knew, any one of them might go to sleep at night only to find himself barricaded in the next morning, a wave of old Wall rubble and Stasi files petrified in his doorway, through which the only recourse was to tunnel.

Among the vendors still left at the Brandenburg Gate after the Wall's fall, the American stopped to check out the Wall's sad remains, undistinguished except for the vendors' historical claims and, if one looked closely, some telltale bit of graffiti. Erickson always thought about buying a piece, just because someday soon it was all going to be gone. He had this idea that on Day X he'd sit in the hotel window clutching his bit of the Berlin Wall like a human time capsule, taking it with him to the other side. On this particular day that he saw Georgie at the gate, Erickson finally picked out a piece, at first glance the most nondescript chunk on the table because the flat outside part of the stone was blank, not a scribble of graffiti on it to note anything of the Wall at all; rather its markings were on the other side. Which didn't make any sense, since the other side was part of the Wall's craggy gray innards, where it wasn't possible for anyone to have written anything. Yet there it was, the fragment of rhetoric: *pursuit of happiness,* and Erickson bought the stone and put it in his coat pocket and turned around and was staring right into Georgie Valis' face.

He was smiling. The writer didn't know whether Georgie remembered seeing him in Kreuzberg or the Ax Bax; maybe he was just hanging around the Brandenburg looking for a tourist to mug. Erickson would have thought it was pretty obvious he wasn't worth mugging. At any rate Georgie was smiling and he started to talk and spoke perfect English, with barely a trace of an accent, or rather he spoke perfect American, which wasn't necessarily surprising since the most interesting thing about Georgie wasn't his repellent political affiliations but what two total strangers had told Erickson on the previous occasions he'd seen Georgie, that on the morning in 1989 when the East German professor left his house ostensibly for work but in fact to begin his life as the Tunneler of legend, Georgie was the ten-year-old son he held so close to him that final time.

In his short acquaintance with Georgie, Erickson never asked whether this was true. It seemed at times too personal and at other times too ridiculous, and there was no telling whether Georgie would have given a straight answer or not. What Erickson did note was Georgie's profoundly ambivalent and furiously mystic obsession with the idea of America. More often than not this was a secret America that Erickson liked to think had little to do with the real one: Georgie was full of stories about great American geniuses Erickson had never heard of, cracked Midwest Nazi messiahs and white supremacists who Georgie assumed commanded the same rapt attention of everyone in the United States. Georgie's obsession with America often got the better of his politics. Ultimately he didn't discriminate between Thomas Paine and Crazy Horse, between sex goddesses and television stars and soul singers; Erickson was never sure Georgie recognized the contradictions. It didn't seem possible Georgie could have listened to that blues tape of his and somehow heard a white man singing. Yet Georgie's corrosive racial romanticism burned the black right off the singer until all that was left was the scarlet muscle of a beating heart.

They didn't talk about politics. The American listened as Georgie rattled on, blithely and earnestly; Erickson would reproach himself afterward for not having said something. He'd reproach himself for not realizing that good manners, even in someone else's country, had their limits. Only once during a Georgie monologue about niggers and fags and kikes and gooks—and it was a monologue rather than a rant; a rant might have provoked more of a response—did the writer suddenly blurt, "Maybe that's just a lot of horseshit." Erickson wished it had been pure moral indignation on his part but it was more reflexive than that, born of some growing dread in the back of his brain that he was going to have to spend the rest of the millennium ashamed of the fact that he hadn't said anything while Georgie conducted his own personal holocaust. So Erickson said it.

Georgie stopped. He'd been staring straight ahead of him and now he stopped, and he didn't turn to the other man or meet his eyes. He stopped as though the distant abrupt backfire of a car had disrupted his train of thought, and then Georgie just got back on the train, he just started back up where he'd been interrupted, and after a while he got onto the subject of America again, the betrayal of its promise, a theme they could both agree on, except Georgie's version of the promise was rather different from the American's version of the promise, Georgie's version of the betrayal was different from Erickson's version of the betrayal, which finally brought them around to Georgie's real interest in the writer, the real reason he'd approached Erickson at the Brandenburg: the small chunk of Wall the writer had bought, with the remnant of its phrase on the back. Georgie had recognized it immediately.

He took the American to his flat in Kreuzberg. In the flat a dull light shone up from the floor. Out of a secret place in the floor against one wall Georgie hauled up a tape player and some tapes, skipping wildly from one musical selection to another, L.A. punk bands and Hollywood movie soundtracks and 1950s Julie London albums. High on the wall beyond anyone's easy reach was what Georgie called his American Tarot. The cards were tacked to the wall in six rows of thirteen. From the floor peering up into the shadows of the wall it was impossible for the writer to see the cards clearly, but they appeared very old, and the thing one noticed immediately was the missing card: a place had been left for it in the seventh spot of the third row, right in the middle. Georgie's flat was empty because in the badlands of Berlin one kept little except what one wasn't afraid to lose, like his tapes, or what he couldn't bring himself to disown, like his American Tarot, or what couldn't be hauled away by scavengers. And in Georgie's flat was also something that definitely couldn't be hauled away by scavengers. It was a slab of the Wall, the old Wall, and it stood in the center of the huge flat towering over the emptiness, where it looked a lot bigger than it had out in the middle of the city ten years before. Erickson hadn't a clue how Georgie got the Wall up there. At its base sat a can of black spray paint, and across the Wall's surface, where the old graffiti had been sandblasted away, Georgie wrote his own, including phrases from the music that was blacker than his love for it would acknowledge.

Georgie and Erickson stood looking at his Wall and the writer thought about Georgie's apocryphal American mother, who had rejected her country so she might drive Georgie's apocryphal German father into the mother earth of the fatherland. That night, leaving the flat and heading for a bar, the two of them turned up a small sidestreet only to see, as though melting into the pavement, an afterthought of the Neuwall jutting insanely onto the landscape from a neighboring alley. Before the American's eyes, Georgie transformed from innocence to ferocity. Struck motionless in his tracks, the young Berliner shook himself free of his stunned inertia to approach the Neuwall's small pitiful sputter, still fresh from someone's efforts only minutes before, where he kicked it, at first almost playfully. After a moment he wasn't playful. Soon he was wailing futilely at the Neuwall as though trying to kick the whole thing down himself, his face black with rage, while the writer watching him realized in a flash that at this moment Georgie's mother was up there with the Brigade in the Reichstag, in whatever wing the Pale Flame wasn't occupying, one of the former informers decimating Stasi files into paste.

The last time he was in the United States, driving aimlessly through Wyoming and the Dakotas for the purpose of being aimless, he heard the news of the Cataclysm the same way he heard all the news that year, on the car radio. He turned the car around at the edge of Iowa and headed back toward the Pacific, assuming the Pacific was still there but never getting far enough to be sure. Every few miles he stopped at a pay phone to try to call anyone in California he could get through to, until it was obvious this was a waste of time, and then somewhere in Utah Erickson came over the ridge of a mountain and saw ten miles ahead on the highway below him the cars backing up in the billowing sheen of the sunset. He met the traffic jam in the middle and they all sat there the rest of the night, no one going anywhere, the cars in front not going and the cars in back waiting for the cars in front to go, until the highway patrol finally came along announcing there was nothing for anyone to do but turn around. At dawn, when he got back up to that mountain ridge, Erickson pulled over and stared westward as though he might see columns of smoke rising in the direction of home, vast and steaming. But there was nothing to see.

Not long before, he'd lived in Los Angeles. For Erickson it had gotten to the point where there was no telling whether L.A. chose him or he chose it; he'd never loved it and had come to distrust people who said they did as much as he distrusted those who claimed they hated it, dismissing the perceptions of both lovers and haters as facile and shallow. He'd been born in Los Angeles, left it at one point in the mid-Seventies to spend some time in Paris and New York, and then returned precisely for L.A.'s profound lack of presence, the way it assimilated the Twentieth Century's dislocation of memory from time into its own identity. He flattered himself as being liberated by the city's abyss.

But by the late Eighties the abyss wasn't liberating anymore, with the end of his marriage and, after that, the most important love affair of his life, in which he invested every dream he still had left. In the midst of this he turned forty. A month later his father died. By 1991 the affair had collapsed and by 1993, with the final failure of his career as a novelist, the ruins around him smoldered close enough to spring him loose in one direction or the other: west, off the edge of a cliff in the Palisades, or east, where the geography offered more potential for emptiness. He gave the west some thought. Being a coward, he went east.

He assumed it was only a matter of time. Over those last two or three years in Los Angeles he kept peering around for the doom that was hounding him. Standing at the corner of an intersection waiting to cross the street, he kept his eyes peeled with passing interest for the stray car that—its driver seized by sudden cardiac arrest—would leap the curb and give Erickson one good bump into eternity. He felt for the throb in his body of this cancer or that virus. Never having been practiced at living in the present, nonetheless he'd been silently shocked by the prospect that his father might not have spent enough of his life being happy, and that the son was doing the same. He wasn't certain happiness was in his genes. When his love affair had ended, his heart had broken in time to the crumbling of history. He came to understand that while in youth it was quite true that time healed the heart, now the revelation of time's passage was that the point finally comes when the heart isn't going to heal again after all. There wasn't much to do but pursue the purely sensual moment. He might have been better at this if he'd only been without conscience.

With his lover he had glimpsed the possibility of a life that included all of him, the dark interwoven with the light, the bad with the good, the weak with the strong, until he was complete and of a piece. After it was over and he knew this completion wasn't going to be possible anymore, he accepted and came to terms with the way in which his literary life, his public life, his private life and his secret life lined up like four rooms, with guests, tourists or temporary residents occasionally straying into one room or the other, none of them necessarily knowing there were other rooms with other guests. There was a door between the literary life and the public one, through which someone might slip back and forth, and a similar door between the private life and the secret, and a hidden passage that ran directly from the secret to the literary. But the only one who ever went in all the rooms was Erickson. The only one who even knew there *were* other rooms was Erickson. No one else was allowed access to all of him again; and when he did things with people in the secret life that remained unknown to those in the private, he understood this arrangement might just be a moral expediency, to justify to himself infidelities and spiritual disarray, even as he also persuaded himself—and sometimes actually believed—that it was the only arrangement keeping him sane.

The rooms became strewn with furious women. Once it would have meant everything to him if even one of them had loved him. Now they all loved him, when he was either too old for it or too unworthy. A friend argued that there was something about him that almost naturally raised these women's expectations, something that persuaded them he was incapable of hurting them and was bound to submit, sooner or later, to their tenacity or patience. But in the wake of everything he finally couldn't convince himself he'd acted in anything other than bad faith, whether he misled them himself or allowed them to mislead themselves, permitting hope to grow into expectation without yanking hope up by the roots, in one room after another repeating the same scene with only a variation of details, the slammed door of a woman's angry exit or his own dreadful walk out that door with the sound of her crying behind him. "Your love was a lie," one of them said on his phone machine, a woman he had loved passionately years before and about whom he'd even written his first novel. "I guess it's the surprise of my life," said another bitterly, on yet another phone message, "to find out you're just a bastard like all the rest." She'd been in some novel or other too, though he couldn't remember exactly which one, or what character she was.

"You're just a real fake," said the last, who had once called him "mythic."

After the Cataclysm he headed on to Iowa and spent some time there with a friend, and then south to Austin and east to New Orleans and north to New York, as purposefully as aimlessness could be. With the crash the next year he sold the car and headed for Europe, settling first in Amsterdam and then Paris, which was no more or less practical than anyplace else until, a year and a half before his fiftieth birthday, he read about Day X on page seventeen of the *International Herald Tribune*. The writer figured they had to have known about it for a while. He had to figure the scientists didn't all just wake up one morning and look at their wrists and tap their watches wondering when, during the night, the small inner coil of infinity missed a beat. Even if he didn't accept the conspiracy theories—conspiracy, after all, to what end?—he figured there had to have been at least a lurking suspicion, quantum whispers of the slowing cosmic timepiece, out of which seeped into the millennium the lost seconds and then minutes and then hours. On maps of outer space, after all, there are the vague shadows that hint at black holes for years before scientists confirm the discovery. In such a way they must have seen in the present the vague shadows of the future.

On the other hand the American writer never believed, as others argued, that the scientists knew something they weren't telling everyone. People said that more in hope than cynicism. Erickson didn't believe the scientists knew much of anything at all. He suspected they knew less than everyone, having finally bumped up squarely against the limits of their vision. Whatever would emerge on the other side of the temporal wormhole fell as much in the imaginational sovereignty of philosophers and fantasists, theologians and crackpots, witches and pornographers and tunnelers: it would be the most purely democratic and totalitarian event ever, having rendered everyone equally subject to its mysteries and revelations. That, of course, was why Erickson had come to Berlin.

Because Berlin was the psychitecture of the Twentieth Century, and if he or anyone should emerge on the other side of Day X in the new millennium as anything more than a grease skid on the driveway of oblivion, they were bound to all come out on the Unter den Linden, the only boulevard haunted enough to hold all of it: dictators and democrats, authoritarians and anarchists, accountants and artists, businessmen and bohemians, decadents and the devout each contradicting their lives with their hearts, SS troops with blood running from their fingers wearing the wreaths an American president laid around their necks and GDR soldiers, wrenched from the vantage point of their towers pulling huge blocks of the Wall behind them, led past the Unter den Linden's grand edifices of delirium and death through the Brandenburg into the Tiergarten by an Aframerican runner with a gold medal around his neck who sprinted all the way from Berlin 1936 into the Berlin games of the year 2000, followed at the rear by a mute army of six million men and women and children utterly white of life but for the black-blue of the numbers their bodies wore, and at the rear the Great Relativist himself doing his clown act, juggling a clock, a globe and a light bulb, tangled in a möbius strip and with a smile on his face that said he for sure knew about Day X anyway, a conspiracy of one.

Erickson received her last phone call the night of the summer solstice. It was around the same time she always called, except as the days had gotten later the night had not yet fallen outside his window, where instead there was the haze of twilight on a street that ran perpendicular to the sun, and therefore never saw either its rise or fall. "Hello," she greeted him.

"Hello," he answered.

"Do you want me?" she asked, and it seemed appropriate that she would betray her accent most on the word want.

"Not on the phone anymore."

There was silence. "It's so much safer," she said.

"No more on the phone."

He knew from what she said now that she'd been thinking about it too. "It was so random like this," she explained. "I called several numbers that first time. Sometimes I got a woman, sometimes I got a man who sounded . . . wrong, and I hung up. Then I called your number, and when they answered they said it was a hotel and they asked what room, and I just said a room number, and they put the call through and it was, by chance, you. I could have dialed any other number instead. A digit higher or lower, or when I got your hotel I could have hung up, as I almost did, or I could have given a different room number, or the number for a room that didn't exist, or they might have asked for the guest's name, and I wouldn't have been able to give them a name. And it seems quite perfect like this, so perfectly random, so perfectly by chance."

"I see."

"But you don't want to do it on the phone anymore."

"No."

"Tomorrow night I'll go to a hotel not far from yours and take a room. I'll take a room hidden away from the street that's very private. I'll call you from there and tell you the number. I'll let the hotel manager know I'm expecting a guest and for you to come straight up. I'll leave the door of the room unlocked. The room will be completely dark. The blinds will be completely closed, and the lights will all be off. I'll be there. Once inside the door you'll wait in the dark for me to come to you. I'll be naked. You can undress, or I'll help you. We won't speak at all or turn on the light. We won't say anything." She paused. "Do you have a tag?"

"Yes."

"I'll wear mine too." She said, "You'll fuck me then. We won't say anything. It will be like the phone, where we see nothing and have only our words, except we will say nothing and have only our bodies. When we're finished I'll find my clothes and dress and leave you in the dark. We'll never turn on the light."

"OK."

"It will be dark the whole time."

"The sun sets later now."

"I'll call later, after the sun sets." She hung up. Erickson put the phone back in the cradle. He was up for several hours, with that humming insistence his body couldn't contain, and when he woke the next morning after a bad night's sleep, on X-191, the day was slightly more than itself, a fraction of X-190 floating freely and haphazardly across the calendar. Erickson opened the window of his hotel room as he usually did and stood back from the light and peered around him. The room was blurred around the edges, and the light outside had an unfamiliar shimmer and he thought some half life of the night's dream was lingering in his eyes. But he kept looking around and the blur was still there, around the furniture and the doorway, and the shimmer was still there in the light and he knew time had escalated almost indiscernibly, that everything was now caught in the pull of X and just beginning the inexorable rush to the event horizon at millennium's end. At the bottom of the stairs, what was left of the hotel's pet cat lay at his feet, torn to shreds during the night. Erickson looked around for some other sign of the Berlin veldt that had invaded the lobby, a rhinoceros perhaps, a python, the beasts of the zoo having begun the final displacement of furry domestic companions. The manager was nowhere to be seen.

By the human logic of time one should always walk, Erickson told himself, from east to west in Berlin. From east to west one walked from Old Berlin through the Brandenburg Gate into glassy synth-Berlin, which had been built expressly for the purpose of rejecting the claims and biases, the suppositions and ghosts of history, the Berlin that in the glare of the nuclear mirror had created itself anew from the ground up and freed itself from history once and for all. But the last time anyone walked from east to west was ten years ago, when everyone on the one side fled to the other, when everyone abandoned the history of Berlin which, in the fashion of the Twentieth Century, had become one more commodity of ideology. In the 1990s the seduction of Berlin was that one always walked from west to east, against the sun and in the face of memory, and then took the U-Bahn back. Now in the new blur of the day the American took the same walk, west to east, maybe on the theory that the city would lose its blur in the process. In Berlin all the small necessary things had broken down while the larger, more ludicrous enterprises carried on: the trains had stopped running at Zoo Station since the last arrival of refugees from the Russian-Slav civil wars, but in the windows of the top floor of the KaDeWe the lights of the government still burned at night, and in the distance to the south of the city construction continued for the 2000 Olympics, an obsession since the beginning of the Nineties that Berlin refused to relinquish regardless of whatever New Year's party eternity had planned.

So on this day Erickson walked from west to east, and with the fall of dusk went to take the U-Bahn back. He ducked into the

Kochstrasse station and descended underground; he was waiting on the platform for the train when he noticed a familiar figure at the other end.

Georgie was slumped on the bench staring straight ahead. Ten-year-old newspapers blew past his feet, and he was so still he might have been dead. Across the tunnel from where Georgie stared, Erickson saw the small hole in the U-Bahn wall that the Frankfurt banker had pointed out; it was as though Georgie were waiting for a father's face to appear in the hole at any moment. A little voice in Erickson's head said to leave him there, but he walked over. He didn't speak to Georgie but waited for him to look up. Georgie didn't turn to look until the American sat down next to him.

He turned to look at Erickson and there was no sweetness in Georgie's face at all. There was nothing in his face of childlike serenity; it was like the night after the two of them had left Georgie's flat when the sight of the Neuwall in the street had transformed the young Berliner's perverse earnest innocence to the malevolent fury that tried to kick the wall down. Except that at this moment, as he sat waiting for a face to appear in the hole of the U-Bahn tunnel, Georgie's transformation had already gone several degrees further. His face was dark like a swarm rising from the other side of a hill, the shadow of having stared too many nights into that hole in the side of the U-Bahn tunnel and having waited too long for a dreamed-of reconciliation that was only met minute after minute and hour after hour and night after night by nothing but the hole's void. Now the sockets of Georgie's eyes were so hollow that all Erickson could see in them was something so black it would frighten even the night, a feeling so lightless it would startle even hate. If Georgie recognized the American at all, he showed no sign. In his face there wasn't the slightest chance a father's face would appear, there wasn't the slightest sign of a Tunneler in the catacombs of memory, not a human sight or sound flickered even in the scurrying of someone's retreat into his own recesses.

Erickson got up. He got up right away. He turned and started walking the other direction, toward the exit of the U-Bahn, where he ascended back to the street and walked, for a change, east to west, which was what he should have done in the first place. For some reason he felt in his coat pocket for the small piece of the Wall he'd bought at the Brandenburg, uncertain whether it reassured or frightened him to realize he'd left it back at the hotel. For a while he thought it was his imagination, for a while he dismissed it as paranoia, but in the last dark block before Checkpoint Charlie he knew the footsteps he heard right behind him were real, and that they were Georgie Valis'. By the time he reached the end of the block the footsteps were all around him, and then he was surrounded in the street by six, then eight, then ten of them, members of the Pale Flame with their heads shaved and their shirts off and their chests bare and each of them with the same tattooed design, a creature with the body of a naked woman and the head of what appeared to Erickson to be a strange bird, rising from a sea of fire against a backdrop of lightning. On all their shoulders they wore tattooed wings. It was as though all of them had been summoned with the snap of fingers, a muttered command, and Erickson turned to Georgie in time to take the first blow, and the last that he would ever count or understand.

And memory broke free once and for all, floating above him like the balloon a child lets go. In that moment the writer was neither quick enough for escape nor afraid enough for panic. He shouted out only once and then succumbed to the only hope left him, that the storm of the assault would blow over him and move on.

Five minutes later Georgie said to the others, "All right."

They stopped with the kicking and beating. They shone in the twilight, six eight ten fiery birdwomen glistening in righteous satisfaction. One of them pushed the body over and they stood examining it. Georgie tapped the writer's face with his shoe to see if there was a reaction, and when there was nothing he started going through the dead man's pockets. He found a wallet and a hotel key, but not what he was looking for. "Shit!" he yelled in frustration, slapping the body alongside its head. For a while he sat slumped in the street pouting at the dead American while his troops stood by waiting. Georgie looked at the address on the hotel key. "Know where this is?" he said to one of the others.

"Savignyplatz."

"I'm going," Georgie said.

"Not real smart, man," one of them advised timidly, after a pause. "Someone will see you." He pointed at the body. "If the cops ask questions they'll wind up at that hotel sooner or later and someone will be able to tell them he saw you."

"If the cops ask questions," repeated Georgie. "What fucking cops? I don't see any cops. Cops don't even pick up all the fucking dead animals," waving his hand at the landscape around him, though at that particular moment there weren't any dead animals to be seen.

"This isn't a dead animal."

"Tell that to him," Georgie said. "Tell that to the cops." He looked at the hotel key and got up off the ground.

"Want us to go with you?"

"No. I'll see you later." He headed back toward the U-Bahn in time to find that his shirt had already been lifted from the bench where he'd left it, and to take the same train the American had planned to catch. He rode the U-Bahn to Friedrichstrasse and changed to the S-Bahn heading in the direction of Wannsee; after several more stops he got off and changed cars because people on the train were looking at the halfbird halfwoman figure of the Pale Flame on his bare chest, before glancing away when he returned their gaze. He disembarked for good at the Savignyplatz station and wandered around the neighborhood looking for the American's hotel. It was dark when he found it.

He was trying to think what he was going to do about the hotel manager. But there was no hotel manager that he could see, only the remains of a dead cat on the stairs, and so Georgie went up the stairs to the room number that was on the key. He opened the door and went inside. While there was something thrilling about the invasion, like a child finding a secret world just beyond the backyard fence, he wasn't much interested in exploring: he quickly perused the room, ignoring its other contents until he found what he was looking for, after not so much effort, in the second drawer of the table next to the bed.

It hadn't been disguised or hidden, it was just there in the drawer, the little shard of Wall with the impossible inscription on the wrong side. Georgie sat on the American's bed contemplating the stone for a while, and then finally returned his attention to the things he'd overlooked. In the same drawer where the stone had been was the American's passport and traveler's checks, cash including German marks and Dutch guilders and French francs, a vaccine tag on its chain with a key in the lock. Georgie unlocked the chain and put the tag around his neck. He stood in front of the hotel-room mirror looking at himself with the tag on. He took it off after a few minutes because the tag kept dangling across the face of the birdwoman and a tag wasn't all that cool anyway,·an insinuation of stigma that was intolerable for a Pale Flame leader.

He went over the rest of the room. He took several of the American's cassettes, Frank Sinatra and a Billie Holiday album, after he threw away the picture of the singer. There was a reggae album Georgie discarded with disgust, and a tape of soul music that the American had apparently compiled personally, the names of the artists written on the label in what must have been the American's hand; the American had titled the cassette *I Dreamed That Love Was a Crime,* a line he took from a 1960s song in which a jury of eight men and four women find the singer guilty of love. He went through the books that were stacked on the hotel dresser, though Georgie never read books, Faulkner, James M. Cain, a 1909 hardcover edition of *Ozma of Oz,* and several that Georgie didn't recognize until he realized from a picture inside that the author of the books was in fact the man he'd just left dead in the street an hour before. On the cover of one of the American writer's books was a picture of a city buried in sand, a black cat in the foreground beside a bridge, a huge white moon rising in the blue night sky. Georgie tore off the cover and threw the rest of the book away. He went back and forth between his new treasures, particularly the stone and the picture of the buried city, and had put the vaccine tag back around his neck and was studying it in the mirror again when the phone rang.

He answered it without hesitation. He said nothing, just listening to whatever was on the other end with the same curiosity he had had while looking through the writer's possessions. He listened as though the sound at the other end of the phone was another thing that had once belonged to the writer but was now his. At first there was silence, in the duration of which the voice on the other end of the line decided to take Georgie's own silence as a confirmation of something: "The Crystal Hotel," she finally said in English with a German accent, "room twenty-eight," and hung up.

Georgie nodded to the dead line as though this made perfect sense. He put back the phone and took from the closet one of the

American's shirts, which he didn't wear but rather used to wrap the cassettes and the piece of the Wall, and then tied it to his belt. He folded the picture of the buried city and put it in his pockets with the passport and traveler's checks and cash and the wallet he had taken off the writer's body. He left the tag around his neck.

On his way back to the S-Bahn suddenly there was the Crystal Hotel right in front of him. It hadn't even crossed his mind after the phone call to go to the hotel and it couldn't be said now that he made a reasoned decision about it; reason wasn't part of the process. Reason would have said to keep on going to the S-Bahn: "Even I know that," Georgie said to himself, laughing out loud. But he had the writer's passport and money and music and piece of the Wall and picture of the buried city, and now the hotel of the writer's phone call had presented itself to him. He was sorry to find that, unlike the last hotel, the lobby wasn't empty but that instead there was a night manager, an extremely old man who worked behind the front desk. The old man appeared even sorrier to see in the doorway of his hotel a bald boy with red wings on his back and fire and lightning and a naked woman with an eagle's head and something dripping from its mouth on his chest. "Excuse me," Georgie said to the old man, "I have a friend in room twenty-eight."

"Yes," it took the manager some time to say it, "she said you would be along. Well," he added with great reluctance, "she said to send you right up."

"Thank you," Georgie said. Beyond the lobby was a bar that hadn't been occupied in years; the stairs were to the left. Georgie went up the stairs floor by floor. He went down each shadowy unlit corridor looking for room twenty-eight until he found it near the back of the hotel, where it occurred to him for the first time that he had no idea what he was doing. He knocked so halfheartedly he could barely hear the knock himself. He slowly turned the door knob and found it unlocked.

For several moments he stood in the open doorway staring into a pitch-black room. He searched the wall next to him for a light but the switch wasn't there. At first he thought the room was empty but then he knew it wasn't empty; he knew someone was close by and he felt the dark of the room challenging him, he felt the night challenging him as though there was one more thing for him to prove. He was inside the room with the door partly but not altogether closed behind him and was surprised how quickly she was suddenly there next to him; all he saw of her was, very dimly, the arm that shot out of the dark to push the door closed. Then he heard her breathing and smelled her hair. He waited for her to say something and wondered what he would answer. He waited for her to turn on the light. He felt her surprise when the tips of her fingers brushed his bare chest; they flinched as though singed by the flames of his tattooed belly. But then her fingers returned to him. He felt them fumble toward his neck to confirm the chain with its tag. She grabbed the chain and pulled him forward into the room until he stumbled against the bed. Though he now understood there wasn't going to be any light, he still waited for her to say something, and then he understood there wasn't going to be anything said. For a moment he was confused, wondering where she was in the dark, until he realized she was on the bed that he stood alongside. Lying at its edge, she unbuttoned his pants and freed him and put him in her mouth. He touched her long hair and her breasts in consternation.

Her breasts felt big to him but he couldn't be sure, since he'd never felt a woman's breasts. Even if he might have been able to construct a mental picture of the woman who lay before him, even if—like a blind man listening to descriptions of colors he's never seen—he wasn't utterly without reference points in the touch of a woman's breast, he would have rejected such a vision anyway. Since he'd never had a woman before, the sanctuary of the dark was immense; he would have killed anyone who violated it. Later, upon leaving the hotel, when she nearly gave in to curiosity and turned on the light after all, she never knew that she had survived only by virtue of having left the light off. In the total darkness he quickly became hard; his erection was a response to the invisibility of the moment, the blur of the frantically waning millennium nowhere to be seen. Within seconds he was already shuddering toward an orgasm. Sensing this she released him from her mouth, and took him in her hand as she knelt on the bed away from him; with trepidation he ran his hands forward along the downward slope of her back to her hair. She put him inside her. Blood roared to his head like a drug. Savagely he pulled her to him. When he heard her gasp and whimper into the pillow where her face was buried, he was at first confounded and then appalled by the lurking presence of love.

The Woman in the Dark says, Everything is humming. The night hums, the city. Everything is seconds ahead of itself, I can feel the whirring of the room. Walking to the hotel tonight I heard the growl of animals in the cellars all along the street, they're disturbed by the hum. They perk up to the sound of time. The dark glows with their eyes. The solstice rushes to catch up with the light of the west. Rudi must be home by now. He's wondering where I am and looking over the loft. Maybe he's found the package from Prague, what will I tell him when he asks about it? What will I tell him when he asks where I was tonight? I don't care any longer. Maybe I won't go back. If I stay tonight in this room, will the American lover stay with me, and what then? It wasn't supposed to be a whole night together. I knew sooner or later he'd say, Not on the phone anymore. I knew sooner or later he'd insist on this. I admit I wanted to as well but I might have waited if I hadn't heard the power in his voice. I might have waited until the end of summer or the beginning of autumn. I might have waited until the eve of the New Year to go into the black hole of X-Tag on my hands and knees being fucked from behind rather than with Rudi, I'd rather feel my tits in the hands of a stranger I cannot see than be with Rudi's dead heart. It doesn't matter. By the New Year Rudi and I won't be together anyway. Rudi and I won't be together by the end of the week. The American lover hums with the night. I could taste on the end of his cock the drop that anticipated his satisfaction. On the New Year I'll pop him at midnight like a champagne bottle, his splash will precede us into the future. Perhaps he won't be here on the New Year. Perhaps he won't be in Berlin anymore. Perhaps the power in his voice on the phone was because he's leaving. But I don't believe he's leaving. I don't believe he has anywhere to go. I believe he's come to Berlin for the

New Year, it's the only reason to come to Berlin, for what's to come. Otherwise you get out of Berlin. Otherwise you're me and still in Berlin calling one number after another listening for the voice of what you need. He was shy for a moment when he first arrived, I saw his form hesitate in the doorway. I was surprised that he'd already taken off his shirt, he must have started undressing in the hallway. He must have begun undressing on the stairs, loosening the first buttons in the street. When I cry out, I feel his excitement. He's a beast, of course. I might have known. From the wound in his voice on the phone. From the sound of his orgasm the first time I called, the groan at the end. I've come to learn that nothing can be defiled anymore. I part my legs and open myself at the junction of my soul. It's the ping of freedom in my mind, like the tap of a wine glass that rings through the house, when the first tiny white drop of him falls into the pool of me and ripples outward. When the heart is broken and the dream is gone, annihilation is delicious. I find in it my last place of peace on the journey into the whirl. The only bastion left me before the siege of what I remember, a flash of red across the black in the distance, a kind of deliverance or, even, a miracle.

"A m e r i c a," h e h e a r d her say, and exploded in confusion. As he slumped to the floor at the side of the bed, his mortification was grateful for the dark. He covered his face with his hands as though even in the dark a bystander might have seen the shame of his satisfaction. Five minutes went by and then ten.

Suddenly he heard her rise from the bed. There were only a few more moments in which he heard her rustling in the room, and then the door of the room opened and she paused to think about turning on the light to see him; and then he heard her footsteps hurry down the stairs. Where had she gone? How long would it be before she came back? He picked himself up from the floor and lay on the bed. His enervation, the way he felt as though he'd receded up into himself, was appalling. Everything had been fine until she said it. Even when he was in her mouth it had been fine.

He was convinced he could have stopped himself before he lost control. But he'd had his first orgasm and now the only thing he kept telling himself was that it was dark and there were no witnesses, that even she wasn't a witness. Was the old man downstairs behind the front desk a witness? Would she tell the old man that Georgie had lost control? She wouldn't tell the old man, Georgie reassured himself. But none of this calmed him much because unfortunately there *had* been a witness and the witness was Georgie. There was no lying to Georgie about it. There had been a witness and the witness was Georgie and he saw himself now in the dark standing over him: the eyes of the birdwoman burned with accusation. It was not the fucking, it was the collapse of control and the indulgent expense of his essence. The solitude of the orgasm, the loneliness of it, was disgusting. Everything had been fine until she said it.

What had it meant, that at the height of his power over her and in the depths of his humiliation of her, she had said it and he'd lost everything? She'd said it like a magic word and immediately it had broken his power over her. The more he thought about this the more he knew he had to wait for her to come back so he could strip her and take her by the neck and hold her in the deathgrip of love and fuck her again in triumph without capitulation. She'd be disabused of any meaning she thought his orgasm might have had. He waited in the dark for several hours and only after he decided he could bear to see himself did he get up and find a light and turn it on. He did this because he was seized by curiosity about her and wanted to find out what he could by rifling through her belongings and because he suddenly had this alarming idea that maybe she robbed him of the American's cassettes and the piece of the Wall. But in the light he found on the floor, halfway between the door and the bed, the shirt with the objects wrapped in it.

He also found, to his great bewilderment, the room empty. There were no belongings. There were no clothes in the closet or drawers, nothing in the bathroom. It didn't take even Georgie long to understand the woman might not be coming back at all.

America, she'd said; but she wasn't American. He could tell on the phone she was German. He pulled out of his pants' pocket the American's wallet and began going through it looking for a name, perhaps scribbled on a tiny scrap of paper, but there was no name, there was no tiny scrap of paper; Georgie yelped in fury and frustration. For another hour he sat on the bed and then pulled on his pants, tied the American's shirt to his belt, and went downstairs.

The old man wasn't behind the desk now. During the time Georgie had been upstairs the old man had gone off his shift and now no one was behind the desk, and the hotel door was locked with no key to be found. I'm locked in the fucking hotel! Georgie thought to himself in disbelief. He kicked his foot through the door and glass came raining down in such an explosion he even startled himself, covering his face with his arms; with his bare elbow he knocked out the rest of the glass and stepped through. Animals howled in the distance. Now there will be witnesses, was all he could think; even more miserably he supposed that since he'd broken the glass he couldn't very well return the next night to ask the old man about the woman who had been in number twenty-eight. Everything's fucked up now, Georgie thought disconsolately, looking at his bleeding arms.

The S-Bahn was closed. Georgie walked from Savignyplatz to the Ku'damm, where he might have been in the mood to vandalize a few of the stores if he hadn't had other things on his mind, and if he hadn't already been bleeding from broken glass. It had been some time since he'd been to the Ku'damm and now he noted how many of the stores were no longer there. Two stray taxis rolling up and down the boulevard refused to stop for him; for half a block he ran along the second one pounding on the side, swearing the Pale Flame's eternal revenge. By morning the taxi driver, having thought over the threat, would be halfway to Munich.

To avoid the Wittenbergplatz where most of the city's remaining cops were, Georgie headed to Zoo Station and then northeast through the Tiergarten, constantly on the alert for police and tigers. It was pretty obvious he couldn't allow himself to get picked up by cops with all the American's things. He thought of disposing of the wallet but he'd still have the passport, which was too valuable to cast aside, and Georgie wanted to go through the wallet one more time anyway in case he'd missed something. He had to get rid of the wallet carefully because if anyone found anything that they could connect with the body at Checkpoint Charlie, they might trace the American back to his hotel in the Savignyplatz; in modern day Berlin the police never went to that sort of trouble but this was an American, and maybe that made it different. Georgie found himself giving the various details of this particular murder more attention than usual, and was still thinking about it when he came upon a segment of the Neuwall standing completely isolated in a clearing of the park, gleaming in the moonlight through the trees. It had the impact of a white tomb. Before tonight Georgie would have attacked it mercilessly; now he shrank from it.

It was dawn by the time he reached his flat.

He bandaged his arms and sat up all day looking at the American's things. He burned the driver's license and social security card, and was surprised to find no credit cards; didn't all Americans have credit cards? This afternoon he'd take the passport over to Curt on the other side of Kreuzberg and put him to work on it. Erickson wasn't a bad name; Georgie could make use of it. It could have been worse, Rodriguez or Tyrone Something, but on the other hand Georgie wouldn't have wasted his time with a fucking Rodriguez or Tyrone. Would a Rodriguez or Tyrone have this piece of the Wall? Georgie couldn't get enough of looking at the stone. He unfolded the cover of the American's book, tearing away the title and the author's name and everything else until all that was left was the picture of the buried city and the black cat in the white sand that glistened in the light of the huge white moon like the lump of Neuwall Georgie had seen in the Tiergarten a few hours before. In his flat he went over to where he'd pinned the seventy-seven cards of his American Tarot and stuck the picture of the buried city in the place of the missing seventy-eighth. For a while he played the American's cassettes.

He was not right. I'm not right today, Georgie said to himself, why not? Was he beginning to blur around the edges like everything else? Was he several seconds ahead of his moment like everything else? He couldn't stop thinking about her. He waited impatiently for the dark as though down the hall from his flat, outside in the street somewhere, a phone would ring with the arrival of night and she would have for him another hotel and another room number. He kept his eyes peeled for witnesses; he lay in bed with his hands on his chest and became transfixed, for the first time, not with the head of the birdwoman who walked from the flames, not with what dripped from her mouth, but her breasts. Their violation in his mind reduced them to the ornaments of pathetic degradation they were, and he sprang from his bed and prowled the flat as the animals used to do in the Tiergarten's cages, waiting for their release. The pupil of the night's eye dilated around him. He stood and gazed at his tarot and at the picture of the buried city that replaced the card he'd always missed; he went to his slab of Wall in the center of the flat and now it too took on the appearance of a tomb, much as had the Neuwall in the woods. Georgie seized the spray can that sat on the floor and wrote THE RETURN OF THE QUEEN OF WANDS. Then he sat on the floor in front of his new graffiti and waited.

He'd never watched the graffiti actually disappear before. He had no idea whether it vanished in the blink of an eye or faded away slowly, over the course of hours or only minutes: "This is a good time to figure this out," Georgie advised himself. He sat waiting, staring out of the dim floodlights of the flat at his new black message until he'd fixed his attention on it so long and so fiercely he finally drifted. He slumped on the floor and slipped into a dark room where he saw the bare outline of a woman. He recognized the slope of her back and the fullness of her breasts, he recognized the caress of being inside her even as he couldn't make out her face. When he woke he'd spilled his semen for the second time of his life, within twenty-four hours of the first. On his Wall the graffiti was gone.

Georgie stood gazing down at himself. He would have exchanged in a moment the shame of his semen for the honor of his own blood gurgling from a wound. Once again he glanced around as though someone might have seen him; he was also extremely annoyed that he'd fallen asleep on his graffiti watch. Once again the graffiti had slipped away into the Wall somewhere, through the slit of historical memory to which this piece of the Wall was the livid vulva, like all the graffiti since the first day the Wall came here and SONIC MEN, ANONYMOUS GOD had disappeared. Georgie cleaned himself of his semen, scrubbing himself until he was raw, and then stumbled back to the bed; once again, even in exhaustion—he hadn't slept since before he'd murdered the American—he thrashed his way through the night. Once again he got up and put on another cassette. Once again he returned to his blank Wall to take the spray can and telegraph another message into the void: THE PURSUIT OF HAPPINESS he wrote.

And now in the ultimate subversion of himself it was his graffiti that revolted him. Because suddenly the words lost all banality and history; they throbbed before his eyes and hinted at something he could neither resist nor understand, the Wall seething and the words shuddering with danger as he recoiled from them. He wanted them to disappear immediately. If at this moment Georgie had had the means he would have emasculated himself with the swipe of a blade and sprayed the pursuit of happiness with the blood of his amputated sex, until the whole Wall was the red of death's honor rather than the white of pleasure's shame.

The Queen of Wands is the card of passion. Her throne rises from the rubble of the fallen wall, and the sands of the American plain blow over her from the east. In this way her passion rises from the American earth; she's a thing of the earth and the passion's a thing of her. At her feet is a large black cat. A round white sphere rises behind her against a dark blue sky. The rod in her hand intimates magic but the magic's really in the hand and not the rod. Her brooding beauty cages the very breath of every man who lays eyes on her and blasts loose the underpinnings on which he's confidently and foolishly built a feeble life. She is without true malice. At her moments of greatest fury the rod may take on the appearance of a knife; that she always fails to use it isn't a sign of weakness but of a goodness she can't overcome. Rather her powers of destruction lie not in hate but chaos, just as the antithesis to God is chaos; and her chaos blows across those in her realm like the sands that bury her throne. She's fickle and will betray, without reason or warning, the one who loves her most. She's hungry for whatever love any man can give her and because she doesn't trust either love or herself she'll abuse both, and rush to the next man who might give her a love the previous man could not, in her search for the love that somehow raises her above her own throne, for which she has contempt. She doesn't believe in what she deserves and she deserves more than she'll ever know. Though Georgie imagines her as fair and golden the Queen of Wands is dark, her beauty understands that white is not the color of illumination but emptiness and that black is not the color of the void but eternity. Though the rings of her regeneration grow paler in time the core of her memory becomes the glowing ebony of a collapsed star: in the American Tarot she's not the Queen of Wands at all but the Queen of Slaves.

Georgie doesn't know this since he's never seen her. The card's great presence for him lies in its absence, because the absence of a single card renders all other cards invalid. Since a year ago when he first stole the deck off an old Parisian Jew in Zoo Station, the meaning of his queen has in her absence grown only more magnificent. Now in the dark in his flat, just below the surface of the floodlights, in every fitful dream he sees just a little more of the woman in the dark yet not enough so that he can tell her hair is black and not gold, her eyes are the green of the sea and not the blue of the sky. She inches just a little further into view. She hovers just a little closer into the present. The shape of her becomes just a little more distinct. But Georgie doesn't know that the Queen of Wands, or the Queen of Slaves, is not the creature tattooed on his chest for instance. He's only figured out that his queen is waiting for him in a buried city, like the one in the picture that has replaced her on his wall, and that the buried city is not Berlin but somewhere in America at the future's farthest point of exhaustion, which means he has a long way to go and not long to get there before the big day arrives, the distance growing farther with every day that time grows shorter.

Nevertheless the black hollow of the Reichstag yawns before Georgie tonight. At this point the nights are running together: was it last night he killed the American, or the night before? Georgie hasn't gone to the Reichstag in a long time, frequenting when he does only that part of it controlled by the Pale Flame; he's never gone into the Reichstag basement. The Reichstag basement is verboten by Pale Flame law. But the nights are running together now and there's no sleep for Georgie from thinking about what happened to him in the dark of room twenty-eight at the Crystal Hotel.

Perhaps Georgie thinks that, by his forbidden presence in the basement of the Reichstag, he'll testify as to his control. Perhaps he believes that if he leaves the Reichstag basement with his erection still unspent and slick with the evidence of a woman the night will forgive him; in such an event he may even forgive himself. But mostly he can't get out of his head that she may be in the Reichstag basement and he goes there now not to prove she is but to reassure himself she is not, he goes there to prove to himself that the woman who selects her men by a number on the telephone and takes them in the privacy of room twenty-eight at the Crystal Hotel has no need to wander the Reichstag basement available to whoever gets his hands on her first. The squat Reichstag sits in the center of Berlin just off the Tiergarten, apart from everything around it, as though abandoned by the city in the same way Berlin abandoned everything at its center a half century ago. On the Reichstag's far northern side is the jagged gape where a bomb ripped a hole in the spring of '96.

Georgie circles the Reichstag basement in apprehension that he's going to run into some of the Pale Flame. He's wearing the American's shirt. He hasn't really forgotten why he never comes to the Reichstag, which has nothing to do with Pale Flame law, but for the moment he tries not to think about it; the reason is there in the back of his mind, rejected by him. He finally enters the hollow. Everything's dark. He brushes past people coming and going; through an entryway he sees in the dark the forms of others moving. At a small table with a light, a young woman with short black hair wants some money to let him go on into the arcade. There's no indication she's been authorized by anyone to collect a tariff, since there's no indication any authority exists here at all, but Georgie gives her some money. She hands him a blindfold and informs him he must put it on before he passes beyond the entryway behind her. Other people's clothes are strewn against the walls and before he undresses Georgie goes through them looking for money; he keeps glancing over his shoulder at the woman with the short black hair. But she isn't watching, she doesn't care what he steals. She's here to enforce nothing but the darkness of a blindfold.

In the darkness of his blindfold he reenters room twenty-eight of the Crystal Hotel. Once more he's standing in the doorway of the American writer's rendezvous, the American writer's darkness. He wanders tentatively forward, his hands before him, waiting for her touch to meet his. He's surprised by the heat of the basement, it's the heat of something older than the summer solstice; the smell of ashes is thick around him. The lurking form of the reason he never comes to the Reichstag spies on him from around the corner of his mind, the American bitch. He feels someone grasp the tag around his neck and he feels to be sure it's a woman. Immediately he becomes erect. He pulls her to the ground which is hard and hot, and says in English, "What's your name." When she doesn't respond he repeats the question in German.

"No names," she answers. She sounds drunk. She touches the bandages on his arms.

He takes her by the neck and shakes her. "What's your name?" he demands.

She squirms beneath him. "Christina." He nods, relieved. He opens her and puts himself inside. The reason he never comes to the Reichstag continues to watch from around the corner, treacherous spying American Stasi bitch. Go away, he mutters; the woman beneath him cries out. Go back to your new wall, he seethes, petulant. He now knows the woman beneath him isn't from the Crystal Hotel even if her name is Christina. Her moans and whimpers don't sound at all like the female at the Crystal Hotel and her breasts are much smaller. She feels and sounds much smaller and reeks of beer and cognac. He's sure he sees a flash of light somewhere beyond the darkness of the blindfold, and in the flash he feels the basement freeze around him and it occurs to him he's been revealed. It occurs to him there are witnesses everywhere. It occurs to him he's a fool, that it's all been a trick and he's the only one wearing a blindfold, and as in a child's game everyone's standing around in a circle watching as he stumbles to his next humiliation. Believing this, he doesn't come but rather wilts to nothing; the woman beneath him sighs with audible relief. Georgie rips the blindfold from his face and jumps to his feet: but no one's watching. It's dark, not pitchblack like room twenty-eight but dark nonetheless, a few barely distinguishable forms of people doing indistinguishable things.

He yanks the female up from the floor by the tag chain and drags her out of the basement. He grabs his clothes from where he left them but doesn't bother to look for hers, and pulls her naked out into the Berlin summer night.

They walk south past the Brandenburg Gate through the bankrupt monument of the unfinished Potsdam Plaza. The moon is full. Christina has long red hair and freckles all over that Georgie can see even in the moonlight, and her most exotic attraction besides her small budding breasts is that except for the hair on her head she's completely shaved, giving her the body of pubescence even as her face makes clear she's several years older than Georgie. She's just sober enough to understand she's completely naked and that the light above her is the full moon and that the trees of the Tiergarten are in the distance. Georgie pulls the female along with the impatience of a child disgusted by the way some long-coveted toy hasn't measured up to the coveting, until they reach an S-Bahn station where they ascend to the platform and wait for a train. The few other stragglers waiting for the train see Georgie and his naked woman and desert the platform immediately. The night's final train arrives and Georgie and Christina get on. Most of the seats are empty, and when the few other passengers see the naked woman and the boy with the tattooed wings, they empty their seats as well. Georgie doesn't want to sit down. Christina's legs buckle as she crumples to the ground at his feet. He pulls her back up to her feet by the chain.

Everyone's a witness now, he tells himself. He grimly believes he's passed some point of no return, that the Pale Flame will cast him from their ranks or kill him when the word gets out about tonight in the Reichstag basement. In a small street-corner market that's open late, Georgie buys a beer while Christina stands stunned in the market's stark overhead light; she covers her face with her hands. The store owner, a Turk, stares at them, not sure which holds his greatest attention, the completely naked shaved woman or the boy buying the beer with the sign on his body of the Pale Flame, which savagely kill Turks as a matter of course. Tonight, however, Georgie says, "Thank you very much," when the owner returns his change. Georgie pulls Christina back out into the night and to his flat. Just inside the flat, slipped beneath the front door, is the result of Curt's efforts with the American's passport. Georgie examines the passport as Christina collapses to the floor.

Georgie puts on a cassette. "This is a good one," he assures the semiconscious woman. He turns the music up, then down, then back up, and undoes the bandages that have been wrapped around his arms. He ties the bandages into several long strips and binds Christina's wrists and ankles, lashing her to his slab of the Wall in the center of the flat. In her stupor she groans. Around and around his Wall Georgie circles, stepping over or around Christina's prostrate body and taking swigs of beer and listening to the cassette. Christina writhes in dazed confusion. Georgie takes the paint can and sprays across the Wall I DREAMED THAT LOVE WAS A CRIME and then returns to his orbit, wishing he had another beer when he finishes the one he bought. Then he goes over to the floodlights and turns them off.

The flat's dark now, nearly as dark as a room at the Crystal Hotel, darker for sure than the Reichstag. He stumbles to his Wall and touches it; he feels the wet black paint of the new graffiti. He finds her in the dark. He strips off the rest of his clothes and lowers himself to take her, but he's wrapped her ankles too tight and there's no separating her. He turns her around but no matter how he tries he can't get inside her. He thinks perhaps he'll put himself in her mouth but he can't even get her mouth open; he keeps turning her this way and that. He keeps telling himself she's someone else. He tells himself it's another's breasts and that the sound that comes from her is another's sound. But she's already been too exposed to the light of trains, to the light of late-night markets, to the light of the moon, for him to trick himself into believing he's never seen her. All his wrath cannot inflate his loins with enough semen and blood to make him erect; his impotence is bigger than the dark. He wails at his situation, rises from the floor and hurls himself in the dark at his Wall so that the wet black paint of his manifesto will leave its imprint on him and tar his wings. But when he hits the Wall there's no wet black paint anymore: Day X has already sucked his message to the other side through the Wall's portal, and the Wall is already blank.

He turns the light back on. For a while he sits against the blank Wall. The Female doesn't move in her bondage except to shiver; in the still of the flat, in the hushed haze of the floodlights, Georgie looks over in the light and sees her eyes are open. A single tear runs down her face. "Don't cry," he says and, aiming carefully, reaches over to crush her tear beneath his thumb as he would an insect, or the flame of a candle. The black paint of his graffiti is long gone from the Wall but the paint on his thumb leaves a vague print on her cheek. Outside, the solace of Berlin meets the new upward tick of the hour, the hum of everything indiscernibly escalates to a new pitch, and for a few minutes, perhaps even closer to an hour, Georgie actually dozes in the light without dreams. When he gets up Christina still hasn't moved, hopelessly bound as she remains to the Wall. Georgie shuts the door of the flat carefully behind him so as not to wake her.

In the Kochstrasse U-Bahn it's probably half an hour before dawn. The trains will begin running soon. No one closes the stations in the offhours anymore and homeless people sleep on the station platform, those desperate enough not to care who robs or knifes them in their sleep. In this final hour of the night Georgie isn't here for robbing or knifing. He stands on the platform just feet from where the American writer made the mistake of sitting next to him; but Georgie isn't thinking of that either. He's forgotten everything about the American except what he's taken from him. Georgie lowers himself from the platform and carefully steps over the rails of the track. He crosses to the other side of the tunnel. A gypsy lying on the platform wakes just long enough to look over and mutter a warning before falling back to sleep; on the other side of the tunnel Georgie pulls himself up alongside the wall. Several times he has to jump up to get a grip on the opening of the hole; he tries to hold himself up long enough to peer inside. Beyond the breach of the hole is a relentless darkness, the kind of darkness he's been looking for since the Crystal Hotel, only to find it now when he doesn't want it. Now he'd settle for light. Now he'd settle for a window or a bulb or a moon; with a spare hand he'd flick a switch if he could, or light a match. All he can do is look into the dark as hard as he can.

Into the hole he calls, "Papa?"

There's only one response to his question as he drops from the hole. He hears it come first from the tunnel of the U-Bahn and with some concern he believes, at first, that the sound is the first train of the day. He thinks maybe he should get off the track. Georgie doesn't know, no one really knows, about the new pitch to which Berlin has escalated; one or two of the gypsies on the station platform also wake to the rumble. At that point Georgie decides the rumble isn't a train. He steps over the rail and stands in the middle of the track staring down into the black tunnel of the U-Bahn. The din slowly breaks the surface of the city's hush. And then, so quickly it startles Georgie, a hyena darts out of the blackness of the tunnel and across the platform, creating a small furor among the waking sleepers who have begun to gather themselves up in apprehension. The animal lurches up the stairs of the U-Bahn to the street level. People on the platform are looking around them, expecting something to happen.

Georgie raises his eyes. Now the sound has risen above him. He looks down into the tunnel once more, following the string of small white lights that line the hills and curves and valleys of the track for as far as he can see; he crosses back to the platform. He hoists himself back up onto the platform and heads back up the stairs to the station entrance. At the top of the stairs he freezes. In front of him an albino peacock spreads its white fan and furiously shudders. Beyond that an emaciated antelope bolts. At the station entrance the rumble is louder; on the street the new pitch is almost audible. On the street Georgie turns to see, thundering toward him from the other end of the block, the last escapees of the Tiergarten's autumnal cages, purring panthers which hunger has left no longer fleet, spindly ostriches and hobbling kangaroos and barely lumbering bears, the surviving cats and wolves and reptiles shaken loose from the cellars of Berlin by the growing roar of the rush toward the black twenty hours that wait beyond the millennium's final chime. Georgie leaps up onto a U-Bahn signpost, where he clings for safety as the animals stampede past him in the silvery blue of the unlit dawn, their ragged sprint westward as though from a pursuing inferno in the jungle.

Curt did a good job, Georgie thinks to himself on the airplane. Once Georgie has finally begun to relax from the takeoff, he studies the passport carefully. Curt has put Georgie's picture in place of the American's and changed the birth date from 1950 to 1980; the name's been left alone. Georgie leans forward in his seat to put the passport back in the bag under his feet, but it means unlatching the seat belt; Georgie hasn't unlatched the seat belt since he got on the plane. This is the first time he's ever been on an airplane. On takeoff he clutched the armrests so hard that for several minutes he didn't notice how the old woman in the next seat, taking pity on him, was holding his hand. If he hadn't been so terrified he probably would have yanked his hand away from her, but he let her go on holding it; they were well in the air before he let go. She's an old woman, Georgie tells himself; with some concern he suspects she's Jewish. But she makes jokes about the flight and puts Georgie at ease, and soon he's doing things for her, walking up and down the aisle of the plane getting magazines for her and a pillow, and the stewardesses are charmed by the friendship between the older woman and the disconcertingly sweet young man with the shaved head. In New York City, as they're going through customs at the airport, the woman tells him he's in the wrong line: "The one for U.S. citizens is over here," she says, pointing at the blue American passport Georgie holds in his hand. When they say goodbye she offers him money, which he politely but firmly refuses. Two hours later at Fifty-fourth Street and Seventh Avenue, a black girl offers to sell herself to him; he accepts and follows her long enough to push her into a trashcan and rob her.

Is something wrong with America? he wonders. He sees more human flotsam in New York than he ever saw in Berlin, even in the early Nineties, coloreds everywhere and obvious queers, and a fuckload of Jews. He regards them all with more curiosity than hostility, like someone who's wandered into the freak tent of a circus. When his bed in the flophouse on Eighth Avenue winds up in the same room with an Ethiopian, Georgie protests, arguing with the manager in the hallway while the Ethiopian watches; but there aren't any other available beds and Georgie doesn't have the money to sleep anywhere else. The Ethiopian understands what's happening well enough to keep his eye on Georgie with stony wariness the rest of the night. Tomorrow, Georgie tells himself, I'll get out of New York and make my way west to the real America.

But the next morning he's violently sick. For several days he can barely move from the bed except to crawl to the toilet, not sure whether to straddle it or wrap his arms around it as his stomach erupts upward and his bowels explode downward. In his fever he feels infested with the American bacteria, struck low among Africans and fags, a prisoner without pity in New York. Almost four days have passed before, in the swelter of the night and the light of the streetlamp that shines through the window, he's well enough to climb from bed out onto the flophouse fire escape, where he can unfold his picture of the buried city to remind himself where he's going and why. He counts his money, including what he took off the black girl that first afternoon. The next day he slinks out of the flophouse and catches a cab to Penn Station, where he buys a bus ticket for as far west as he can go.

X-148. She's waiting for him and he doesn't have much time.

He takes the bus to Philadelphia and then Memphis, and from there to St. Louis. He likes the bus better than the plane. Watching out the window his heart leaps at the sight of the red, white and blue crucifixes that line the highway and the billboards of a ferocious Jesus with piercing blue eyes who holds an American eagle in his arms. On the horizon in the distance he spots the old drive-in movie screens from the Fifties that have been painted black as monolithic signposts of the converted plague camps. He dozes and her outline becomes more distinct before him. A light from an unknown source reveals her inch by inch. Sometimes he thinks about Berlin; he wonders if anyone has found Christina yet, tied to the Wall in his flat. In the dead of night, as the bus rolls on and everyone sleeps, Georgie slips from his seat and lifts a watch off another passenger two rows back. He winds the watch and puts it in his pocket; at the next stop he'll get the exact time.

In St. Louis it's X-134. The blur of edges gleams shinier and faster, the light of the days grows more metallic. Time is a mineral.

X-132 and it's Kansas City. X-129 and Georgie sets out on foot, few cars stopping to give him a lift. X-124 he sits in the back bedroom of Lauren's house on the Kansan flatlands and shows the piece of Wall to Kara, who says, "It's a nice rock. But you have to admit, it's not as good as a bottle with eyes, or even wings on your back."

He walks out of the summer into the west. The spasms of the last solstice barely reach him anymore. His progress is reduced to ground level; he's tapped out of money and in these final days must rely on people's good will. He's struck and confused by the kindness of Indians he meets in New Mexico. Sometimes when people ask him he tells them his real name and sometimes he doesn't. In the middle of the desert far from civilization he finds written on the concrete bridges of highway overpasses graffiti hailing thrash-metal bands, and stops to listen for nomads in the desert playing boomboxes. By Arizona, people sit rocking on the front porches of their desert houses cradling clocks in their arms. The lines of ink that streak the front pages of newspapers become increasingly indecipherable until finally the news takes the form of a lost hiero-glyphic. Tumbleweeds skitter along the highway before him, the dust of the desert rushes past him, though no wind blows; the weeds and dust blow to a different force. Soon it occurs to him that none of the cars on the highway go his direction anymore. Every car passes him heading east; he hasn't seen a single car going west for as long as he can remember. By X-52 there aren't any cars going east either. He constantly checks the time of the watch he stole on the bus. He constantly asks convenience-store clerks if their clocks are right, and calls the time-of-day on the pay phones along the highway that still work, as he slips from time zone to time zone picking up one hour after another. With his sweetness that catches people off guard he gets a bite to eat here and there, but he isn't hungry much. He's long since discarded the American's passport, back around the Texas Panhandle. At night when he closes his eyes there's only blackness; the west has drained his sleep of dreams.

By X-37 it's begun to get cold. In Flagstaff Georgie tries to steal a coat from the front seat of a four-wheel drive and almost gets caught. He's pushing himself beyond hunger and cold and exhaus-tion, exhorted onward by the signs of his progress. He keeps check-ing the watch. He keeps checking calendars. He keeps track of the days and hours. By the time he reaches what was once the Mojave Desert he's passed the highway checkpoint beyond which no one's allowed without authorization. Except now it's X-18 and the checkpoint's deserted of soldiers or guards; no one's around to stop Georgie and turn him away. The desolation of the Cataclysm's landscape is bitter and overwhelming, rolling dead-white hills. He has some water and not much else; every time he feels hungry, every time he can't bear the cold, every time he wants to sleep, he looks at his picture of the buried city and thinks of room twenty-eight in the Crystal Hotel. He reads his picture of the buried city like a map, he examines the contours of the Cataclysm dunes and compares the moon in the picture with where the moon now hangs in the night sky. On the night of X-6 a small light glimmers in the distance, and when it shortly becomes two lights, he grows excited by how close they are. Then he realizes the lights are coming toward him, and it isn't long before a pickup truck pulls to a stop.

In the back of the truck Georgie can see shovels and pickaxes and rags. The driver's a big man with a beard and a cap pulled over his head and ears; a windbreaker is zipped to his neck. He looks at Georgie in disbelief. "Who the hell are you?" he says.

"Erickson," says Georgie.

"Well, good lord, Erickson, what the hell do you think you're doing out here?"

"I'm going to the buried city," Georgie explains.

The driver's stunned. "I don't know where you heard about that," he shakes his head, "that's totally hush-hush."

"Is it much farther?"

"I'll bet you ran into Fred in Flagstaff, that fuckhead. Get a little tequila and beer in him and Fred'll tell everyone the secret of the atomic fucking bomb if he knows it, which fortunately he doesn't. Two weeks ago you couldn't have gotten within fifty miles of here. But I guess the party's over now and everyone's gone home, which is where I'm going, or at least someplace that makes for a passable facsimile."

"It was in the cards," Georgie explains about the buried city.

"Hop in, pal. I'll take you back to Kingman. There's nothing back there," he nods in the direction he's just come from. "Like I said, everyone's gone home while there's still time. There's a waitress I know in Kingman. She works in one of the worst restaurants in the civilized world and we're going to get a room together, at a motel on the main drag of town."

"It's a very old city."

"Yeah, I know it's an old city, pal. You ever find out how old, drop us a postcard, will you? We just spent the last year and a half trying to figure out exactly how old."

"You'll have to give me your address so I know where to send it."

The driver considers Georgie solemnly. "I was making a joke," he finally says, slowly. "I don't really want you to send me a postcard." He leans over across the seat and opens the passenger door. "Hop in."

"I have to go."

"Man, I'm telling you there's nothing back there. A few buildings that were probably houses once, and the rest of it so far buried beneath the rubble no one would have ever known it was there if that big dust-up a few years back hadn't opened up everything. Take my word for it. I can't believe that asshole Fred. What a mouth."

"I have a friend there."

"Man, you do not have a friend there. *There's no one there,* I'm telling you." He motions to the open passenger door.

"No thank you."

"From this point on you're on your own. I'm the last soul you're going to see."

"OK."

The driver shakes his head again wearily. "Here." He reaches behind the passenger seat and pulls out a blanket and a plastic bottle of water. "The blanket's dirty, but . . ." He hands them to Georgie through the window.

"Thank you. Do you have the time?"

The driver looks at his watch. "About a quarter to seven."

Georgie is setting his own watch. "Do you have the exact time?"

The driver looks again. "I've got six-forty-eight." He reaches back across the seat and pulls the passenger door closed. "Take it easy," he says. He starts the truck and drives off, and Georgie doesn't wait to watch the tail lights disappear down the highway; he's continuing on, exhilarated. He puts the water in his pack and wraps the blanket around him.

He reaches the excavation site on the afternoon of X-4. The Cataclysm has cut a savage swathe through the earth, and on the edge of the divide Georgie can make out in the distance the gray befuddled sea. Georgie stares down into the rocky gash where the earth has wrenched loose of itself and, from one end of the Cataclysm's gorge to the other, he sees staring out of the black rock the dim ravaged faces of ancient white houses, ladders, and scaffolding drooling down the cliffs. Georgie begins his descent. The world is soundless. The crash of the sea is too far away and no wind blows through the canyon, and Georgie hasn't heard or seen a single stirring of life for days. After months of the flash and clatter of birds in the skies of Berlin this sky is empty and he becomes all the more aware of the crunch of rocks beneath his feet as he makes his way down into the site. By dusk he's at the bottom. For the first time in days he collapses into the blanket the truck driver gave him and sleeps the whole night, without a single dream's glint or whisper.

In the morning he wakes in panic. He looks at his watch and then looks again; for a moment the watch has stopped. He taps the face of the watch and the second hand starts back up: was the watch running just a moment ago when he first looked at it, having lost only a split second, or has it been stopped all this time, maybe all night? Perhaps he hit his wrist against one of the rocks on the cliffs. The watch says 8:21. Georgie tries to tell himself calmly that he wasn't climbing the rocks at 8:21 last night, he'd already reached the bottom by then and fallen asleep; in all likelihood it's now 8:21 in the morning. But in his disorientation Georgie has a lapse on the day: X-. . . 3? 2? What, Georgie thinks to himself, does X-3 mean anyway? Does it mean X is three days away, or two? Or four? Stooped deep in the earth's crevice, rocking on his feet, he miserably holds his head in his hands trying to straighten out everything in his mind. Finally he begins to walk down the gorge in the direction of the excavation. The scaffolding constructed alongside the cliffs has the abandoned air of something deserted quickly. Above one makeshift rampart is a pair of ancient windows and in another clearing he finds the unearthed remains of something resembling a plaza or town square. In the black volcanic earth beneath the gray light of the sun is the outline of a white circle. At its center is the dark stump of some kind of pillar or obelisk.

Georgie spends the rest of the day searching through the unearthed city. By the next day his panic is of a different sort. It's a panic about food, to begin with; he cannot will away his hunger any longer, and despite all his attempts at conservation his water will last only another day at best. He's also having more difficulty keeping track of the time. He keeps looking at his watch. When he stares up through the mouth of the gorge, which gets smaller and smaller the further he goes, he sees passing overhead in the sky high above him tumbleweeds and wheels and machine gear and office equipment and supermarket sundries and newspapers and pages from diaries, a panoply of general uselessness spinning wildly westward on a current no wind has ever blown: time is almost up. Most profoundly, Georgie's beginning to have grave doubts that the Queen of Wands is here. Georgie's beginning to suspect that the driver of the pickup truck on the highway was right, that no one is here. Growing weaker and more delirious he rushes through the buried city from one room to another looking for her. Trying to sleep on the hillside in one of the ancient houses, when the unleashed night of the desert couples with the unearthed night of the timeless city, he bolts upright again and again to his expectation of ghosts, any of whom might be the one he's come so far to find. He shivers in the dark. He awaits her touch, for her deliverance into his hands. He would be erect with desire, he assures himself, if he had the strength for it, if delirium were enough to fuel desire, as it nearly is.

X-1.

Deeper into the city he wanders. The mouth of the gorge above him has finally disappeared altogether. Like his legendary father tunneling subterranean Berlin Georgie's becoming lost, beginning to circle back on his own steps through one after another of the Cataclysm's revealed rooms. He doesn't have the strength to climb another scaffold. He doesn't have the strength to call her name. Piece by piece he's stripped himself down, casting aside the shirt and vaccine chain and the contents of his pockets, the water and blanket and even the picture of the buried city, which, in retaliation for its betrayal, he rips to bits and flings above him as though to hurl it out of the canyon altogether. The bits of the picture only rain back down on him. Foolishly he brushes some of the confetti from his wings, comically he wears some on his bare head. He tears his watch from his wrist and holds it in front of his eyes desperately trying to focus on the hour. In his other hand he clutches the only thing he can't bear to discard, the piece of the Berlin Wall. He stumbles further into the gorge in his fevered daze, sometimes dozing against the canyon's side; in hallucinatory moments he misses Christina with the shaved freckled body writhing in the bondage of his bloody bandages on the floor of his flat. As he lies beneath the gorge's shelter the hours pass and then the rest of the day, until he hears the gray twilight sun sink far beyond the edge of the earth. Not long before midnight, when it's too dark for Georgie even to read the time on his watch, he hears the shadow of the millennium advance across the eastern horizon.

In the dark of the shadow he sees something.

It's so faint he looks again and again, by now distrusting his own eyes, but further into the gorge, suspended a few feet above the ground, is the outline of something. In his delirium the first and only thing he can think of is a coffin, set in the side of the canyon like a jewel. He crosses the crevasse. When he sees the climb he must make he nearly turns back, but slowly he begins, with his watch and his piece of Wall. In a rocky hollow of the canyon he sees it isn't a coffin; within several feet he sees it's another of the city's ancient doors. It doesn't seem possible he could have missed this door. It doesn't seem possible he could have missed anything. He's been over everything again and again. But there's a door now and the only reason he could see it at all from the other side of the gorge was because coming from behind the door is, unmistakably, a light.

He's terrified. He backs away from the door: terror wars with desperation. He steps back to the door: as he tries to get a grip on it, desperation refutes terror. He holds the watch up to the sliver of light coming through the crack of the door and, behind and below him, the ghost city splayed across the Cataclysm's breach slides into oblivion.

At 11:59, the second hand of the watch hurtling toward twelve, he yanks open the door and steps through.

The old man stirs in his chair at Georgie's entrance but doesn't wake at first. The bareness of the room is blinding to Georgie; he holds his hands up to his eyes. In the glare he can barely make out the sink and toilet in the corner and the unmade bed against the wall. On the table in front of the lone old man sits a radio that's turned off and Georgie's piece of the Wall, though even as Georgie now looks at the evidence of his empty hands he can't remember putting it there. Beyond the old man on the other side of the room is another door. It's slightly open. Beyond the door is a dark hallway.

The stillness of the room is even more striking to Georgie than the lifelessness of the last several days, though now he isn't so sure about the last several days, whether they were several days ago or several years, or whether days or years still mean what they did moments before. The stillness means to deny the presence of the old man. A buzz in some other part of the building, beyond the door on the other side of the room and down its dark hallway, takes on the audible outline of a TV. The old man looks at the room around him much as Georgie has been looking at it, and he's been staring at the bed for some time and is still staring at it when he asks, so quietly Georgie can barely hear him, "Is there any wine?" He finally turns to Georgie only because Georgie hasn't answered.

The old man smiles. He raises his eyes to Georgie. With his heart in his throat, Georgie stares back into the old man's eyes and knows he's insane.

It isn't like the people on the U-Bahn when they used to stare at Georgie. The old man sees Georgie from the perspective of a finished life: the boy is already drained of the disproportionate meaning of the present. The wings on Georgie's shoulders, the woman with the head of a bird on Georgie's chest, have no impact on the old man at all. The dagger of time hanging by a thread over the old man's wild auric hair dreads its own fall while he anticipates it; his fearlessness fills Georgie with loathing. In the subsiding blaze of the room the old man's face appears like a vision in the hole of the U-Bahn tunnel at Kochstrasse; and now Georgie is repelled by this grotesque old man in ragged clothes, the torn pants on his long legs and the shoes with holes and the lining of his coat drooping from the hem, who's invaded Georgie's long dream. But the feeling gets much worse when Georgie says, "Who are you?" and the old man answers, his stare unbroken and his smile unchanged, "America," and laughs softly afterward as though he's made a joke.

Liar, is the word that catches in Georgie's throat. But he warns instead, "That's where I came from." The old man continues to smile at Georgie the way a stranger smiles lewdly at another man's woman even though the other man stands right next to her. Georgie can't even look at the old man. Fury laces hunger and exhaustion to the point of lightheadedness, and he's been sitting in his chair across from the old man rocked by this fury and hunger and exhaustion, staring at the bare wall beyond the bed for four or five minutes, before he realizes with a start what's been right in front of him the whole time.

Someone is sleeping in the bed.

Her back is to him. He has no reason to know it's a female except he just knows, and the horizon of the white sheet displays the shape of her, and Georgie can't believe she's here after all. He had reconciled himself to not finding her, and now she's in the bed right in front of him. "There's someone sleeping," he says.

Thomas nods. The smile on his face hasn't changed, and Georgie thinks perhaps the old man is mocking him; but then the smile gives way to fierce pain. Thomas takes his head in his hands. He squeezes his head as though to wring the pain out of it, until he can't hold on anymore and slumps back in the chair. His face glistens. Exultation sweeps Georgie, because the old man isn't smiling anymore and Georgie has found her sleeping in the bed in front of him; at one point she moves slightly in her sleep. Out of the haze of his pain Thomas picks up the piece of the Wall on the table and peers at it for some time. He examines the back of the shard as though it's the longest sentence in the world, Georgie thinks indignantly to himself. The part of Georgie that recoils from the inscription, the part of him that regards it as something infectious, swarming with moral bacteria, fears that a secret hovers between him and Thomas that will demand its exposure if the old man doesn't put the stone down soon, which he does only at the last moment.

"What are you doing here?" Georgie says.

Thomas rubs his temples and the back of his neck. He speaks so softly Georgie can barely make him out. "Is there news from Virginia?"

"I don't know," Georgie answers.

"What finally loses a man's soul," Thomas says, "the betrayal of his conscience or the betrayal of his heart?" He looks up at Georgie as though the boy with tattooed wings will actually have an answer to this question; the old man's beatific smile struggles to surface above the pain in his head. He raises an old finger. "Both, you're thinking. Aren't you? You're thinking both." He nods. "But what if you have to choose? What if your life is forced to one or the other and there's no avoiding having to choose? What if your life chooses for you, or she does," and Georgie is startled, because Thomas is indicating the woman in the bed. The old man tries to unbend himself from his chair but doesn't have the energy; he collapses from the effort. He glares around him at the affront of the room's light. He mutters, "Virginia runs with blood, like my dreams of Paris," and he smells of smoke.

"You're a disgrace," Georgie charges. But his voice cracks. Trying again he manages, "You're drunken scum and it isn't right you call yourself that name." America is the name he means.

Thomas knows it's the name Georgie means. "Of course," he nods, "the flesh," and he pulls at the old weathered skin on his face, "is too pale to be American flesh. Isn't it?" and he keeps pulling at his face for the momentary hot rush of blood to his fingertips. He massages his wrists and Georgie sees how raw they're rubbed, as though they've only recently been released from chains. Thomas looks at the bed and says, "And what if she had answered yes? When I asked her to go back to America with me, what if she had promised different? What if, there in the square of the Bastille among the glass and blood and gunpowder, she had said Yes I'll return with you to America as the slave of your pleasure, instead of turning as she did and disappearing from my life forever into Paris' roiling core, while I stood at the top of the street screaming her name? What if my life had chosen my heart rather than my conscience? What if I'd put a price on her head and shackled her naked in the cabin of my ship like the property she was, what if I'd smuggled her back to Virginia pleasing my heart every day for the rest of my life and left my conscience to God or the hypocrites who claim to serve him? Let them try to stop me from taking her back, Paris and its revolution. Let it shrivel and petrify like a small black fossil, my tyrannic conscience. Happiness is a dark thing to pursue," the old man hisses at Georgie, his eyes glimmering brighter and madder at the bald boy, "and the pursuit itself is a dark thing as well. Even God knows that. Above everything else, God especially knows that." Thomas seizes his racked head. When the pain subsides just enough he whispers, "What if I'd loved her my whole life." His old eyes are wet. "Would the conscience be as shriveled and petrified as the heart is now? Where's the frontier of the first irrevocable corruption? Where's the first moment in the negotiation of the heart and conscience when one so betrays the other that the soul's rotting begins? God's hypocrites will say there's no difference between one corruption and another, that the smallest is as damnable as the biggest: but I made a country once. It was the country of redemption, somewhere this side of God's. It was the frontier of the first irrevocable compromise between the heart's freedom and the conscience's justice, past which the soul can still redeem itself." He clutches his head again and moans, "The blood."

There floods into his face the sound of every promise, the claim of every choice, the crash of his heart into his conscience and everything of himself that died from the collision, the stricken memory of happiness that abandoned him, the mourned wife and departed black fourteen-year-old lover, the shouts and gunshots of revolution, the shattered ideals in which even his own betrayal cannot stop him from believing; the ideals still believe him even as he can no longer believe them. And suddenly he appears ancient. Suddenly the misery sags his face and he can't decide which to hold, the racking thunder of his head or the red burn of his wrists, and he says, "I have to sleep." He pulls himself from the chair and gropes toward the bed. He can hardly move from the pain and stumbles in the glare of the room. He holds himself up against the far wall and lowers himself slowly onto the bed, and seems to float the rest of the way to the pillow, laying himself down beside her as Georgie watches in horror.

The revulsion that washes over the young Berliner, to see the old man lying in bed next to the one for whom Georgie's come so far, displaces exultation; rage nearly paralyzes him in his place. "What if she'd said yes," the old man whispers, trailing off; beneath their lids his eyes dart madly to dreams of his black slave queen emerging from the carriage in Virginia pregnant with his son, managing as the mistress of his house and lands. Georgie rises from his chair and stands looking down at the bed. "Liar," he says when he brings the last extant piece of the Wall crashing down on the old man's skull; the wound seems as tidy as it is fatal. It seems a full minute before the blood trickles from the old man's ears, though the eyes immediately stop darting, their dreams having shut off like a light. Georgie stands examining the tainted stone in his hand with sorrow, to see if some small part of its inscription has been left in the creases of the old man's brow or the roots of the white-fire hair. He sits down at the table still holding the stone and turns on the radio, but then returns to the bed.

The old man is bleeding more. For the first time the woman responds in her sleep to the room's turbulence, rearranging herself where she lies, confusion flashing across her sleep as she turns to Georgie for the first time. For the first time he actually sees her face. The ecstatic blackness that comes rushing up from her staggers him where he stands.

It isn't simply her blackness but her beauty that is the worst trick. He can deny neither her blackness nor beauty even as he's sure the one must deny the other. Her raven hair falls across her face, and in the corner of her mouth like a drop of wine is a word that begins to run down her chin; a tear waits beneath one fluttering lash. She lies lushly delivered of something she doesn't know and won't begin to suspect until she wakes from the dream that's now devouring her life, at which point only the devouring will be left. She doesn't suspect what's only moments beyond her eyelids. It's as though Georgie would deliver her from the waking world, as he's delivered Thomas to the last mad dream of his life, it's as though for something more than reprisal against the terrible trick of her beauty and blackness that Georgie lifts the piece of Wall once more in order to bring it crashing down onto Sally's head as well. Several times he raises the stone over her before he lowers his arm without striking. He's only slightly more confounded when she turns again and he sees dangling from her fingers, poised to fall beside her, the knife. He turns and walks out of the room into the hotel hallway, leaving the door open behind him. He walks down the hallway and the hotel stairs and through the empty lobby; the buzz of the distant TV becomes clearer.

Outside, in the dead calm of the city, he can smell the sea.

Now it's not even exhilaration and rage anymore, it's the bitterness of futility and the pointlessness of continuing, along with exhaustion and adrenaline and memory. Georgie sobs hysterically at the cruelty of his eyes that insisted on both her blackness and her beauty, at the treachery of a hand that couldn't kill either. As he wanders the dead of night from circle to circle and obelisk to obelisk, halfnaked and crying, it's a wonder he doesn't arouse the entire city; three hours later Dee, behind the bar of the Fleurs d'X, concludes from the look on Georgie's face that he's under the spell of a drug she's never seen before, brought from some city she's never heard of. He's stopped crying by now, but the look in his eyes makes uneasy the Fleurs d'X girls who have learned to be unnerved by nothing. It's also clear that the boy with the tattoos has no money, that he literally hasn't the shirt on his back. Dee sends over a shot of whiskey anyway, figuring Georgie will finally just pass out on the floor, from where he can be dragged down the hall and dropped down the stairwell.

Exhaustion and adrenaline, whiskey and memory whip Georgie back and forth between silent stupor and desperate outbursts. By deep into the evening he doesn't really know anymore who he is or where he is or how he got there; every once in a while he's aware of a naked woman presenting herself to his inspection but not his touch. The dream of room twenty-eight at the Crystal Hotel is far away. Girls keep putting shots of liquor in front of him as he babbles; sitting at the stage he's just sober enough to understand that when the girls dance the other men give them money. Two or three times Georgie actually searches his own pocket as though he's going to find something to offer.

This has been going on for a while when he feels a drop on his chest.

He looks up at the ceiling. "There's a leak," he mutters to no one. He momentarily grabs one of the girls by the wrist: "Got a leak up there," he slurs, staring into the dark above him. The girl thinks it means he's got to piss. He keeps running his hand across his belly and his chest to wipe something away but nothing's there, even though he feels the drops. He moves to another seat, but wherever he moves he feels something dripping, and the more he wipes his hands over his body the more frustrated he becomes to find nothing, not water or whiskey or blood, just drip drip drip. He cannot, in the dark of the Fleurs d'X, see the drops falling from the mouth of the woman with the head of a bird on his chest.

He feels the shudder in his shoulders of wings trying to break free, flapping.

There, at the side of the stage, a vision rises from the dark before him.

She rises from the dark on the other side of the stage, head first into the light until the light holds all of her, from the gold of her hair to the black stockings of her long legs; and Georgie knows that though she's not the Queen of Wands, she is the Woman in the Dark. If he were either a little less drunk or a little more he might reach out to fill one hand with one breast so as to measure it against the memory of room twenty-eight at the Crystal Hotel, what remnants of its memory remain. He would have her say the word America to see if it matches memory's echo, faint as it may now be. In the light she smiles at him like a child. None of the others have smiled like this. He's too naïve to understand that they haven't smiled because he has no money and they're waiting for him to intoxicate himself into oblivion, all he knows is that the Woman in the Dark is smiling at him and, for the first time in so long, nothing seems quite as hopeless. She's pure white and gold. There's not the flicker of blackness across her face. In the light she consumes his existence and leaves only the trace of his relief; he settles into a rapturous peace.

But something is happening in his shoulders. Something is happening on his chest. Somewhere in time a trolley disappears and an obelisk moves several feet; on a back alley official graffiti gives way to heresy written on a slab of Wall into which messages disappear one by one. Something is unraveling memory by memory, not only the memories of the moment but of the moments to come and the moments that have already come.

And for a moment, while there's still time, Georgie returns to his rapture. Shamed by her smile, shamed by his poverty, he places the piece of the Wall at her feet, the only thing he has to offer, entirely confident it must mean as much to her as it does to him. When the dance is over she picks up the stone and looks at it: there's something written, Georgie almost says to her, when she thanks him and disappears before he has the chance.

Raising his hands to his chest, he begins to scratch.

M a n y   y e a r s   l a t e r,   w a t c h i n g the new girl audition, Dee had completely forgotten the strange young man with the tattoos. But she did remember Wade, who thought he had come to the Fleurs d'X looking for a dead body and turned out to be looking for another kind of body altogether. Dee may not have remembered the first time Wade talked to Mona but she remembered the second, when he waited hours for her and kept throwing men out of their chairs, and she remembered the time he tore off his clothes and mauled one of the other customers who had shown too much interest in her, or perhaps it was that she had shown too much interest in him. At any rate, that was the night Mona disappeared forever, and the last time Dee ever saw Wade in the Fleurs d'X, though like everyone she'd heard the stories about the naked giant who wandered the Arboretum year after year searching for his lost dancer. And so from time to time she had occasion to be reminded of Wade even as the boy with the tattoos was blotted from memory within twenty-four hours of the cops' dragging from the back room his shredded corpse.

Halfway through the third and climactic part of the routine, the new girl auditioning for Dee finally balked. She froze midmusic and scooped up her clothes and rushed from the stage, standing off to the side of the club now, probably feeling like a fool. Oh God, don't start crying on me, Dee thought to herself, watching the dim form of the girl struggling in the shadows to regain composure. This was why Dee held auditions in the slow hours, when it was less overwhelming and the customers were at their least demanding; she wasn't surprised about this one, sharing the men's disappointment and the other dancers' relief, because this particular girl was the most beautiful to walk into the club for as long as Dee could remember, which was one of the things that had gotten Dee to remembering Mona and Wade. Beautiful girls often failed auditions because they weren't damaged enough or not damaged in the right way or too damaged in the wrong way, or not so innocent of damage they'd take off their clothes in the street for the fun of it, if fun were legal.

The new girl reminded Dee of Mona for the way she was beautiful and of Wade for the way she was a glimpse of black. She pulled on her white dress and turned in the dark, walking past the stage toward the bar. "Sorry," she muttered, half chastened and half defiant.

"Forget it," Dee said. "Maybe you're just not cut out for it. Why do you want to do this anyway?"

Once the sense of defeat passed, the girl didn't really look too crestfallen: damaged in the wrong way, Dee concluded. The girl's selfpossession, which had so dissolved in the glare of the stage light, slowly reasserted itself. She was tall and big-boned, gangly in her negotiations of light and shadow; stray genes wandered across her wild dark hair and liquid mouth, the blue in her eyes hijacked from some other eyes, the hair's transient glint of gold that ran the border at midnight from another country into her own. Every head in the Fleurs d'X had turned when she walked in, which was something Dee hadn't seen in a while; it took a lot to turn a man's head in a room full of naked women, or maybe the point was it didn't take much at all. The girl had been all bravado in the beginning, a little too much bravado in retrospect: she was accustomed to demanding the chance to prove herself. "I need the work," the girl answered.

"Yes, well, everyone needs the work," Dee said, "but people choose this kind of work for a reason. Maybe all your life you've been told you're beautiful. Maybe it's the only thing you know about yourself. But up there," she pointed at the stage, "you either didn't believe it or didn't care, it wasn't worth anything to you. Up there beautiful not only isn't everything, it isn't even the main thing." Dee guessed the girl had just arrived in the city. "Where's your family?"

"The theater," she answered, "on the other side."

"In the Arboretum?" For the first time tonight Dee was amazed, and in the Arboretum tonight was always a long time.

"I don't want to talk about my father," the girl said with such a hard look in her eyes that Dee immediately thought to herself, So that's what this is. We take off our clothes and humiliate daddy. And as if she'd read Dee's mind, the girl continued, "It has nothing to do with him. I've been looking for someone."

"And you thought you'd find him here?"

"All the men come here sooner or later, don't they?"

"Maybe yours already came through and moved on. Or maybe he won't come around for a while yet. You could take off your clothes for a lot of men waiting to take them off for one in particular."

The girl nodded.

"Does he know you're here?"

"I don't see how."

"I mean your father."

"No."

"Go home and forget it."

"I don't care if my father knows," the girl insisted. "I think this is about the only thing I could do that would bother him at all."

"Sounds like maybe this does have something to do with him."

"Thank you for giving me the chance," the girl said.

"Come back if you ever want another shot. The men would love you and the girls would get used to it."

From the Fleurs d'X the girl carried Dee's memory with her; with the snap of her fingers the two large gray dogs curled up against the wall followed. She returned to the theater where her father lived with the other actors; he didn't ask where she'd been. She didn't expect he would. Once or twice she considered bursting his self-absorption with an announcement, once or twice she thought some guy might stumble into the theater who just happened to have seen her feeble audition; he'd point her out and create a small furor, perhaps. Instead, in the silence of her stoicism, the seed of Dee's memory flowered in the girl's own consciousness until she recognized it one hour in the Arboretum corridor. It also recognized her.

She turned her corner as Wade, crazy with drugs and cognac

and loss, turned his. He was far more stunned by the sight of her than she was by him. What shocked her instead was when he said, with the strangest look on his face, "Sally?" and then said it again and started toward her until she shook herself free of the sight and sound of him and ran. The next time she saw him, she didn't run. She found him in a flat at the far end of the Arboretum lying in a heap against one wall. He was sweating profusely, mumbling nonsense and slipping in and out of consciousness. She approached and stood at his feet; when he opened his eyes, just cognizant enough to say the name again, she shook her head. "I'm not Sally," she answered. "Sally was my mother."

In his drunken haze, he narrowed his eyes to think. "Was?"

"I'm looking for a man," Polly said. "His name is Etcher."

She searched for him a year. She searched the Arboretum, sometimes returning to Fleurs d'X and the wary glances of the dancers; and then she left the Arboretum and began looking for him in the city. She wandered Downtown and the Market, occasionally sleeping in the street, and even spent a couple of nights in the same hotel, though not the same room, where her mother had awakened to a body many years before. It wasn't likely she was consciously retracing any steps when she walked up the rock to Church Central. Working in the archives was a priest only a few years older than she, no less alarmed by her than Etcher had been the first afternoon he saw Sally Hemings with Polly in tow; if anything, Polly's inquiry brought greater consternation. "You have to go now," the priest croaked, as though the name she'd spoken was reverberating upstairs at this moment and he would be held accountable.

She waited for the archives clerk at the bottom of the rock. When he emerged from Church Central one twilight on a bicycle, Polly followed. He carried a large bag in one arm. Slowly he rode through the city, leaving Downtown and heading east with Polly hurrying along behind at a distance, her big gray dogs dawdling behind her. He crossed the peripheral highway and began pedaling over the lava fields in the direction of the volcano; perhaps, as she followed, she was cloaked in darkness. Perhaps, as she followed, she was cloaked in the rage of her abandonment by the mother's death and the father's ego. Perhaps crossing the black fields under the light of the moon in her white dress she would have appeared to the priest, had he looked back, as nothing more than a ripped veil blown over the waves of a black sea, or a robe discarded by a priest at the foot of the road. But no one saw her or the dogs: had she dropped her dress in the midst of the fields and walked naked, in the cloak of her ashy skin, she could not have been more invisible. She never meant to be unseen. She meant, rather, to ask the priest the same question she had asked in the archives. He disappeared in the distance and then returned an hour or so later, gliding right past her as he headed back to the city. Under one arm, where he'd held the bag, he now clutched some papers.

Polly didn't turn back to the city but pressed onward. She reached the base of the volcano when light began to appear from the other side, and she made out the bicycle's track as it veered off to the north and ascended the mountain. The track ended in a rocky cove, where she found a red mailbox standing alone with no address or name. The mailbox was empty. At the base of the mailbox was the bag left by the priest; inside were bread and cheese and fruit, water and wine. Her dogs, now thirsty and tired, sniffed at the bag. Polly left it and continued up the trail to the volcano. Not long before noon she reached the highest ridge of the volcano in time to meet the sun coming up the other side. Behind her she could see all of the lava fields and Aeonopolis beyond them and the sea beyond it, the zipper of the train's tracks heading up the coast. South of the city where the beach twisted was the penal colony, attached to the landscape like a leech.

Below her was the crater. It smelled of sulfur. On the far east side oozed the white molten part of the mountain, the surrounding ground dead except for an occasional shrub or flower, a whimper of green from the black lava. Just inside the crater's edge, teetering on a volcanic shelf, a tiny hut seemed to grow out of the rock. As the panting dogs ran ahead, sniffing at the crater in search of a lake to drink from, Polly sat watching for some time, once or twice deciding on retreat before she convinced herself she'd come too far to give up. The day began to slide toward the city and the sea.

She made her way through the shadows of the crater toward the house.

When she came to the door she knocked quickly, leaving herself no time to change her mind.

Her knock went unanswered. She opened the door and pushed it ajar. "Hello?" she began to call, but it caught in her throat. She stepped into the house. A mattress lay in the corner not far from an unused stove. On the other side of the hut a box of dishes and utensils crumbled beneath the sink. Above the sink a cupboard sagged with the weight of wine bottles that threatened to tumble off any moment and shatter; Polly counted twenty or thirty empty ones rolling along the floor with little red puddles inside. On the other side of the room was another doorway.

A desk sat in the center of the second room, so buried beneath papers and manuscripts and writing implements that not a square inch of the surface showed through. Behind the desk was a shelf of books in old red covers. The binding of the volumes had been ripped apart and the pages were torn and loose, as though attacked by a wild animal. Covering the wall facing the desk was a huge map. Only after she'd studied it some time did Polly understand it was a diagram of the city. Lines were drawn in frantic flourishes from one end of the map to the other, from the volcano in the east to Church Central in the west to a place just north of the city boundaries, which examination revealed to be the Arboretum, crossing at a point of no distinction, a small alley off the Downtown streets of Desolate and Unrequited. Some zones were clearly designated—Sorrow and Ambivalence and Humiliation—and others not, the most confused being the name Redemption, which the map's author had replaced with Desire, only to cross that out and rewrite Redemption, only to obliterate the first again for the second until all that was left was a crazed blotch of confirmation and denial.

Polly stood looking at the havoc when, without hearing a sound, she knew someone else was in the room. It took several seconds to find the courage to peer over her shoulder. The shadow of the volcano's ridge rumbled across the floor from the outer doorway to billow up at his feet and engulf him, until all she could be sure of was the cobalt blue of his eyes, as close to the blue of her own as she'd ever seen. They loomed all the larger behind his glasses.

It was the only thing of him she recalled immediately; his life had long since been cut loose of not only her memory but his own. His clothes were tattered and filthy. His black hair was splattered with white and gray and, at two or three inches shorter than her father, he might have seemed smaller than she remembered if his humanity hadn't imploded long before to leave the huge void of him howling at everything within range. The reek of him was more than wine and dirt, it was the stink of a life that had died years before, briefly preserved in ice but having begun its mortifying thaw just in time for her to greet the remains. There was nothing merciful about his impact, nothing compassionate or caring or reachable. She tried to say something. "My name is—"

"Yes," he said. His eyes finally left her, to assess the situation of his books and papers.

"I didn't touch anything," she promised, though she couldn't imagine how anyone would know, or whether he cared. Taking one or two steps he kicked papers on the floor beneath his feet. He went over to the chair behind the desk and sat down. He paid her no more attention, staring instead at the disarray before him and reaching below the desk to fumble for and hoist up a bottle of wine, which he poured into a dirty glass. She kept waiting for him to say something, even as she tried to think of what to say to him. But he just sat drinking his wine, pouring himself another glass and then another, shuffling about his desk in the dark of the room for a page he could have found only by some mad system. When he lit a candle on the desk and picked up a pen and began to write as though she weren't there, still not saying a word to her except the yes that had evolved over the minutes into a no, having in the process completely banished her from his awareness, she raised her hand to her mouth to stifle a sob. Turning, she ran from the room.

She almost ran from the hut and the volcano but got as far as the front door. The voice that called her back wasn't his but her own; she slid along the door to the floor and cried, wondering if there was anywhere in time she belonged. The exhaustion of the previous night caught up with her and she fell asleep. It was some time after she awoke in the dark, it was some time after she woke to the red glow that came through the window and she remembered she was sleeping in a volcano, that she also remembered she had passed out by the front door but was now lying on the mattress. In the dark of the night and the glow of the mountain she sat up and searched for a sign of Etcher in the room with her. When she couldn't find him she went back to sleep.

He wasn't there either when she woke the next morning, and he didn't show up until the late afternoon when he came walking over the ridge of the volcano from the west. He was dressed in the same terrible clothes and carried in his arms the bag of food left at the red mailbox on the other side of the mountain. In the hut Etcher didn't say a word, he didn't look at Polly at all; but when he put some fruit from the bag in a dusty bowl to set on the floor by the mattress where she'd slept, and she reached to take it from him, he flinched at her hand as though it held a weapon or was raised to accuse him. He hurried into the other room, closing the door behind him. The rest of the day passed without his reappearance.

Over and over she told herself to leave. Every time she convinced herself to go, she convinced herself to stay. She took walks with the dogs around the volcano but mostly stayed close to the house, in case he should emerge from the back room. She had hoped to charm him or ingratiate herself, something she'd been good at since she was small, but he gave her no opportunity. The next day went by and then the next, without one word exchanged between them. As the days passed, her white dress became darker and darker until it was black, and Etcher drank more and more wine until by nightfall she'd look out the window of the house to see him dallying precariously on the crater's edge, as though daring sobriety to prevent his toppling over. Any moment she was prepared to rush and save him, except that she remembered how he had flinched at the sight of her hands that first day and she was afraid if she sprang to retrieve him he'd take a fatal step back. Eventually he always wound up, by his own maneuvers, asleep in the chair behind the desk, while she lay on the mattress thinking of the Arboretum. By now she knew her father had noticed her absence. By now she assumed her father had noticed some part of him was missing, like a limb or an eye; he'd raised one of his arms by now to blithely observe that the appendage usually found at the end was replaced by a stump. She couldn't be sure which tormented her more, that he might be wrenched by the discovery she was gone or indifferent to it.

On the third day Polly followed Etcher in the early hours of morning as he set out on another walk to the red mailbox. From the highest summit she watched him leave the papers he'd written the previous night, to be picked up by the priest on the bicycle, who left in return the bag of food and water and wine. Often Etcher seemed so drunk or hungover that Polly couldn't see how he got beyond the hut's porch, let alone all the way over the top of the mountain; and one morning after she'd been there a week, when he still hadn't said a single word to her beyond that first yes, she found him snoring in his chair behind the desk with the night's tortured pages wadded in his fists. She took the pages and smoothed them out on the floor and set off with the dogs for the mailbox.

Hours later she met Etcher on the way back, huffing and puffing up the side of the crater. Within twenty feet of her he stopped, his furious magnified eyes regarding the bag of food in her arms. "I took the papers to the mailbox for you," she said. He answered this news with more of his black silence, approaching to take the bag from her. "I can carry it," she assured him, and for a moment they tussled over the bag until he grabbed it away. He turned back toward the house and she followed in a hush. She had resolved over the course of the days and nights that she wouldn't go until he told her to. She would outrage him from his wordlessness, if she had to. At the house, in the doorway, he suddenly turned to her.

"Where's your father?" he said.

"Behind me," she said, and he looked over her shoulder at the volcano's horizon, but then realized that wasn't what she meant. He went on inside the hut. She believed the opportunity was at hand: "I can barely remember you," she said, directing her words straight at the past. "That's good," he answered, and ripped the bag ferociously to liberate some bread at the bottom, taking a bottle of wine from the cupboard above the sink and storming into the back room. For several minutes she stood staring at the closed door, trying to talk her anger into bursting through it and confronting him.

She had a dream that night in which a dead woman who looked much like her lay on the mattress in the corner of the hut where Polly herself was now sleeping. How the woman had died wasn't clear, and for a moment, when she seemed to turn her head, Polly thought perhaps the woman was alive after all; then the woman disappeared, and Polly's relief gave way to the certainty that the disappearance and not the death was the delusion. At the end of the dream Polly had the strangest impression she was dead herself, even though her life didn't yet understand this: the circumstances of her life had gone so awry that ending it seemed the only viable option. Everything in the dream simply seemed so hopeless and involved such futility that suicide wasn't an emotional decision but a practical one; she didn't want to do it but was overwhelmed by the feeling that it was the only out.

When she woke, it was as though a noise had awakened her. But the hut was still and she felt entirely alienated from her dream, until she realized it wasn't hers: rather this dream had smuggled itself from the other room, slipping through the doorway and across the floor to the mattress, where it invaded her ear and ate its way voraciously into her mind. She could see its form in the dark of the hut, like a crustacean from the lava sea outside skittering across the room. The dogs on the porch whimpered and sniffed at the door. Then there was the abrupt crash of glass in the back room, which gave way to a strange commotion, and she jumped from the mattress and pushed opened the back door, where she half expected to find a battle taking place between Etcher and some beast lurking in the shadows.

Wine ran down the large map on the opposite wall where he'd thrown first the glass, then the bottle. The glass had broken and the bottle lay at the base of the wall gurgling out the remains of its contents. He sat hunched over the desk with his face in his hands and, as though gripped by a seizure, suddenly flailed at the desk so recklessly that the candle was about to tip over and set everything on fire. Polly grabbed the candle. Light darted over the room. In the darting light Etcher didn't look up, he didn't move his hands; his glasses lay on the papers in front of him. In the privacy of his hands he said, "Do you know what it does to me to see you?" She had to clutch the candle hard to keep from dropping it; he still wouldn't show himself, he still wouldn't look at her. "To see *her* face looking at me over your shoulder . . ."

"I'm sorry," Polly said.

"You're sorry?" and that released him. His hands fell to the desk and his cheeks were streaked and flushed. "You're sorry for your *face?*" The force of his fury seemed to raise him up from where he sat, though in fact he didn't move at all; in his blind eyes, their glasses still lying on the desk, flashed the last freak moment left of a vision's halflife from years before, when he loved Polly's mother and saw everything. "She must have been sorry every day of her life," he said in a furious whisper. "I must have heard her say she was sorry more times than I could count. She was sorry for her face and she was sorry for her heart, she was sorry for the way everyone told her she had something to be sorry for. She was sorry for the right choices and sorry for the wrong ones and sorry for not knowing which was which, which was almost all of the time. She was sorry for me and she was sorry for the others, but she was never sorry enough for herself except when it was time not to be sorry anymore. Are you here for revenge?"

"Wh-what?"

"It's a waste of time, if you've come for revenge. It's a waste of time, if you've come to hate me. Because there's no hate you can muster half as good as mine. No revenge you can take half as final as me getting up from this chair and walking out that door and off the edge of the precipice into the fire, a course of action I consider daily, or perhaps it's hourly. Do you want to be the one who pushes me?"

"I . . ."

"Come on then," he said, rising from the chair. He leapt around the desk and grabbed her by the wrist; she screamed, nearly dropping the candle. He pulled her through the front room and out of the house across the porch, past the dogs out onto the ledge, the red mist hanging in the night around them.

"Please," she begged.

"Do you remember the train ride back, after she died?" A thousand times over the years he must have told himself he was over her. A thousand times in response he must have called himself a liar. Like a wild animal that returns to a habitat it's never known, but which is its natural one nonetheless, Etcher had come to the mouth of the volcano, and now overlooking the lava he staggered as though to slip over. She screamed again, pulling him back. "It went on forever, all the way back to the city, and you wouldn't talk to me except to say, like you had a hundred times before, 'I'm not your friend.' And then on the station platform you ran to your father and he picked you up in his arms and took you away, and I waited for you to look back at me just once, and you never did. And I knew I'd lost both of you."

"I was just a little girl."

"I didn't mean to kill her," he cried. In the sheen of the fire his eyes grew wide with the sound of it, as though he could see the admission floating in front of him over the crater, and he wanted to reach out from the void of his life and pull it back.

"You didn't kill anyone," she pleaded. "Please come away from the edge."

"I meant to save her, like I did before."

"You couldn't save her either. You didn't kill her and you couldn't save her."

"I was supposed to take care of you. She said, Take care of Polly, and I let him take you."

"He was my *father,* Etcher. And I was just a little girl. And I don't remember much of what happened except that you loved my mother, even then I knew that, and that's why I've come back. And if you hate yourself now then you let me down when I need you most, when I need you to tell me all the things about her that my father won't or can't because he never really knew her, when I need to know there was someone in our lives who loved us more than his own life, and that was you. So you have to come away from the fire now, and tell me. Please."

In the glow of the crater, his face in his hands, he wept. The tears ran through his fingers and down to the ragged sleeves of his shirt. When he finished and came away from the fire he seemed very old to the girl, as though his legs would buckle beneath him, and there was enough of the father in her to find selflessness a revelation, to find the human burden of carrying an old man away from the fire a frightening thing to accept. She sat against the wall as he slept, not at his desk but on the mattress at her feet, spent of his nightmares that plopped one after another from his brain to the floor, scattering helplessly for shelter.

W h e n   h e   l e f t the city, the beggars followed.

He had returned in broad daylight years before, met by neither cops nor priests, who were only beginning to adjust to the trauma of his escape and therefore hardly expected his reappearance. In the voggy glare of midafternoon, under the eyes of the city, he moved himself and the red books to the volcano, and only the beggars took note, the beggars who had zeroed in on his unguarded conscience from every alley and corner, in the midst of every crowd. Now they poured into the streets from the curbs and door-ways, following along behind not to beg anything more of him but simply to say goodbye, the broken army of the city's forsaken standing at the edge of town alongside the peripheral highway silently watching him disappear into the lava fields. It was only this demonstration that alerted the authorities of Aeonopolis, half a day late, that Etcher had again slipped in and out of their grasp. As the Arboretum had long since proved, authority was never partic-ularly equipped for dealing with audacity.

Larger audacities were to confront them.

Page by page, Etcher was rewriting the books.

Page by page he left the Unexpurgated Volumes of Unconscious History in the red mailbox at the volcano's base, as had been ar-ranged with the Church; what had not been arranged was that, leaf by leaf, each was transformed by him. As the years passed, the precarious placement of the volumes on the shores of the crater's fire, where Etcher might drop them one by one into the lava, un-raveled the nerves of the priests while discouraging the plans of police to swoop down on the tiny house and seize what was in it. Etcher had taken the lessons of stalemate to the ultimate edge of stalemate, and then began to write. He wrote every day that he didn't throw himself into the crater with as many of the books as his arms could carry.

He did it because, having not had a single night since her death when he didn't dream of her, having plummeted into the dark hole of his heart, all he could find in his control was history. As his heart had been undone, as he would undo his own memory in some pointless effort to forget her, he would now undo history minute by minute, detail by detail. He gave history its false cues, he misspoke its passwords. In his rewritten history bombs failed to detonate, assassins' guns misfired in the theater. Secret tunnels were dug from the killing grounds of the Commune by which escaped whole revolutions; invasions were distracted by the pornographic obsessions of dictators. Motorcades were delayed by a flat tire. The earth of Etcher's new history shimmered with the fission of reactor meltdowns, and wars that had once ended in four years went on for forty. Hard moral lessons were corrupted. The conscience of history became as relative as its science, and memory became a factor of expedience in the equation of power.

Complicit in Etcher's assault were the priests themselves, who gave no indication they understood the revisions. Perhaps they actually believed it didn't matter, as long as the books were returned to their vault where they might again become sacred. Likelier they suppressed their worst suspicions, flinging the returned pages back into the dark and lunging the door closed behind them to secure the books not from thieves but themselves, who might come to know what they couldn't stand to know. Likeliest was that the priests had rarely read the history in the first place and wouldn't have known it was not the same even if they bothered to read it now. Rummaging in the heart's basement, stepping into history through the doorway of the heart as the second hand hurtled toward midnight, perhaps not unlike the priests Etcher believed he would find a resurrection. Not his own, since he didn't believe in that anymore, but hers, since hers was his anyway. Failing such a discovery he thrived on the energy of destruction and anarchy until the night of his confession to Polly, at which point he thrived on her. At least for a while the mad storm of his work calmed. The molten flow of the mountain receded into the earth and the fire of the volcano cooled to embers, around which the old man and the girl circled to stories of her mother, which often broke down early in the telling.

He would compose himself and begin again. Sometimes they talked so long into the night that history, for a night, passed unviolated, returned to the red mailbox intact and without changes,

though in new contexts from changes that had come before. Etcher
drank less. And then, from the choke in her voice at the mention
of her father, he knew that sooner or later Polly would leave, that
her fury at her father was the defiance of a heartbreak that sooner
or later must reconcile itself to the source. And that was when he
knew she'd go back to her father because she couldn't leave as far
behind as she might have hoped or believed the little girl who had
run to her father on the station platform, who adored him more
than anyone else in the world and always would. So once more
Etcher began to drink. Once more he began to write. He was back
in the heart's doorway, passing through to seek its most malevolent
possibility. If he could not, once more, find a resurrection, he
would locate a trapdoor instead, a lever to pull through which
Gann Hurley would plummet to oblivion. But though he might actually find such a trapdoor, though he might actually find such a
lever, the fact was that this was *his* heart, not Polly's, where her
father was safe and untouchable, arrogantly secure, forever protected from even his daughter's own rage.

In the back room he wrote faster and more furiously. At first he
thought, on the night the knock came on the door, that it was the
pounding in his own head; and when he realized it was not in his
own head, when he realized it wasn't Polly banging around in the
other room or the dogs sniffing at the residue of wine in the empty
bottles, he assumed any other possibility but the fantastic truth.
He assumed it was the clerk from Central on his bicycle, though
the clerk had never before passed the red mailbox. He assumed it
was the cops. He assumed it was Hurley, who had come for his
daughter. When Etcher called out the girl's name and then called
again, and went into the front room where Polly was frozen in the
open doorway, he never assumed it would be Sally Hemings standing there on the porch outside, on the eve of a choice that would
change everything, staring aghast into Polly's face, which stared
back. The mother, at fourteen, was several years younger than the
daughter.

He nearly fainted.

Polly rushed as though to catch him but he caught himself, gazing
from one girl to the other. Since the thing that terrified him most
wasn't simply her ghost but how in the doorway Sally looked at

him as though she'd never seen him before, he said her name
almost as a question. It didn't entirely get past his lips, part of it
caught in that doorway of the heart where it had lingered so long.

Sally turned from the door. She ran past the gray dogs curled on
the porch, up the side of the crater toward the ridge of the mountaintop. She ran down the other side of the mountain toward the
lava fields. She hadn't a thought in her head of water or prison or
slavery; later she would have liked to believe it was a dream, she'd
have given anything to believe it was a dream. But at this moment
she knew it wasn't a dream and so she ran parched and exhausted
and half out of her mind. She never looked back at the crater or
the house or Polly standing in the doorway watching her go; when
she finally reached the bottom of the volcano she went on running
and stumbling across the black plain. Sometime in the night a
wagon picked her up. Sometime in the night she felt and heard
beneath her the turning of wheels; she felt and tasted on her lips
the trickle of water. Into the night she didn't dream or think at all.
The wagon took her back to Paris.

In the early hours of morning she pulled herself off the back of
the wagon. She wandered aimlessly as she'd done the night she
buried the carving knife in what she believed was Thomas' sleeping body back on the rue d'X. Pulled by the tides of the city, Sally
returned to the center of the Parisian moment: the black prison
with eight towers, which the revolution had stormed forty hours
before. Smoke still hung on the square. Blood had long since overcome the scent of lilac from the broken window of the perfume
shop. People streamed freely across the prison drawbridge in and
out of the prison gate; high on the dark red pikes that surrounded
the square were the heads of garrison soldiers. Women wept over
the cobblestones where their men had died. Moving from widow
to widow, talking to them, holding them in comfort, was Thomas.

Sally watched for some time. To each of the women Thomas
gave some money. It reminded her of when she was a little girl and
one day had seen him seize the whip from a man beating a slave.
She sat dazed in the street amid the glass of the perfume-shop
window; pieces of glass glittered in the dawn sun. Finally he saw
her. In the smoke he stood staring at her. When he came toward
her she couldn't help but find his judgment terrifying. He looked at
the glass all around her and said, "You're going to cut yourself,"

and picked her up and caught himself on a shard in the folds of the tattered dress he'd bought her; together they watched his hand bleed. As he carried her in his arms she tore from her dress a long strip and wrapped it around his hand. She wanted to sleep in his arms but said, "Put me down."

He put her down. Her knees buckled beneath her and he had to catch her from falling in the street. She pulled herself from his arms and began walking away. "You're too weak to walk," he said.

"No."

"You have nowhere to go."

"Your hand's bleeding," she said; "you should go home."

"If you leave now you'll never see your family again. You'll never see America again. You'll be in a strange country forever, with strange people and a strange language you don't know—"

"I'll learn."

"In Virginia you will be the mistress of my house. The queen of my bed." He ran after her.

She turned to confront him. "I would just try to kill you again," she said. "I'd keep trying until I did."

"Where do you suppose you'll go? How will you live?"

She resumed walking from the square down the winding street. This is the way to the river, she thought to herself. She heard him behind her.

"You belong to me," she heard him say.

"Not anymore."

"You belong to me," he asserted, "I'll take you back forcibly. I'll put a price on your head and shackle you naked in the cabin of my ship like the property you are. Sally."

"Goodbye."

"Sally?"

She kept walking. The river is this way, she told herself. The smell of gunpowder wafted by.

"Sally," he called from the top of the street. Above her she saw windows opening at the sound of his voice and people sticking their heads out to look. "Sally!" The violence of his voice was unbearable. In all her life she'd never heard him raise it. In confrontations with kings and revolutionists and priests and slaves alike, in his angriest, most determined and demanding moments, she had never heard his voice rise to a shout but rather fall to a whisper, except for that sound he made on the death of his wife, that word-less abysmal sound that sent Sally at the age of nine running from the deathbed. Down into the winding center of the city she made herself walk on, not daring to stop let alone look back at the figure of the tall man screaming her name at the top of the street littered with glass and blood.

He did not follow her, though she might have expected him to, or even hoped it. All that followed was her legend, which swept her along in its path through the riots and famine, massacres and purges, around fountains and under archways, beneath streetlights and over bridges and past cafés of swirling leaflets and ringing declarations: she moved through the Revolution like a shudder. She was the ultimate insurrectionist, who had liberated herself of the world's greatest revolutionary, leaving him proclaiming his ownership and crying her name. Her eyes did not lose the druggy glow of her dreams. She did not take off the fine dress he once bought for her, now spattered with blood that many insistently mistook for the carnage of the Bastille even as it was in fact from Thomas' own hand. Her legend swept her from the flat-topped smoking mountain of her vision, where she saw the daughter she never had, to the Mountain of the convention hall, where the new Republic's leaders sat against one wall overlooking the wreckage of their wrath, Sally on the top tier in a gown of blood that became brown with years, the black muse of a new calendar with a choice she never made lying in rubble at her feet, the throne of a Queen of Slaves rejected for a revolution's realm.

On the top tier of the Mountain, the squalling deputies of the convention below them debating the law of a new era and whether under that law blood flowed uphill, Maximilien sat on one side of Sally and on the other Georges, whom Sally called Jack. They were hyena and lion respectively. In the mornings she stared at Maxi-milien across his sitting chamber, waiting for whatever inspiration would unlock him from his impotence; because Maximilien meant to be a god the prospect of an erection only terrified him, every failure only convincing him anew of how godlike he was. Because Jack had no interest in being a god he slipped Sally from Maximi-lien's bedroom in the dead of night and fucked her heartily, return-ing her to his rival's chaste contemplation by sunup. I've exchanged a complete American revolutionary for a couple of half-finished

French ones, Sally laughed to herself one rainy afternoon, wondering if the two added up to something more or less than the one. She was watching, for what must have been the thousandth time, the earthbound glide of the guillotine in the place de la Concorde. In the gray wet sky the blade gleamed like a dead star doomed to fall from space again and again. When her ecstasy reached the point of delirium, when in her mind she had brought the knife down into Thomas' body so many times she just couldn't do anything more to free herself of him, Sally returned from the guillotine one twilight to stand in Maximilien's atrium, her dress soaked with more blood than could ever dry to brown in a lifetime. Blood was on her hands, blood was smeared across her face. Maximilien appeared in the archway and looked at her. "What kind of monster have I become?" she asked him.

"You've become," was his cool answer, "the symbol of the Revolution's glory, its purity of purpose and pitiless justice."

"It's enough blood, Maxime. It's been more than enough."

"There's yet another head to drop," he advised. "So take your animal pleasure from him tonight while he's still around to give it."

It took every argument and entreaty, every tactic and ruse for Sally to persuade Jack to flee France that night and save his own life. Finally it took her promise to go with him, since he insisted he would not go without her. They lived together in London not far from the house of the American couple where Sally had stayed her first night after crossing the Atlantic five years before. What was left of the Eighteenth Century passed in Sally's whispered counsel and Georges' underground manifestos smuggled to France, where with his departure the Revolution had been deprived of its last chance to consume itself. With the collapse of the Bonaparte Putsch of '98 and the beheading of its leader, and the Revolution's uninterrupted metamorphosis into totalitarian state, Jack lost heart, trying to pinpoint where everything had gone wrong, when the Revolution had first foreshadowed the terrorist tenet of the modern age, which holds that freedom is not the ideal of the slave but the luxury of the bourgeois, that one is not a victim in spite of his innocence but because of it, because the terrorist holds innocence to be the guiltiest and most contemptible of political infractions.

Mostly, in the tradition of all egoists, Jack mourned his own irrelevance. Sally could not mistake his resentment toward her for it, how he held her accountable; in retrospect he would rather have given up his neck than his place in history, though he could bear to give up neither if it meant relinquishing his claims on her body. "My God," he sputtered one night in an exceptionally lucid moment, "does all of history think with its dick?" His happiest moment may well have been his last, on the eve of the Nineteenth Century, when he discovered that history remembered him after all. A stranger entered a tavern where he found Jack having supper. Throwing wide his arms the stranger exclaimed, in French, "Can this honor actually be mine? Is it really the great Danton I see before me?" and before Sally could take the ale from her mouth to warn him, Jack, literally flattered to death, expansively allowed as how he indeed was that person. The stranger smiled, pulled a pistol from under his cloak and blew Jack halfway across the room. Three other diners rose from their tables to reveal themselves as revolutionary grenadiers. "By the judgment of the Committee on Public Safety," the stranger pronounced to Jack's dead body, and then turned to the shocked twenty-five-year-old Sally: "Citizen Robespierre sends for you, madame." Six hours later she was crossing the Channel back to France.

As it happened, her reunion with Maximilien was limited to his image on the edifices and banners and statues of Paris, where he had become deity of the Revolution's secular religion. Sally and her guards arrived at the Luxembourg Palace just in time to hear the news that, at the moment the assassin's bullet shattered Jack's chest, Maximilien had clutched his own heart with a cry and tumbled from his seat at the very summit of the Mountain. Only the rush of several flacks to the podium of the convention hall broke the fall, prolonging life one more day until its final agonizing rupture. In her carriage the soldier who had shot Jack took the news with relative calm. "Robespierre is dead. Citizen Saint-Just is Dictator now," he announced. "May I drop you elsewhere, madame?" and Sally allowed as how she'd just as soon be taken across the river to the Hotel Langeac. By the time her carriage reached the rue d'X her legend had transformed yet again, from the woman who had declined a queendom of slaves and a place as mistress of the Revolution to become instead a subversive's whore. Perpetuating this legend was not the folly of her choice but the sanguine conviction of it. In the Hotel Langeac she had a room with a fireplace and a four-poster bed, and a window that pointed the other direction from where Thomas' balcony had looked the night he watched her run from the hotel for the last time as his slave. At night she could see from her window the streetlights of the boulevards in the distance and the carriages that brought the men to her. They left her gifts, small porcelain figures and little snowstorms imprisoned in crystal balls which adorned the shelf of her room.

During the day she made jewelry, necklaces and earrings, and recalled her greatest creation. I invented a country, she had heard Thomas say, with the arrogance of a man who thinks it's the business of men to make countries and the business of women to make jewelry. But it had taken her all her life to realize it was she who made the country and that the country had always been hers to make, that it waited for either her yes or no that afternoon in the place de la Bastille so as to be born one thing or the other, as an embryo waits for one chromosome or another to be born man or woman. It had taken all her life to hope that in saying no, thus denying herself the chance ever to see her country again, she had made it a purer thing. But she wasn't so sure about purity anymore, having survived a revolution so obsessed with purity of conscience that its heart had gone first to stone, then to dust, before scattering to nothing.

She couldn't be so sure about America either. A visiting mystic brought her news in the first year of the Nineteenth Century about the slave wars and the mad philosopher general who led them after he'd sold himself to his own slaves in bondage. "No more," Sally said, "I don't want to hear any more." But when her visitor was leaving and she extracted from him the obligatory gift, she begged that it be something of America; and though there was no real way for her to be certain that the deck of cards he produced was an American Tarot, as he insisted, she took his word for it, convinced of the momentousness of the sacrifice when the owner gave up a single card, without which none of the deck's other seventy-seven had meaning. Tacking the Queen of Wands to her bedchamber wall, she looked at it the last thing on going to sleep at night and the first thing on waking in the morning and, lost in its message in between, every night and every morning for the next thirty-four years until the day she died in the Hotel Langeac on the rue d'X at the age of sixty-two. The year was 1835, or year XLIII of what was once called the Revolution but which Maximilien had renamed before his death, with the obvious self-referential implications, the Deliverance.

In 1790 her legend swept Thomas home. Halfway across the sea the ship's crew became alarmed to find Thomas missing from his cabin and nowhere on deck. He was finally located in the ship's hull, looking for the deepest and coolest place to soothe the blinding pain in his head. When he wouldn't leave the hull, living there like a rat all the way back to America, James Hemings took over Thomas' cabin, sleeping in Thomas' bed and eating Thomas' meals, reading Thomas' books and drinking Thomas' wine, making the arrangements for the rest of the voyage. At the harbor in Norfolk the ship was met by a carriage with black window shades, behind which a semiconscious Thomas hid from sunlight and America in equal measure.

When he reached home and his slaves turned out to welcome the carriage's return, their enthusiasm dissolved into confusion as minutes passed into hours with no one emerging while the carriage sat in front of the house. Again and again James would open the carriage door and peer in, the slaves watching as whispers passed back and forth between driver and unseen passenger, each exchange concluding with James shutting the door and the master declining to appear. Occasionally the slaves would lend the situation an increasingly tepid cheer as though to encourage Thomas out of the carriage; but finally the crowd simply dispersed, returning to their labors, the carriage left alone in the yard. Darkness fell. James unhitched the horses. He spent the rest of the evening with his mother, to whom he broke the news that she would never see her daughter again. Whether it was her wails of despair or simply the cold dead of night that inspired Thomas to make an escape, in the morning the slaves found the carriage open and empty, and word spread over the plantation that the master was finally in the house.

The country was riveted by the news of Thomas' return. Its elite flocked to his porch only to find themselves rudely rebuffed by James, who announced to all that the master would be receiving no one. The plea of the country's government that Thomas accept a seat of power went unanswered except for the laughter heard coming from the house's darkest quarters. James ran the affairs of the plantation as he had managed the business of the oversea voyage. Several years passed. One summer day an erstwhile visitor to the plantation, undeterred by the rumors of the Monticello Madness, rode up within sight of the house on a far hill and found his way blocked by a particularly grisly wall of wood and wire and thistle. It was the sort of fence constructed not as demarcation but barricade. Much more astonishing, the wall was guarded by armed slaves. "See here, boy," the visitor ordered one, "let me pass that I may have an audience with Mr. Jefferson." The slave cocked his musket with an aim as true as the light in his eyes. "Beyond this point is Free Virginia, your fucking majesty," the black guard answered. "Go let your horse shit somewhere else."

Free Virginia? the man thought in horror riding away. By nightfall Richmond had heard and by dawn the rest of the nation. By week's close the realization that Thomas' plantation had been transformed into an armed compound was supplemented by bulletins of arriving black guerrillas from Haiti and Santo Domingo slipping through the South Carolina coast. By the end of the month the world knew that a slave army of hundreds, perhaps thousands, led by their silent pale general, was camped in the heart of America. By the last days of summer the terrified white citizenry was mobilizing in haste as the country's new president went to Virginia to talk to an old friend.

The president arrived at dusk in a carriage of his own, protected by superfluous guards who could be made short work of by the black troops that spread over the hills beyond the barricades. Watching from his carriage window the president saw bonfires on the knolls, cotton fields completely uprooted and cleared away for training grounds, free blacks and former slaves with guns and what had once been the plantation slave quarters converted to barracks, food bins and munitions sheds. A white flag flew from the president's carriage top. Another white flag was draped across his chest, though whether it provided a better target than sanctuary became a joke that traveled so quickly among the slavesoldiers that James Hemings had already heard it by the time the president reached the door of the house.

The house was utterly dilapidated. Doors hung on their hinges and shutters from the windows. Vines from the growth outside slid through the guest chambers like snakes. The ballroom had been gutted to become a strategy room, with a huge topography of the countryside laid out on a table and a flurry of markers depicting lines of attack so ominous the president averted his eyes, afraid he'd see something that jeopardized his life. "Doesn't matter, Mr. President," James assured him, "nothing there your white ass would understand anyway." James led the president deeper into the house until they came to a back room where two armed sentries stepped aside to let them pass.

The dead smell of the room was overpowering. The president stood in the dark long enough to believe his eyes would never adjust to it. A dim form finally began to appear on the other side of the room. "Could you please light a candle?" came a familiar whisper to the form of a second guard, who lit a candle to reveal the form of yet a third guard. The white flag on the president's chest soaked up the candlelight like a sponge, glowing back. "Hello, John," the man seated on the other side of the room whispered.

The president stepped forward. "My God, Thomas," he answered.

"How's the country these days?" Thomas didn't look directly at the president but shielded his eyes from the dull throb of the pinpoint of candlelight.

"The headaches," John surmised, remembering.

"It's not even a headache anymore, John. There are rare moments when the pain actually goes away, I mean *moments,* ten or fifteen seconds, and you know what I think when that happens? For those ten or fifteen seconds I'm afraid I've died, because it's the only thing I can imagine taking away the pain. It's become the kind of pain that reminds me I'm alive."

"The country is damned terrified, to answer your question. Are you planning to take over with your slaves? You never fooled me about your appetite for power, Thomas. The others, Abigail, well, she's always been irrationally fond of you, with a preternatural faith in that part of you that was always so good at being all things to all men. But you resent it that I'm president, I know that. It's been like this between us ever since we've been friends. You resent it deeply." He whined, "I *deserve* to be president." He stepped closer. "What the hell has happened to you?"

The tawny circle of the candlelight widened now to reach Thomas' brow, and it was with a shock that John then saw the other man was naked.

"Thomas," he croaked, his throat becoming thick, to which Thomas raised his hand to his eyes once more and John heard the clanking of the chains and saw the shackles on his wrists. "Oh no," he said. He looked at the two armed guards standing to each side of the naked white man. "Oh no, Thomas." He looked around him for James Hemings, unsure whether he was still in the dark of the room by the door. Vehemently he cried at the two guards, "This is an abomination. This is an outrage." He lunged at Thomas as though to rip him free of the chains, but Thomas raised his hand just a half a second behind the guards raising their guns; whether Thomas was signaling John to stop in his tracks or the guards to refrain from shooting John wasn't clear, perhaps even to Thomas.

"Please, John. My head hurts badly enough. No one has taken me prisoner. I sold myself."

"What?" said the president.

"It was all above board. As legal as a transaction can be." He turned to one of the guards. "Is there any wine?" he said. "Would you like some wine, John?" The guards didn't move or answer. "I can't take this light anymore, please snuff the candle." The guard on Thomas' left leaned forward and, with a quick puff, blew the room back into darkness. Instinctively the other white man recoiled. "It's the final resolution of the dilemma of power," he heard Thomas say in the dark, "to be at once both king and slave. To at once lead an army and be its waterboy. To command every man and woman within miles, and be subject to the whim of any little colored child who wanders in and orders me to dance like a puppet, or make a funny face, or wear something silly on my head such as the peel of an orange or an animal turd. Sometimes I just wish for a woman, is all. Sometimes I wish for just one, who in turn may ride me chained through the hallways of the house like a beast of burden. I wish there was just one woman who could come into the dark and arouse me, and drain the pain from my head to my loins through her lips. But there's no woman who can do that anymore, try though I might, beautiful though one might be."

"You're mad," John's voice cracked.

"You haven't even asked what my price was," Thomas sulked. "Ask me what my price was."

"You're insane."

"The first price was too high, of course. The first price was too impossible. It was her, naturally: she was the price. When they refused that, I would have settled for a single night with her, and when they refused that I would have settled for an hour. But she simply wasn't part of the bargain, was she? They couldn't have sold her to me even if they wanted because, you know, it's a funny thing, but she had entirely other ideas about it. So finally I settled on a bottle of wine. It was a good bottle of wine. You should make that clear to others when you go back, it was a *good* bottle of wine. You should make sure they understand it was a bottle of French vintage that James brought back from Paris. I drank it in an hour. While I drank," he said, "I saw her face and touched her hand, and it was hours before she left me again, before the edges of her began to dissipate in the dark until she was just a small black pool on the floor next to my bed."

"It was that girl in London," John said.

There was a pause that seemed momentous to John only because it was so dark, and then he heard Thomas say, "I can't see your white flag anymore, John."

"It was that girl in London, who brought over your daughter. And Abigail said, She shouldn't go to Paris; and I was a fool, not because I didn't believe her but because I knew she was right and I wouldn't admit it. She shouldn't go to Paris, Abigail said. If you had come to get your daughter in London as had been planned, everything would have been different. You would have gotten your daughter in London as planned and taken her back to Paris with you, and that girl would have been on the first ship back to America."

"I can't see your white flag anymore so I think you better go. If you stay longer, no one will be able to see your white flag. Nothing stays white here very long."

John turned, stumbling in the dark toward the door. He grappled for it so frantically that the white flag ripped from his chest. He ran from the room clutching it in his hand; he ran down the hall of the house past the armed slaves and through the house's entryway. He virtually leapt into the waiting carriage, jarring it so hard the horses took the impact as a signal to lurch down the road in full gallop. Half of Virginia was behind them before they stopped.

Thomas' army moved that night. Thomas rode with James in his black carriage, chains around his wrists and clothed in an Indian blanket; the president's militia reached the plantation in time to find squealing pigs and lingering mules as its new custodians. The slave army alternately lumbered and darted across the American countryside, disbanding in one hamlet to reassemble in another valley, engulfed by skirmishes from Virginia to Ohio to Pennsylvania and New York, back down to Maryland through the fall and into winter, never quite deciding whether to try to seize the country or leave it. Every once in a while Thomas would emerge after sundown from his carriage or tent. He would walk through the camp, directing his army's maneuvers on their march west to the Louisiana territories while the autumn wind blew his tall frail body and tattered rags and his masters ordered him to feed the horses and clean the rifles. When the campaign's climactic battle decimated the forces so disastrously even retreat wasn't feasible, when America washed itself in a tide of slave blood, James chained Thomas to the carriage seat and they made their escape into a country that had no name but west. Eventually they came to an Indian village.

The village stood high on a mesa that overlooked the world for as far as Thomas could see. Abandoning the carriage James unlocked Thomas' chains and the two men made their way by foot up the path alongside the mesa, where they were greeted by the natives, into whose arms Thomas collapsed. Two Indians carried him across a narrow stone bridge that connected the main mesa to a smaller one, so high above the ground that Thomas was overcome with the fatalistic calm of having placed his life utterly in the hands of others. He was taken into an empty adobe house, where he was set on blankets with a bowl of water beside him. When he lay down, his head hurt even more; and so for some time after the natives left he sat upright, soothing the pounding at the back of his skull against the coolness of the dirt wall. He was thirsty for some wine. He kept thinking he should drink the water in the bowl but he hadn't the energy to lift it to his mouth, and a few moments later he regretted not having taken the opportunity when he woke in the hotel room to find the water gone, displaced by the long-forgotten scent of someone sleeping in the bed several feet away, the strange bald boy with the pictures on his body coming through the door.

Sixteen years after the murder of the unknown man in the Downtown hotel, the police arrested Gann Hurley not far from the peripheral highway where he'd been sighted for the past two months staring out at the lava fields. As it happened Polly was just crossing the fields with her two dogs on her way back to the city, and was just on the other side of the highway, when she saw the officers swoop down on Hurley and drag him to the car. She cried so desperately as she ran alongside the car that all the way back to headquarters the cops shot sullen, reproachful glances at their boss; at headquarters the girl begged them to let her see her father, until she collapsed in the hallway. The boss was unimpressed, unless one counted sheer satisfaction. Even the scar of his face appeared content.

Most of these years Mallory hadn't really cared much about the unsolved murder, his attention entirely absorbed by Wade's apprehension in the bowels of the Arboretum. But now the Hurley arrest represented for Mallory the final closure of an obsession that began in earnest the afternoon his face was peeled from the front of his head onto an alley wall. There were still loose ends in the matter, which Mallory might have spent the rest of his life tying up if he seriously believed there was a point; but even Mallory accepted that no one was likely ever to know exactly who the dead man in the hotel had been or what had happened between him and Sally Hemings, though whatever had transpired was presumed motivating enough for Hurley to kill him. The evidence was slim but, thought Mallory to himself, fuck evidence. It was a process of elimination, and when everyone else was eliminated Hurley was left, and his throat was as good for ramming a murder down as anyone's. Mallory had been so relentless in his pursuits for so long he didn't know how to stop, and he had half a mind to arrest the daughter as some sort of accomplice, if at the time of the incident she hadn't been two years old.

Forty-eight hours after Hurley's arrest, however, Mallory knew something was amiss. The directive came down from Primacy to move Hurley not to the penal colony, where Mallory expected to send him, but the train station. "What bullshit is this?" Mallory asked whoever was within asking range. Hurley was put back in a car and taken to Vagary Junction, where not only a train was waiting but also, on the platform, a flock of white-robed priests, more of them in one place than Mallory had ever seen at one time. Standing in the doorway of the train was Hurley's daughter and her dogs. The rosary was removed from Hurley's wrists and now Mallory definitely had this queasy feeling in his stomach. As he became more and more furious his face began to bleed, small red rivulets trickling into the lines and wrinkles.

His daughter threw her arms around him as Hurley got on the train, and Mallory could see them through the windows as they made their way down the aisle of the car. The priests signaled the conductor and the train responded with a lurch, and a minute later obsession's final sweet resolution was irrevocably beyond Mallory's reach; all that was left was the volcano in the distance and the steel rails gleaming in the Vog and the man on the other side of the track with the red books in his arms and the blue eyes floating in his glasses like crystal balls. Like Mallory, Etcher stood watching the disappearing train for as long as it was in sight, and then stepped over the rail and up the steps to the platform, where he delivered the books into the possession of the priests, and the rosary that Hurley had worn was snapped around his wrists and he was put in the police car. He was driven down the highway to the penal colony south of the city. Within the colony's gray walls he was given a gray prisoner's robe and placed in a large black cell with no windows, for which the sound of the sea in the distance, Etcher told himself, was soothing compensation.

He had his own mattress and was allowed one small bag of

personal possessions as long as they didn't include reading material. He had been in the cell an hour before he realized he shared
it with other prisoners, some of them lying so still in the shadows
they might have been dead. He was taken to a yard where the
ground was littered with forbidden artifacts that had been seized
during altar searches; on the rocks of the yard, under the watch of
armed priests in black robes, the prisoners smashed the artifacts
with dull mallets. Iconic carvings and blasphemous jewelry and
children's books were hammered and pulverized into pulp. First
the sensual quality of the object was disfigured and then its meaning, and then its form; and when the object had been pounded into
a misshapen lump of wood or mineral or paper, the remains were
then beaten into the rock itself until the whole ground throbbed
with heresy. Since new artifacts were being delivered every day,
this work never ended. The prisoners had no conversation among
themselves and gave what they were destroying no special attention.

The days passed and then the weeks. Etcher became old and
exhausted by the work. He didn't eat and in the mornings he had
to be brutally awakened by the black-robed guards as though from
a stupor. He opened his eyes every day to the devastating regret
that he was still alive. Though visiting day was once a month no
one came to visit him, nor did he expect anyone; but loneliness
that he not only reconciled himself to when he lived in the volcano
but coveted was now harder to bear. Though he tried very hard
not to think about anything, to drain his mind of any wandering
impulse, after a while he found that in the yard beneath the blis-
tering sun he couldn't help but occasionally gaze through the
barbed wire of the penal walls to the volcano in the east and the
city to the north. He told himself he had no reason for this reverie,
but soon it was the thing he lived for and from which the guards
interrupted him. Months went by before Etcher realized one day
who it was he was looking for, as though she would appear around
a bend or over a hill; and then his heart pleaded with him not to
torment it. He reasoned with himself that she was safe now and
free and where she belonged, that this after all was why he had
made his bargain with the priests, to give back her father after
having taken away her mother. He pointed out to himself that if

she were to come back to the city she might never be able to leave again and would therefore only risk never seeing her father again. It was not only a preposterous hope to inflict on himself but a cruel one to expect her to fulfill.

Nonetheless, he couldn't help but look for her. With every day she didn't come, the wound of his heart grew a little larger and deeper and he got a little older and sicker, until one afternoon as he was slamming his mallet against a rock in the heat, trying to remember what the artifact was he had just destroyed, he realized it was his glasses. Pitching face first into his heartbreak he collapsed not into the black robes of a guard but the black arms of another prisoner.

Etcher didn't recognize the other prisoner. That time so many years before in the hallway of the Arboretum all he'd been aware of was his own blood and the assailant's looming form. Now when Etcher regained consciousness on the mattress in his cell, the other man was there to give him a drink of water and a bite of bread. The two of them didn't speak for a long time. The first thing Etcher asked several mornings later was, "Did she come today?"

Wade didn't know what he was talking about. "No," he answered.

After a moment Etcher said, "I thought maybe she came."

"Get some sleep," Wade said. After that Etcher asked every time he woke, sometimes only hours apart, since in his growing delirium he lost track of the days. Wade dreaded Etcher's awakenings, when he always had the same answer to the same question. "It makes no sense that she should come," Etcher reasoned out loud. "She shouldn't come."

"You're not well enough to see anyone anyway," Wade said. "You haven't moved from this mattress in three weeks."

"I'll get up if she comes," Etcher insisted.

"OK."

"Promise you'll tell me."

"OK."

But of course she did not come. Soon, working in the yard, Wade found himself searching for her as Etcher had, his eyes constantly peeled for a sign of her up the road in the distance. Now he had a pretty good idea who he was looking for. And when the sun set he returned to the cell wondering whether it took more courage to tell Etcher a lie or the truth.

Etcher's moments of cognizance dwindled. Soon he was spitting blood, and after that pissing it. With one arm the black man held the white man up over the hole in the corner of the cell that served as a toilet; in his other hand he held Etcher's dick for him while he watched the stream of blood in the dark. When he carried Etcher back to the mattress he could hear the pieces of the man's heart rattle in his chest. It was the sound he thought of when Etcher gave him the box.

Etcher had awakened one last time. Wade held him in his arms. Etcher barely had the strength to speak, so his eyes asked instead and Wade answered, "She came today." Etcher gripped the other man's arm harder than Wade would have thought he could grip. His eyes pleaded with more longing than Wade would have thought blind eyes could plead. Wade swallowed and went on, "She was here. I saw her. I talked to her a second or two through the wall. She asked about you. She'll be back tomorrow." It was an awful gamble. He was gambling that Etcher wouldn't make it through the night. He was gambling against Etcher's life that Etcher might take with him into death one last dream. Etcher pulled Wade's ear down to his mouth.

"Listen to me," he whispered, "there are only three things you die for. Love, freedom, or nothing."

That was when Etcher gave Wade the box. He had Wade bring his bag of possessions and he dug it out from the bottom. It was an old black box, once very beautiful but now battered and nicked, with a rose carved on the top. Etcher shoved the box into the other man's hands and Wade opened it as though it held something significant, the final revelation of a man's life. But the box was empty except for some rubble that rolled in tiny pieces from corner to corner, and though Wade hadn't the faintest idea what use he would ever make of a box, since he would never have anything to put inside, he accepted it as the momentous gift he assumed it was and held it while Etcher died, one final word rising to the dead man's lips where it stuck unspoken. Wade knew what it was.

It   w a s   o n l y   a f t e r the priests had come for the body, wrapping it in sheets and taking it from the cell, that Wade examined the remains of the rubble in the box more closely and, piecing together several tiny fragments, realized that with a little patience he could reassemble nearly all of *pursuit of happiness.* And then he knew that in his possession he had the most forbidden artifact of all, and buried it so deep in his corner of the cell that he gladly risked never retrieving it again, if it meant it would never be obliterated into the ground outside.

In the yard the next day he saw, through the penal walls, the wagon come up the road. The girl at the reins had found the charred wagon out in the lava fields, its horse wandering in confusion looking for a patch of grass if not a familiar street, the blaze of the Bastille still in its eyes. Two large gray dogs ran alongside. Wade watched the wagon pass the wall nearest him, and Polly was met at the colony gates by several priests who loaded the body in the back, draped in the same sheet with which they had wrapped it the night before. If he could have talked to her for only a moment, Wade would have asked whether she had known he was dead or whether she just came a day too late; but all he could do was stand and watch her go, even as the guards barked at him to return to work. She disappeared up the road. She came to the highway that led to the city and crossed the highway, continuing on over the hard lava. She neared the volcano and was wondering how she was going to get the body up beyond the ridge and as far as the crater when, though it might have been simply the sound of the ocean breeze, she stopped the horse to turn and see the breeze lift the sheet right off the body, because she thought she had heard someone say something.

And she watched take flight, like a black moth from his dead mouth, the name of the woman he loved.

About the Author

Steve Erickson was born in 1950 in Los Angeles. He graduated from UCLA with degrees in cinema and journalism, and over the years has lived in New York, Paris, Rome and Amsterdam. He has published three novels—*Days Between Stations* (1985), *Rubicon Beach* (1986) and *Tours of the Black Clock* (1989)—and a political memoir, *Leap Year* (1989), in England, France, Germany, Spain, Italy, Holland, Greece and Japan. His work has also appeared in *The New York Times, Esquire* and *Rolling Stone,* and he is curently the film critic for *L.A. Weekly.*